QUEST FOR THE UNICORN HORN

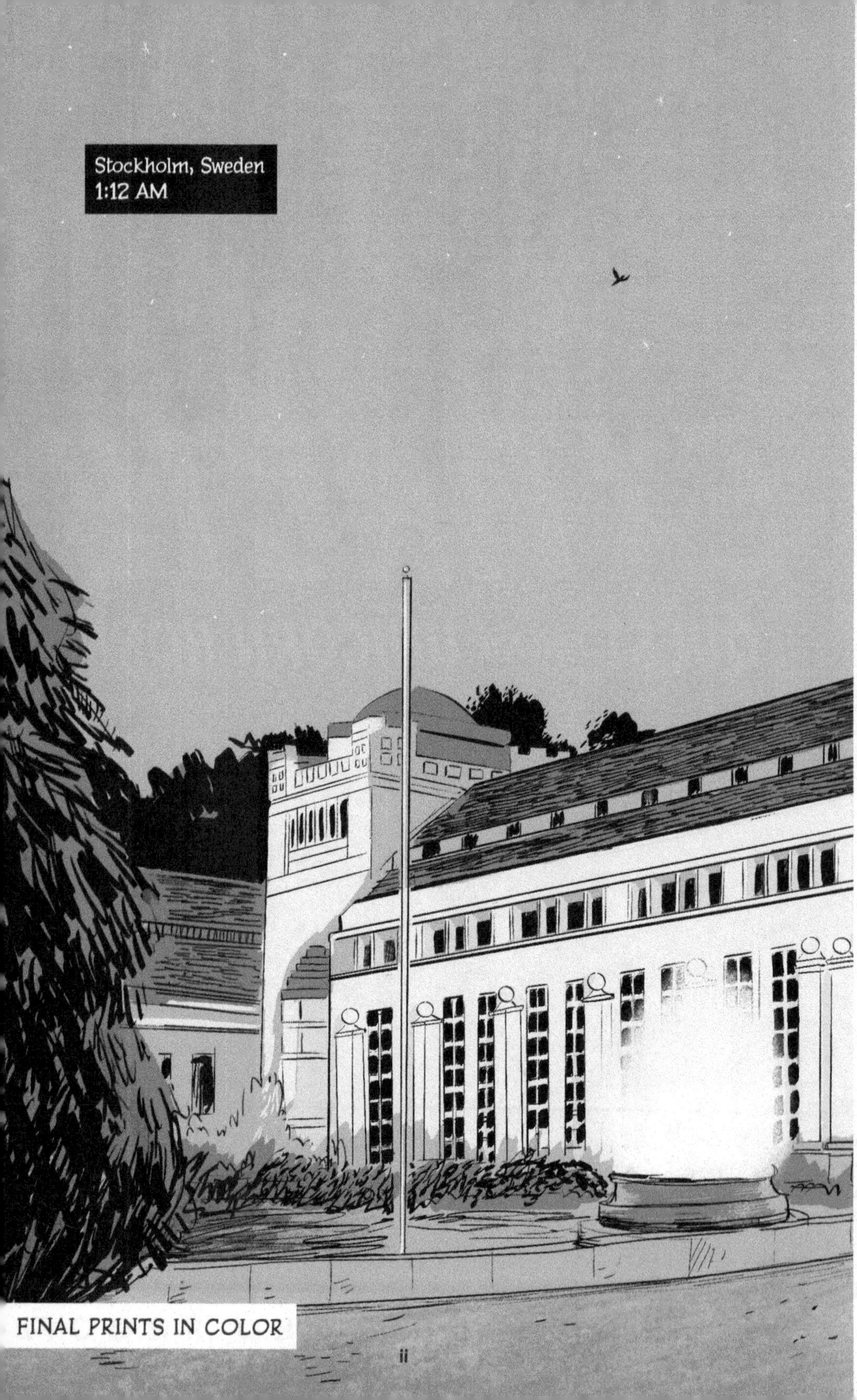
Stockholm, Sweden
1:12 AM
FINAL PRINTS IN COLOR

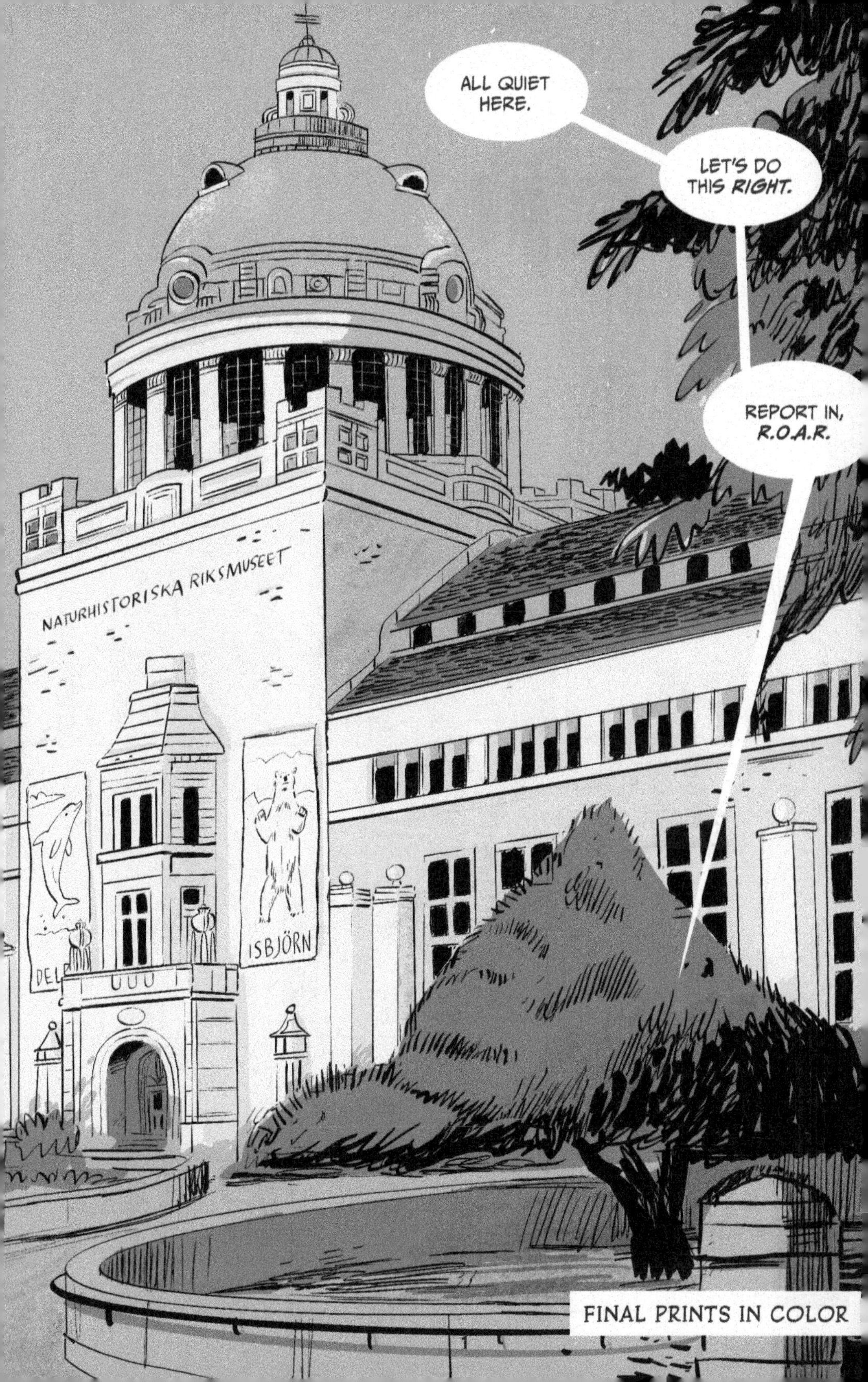
ALL QUIET HERE.
LET'S DO THIS *RIGHT.*
REPORT IN, *R.O.A.R.*
NATURHISTORISKA RIKSMUSEET
ISBJÖRN
FINAL PRINTS IN COLOR

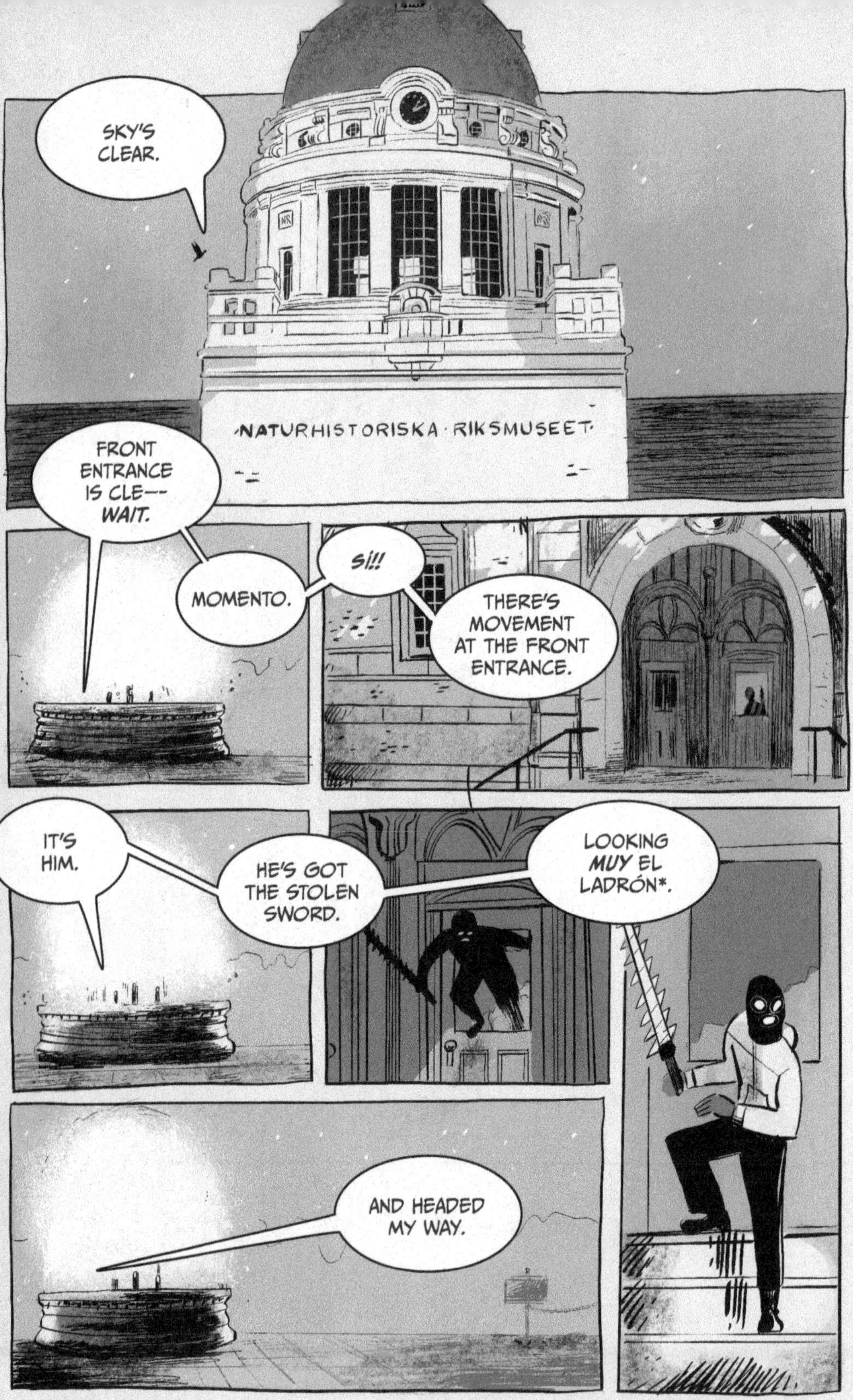
SKY'S CLEAR.
NATURHISTORISKA · RIKSMUSEET
FRONT ENTRANCE IS CLE-- WAIT.
MOMENTO.
SÍ!!
THERE'S MOVEMENT AT THE FRONT ENTRANCE.
IT'S HIM.
HE'S GOT THE STOLEN SWORD.
LOOKING MUY EL LADRÓN*.
AND HEADED MY WAY.

*Thief, in Spanish

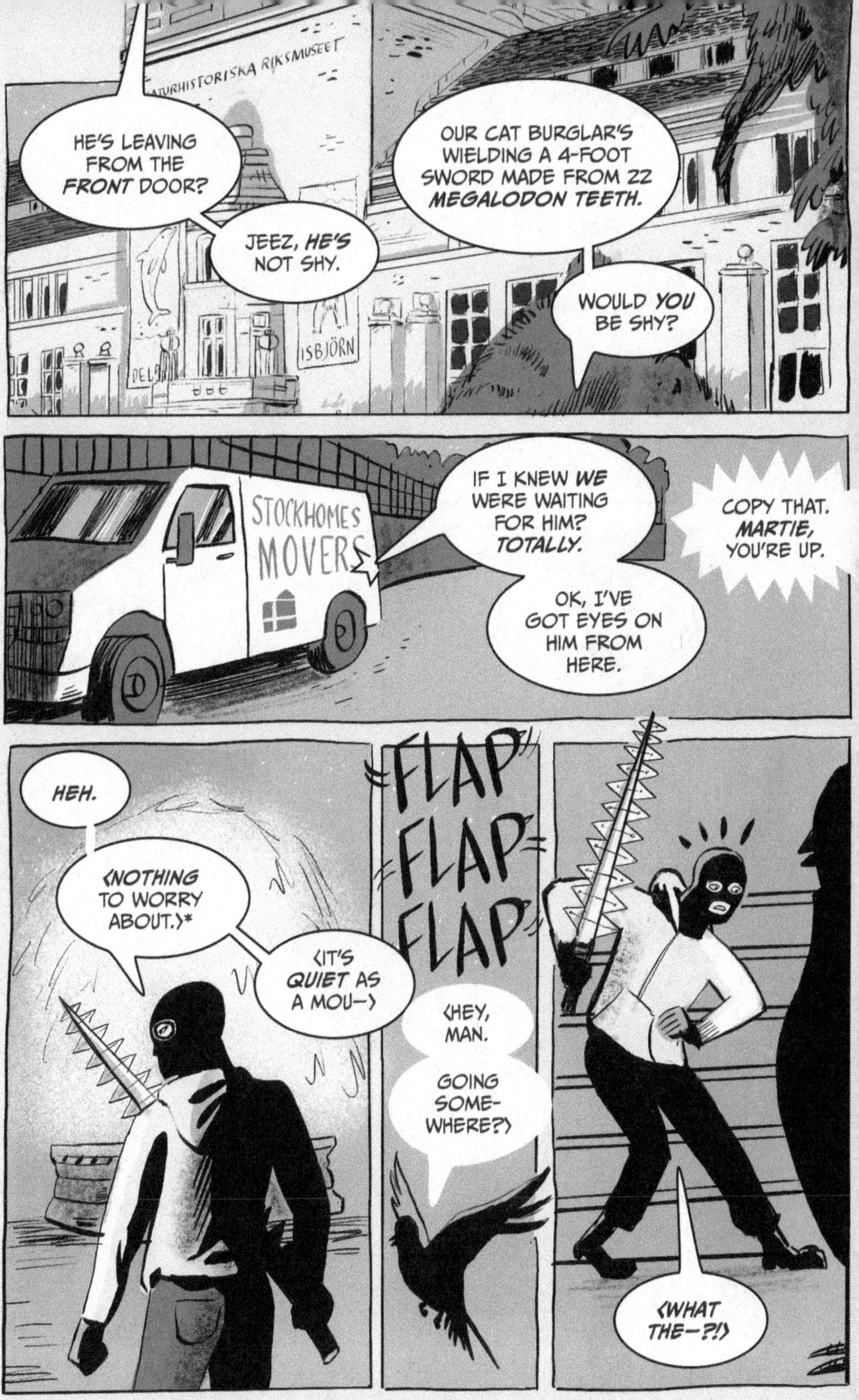
NATURHISTORISKA RIKSMUSEET
HE'S LEAVING FROM THE *FRONT* DOOR?
JEEZ, *HE'S* NOT SHY.
OUR CAT BURGLAR'S WIELDING A 4-FOOT SWORD MADE FROM 22 *MEGALODON TEETH.*
WOULD *YOU* BE SHY?
ISBJÖRN
STOCKHOMES MOVERS
IF I KNEW *WE* WERE WAITING FOR HIM? *TOTALLY.*
OK, I'VE GOT EYES ON HIM FROM HERE.
COPY THAT. *MARTIE,* YOU'RE UP.
HEH.
⟨*NOTHING* TO WORRY ABOUT.⟩*
⟨IT'S *QUIET* AS A MOU—⟩
FLAP FLAP FLAP
⟨HEY, MAN.
GOING SOME-WHERE?⟩
⟨*WHAT THE—?!*⟩

*Translated from Swedish

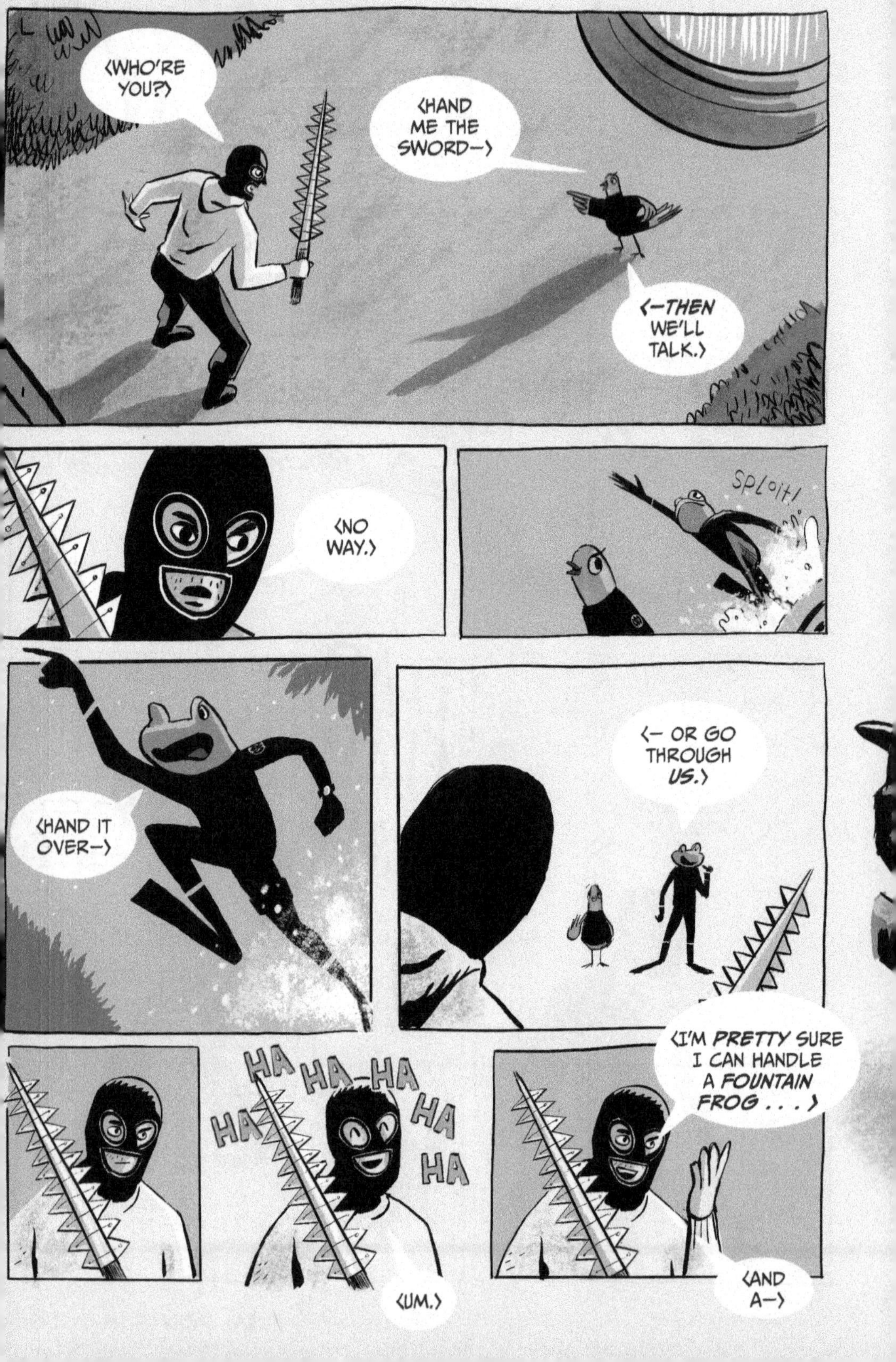
⟨WHO'RE YOU?⟩
⟨HAND ME THE SWORD—⟩
⟨—THEN WE'LL TALK.⟩
⟨NO WAY.⟩
SPLOIT!
⟨HAND IT OVER—⟩
⟨— OR GO THROUGH US.⟩
HA HA-HA HA HA HA HA
⟨UM.⟩
⟨I'M PRETTY SURE I CAN HANDLE A FOUNTAIN FROG . . .⟩
⟨AND A—⟩

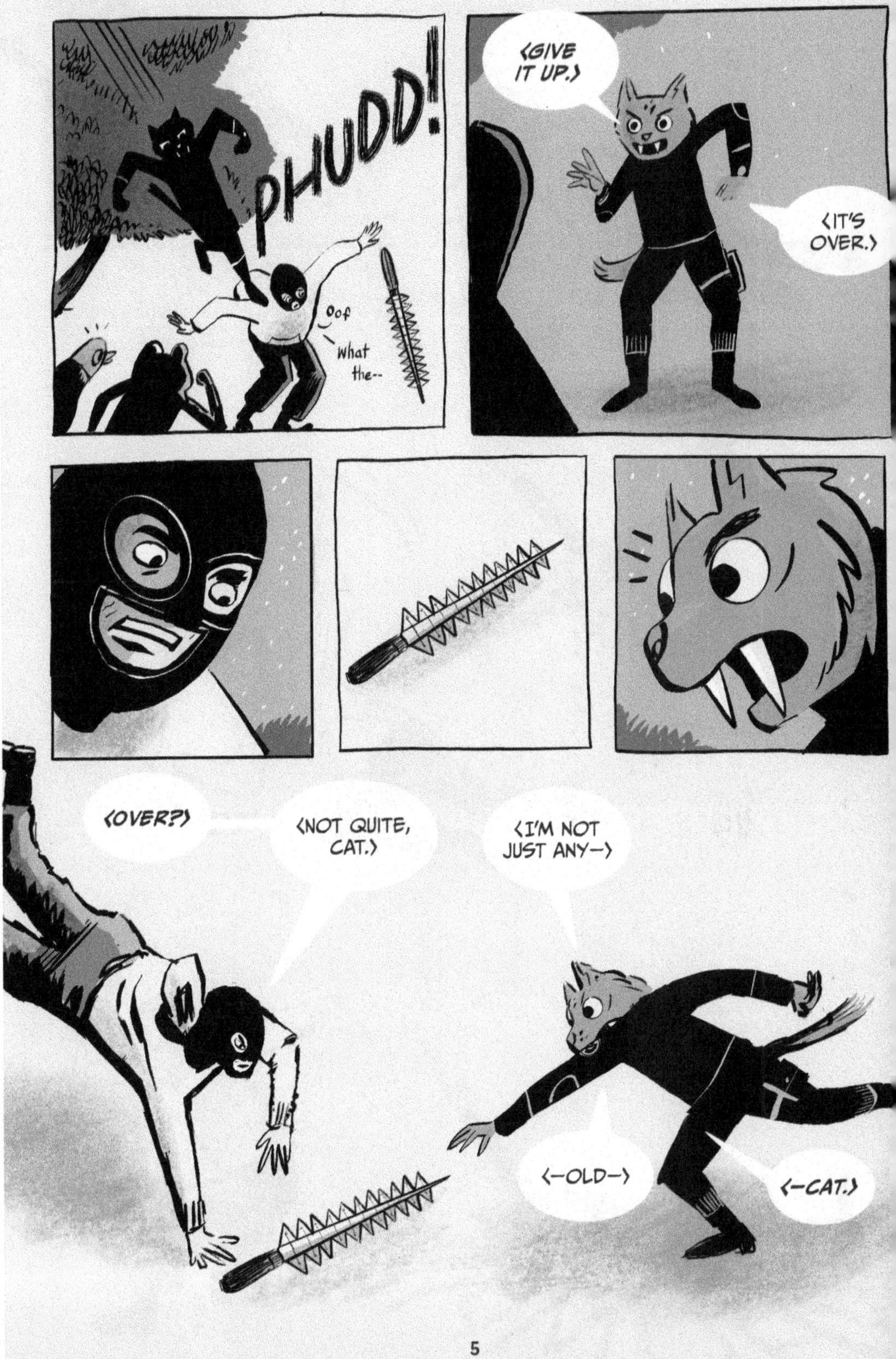
PHUDD!
Oof
What the--
⟨GIVE IT UP.⟩
⟨IT'S OVER.⟩
⟨OVER?⟩
⟨NOT QUITE, CAT.⟩
⟨I'M NOT JUST ANY—⟩
⟨—OLD—⟩
⟨—CAT.⟩

FINAL PRINTS IN COLOR

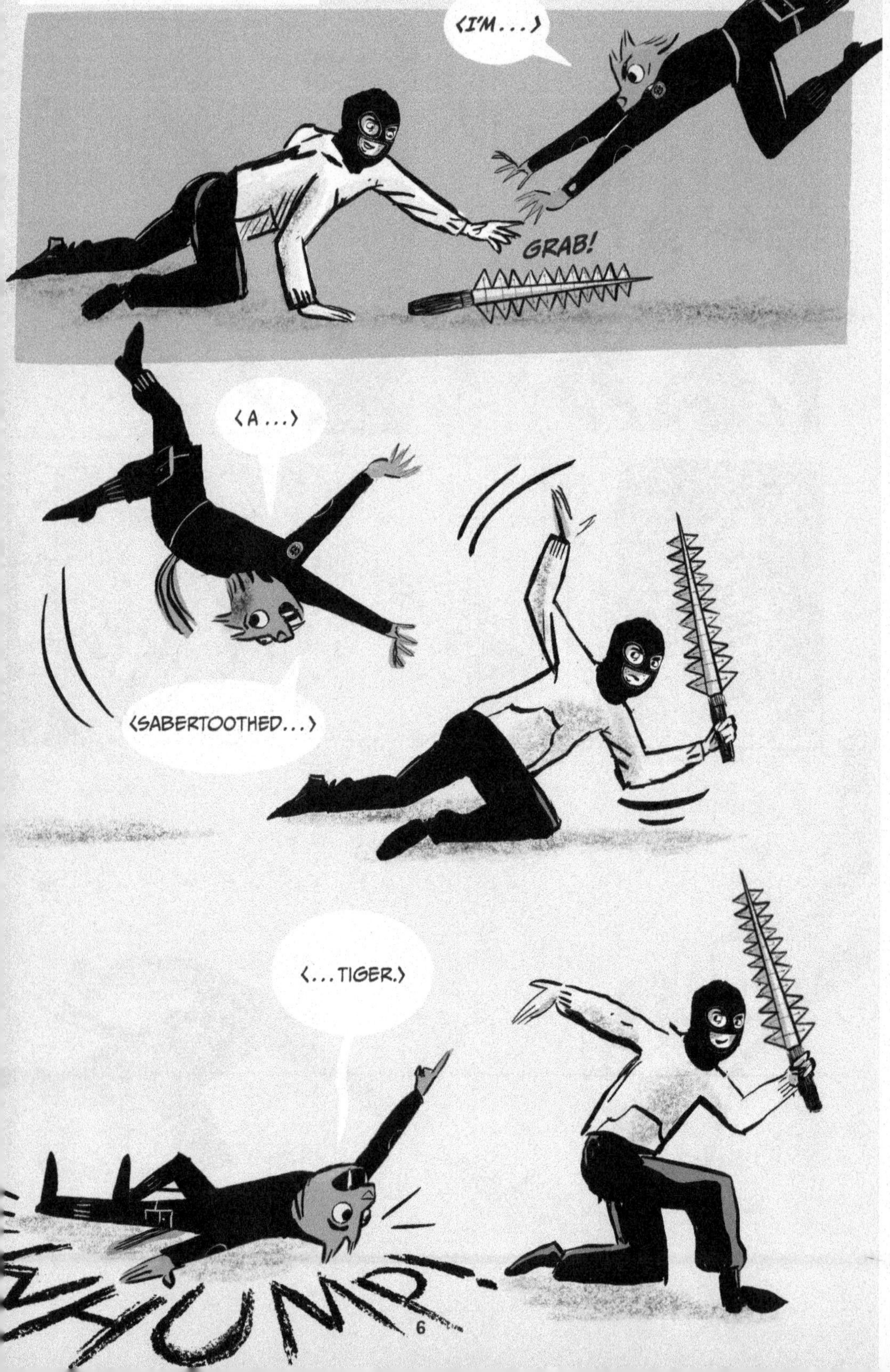
‹I'M...›
GRAB!
‹A...›
‹SABERTOOTHED...›
‹...TIGER.›
WHUMP!

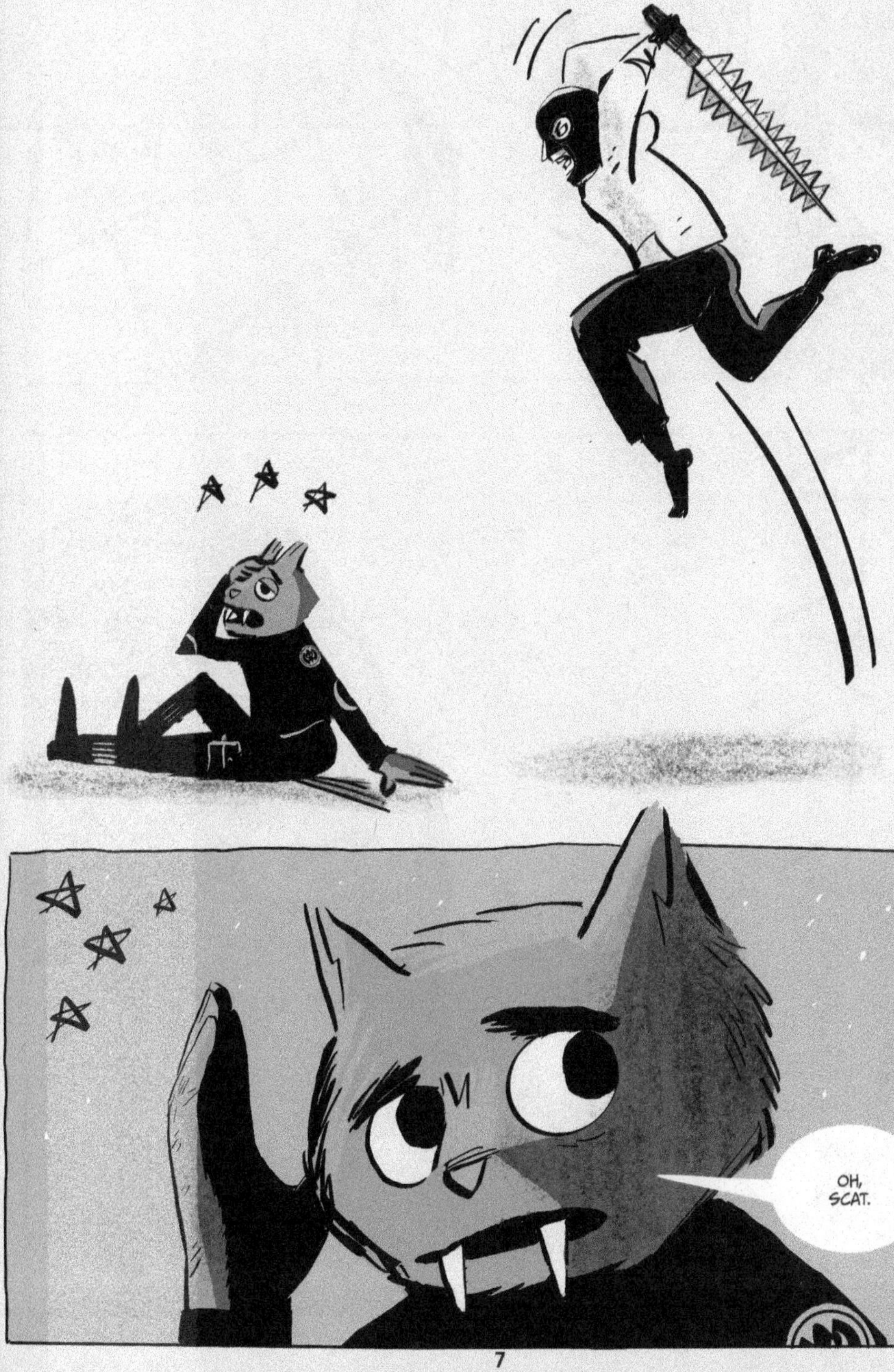
OH,
SCAT.

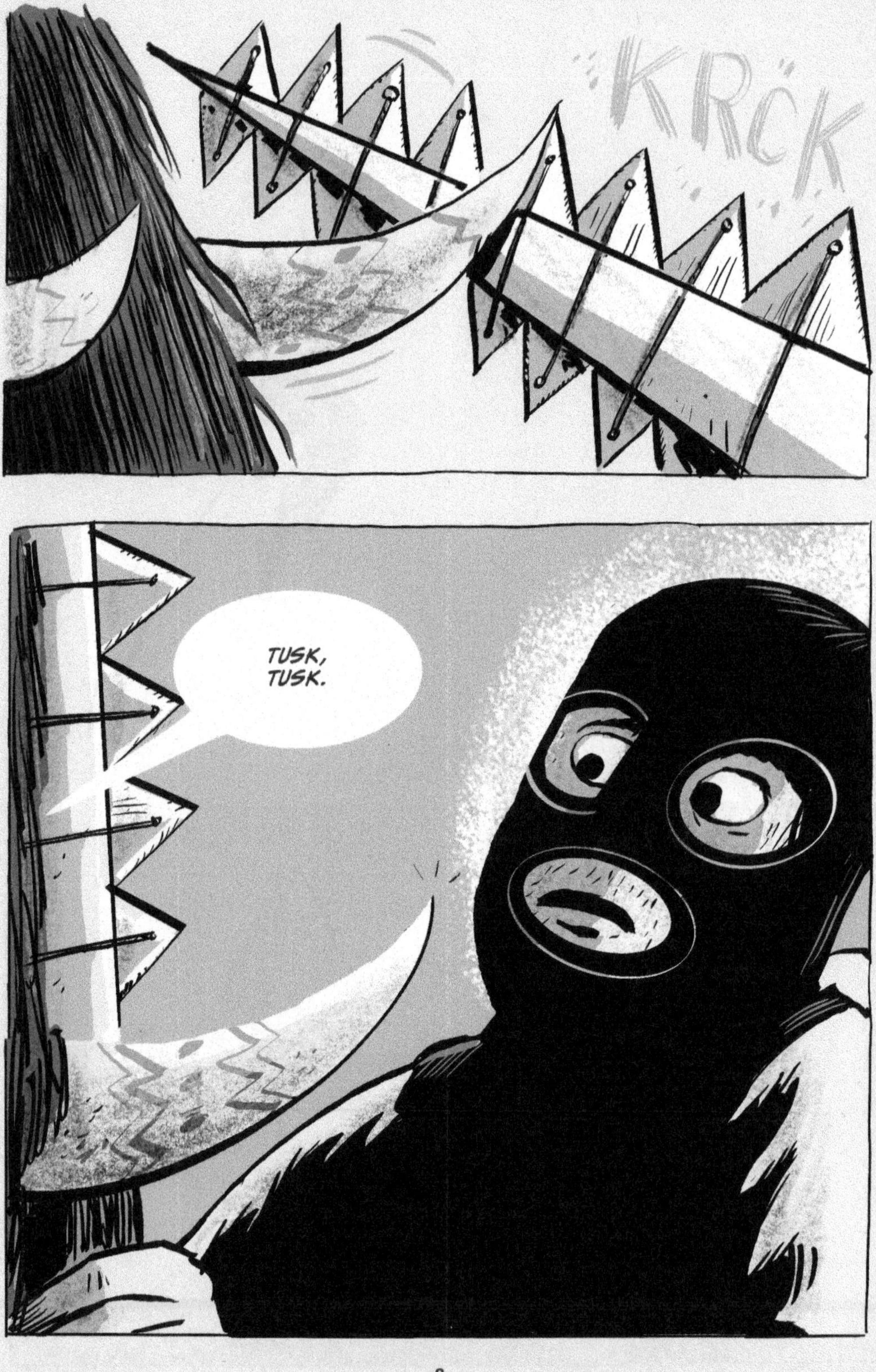
KRCK
TUSK, TUSK.

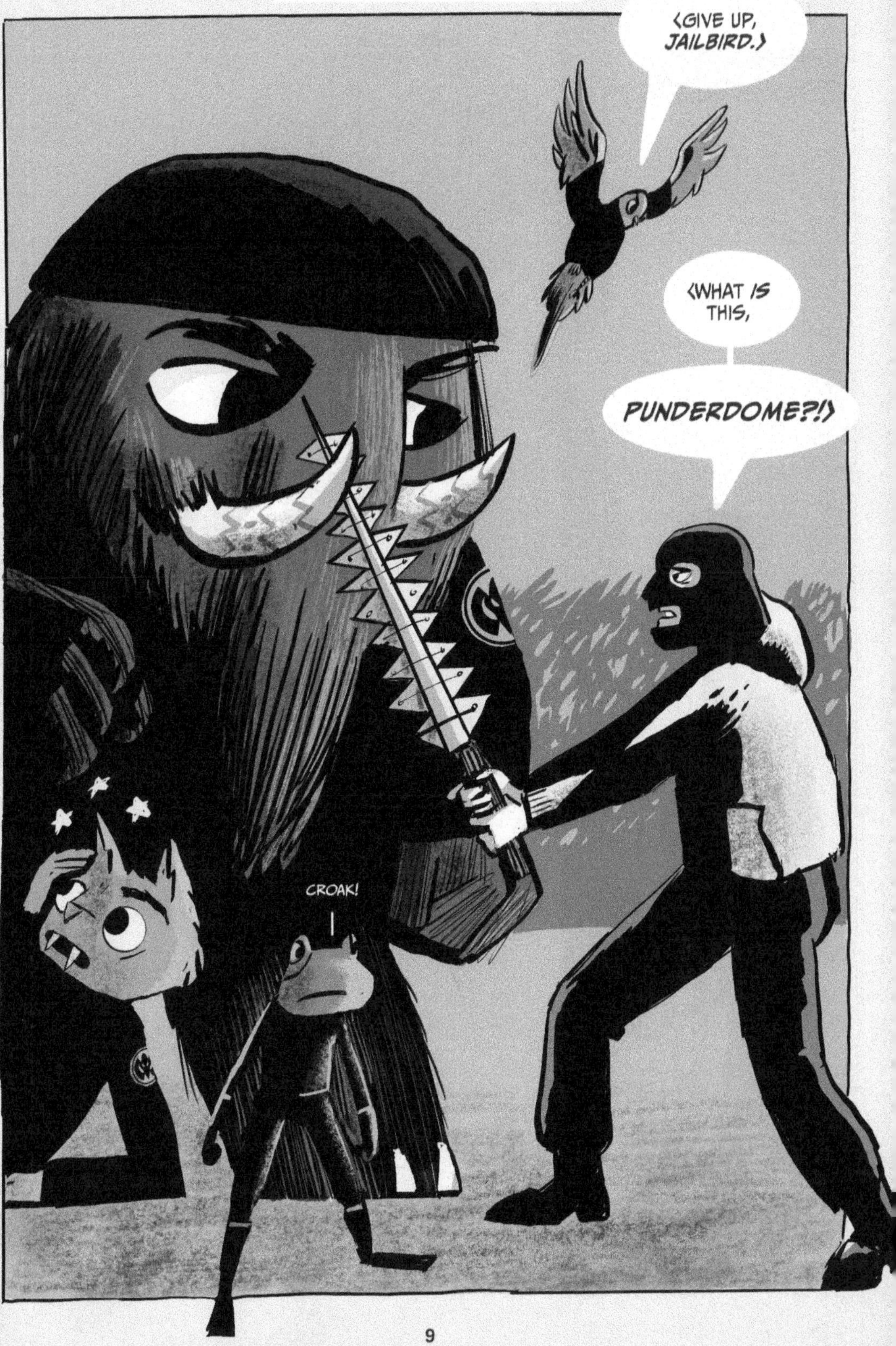
‹GIVE UP, JAILBIRD.›
‹WHAT IS THIS,
PUNDERDOME?!›
CROAK!

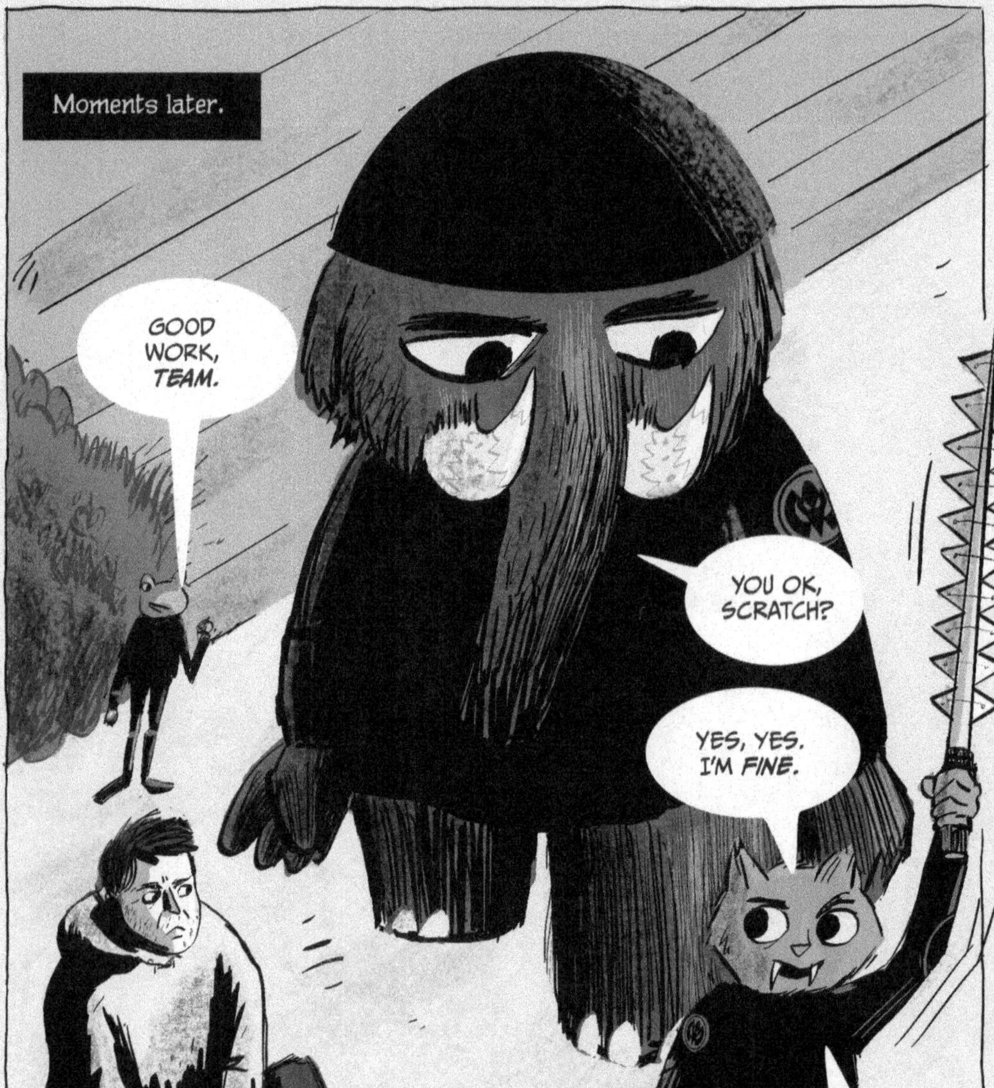
Moments later.
GOOD WORK, *TEAM.*
YOU OK, SCRATCH?
YES, YES. I'M *FINE.*
I'LL REPORT BACK TO *DR. Z—*
I HAVE THE *SWORD!*

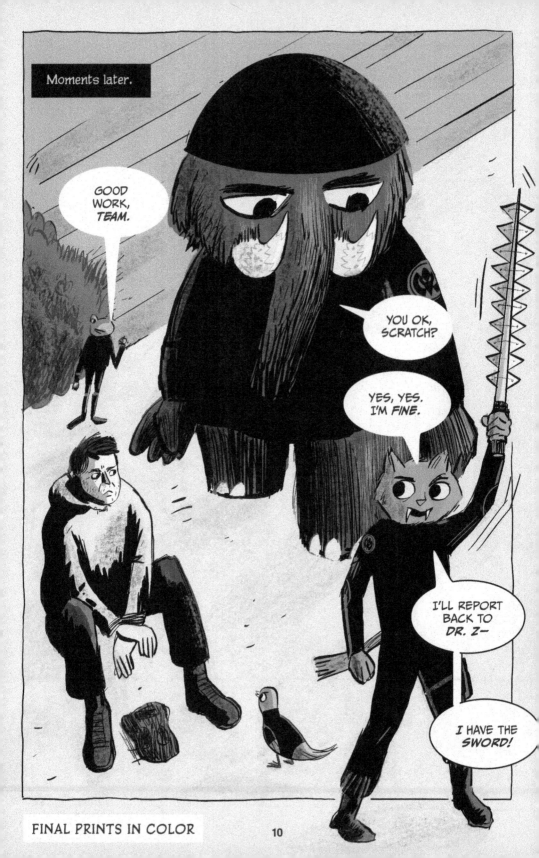

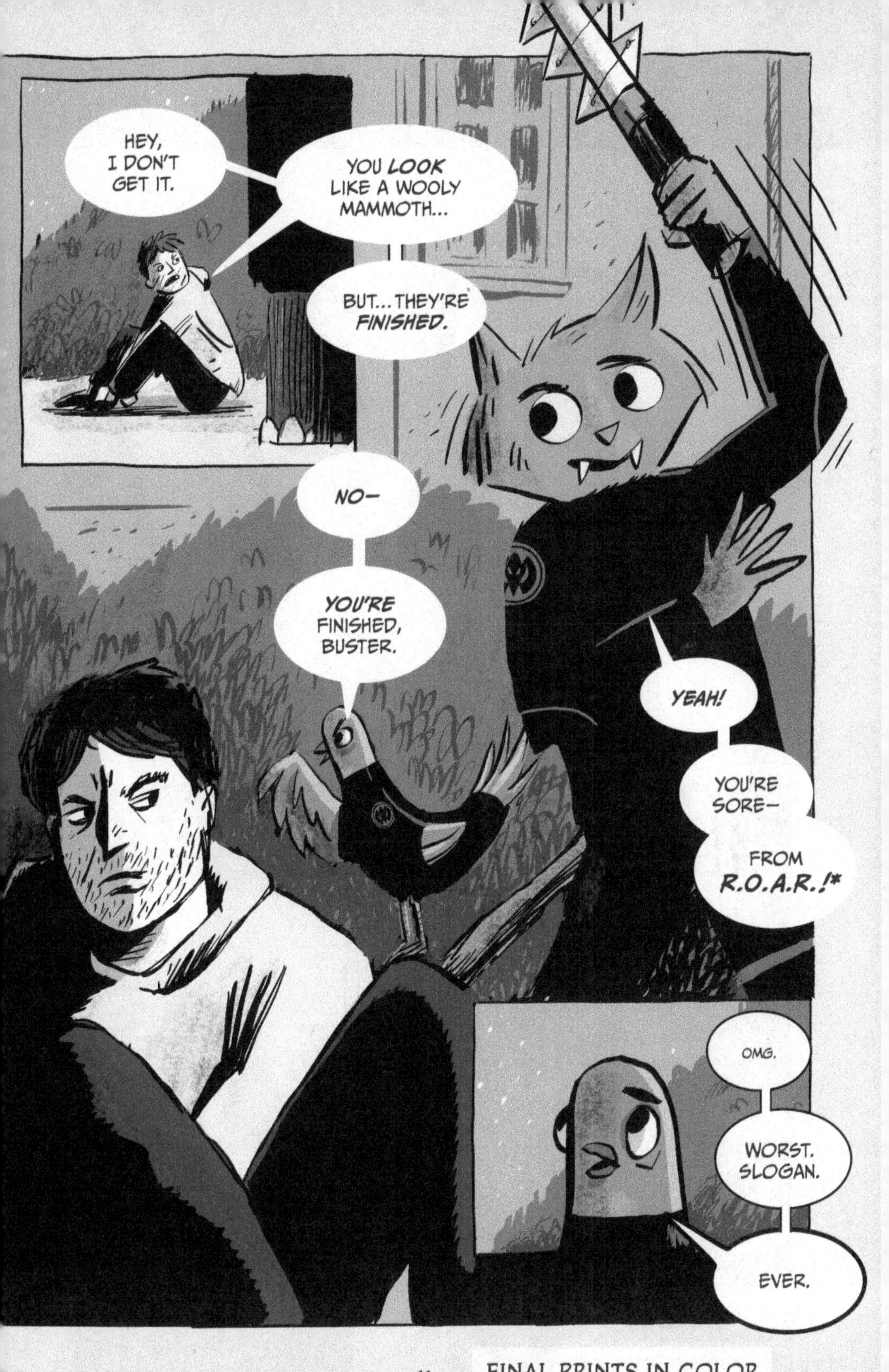
HEY, I DON'T GET IT.
YOU *LOOK* LIKE A WOOLY MAMMOTH...
BUT... THEY'RE *FINISHED.*
NO—
YOU'RE FINISHED, BUSTER.
YEAH!
YOU'RE SORE—
FROM *R.O.A.R.!**
OMG.
WORST. SLOGAN.
EVER.

* Rescue Ops Acquisition Rangers

THE EXTI

Starring:

LUG

MARTIE

NCTS

QUEST FOR THE UNICORN HORN

SCRATCH

QUITO

FINAL PRINTS IN COLOR

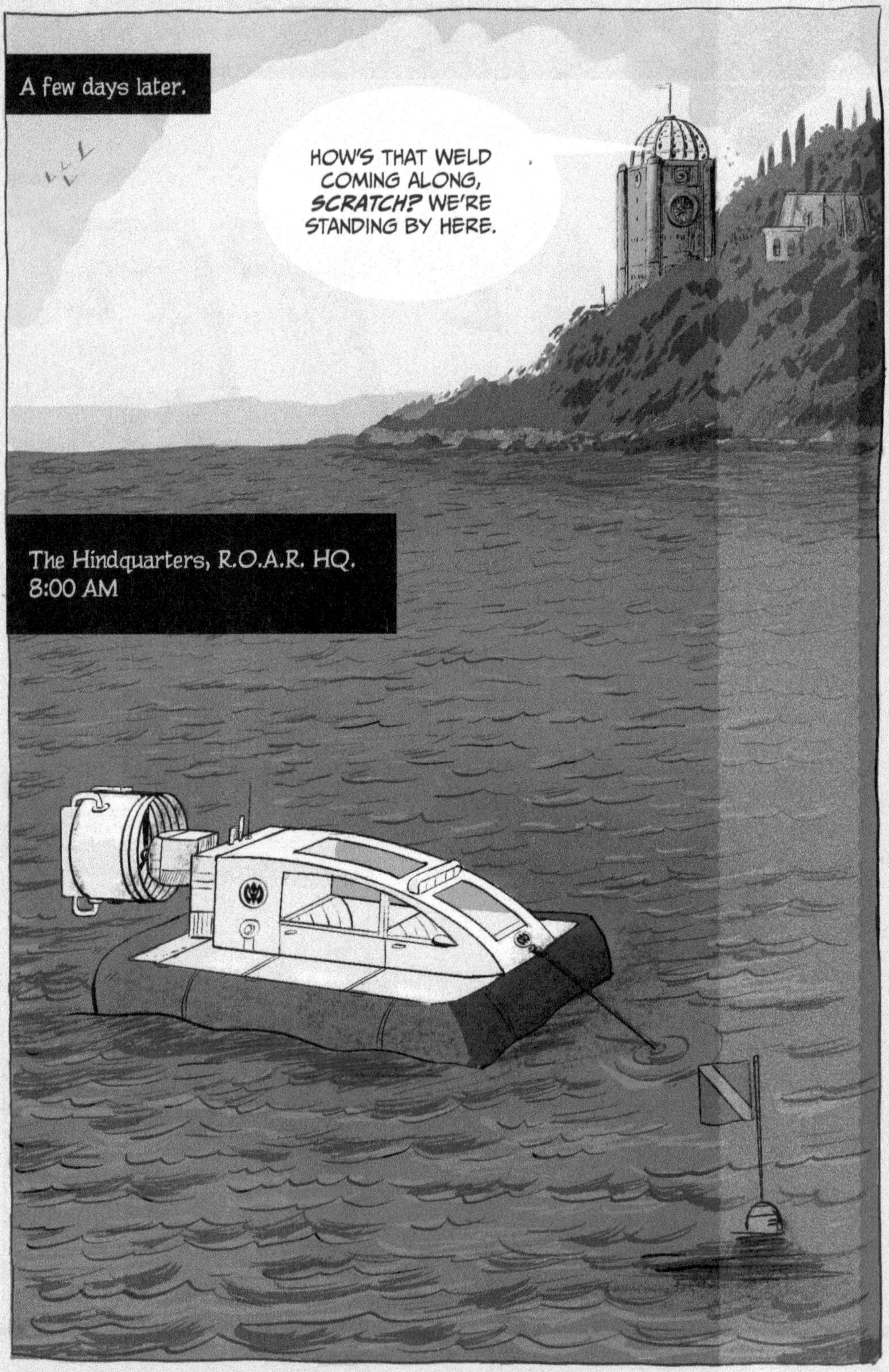
A few days later.
HOW'S THAT WELD COMING ALONG, *SCRATCH?* WE'RE STANDING BY HERE.
The Hindquarters, R.O.A.R. HQ.
8:00 AM

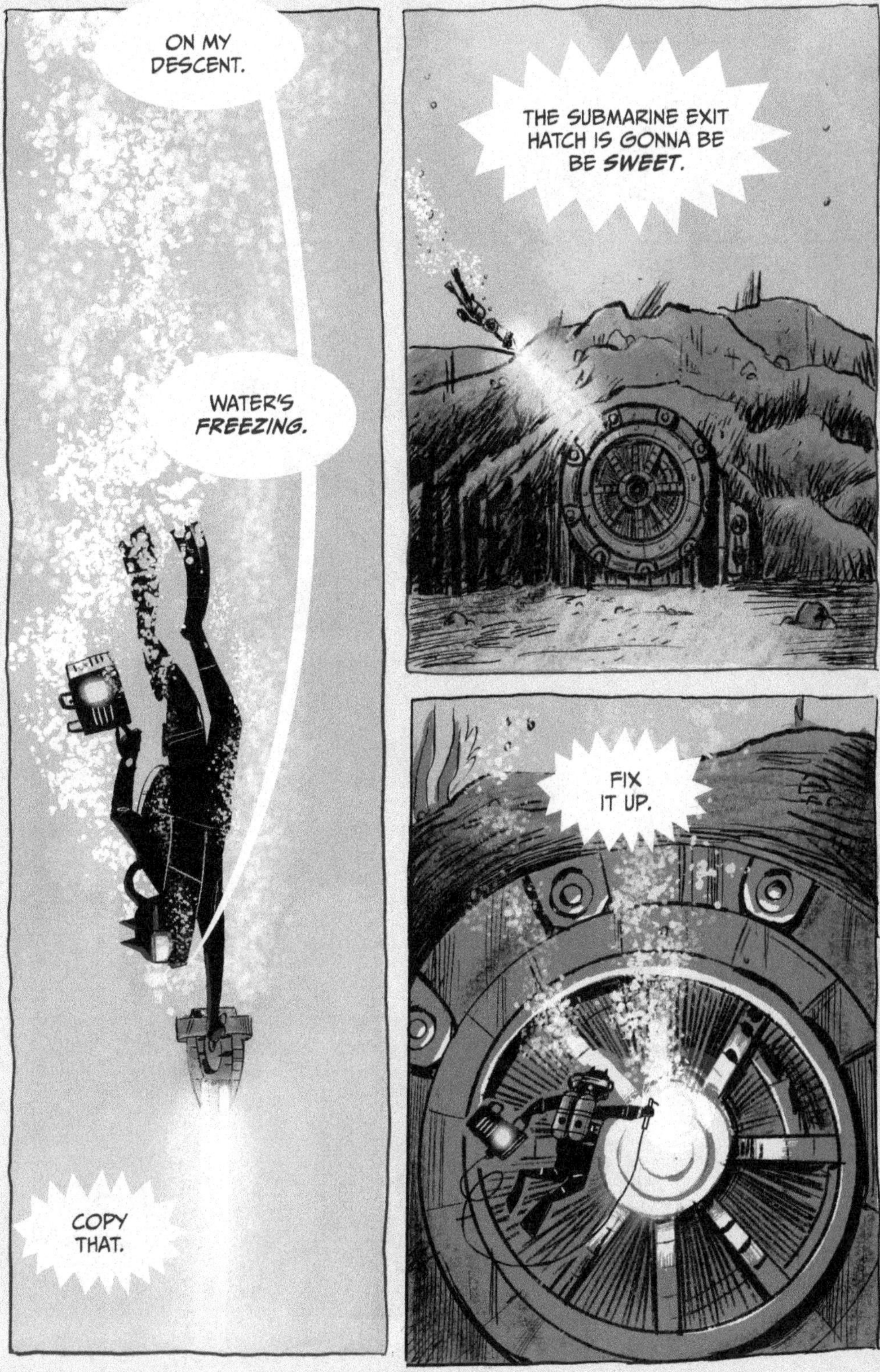
ON MY DESCENT.
WATER'S *FREEZING.*
COPY THAT.
THE SUBMARINE EXIT HATCH IS GONNA BE BE ***SWEET***.
FIX IT UP.

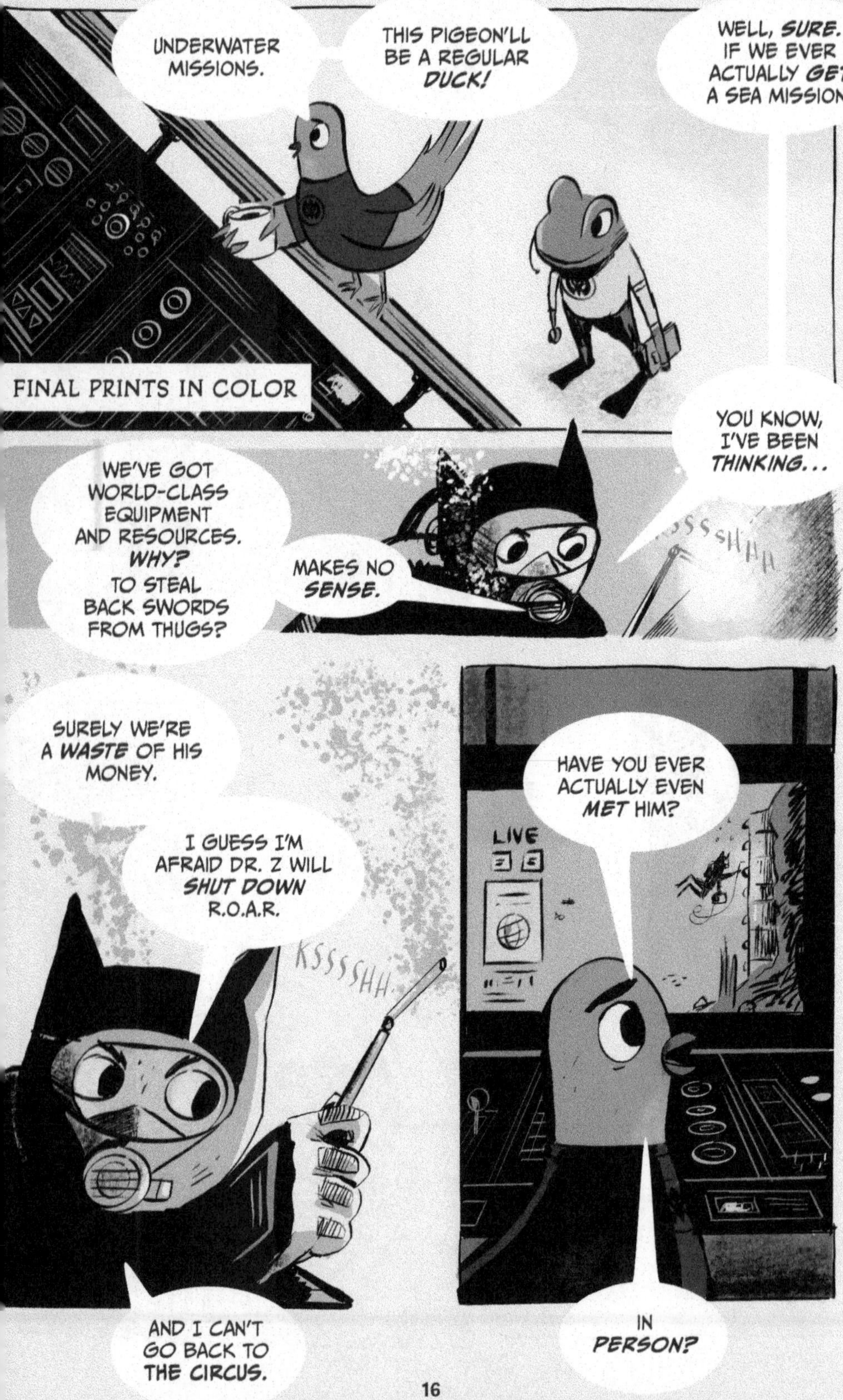
UNDERWATER MISSIONS.
THIS PIGEON'LL BE A REGULAR DUCK!
WELL, SURE. IF WE EVER ACTUALLY GET A SEA MISSION.
FINAL PRINTS IN COLOR
YOU KNOW, I'VE BEEN THINKING...
WE'VE GOT WORLD-CLASS EQUIPMENT AND RESOURCES. WHY?
TO STEAL BACK SWORDS FROM THUGS?
MAKES NO SENSE.
SURELY WE'RE A WASTE OF HIS MONEY.
I GUESS I'M AFRAID DR. Z WILL SHUT DOWN R.O.A.R.
KSSSSHH.
AND I CAN'T GO BACK TO THE CIRCUS.
HAVE YOU EVER ACTUALLY EVEN MET HIM?
LIVE
IN PERSON?

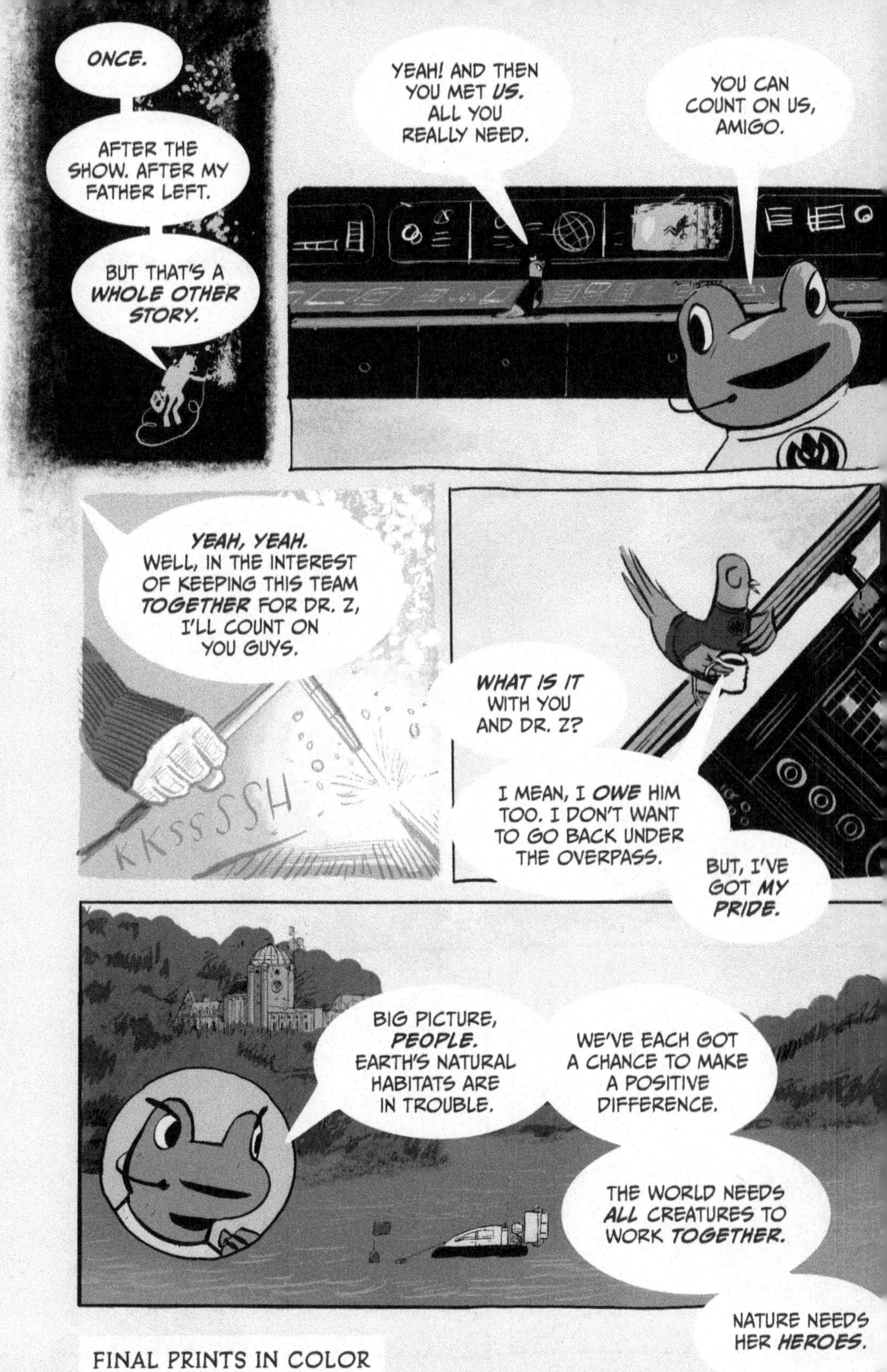
ONCE.
AFTER THE SHOW. AFTER MY FATHER LEFT.
BUT THAT'S A WHOLE OTHER STORY.
YEAH! AND THEN YOU MET US. ALL YOU REALLY NEED.
YOU CAN COUNT ON US, AMIGO.
YEAH, YEAH. WELL, IN THE INTEREST OF KEEPING THIS TEAM TOGETHER FOR DR. Z, I'LL COUNT ON YOU GUYS.
KKSSSSH
WHAT IS IT WITH YOU AND DR. Z?
I MEAN, I OWE HIM TOO. I DON'T WANT TO GO BACK UNDER THE OVERPASS.
BUT, I'VE GOT MY PRIDE.
BIG PICTURE, PEOPLE. EARTH'S NATURAL HABITATS ARE IN TROUBLE.
WE'VE EACH GOT A CHANCE TO MAKE A POSITIVE DIFFERENCE.
THE WORLD NEEDS ALL CREATURES TO WORK TOGETHER.
NATURE NEEDS HER HEROES.

FINAL PRINTS IN COLOR

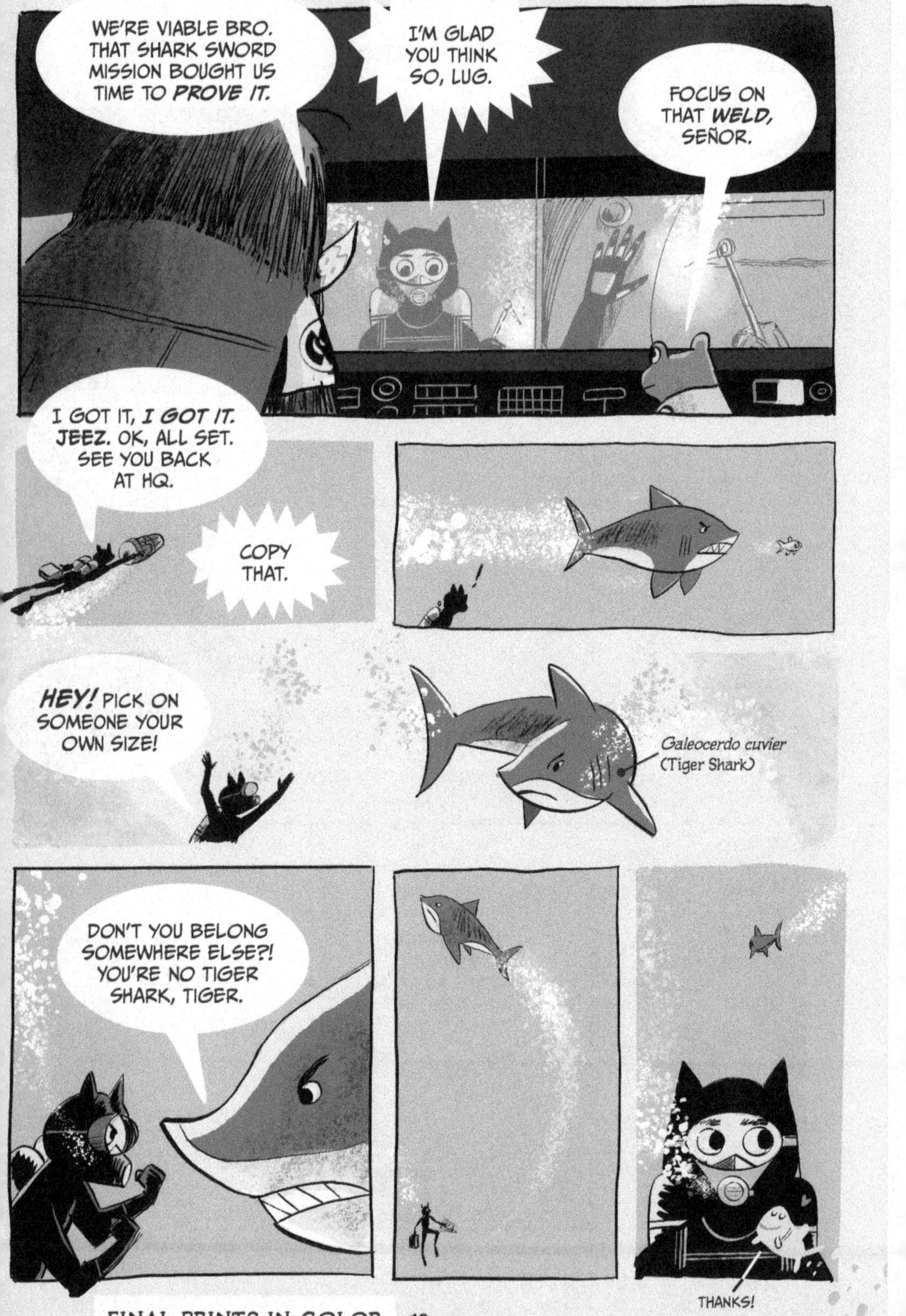
WE'RE VIABLE BRO. THAT SHARK SWORD MISSION BOUGHT US TIME TO PROVE IT.
I'M GLAD YOU THINK SO, LUG.
FOCUS ON THAT WELD, SEÑOR.
I GOT IT, I GOT IT. JEEZ. OK, ALL SET. SEE YOU BACK AT HQ.
COPY THAT.
!
HEY! PICK ON SOMEONE YOUR OWN SIZE!
Galeocerdo cuvier (Tiger Shark)
DON'T YOU BELONG SOMEWHERE ELSE?! YOU'RE NO TIGER SHARK, TIGER.
THANKS!

*GAIA: Global Animal Information Access

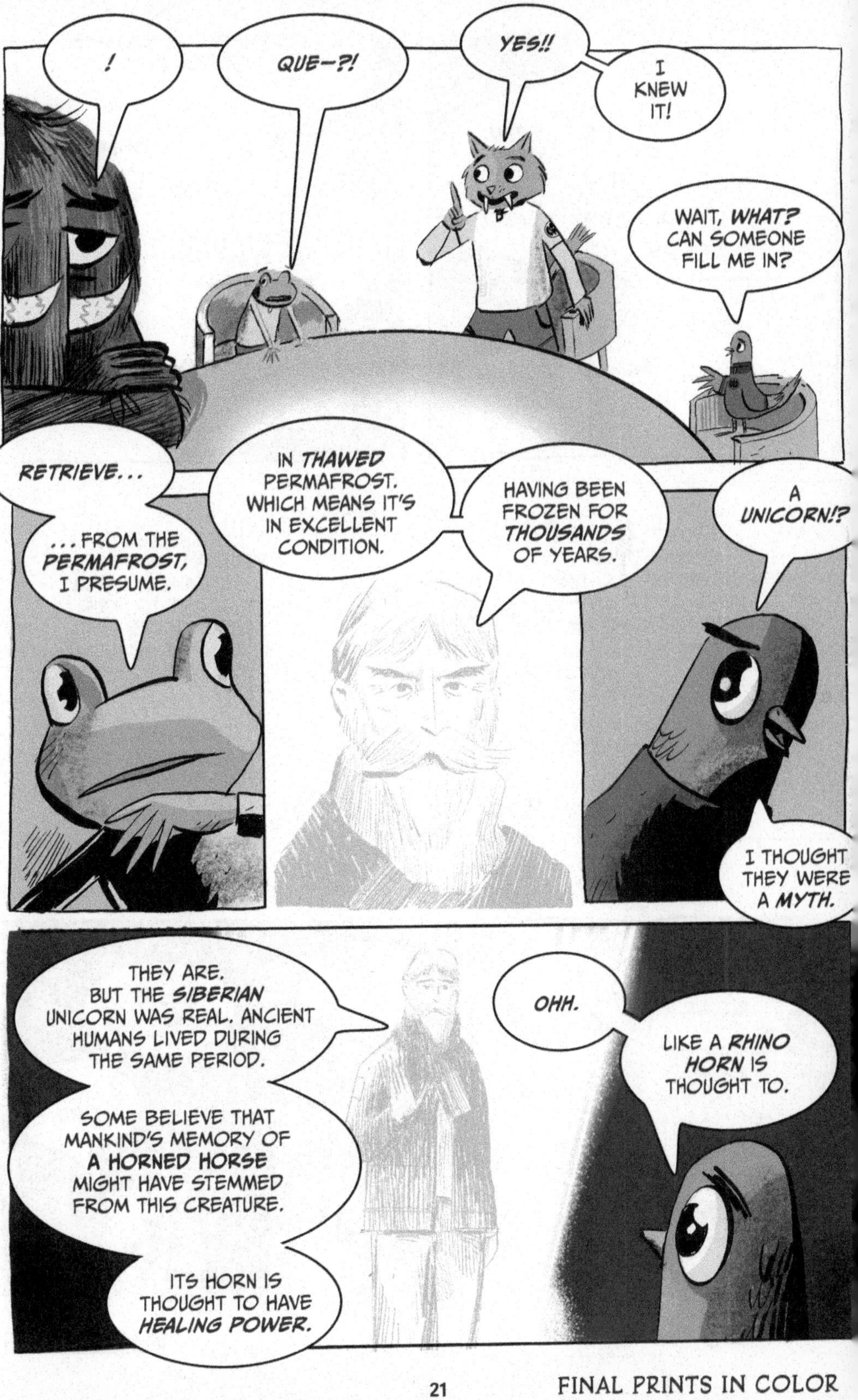
!
QUE—?!
YES!!
I KNEW IT!
WAIT, WHAT? CAN SOMEONE FILL ME IN?
RETRIEVE...
...FROM THE PERMAFROST, I PRESUME.
IN THAWED PERMAFROST. WHICH MEANS IT'S IN EXCELLENT CONDITION.
HAVING BEEN FROZEN FOR THOUSANDS OF YEARS.
A UNICORN!?
I THOUGHT THEY WERE A MYTH.
THEY ARE. BUT THE SIBERIAN UNICORN WAS REAL. ANCIENT HUMANS LIVED DURING THE SAME PERIOD.
SOME BELIEVE THAT MANKIND'S MEMORY OF A HORNED HORSE MIGHT HAVE STEMMED FROM THIS CREATURE.
ITS HORN IS THOUGHT TO HAVE HEALING POWER.
OHH.
LIKE A RHINO HORN IS THOUGHT TO.

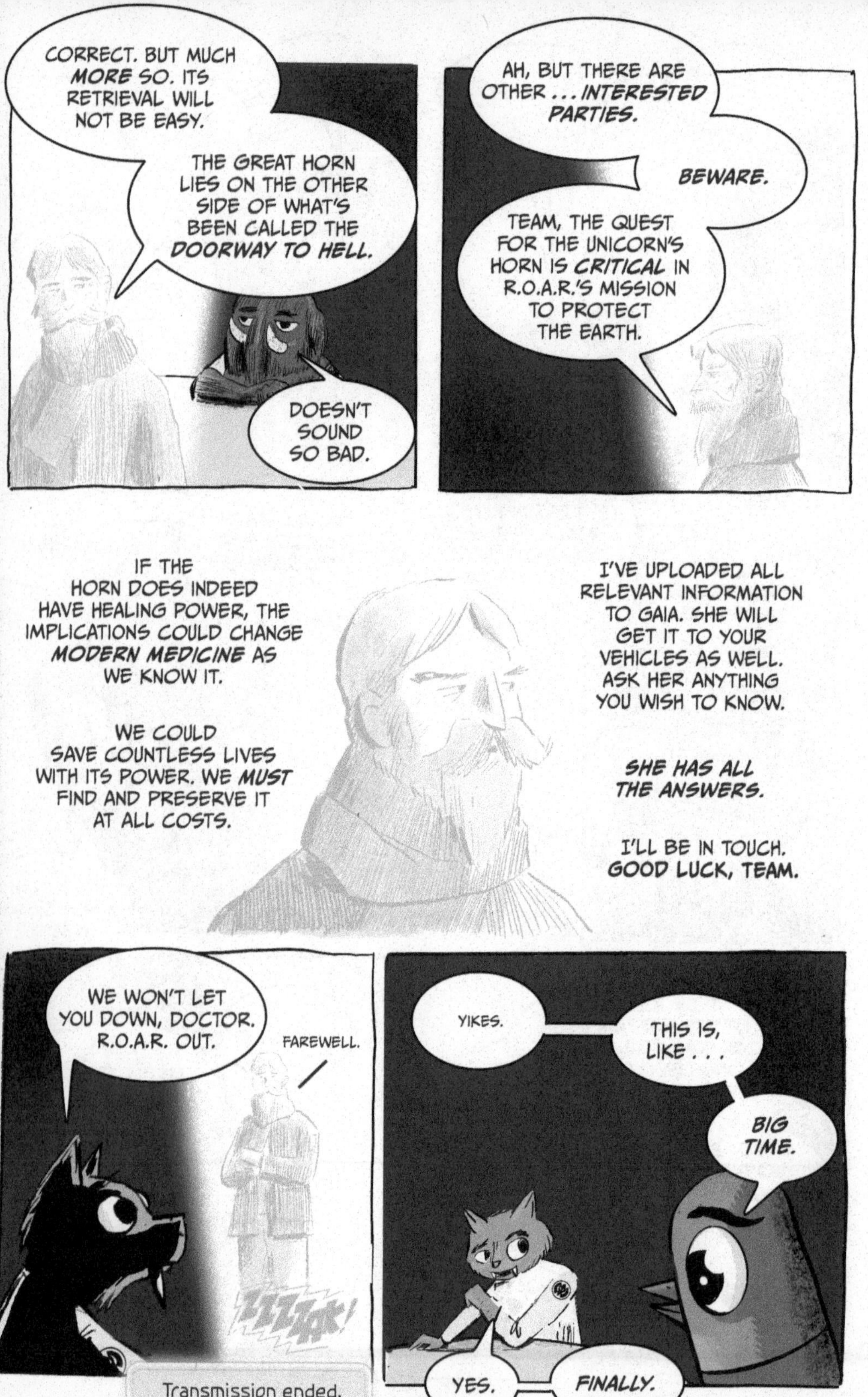
CORRECT. BUT MUCH MORE SO. ITS RETRIEVAL WILL NOT BE EASY.
THE GREAT HORN LIES ON THE OTHER SIDE OF WHAT'S BEEN CALLED THE DOORWAY TO HELL.
DOESN'T SOUND SO BAD.
AH, BUT THERE ARE OTHER . . . INTERESTED PARTIES.
BEWARE.
TEAM, THE QUEST FOR THE UNICORN'S HORN IS CRITICAL IN R.O.A.R.'S MISSION TO PROTECT THE EARTH.
IF THE HORN DOES INDEED HAVE HEALING POWER, THE IMPLICATIONS COULD CHANGE MODERN MEDICINE AS WE KNOW IT.
WE COULD SAVE COUNTLESS LIVES WITH ITS POWER. WE MUST FIND AND PRESERVE IT AT ALL COSTS.
I'VE UPLOADED ALL RELEVANT INFORMATION TO GAIA. SHE WILL GET IT TO YOUR VEHICLES AS WELL. ASK HER ANYTHING YOU WISH TO KNOW.
SHE HAS ALL THE ANSWERS.
I'LL BE IN TOUCH. GOOD LUCK, TEAM.
WE WON'T LET YOU DOWN, DOCTOR. R.O.A.R. OUT.
FAREWELL.
ZZZZAK!
Transmission ended.
YIKES.
THIS IS, LIKE . . .
BIG TIME.
YES.
FINALLY.

FINAL PRINTS IN COLOR

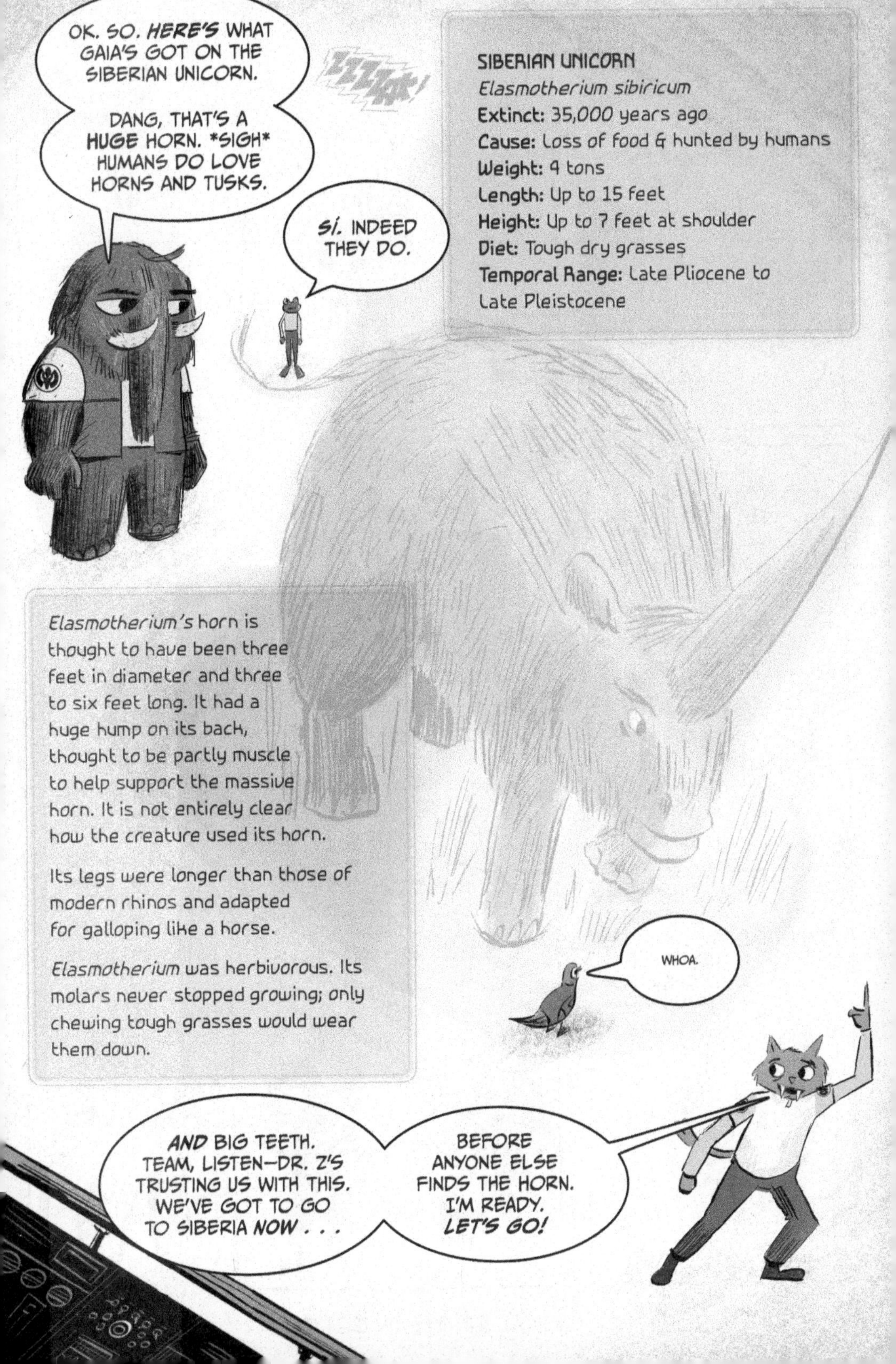
OK. SO. HERE'S WHAT GAIA'S GOT ON THE SIBERIAN UNICORN.
DANG, THAT'S A HUGE HORN. *SIGH* HUMANS DO LOVE HORNS AND TUSKS.
SIBERIAN UNICORN
Elasmotherium sibiricum
Extinct: 35,000 years ago
Cause: Loss of food & hunted by humans
Weight: 4 tons
Length: Up to 15 feet
Height: Up to 7 feet at shoulder
Diet: Tough dry grasses
Temporal Range: Late Pliocene to Late Pleistocene
SÍ. INDEED THEY DO.
Elasmotherium's horn is thought to have been three feet in diameter and three to six feet long. It had a huge hump on its back, thought to be partly muscle to help support the massive horn. It is not entirely clear how the creature used its horn.
Its legs were longer than those of modern rhinos and adapted for galloping like a horse.
Elasmotherium was herbivorous. Its molars never stopped growing; only chewing tough grasses would wear them down.
WHOA.
AND BIG TEETH. TEAM, LISTEN—DR. Z'S TRUSTING US WITH THIS. WE'VE GOT TO GO TO SIBERIA NOW . . .
BEFORE ANYONE ELSE FINDS THE HORN. I'M READY. LET'S GO!

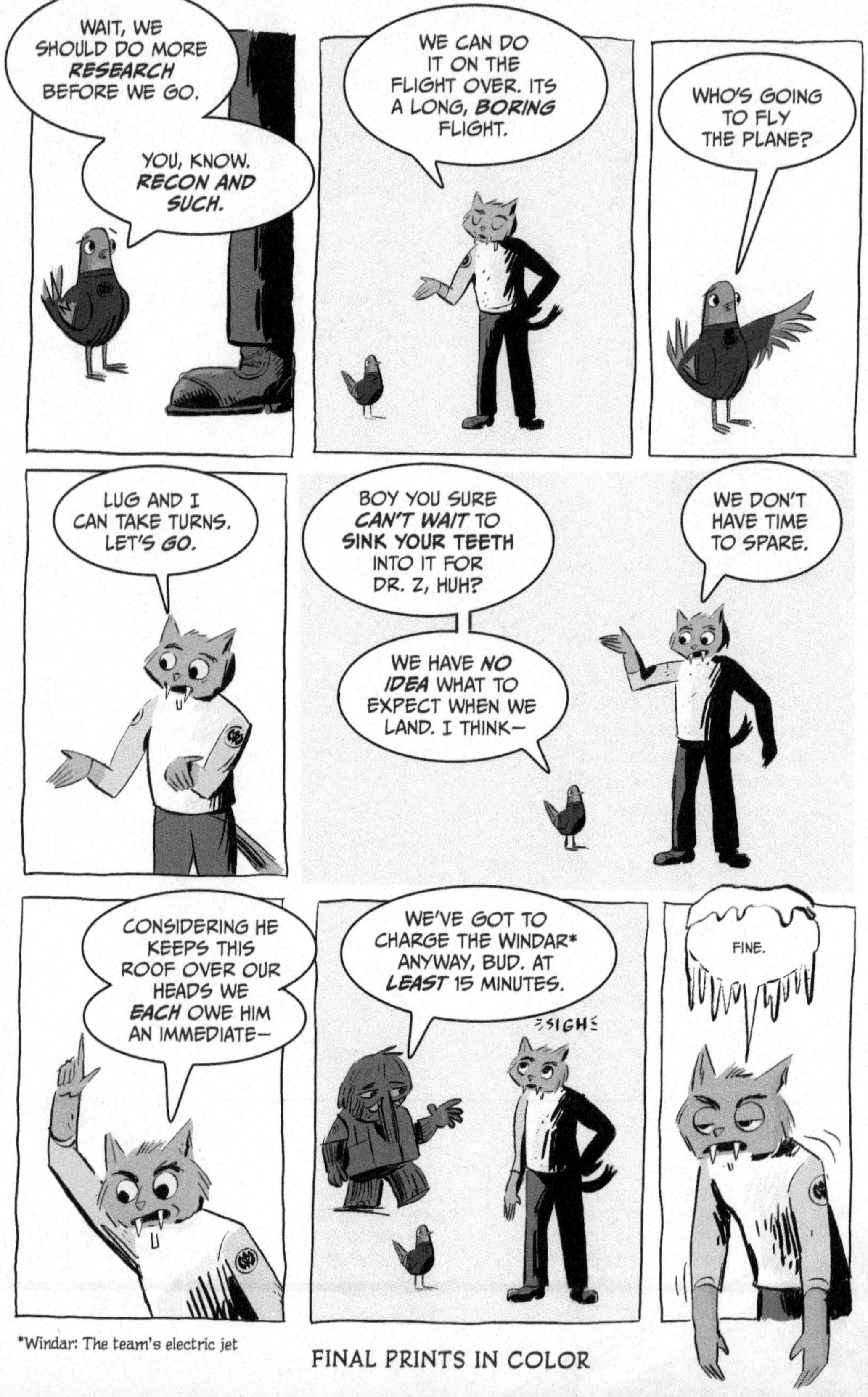
WAIT, WE SHOULD DO MORE RESEARCH BEFORE WE GO.
YOU, KNOW. RECON AND SUCH.
WE CAN DO IT ON THE FLIGHT OVER. ITS A LONG, BORING FLIGHT.
WHO'S GOING TO FLY THE PLANE?
LUG AND I CAN TAKE TURNS. LET'S GO.
BOY YOU SURE CAN'T WAIT TO SINK YOUR TEETH INTO IT FOR DR. Z, HUH?
WE HAVE NO IDEA WHAT TO EXPECT WHEN WE LAND. I THINK—
WE DON'T HAVE TIME TO SPARE.
CONSIDERING HE KEEPS THIS ROOF OVER OUR HEADS WE EACH OWE HIM AN IMMEDIATE—
WE'VE GOT TO CHARGE THE WINDAR* ANYWAY, BUD. AT LEAST 15 MINUTES.
SIGH
FINE.

*Windar: The team's electric jet

FINAL PRINTS IN COLOR

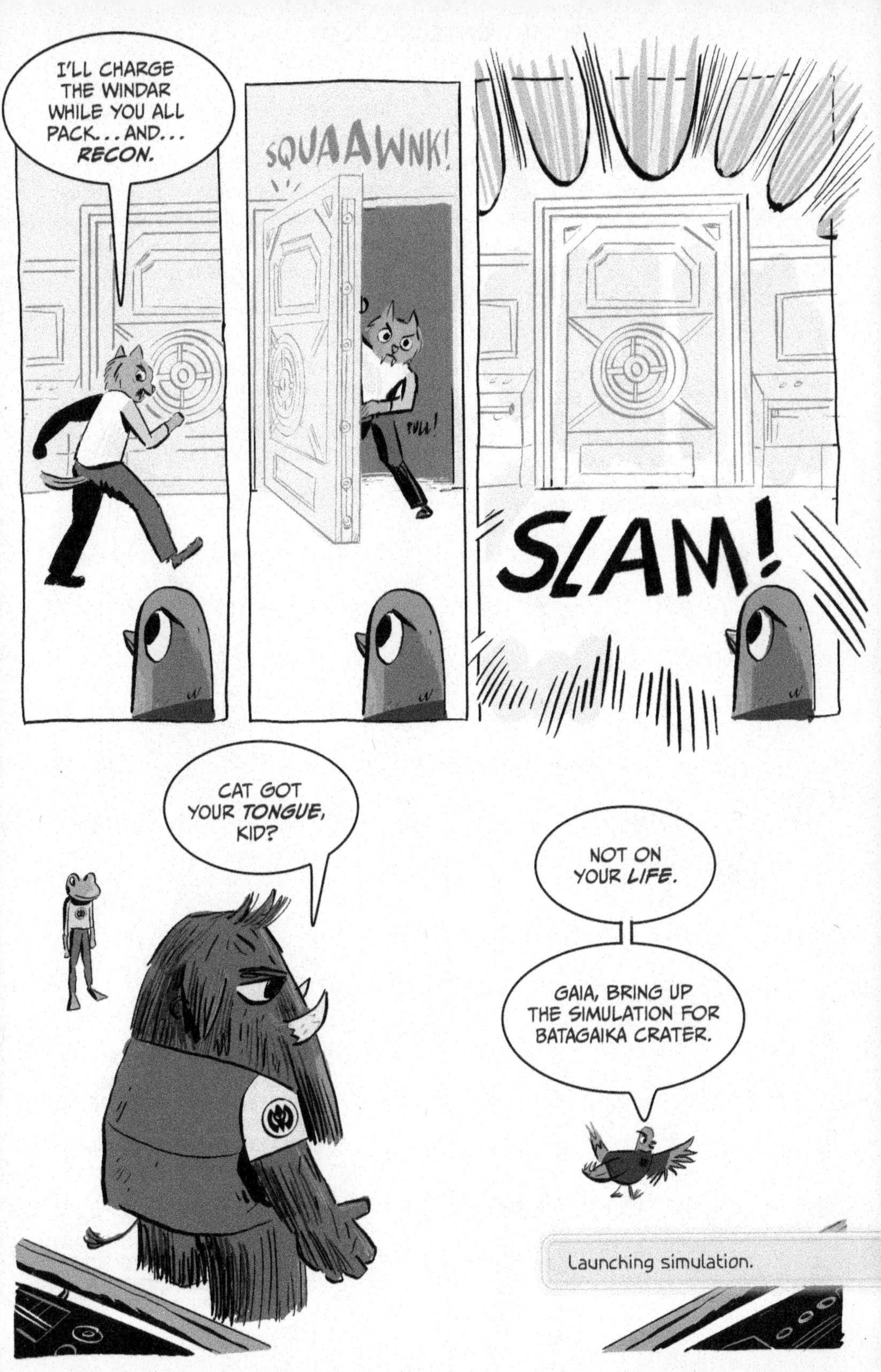
I'LL CHARGE THE WINDAR WHILE YOU ALL PACK...AND... RECON.
SQUAAWNK!
PULL!
SLAM!
CAT GOT YOUR TONGUE, KID?
NOT ON YOUR LIFE.
GAIA, BRING UP THE SIMULATION FOR BATAGAIKA CRATER.
Launching simulation.

FINAL PRINTS IN COLOR

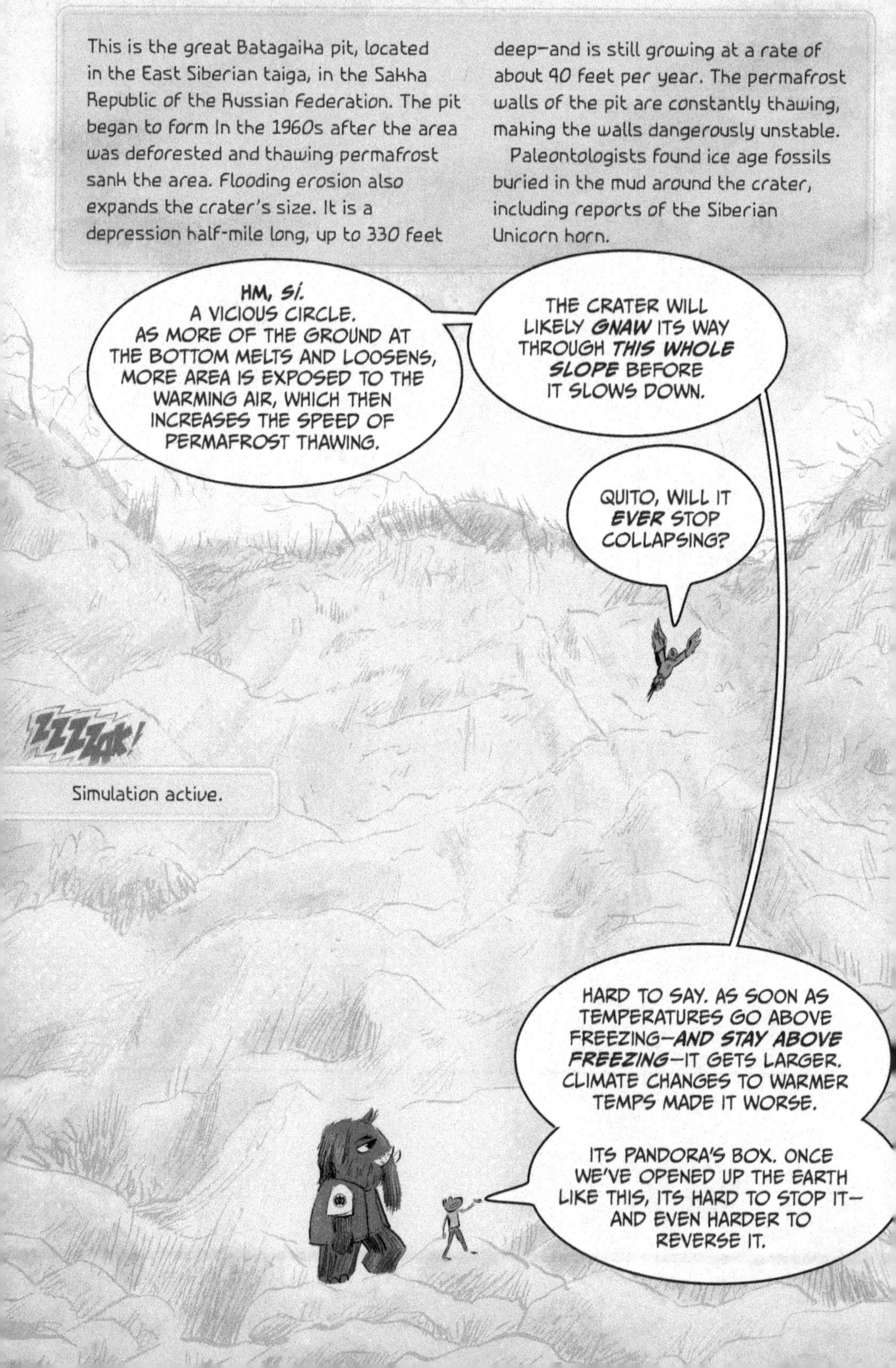
This is the great Batagaika pit, located in the East Siberian taiga, in the Sakha Republic of the Russian Federation. The pit began to form In the 1960s after the area was deforested and thawing permafrost sank the area. Flooding erosion also expands the crater's size. It is a depression half-mile long, up to 330 feet deep—and is still growing at a rate of about 40 feet per year. The permafrost walls of the pit are constantly thawing, making the walls dangerously unstable.
Paleontologists found ice age fossils buried in the mud around the crater, including reports of the Siberian Unicorn horn.
HM, SÍ. A VICIOUS CIRCLE. AS MORE OF THE GROUND AT THE BOTTOM MELTS AND LOOSENS, MORE AREA IS EXPOSED TO THE WARMING AIR, WHICH THEN INCREASES THE SPEED OF PERMAFROST THAWING.
THE CRATER WILL LIKELY GNAW ITS WAY THROUGH THIS WHOLE SLOPE BEFORE IT SLOWS DOWN.
QUITO, WILL IT EVER STOP COLLAPSING?
ZZZZAK!
Simulation active.
HARD TO SAY. AS SOON AS TEMPERATURES GO ABOVE FREEZING—AND STAY ABOVE FREEZING—IT GETS LARGER. CLIMATE CHANGES TO WARMER TEMPS MADE IT WORSE.
ITS PANDORA'S BOX. ONCE WE'VE OPENED UP THE EARTH LIKE THIS, ITS HARD TO STOP IT—AND EVEN HARDER TO REVERSE IT.

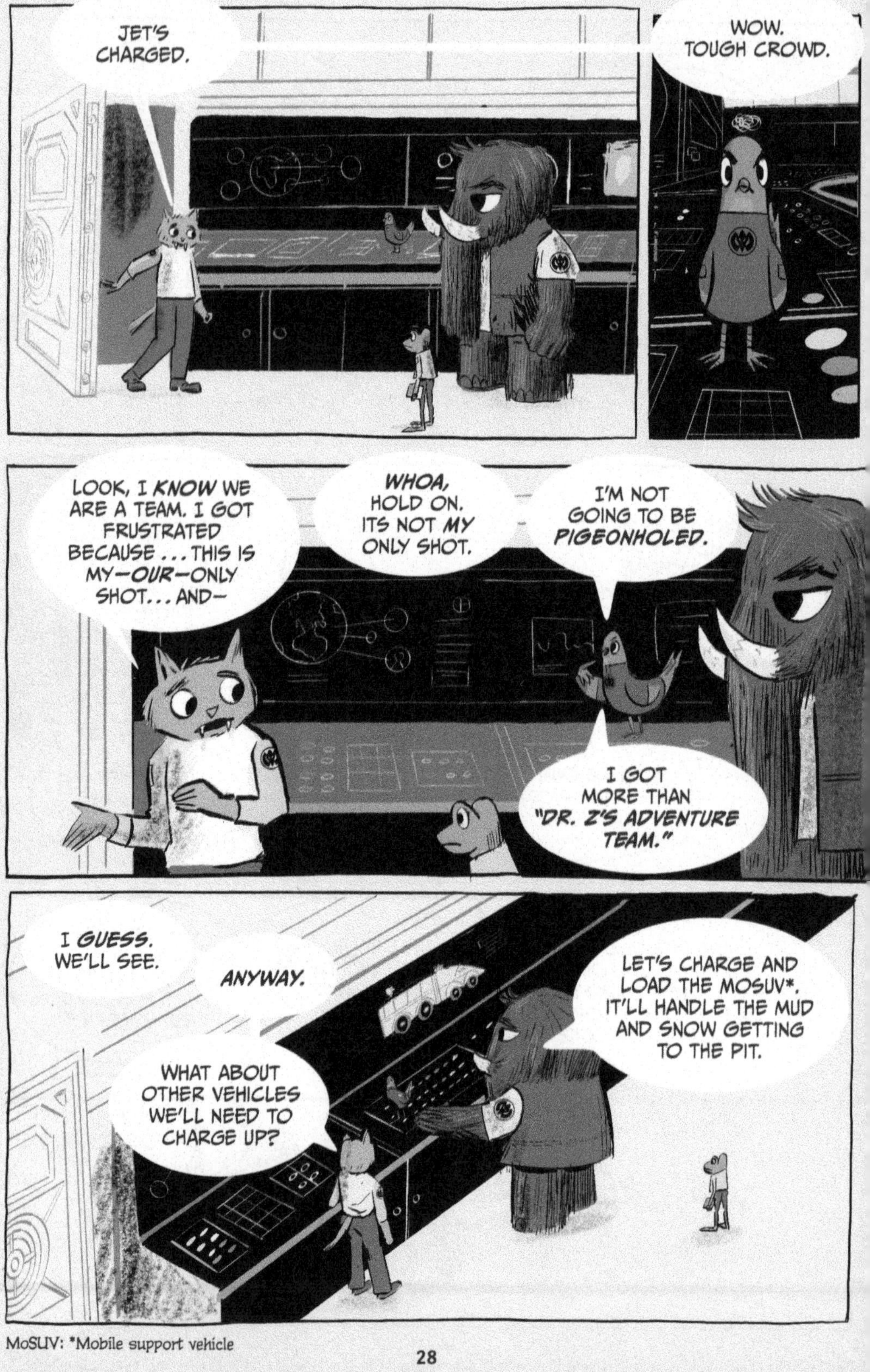
JET'S CHARGED.
WOW. TOUGH CROWD.
LOOK, I KNOW WE ARE A TEAM. I GOT FRUSTRATED BECAUSE . . . THIS IS MY—OUR—ONLY SHOT. . . AND—
WHOA, HOLD ON. ITS NOT MY ONLY SHOT.
I'M NOT GOING TO BE PIGEONHOLED.
I GOT MORE THAN "DR. Z'S ADVENTURE TEAM."
I GUESS. WE'LL SEE.
ANYWAY.
LET'S CHARGE AND LOAD THE MOSUV*. IT'LL HANDLE THE MUD AND SNOW GETTING TO THE PIT.
WHAT ABOUT OTHER VEHICLES WE'LL NEED TO CHARGE UP?

MoSUV: *Mobile support vehicle

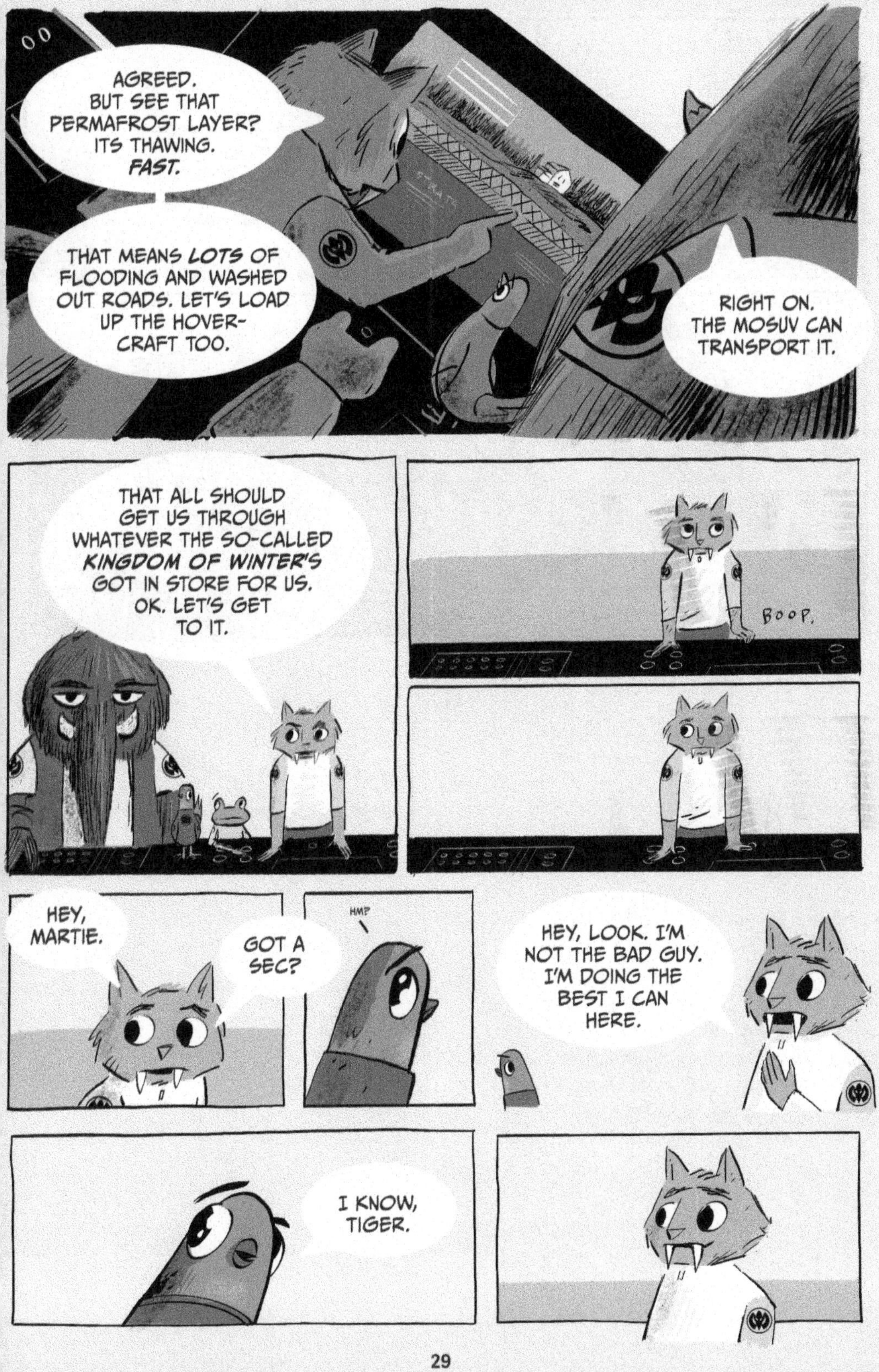
AGREED.
BUT SEE THAT PERMAFROST LAYER? ITS THAWING. *FAST.*
THAT MEANS *LOTS* OF FLOODING AND WASHED OUT ROADS. LET'S LOAD UP THE HOVER-CRAFT TOO.
RIGHT ON. THE MOSUV CAN TRANSPORT IT.
THAT ALL SHOULD GET US THROUGH WHATEVER THE SO-CALLED *KINGDOM OF WINTER'S* GOT IN STORE FOR US. OK. LET'S GET TO IT.
BOOP.
HEY, MARTIE.
GOT A SEC?
HM?
HEY, LOOK. I'M NOT THE BAD GUY. I'M DOING THE BEST I CAN HERE.
I KNOW, TIGER.

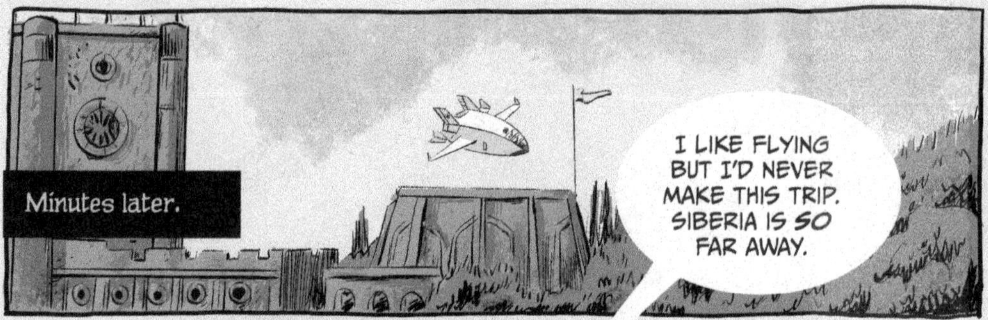
Minutes later.
I LIKE FLYING BUT I'D NEVER MAKE THIS TRIP. SIBERIA IS *SO* FAR AWAY.

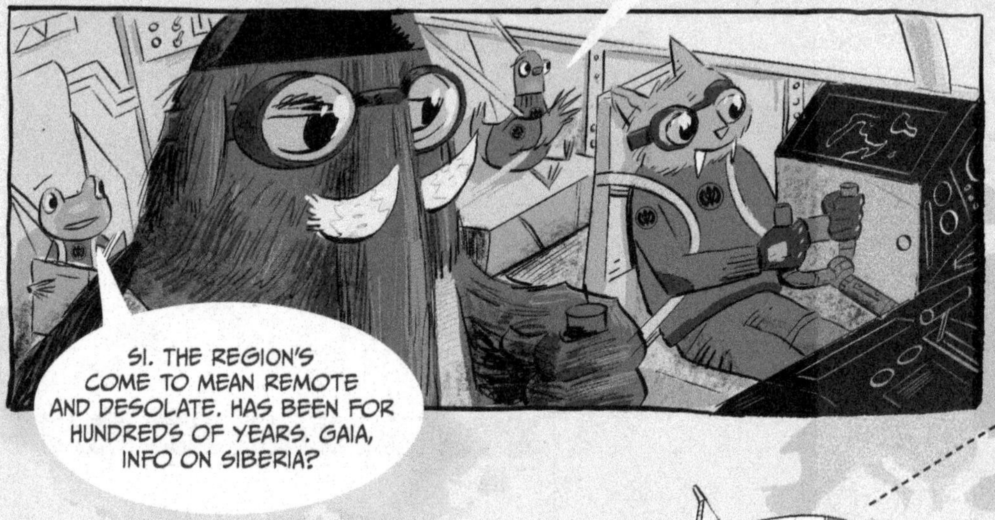
SI. THE REGION'S COME TO MEAN REMOTE AND DESOLATE. HAS BEEN FOR HUNDREDS OF YEARS. GAIA, INFO ON SIBERIA?

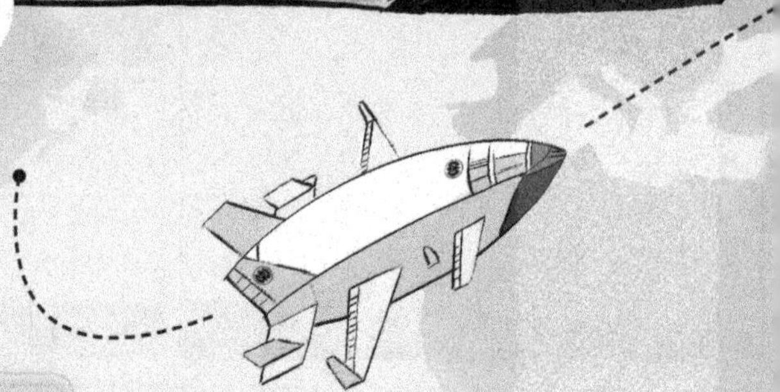

Empress Elizabeth exiled prominent political prisoners to Siberia beginning in 1744. It took a year's journey to reach Siberia from St. Petersburg in those days. Today, it's still remote. There are only two highways in Yakutia. The one built using Gulag prisoners labor under Communism is mostly unpaved dirt.

Flight time: 16 hours 47 minutes 10 seconds

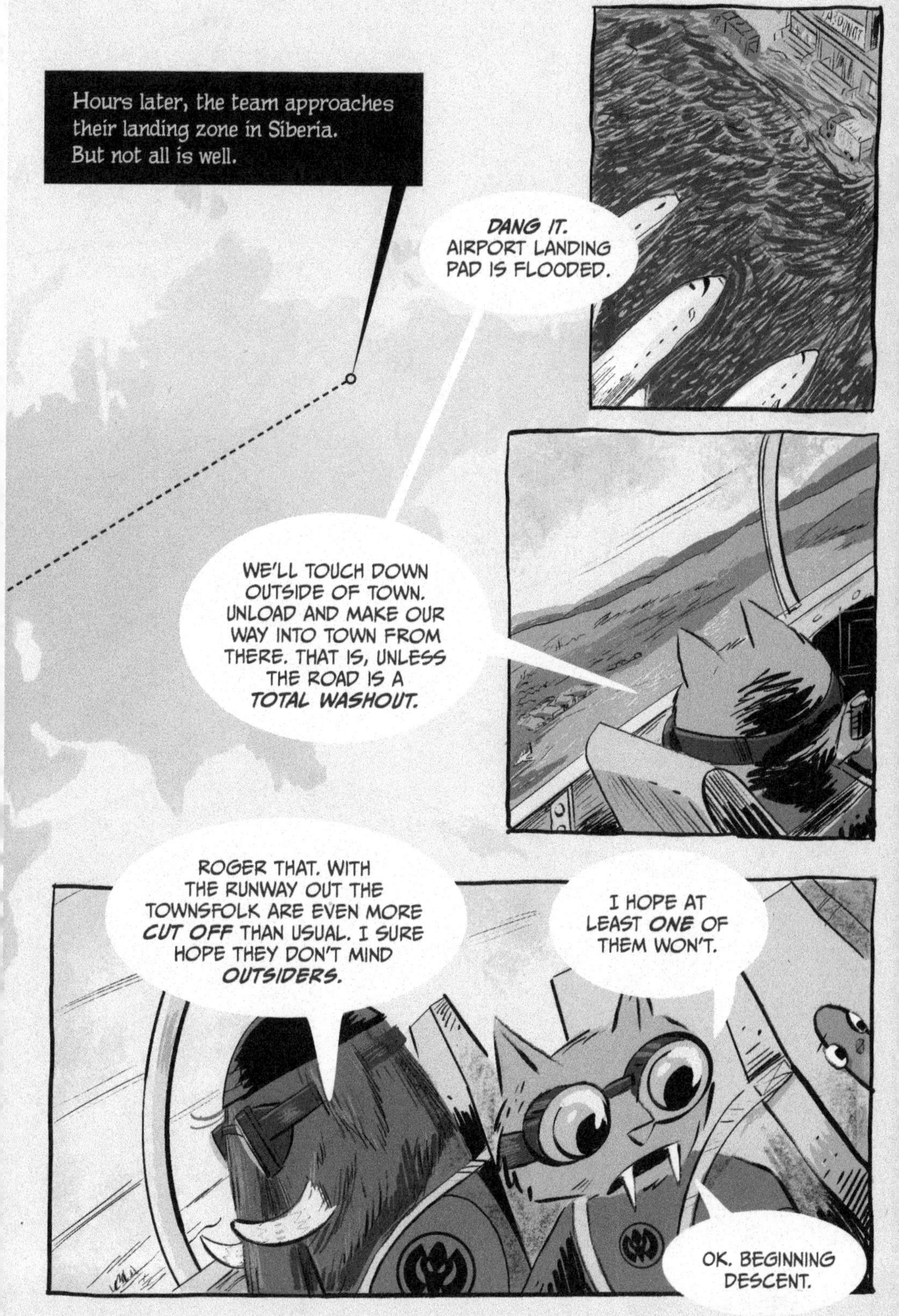
Hours later, the team approaches their landing zone in Siberia. But not all is well.
DANG IT. AIRPORT LANDING PAD IS FLOODED.
WE'LL TOUCH DOWN OUTSIDE OF TOWN. UNLOAD AND MAKE OUR WAY INTO TOWN FROM THERE. THAT IS, UNLESS THE ROAD IS A TOTAL WASHOUT.
ROGER THAT. WITH THE RUNWAY OUT THE TOWNSFOLK ARE EVEN MORE CUT OFF THAN USUAL. I SURE HOPE THEY DON'T MIND OUTSIDERS.
I HOPE AT LEAST ONE OF THEM WON'T.
OK. BEGINNING DESCENT.

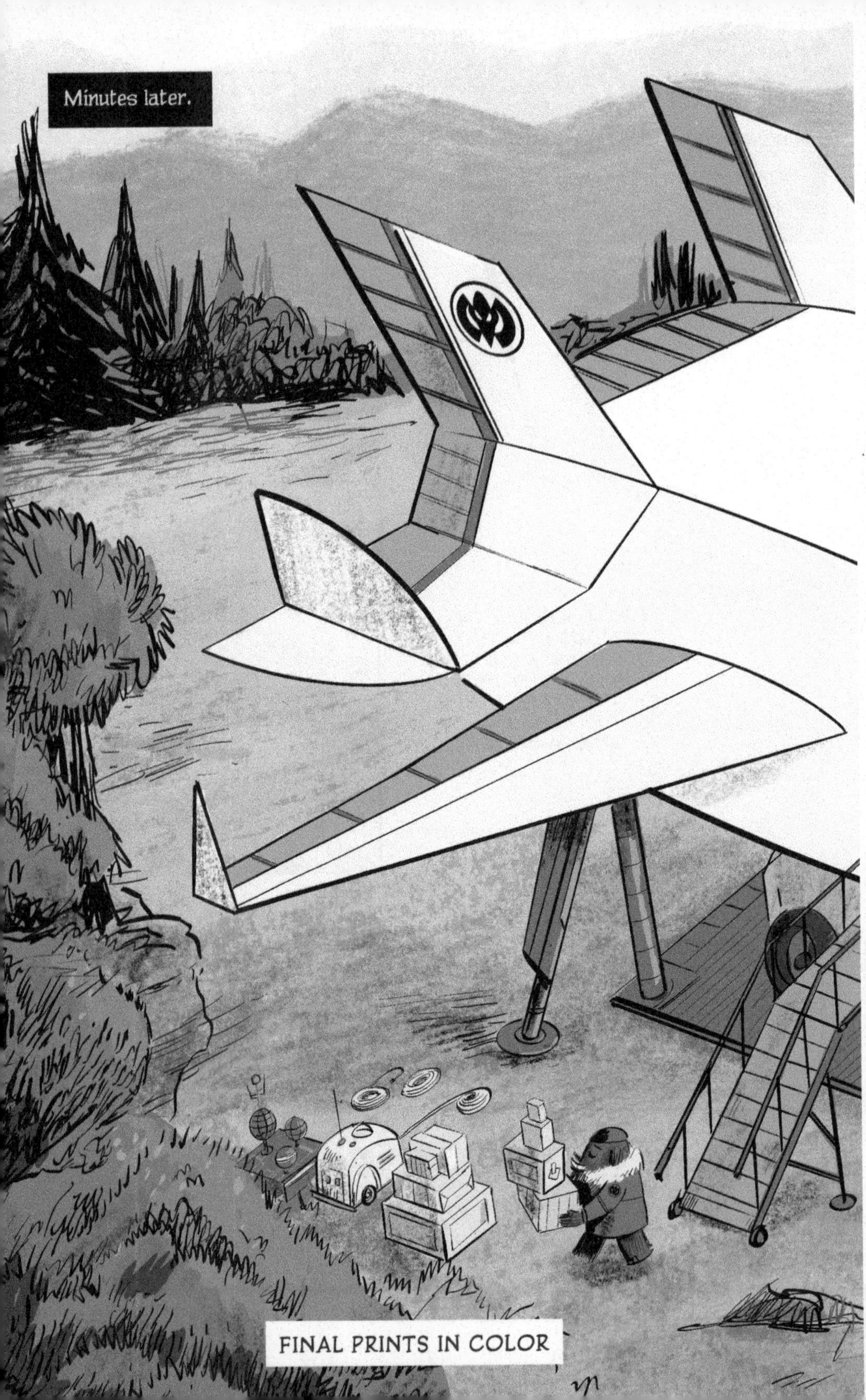
Minutes later.

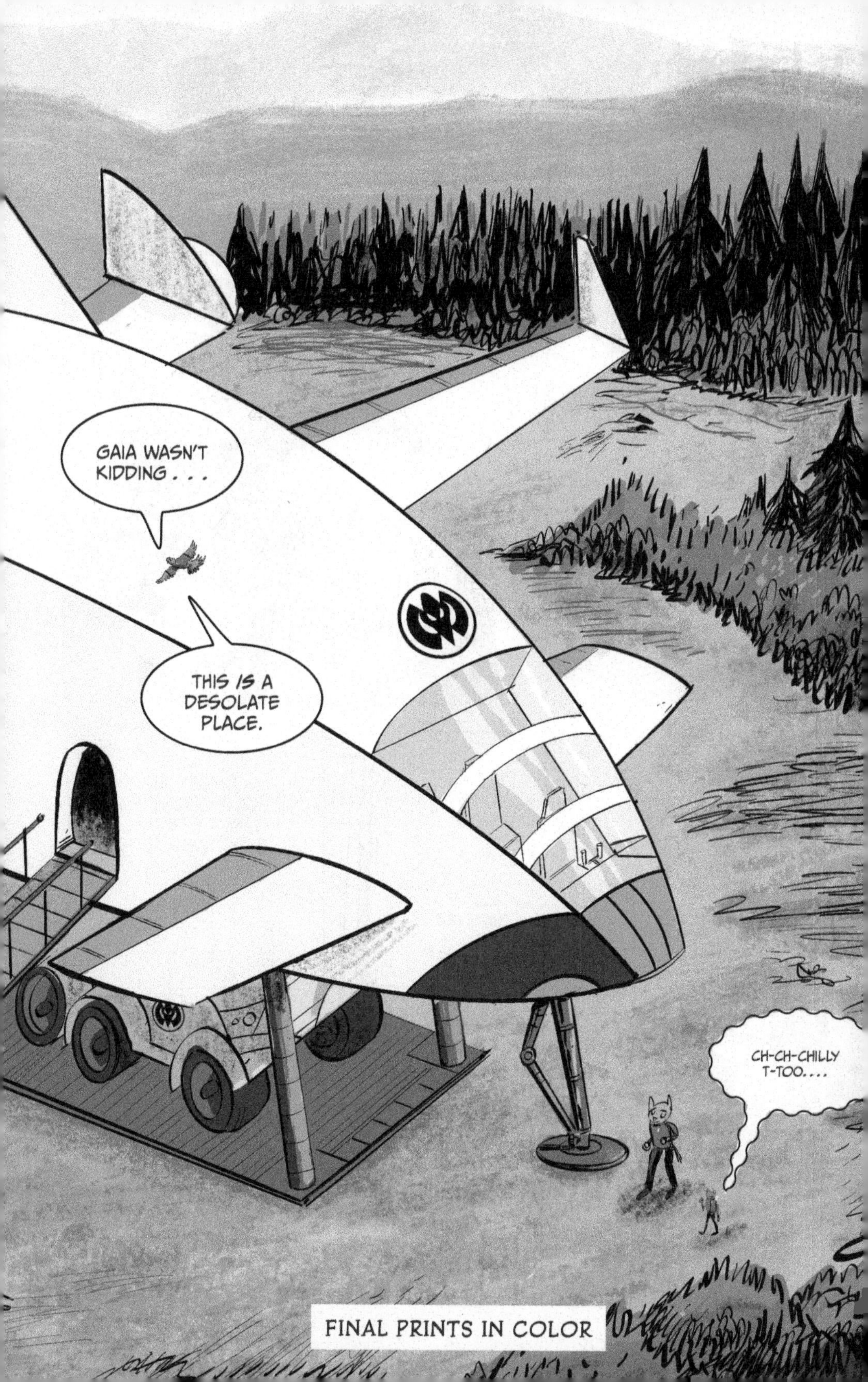
GAIA WASN'T KIDDING . . .
THIS IS A DESOLATE PLACE.
CH-CH-CHILLY T-TOO. . . .

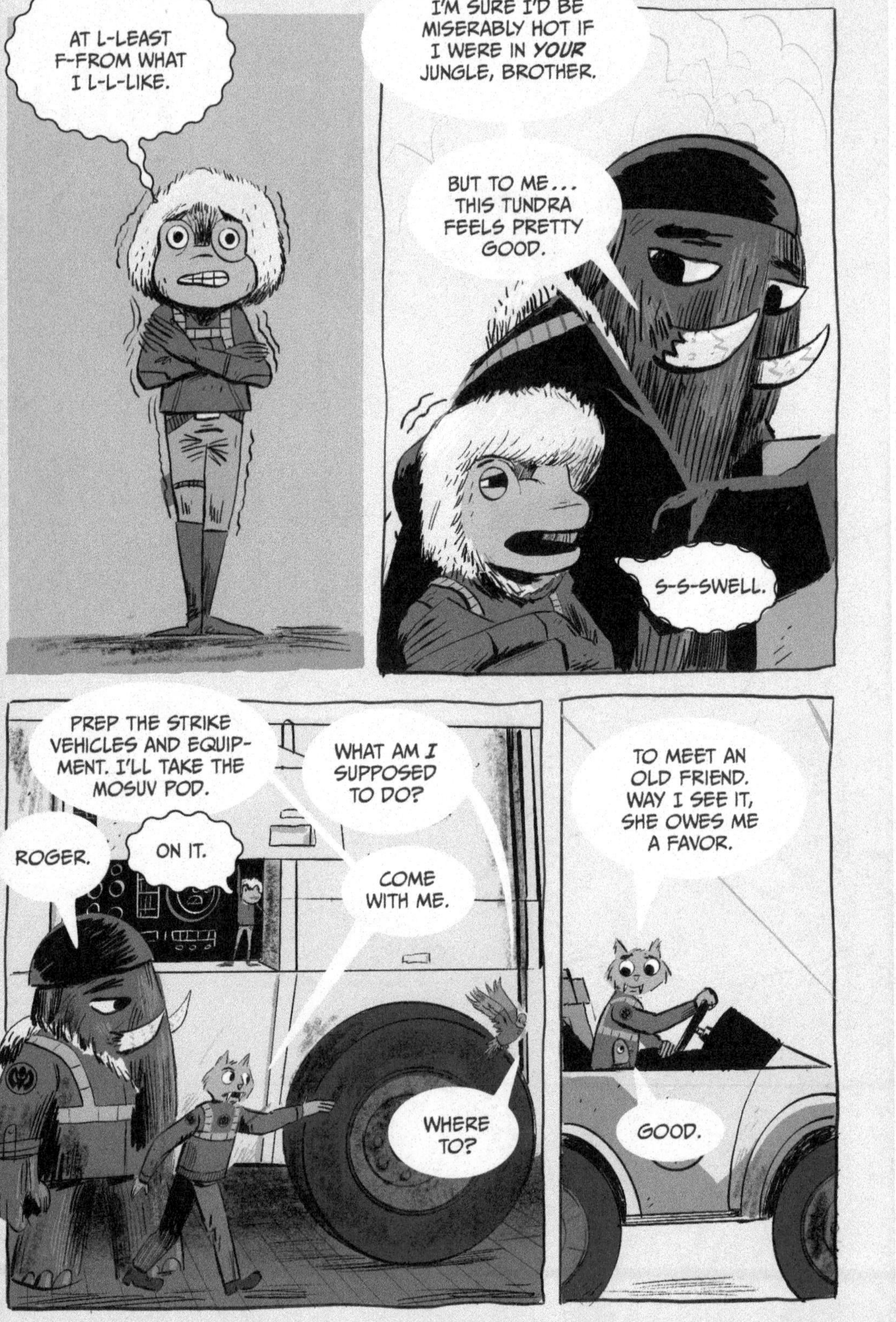
AT L-LEAST F-FROM WHAT I L-L-LIKE.
I'M SURE I'D BE MISERABLY HOT IF I WERE IN *YOUR* JUNGLE, BROTHER.
BUT TO ME... THIS TUNDRA FEELS PRETTY GOOD.
S-S-SWELL.
PREP THE STRIKE VEHICLES AND EQUIP-MENT. I'LL TAKE THE MOSUV POD.
ROGER.
ON IT.
WHAT AM *I* SUPPOSED TO DO?
COME WITH ME.
WHERE TO?
TO MEET AN OLD FRIEND. WAY I SEE IT, SHE OWES ME A FAVOR.
GOOD.

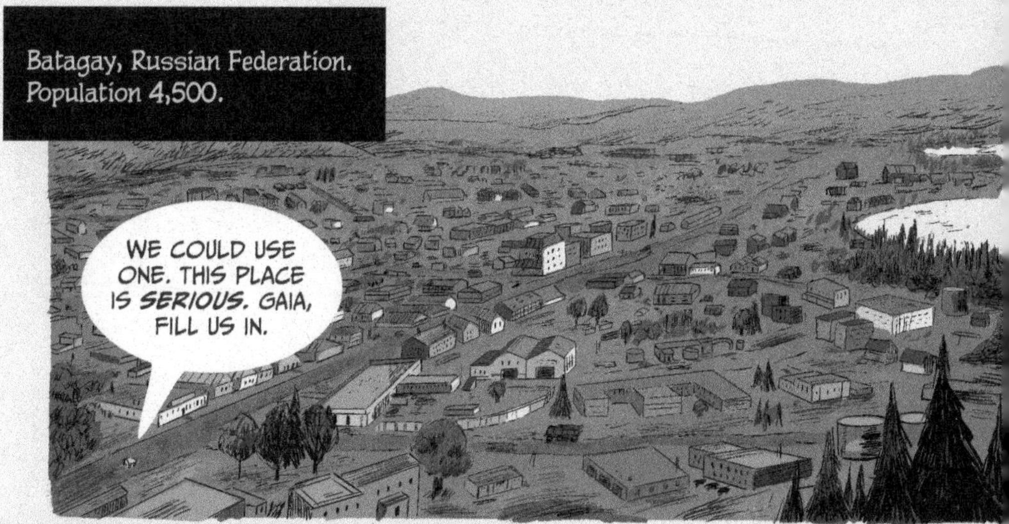
Batagay, Russian Federation.
Population 4,500.
WE COULD USE ONE. THIS PLACE IS *SERIOUS.* GAIA, FILL US IN.

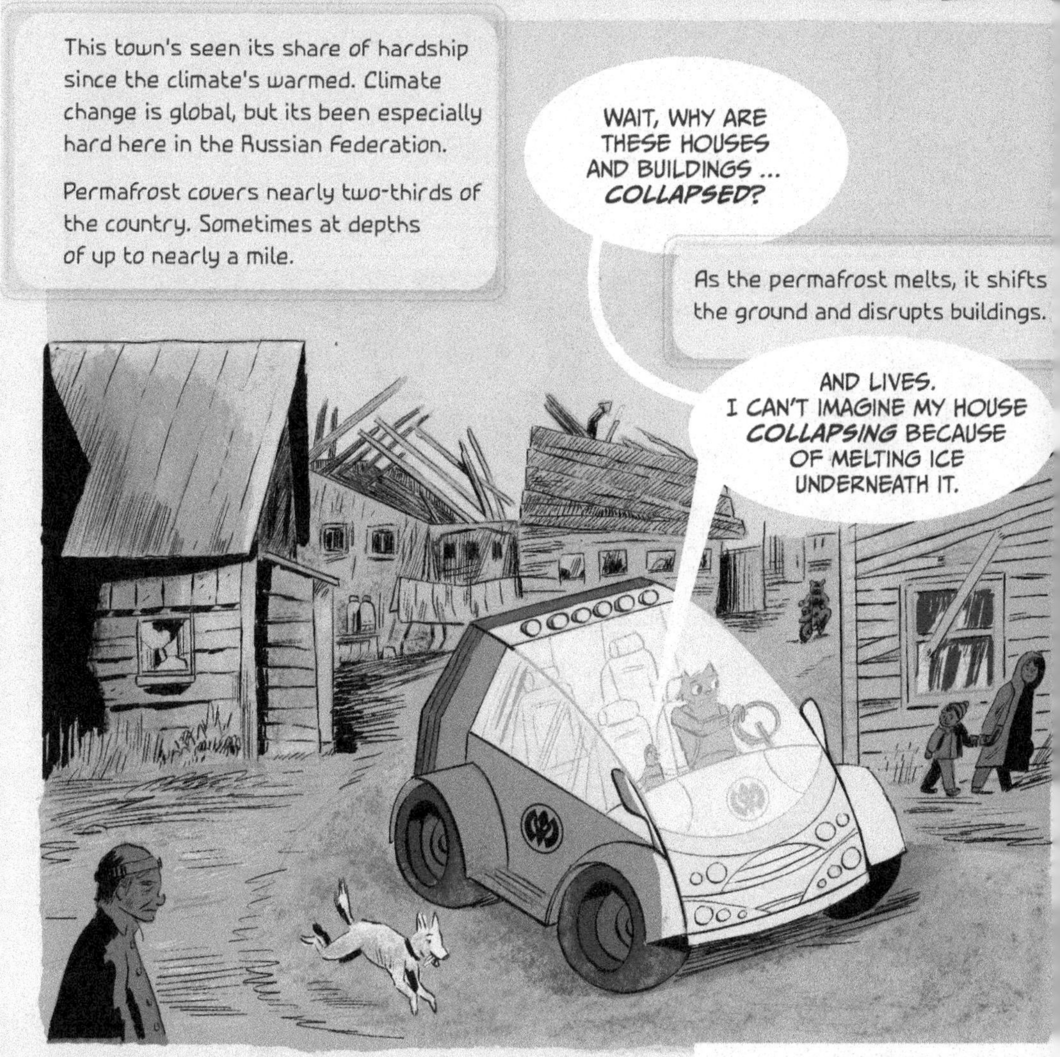
This town's seen its share of hardship since the climate's warmed. Climate change is global, but its been especially hard here in the Russian Federation.
Permafrost covers nearly two-thirds of the country. Sometimes at depths of up to nearly a mile.
WAIT, WHY ARE THESE HOUSES AND BUILDINGS ... *COLLAPSED?*
As the permafrost melts, it shifts the ground and disrupts buildings.
AND LIVES. I CAN'T IMAGINE MY HOUSE *COLLAPSING* BECAUSE OF MELTING ICE UNDERNEATH IT.

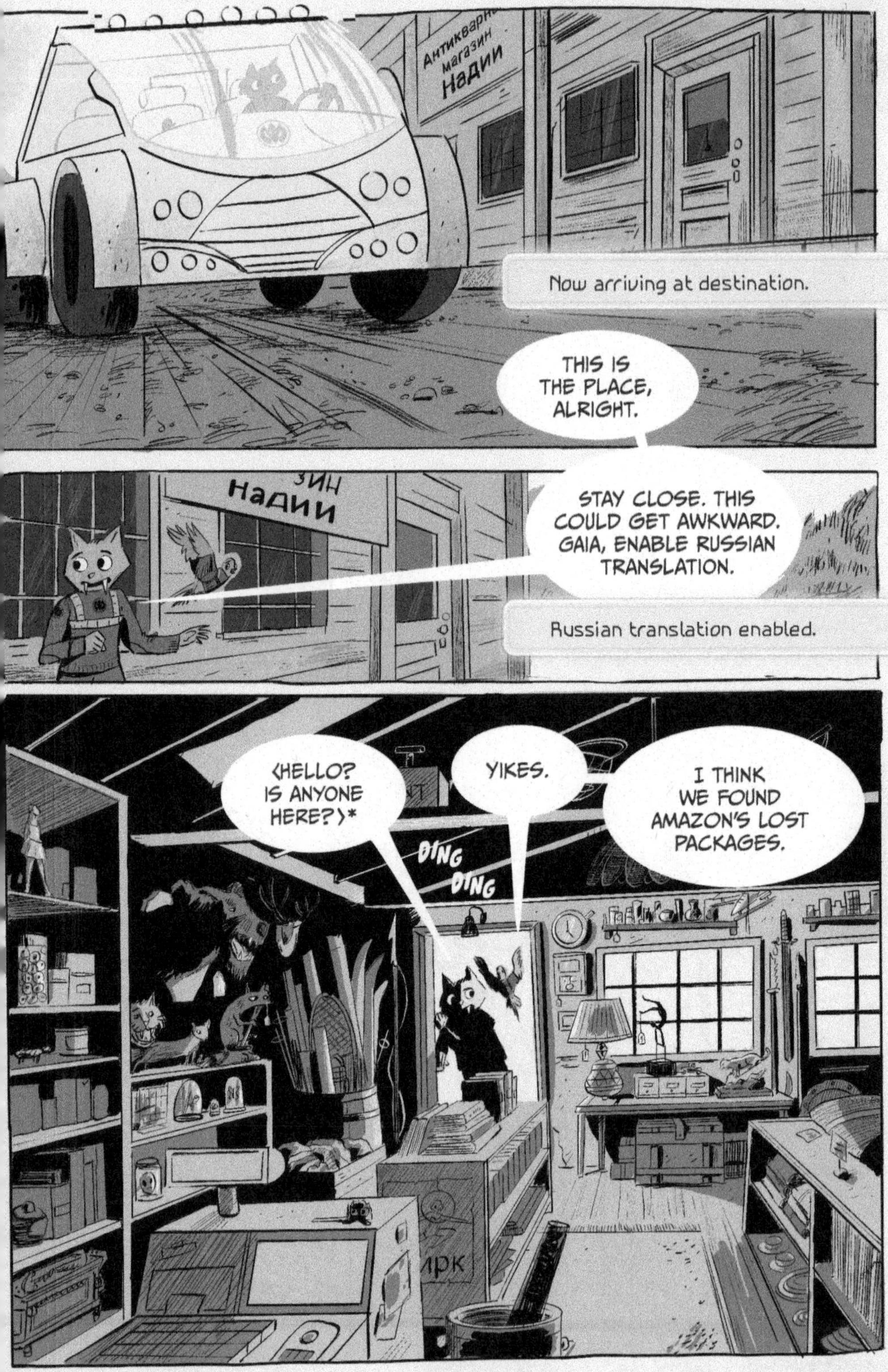
Антикварн
магазин
Надии
Now arriving at destination.
THIS IS THE PLACE, ALRIGHT.
Надии
STAY CLOSE. THIS COULD GET AWKWARD. GAIA, ENABLE RUSSIAN TRANSLATION.
Russian translation enabled.
‹HELLO? IS ANYONE HERE?›*
DING DING
YIKES.
I THINK WE FOUND AMAZON'S LOST PACKAGES.

*Translated from Russian

FINAL PRINTS IN COLOR

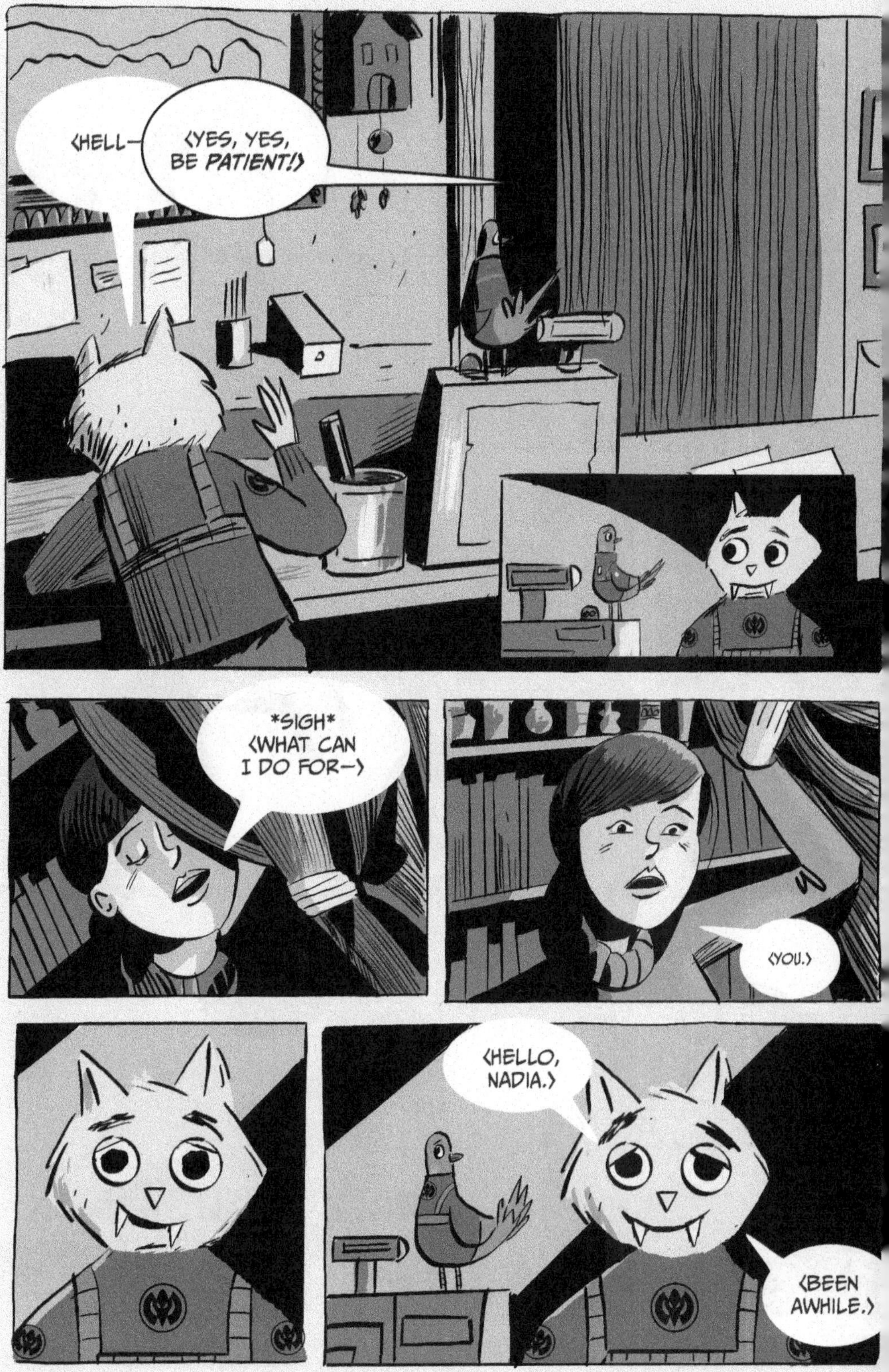

<HELL—
<YES, YES, BE PATIENT!>
SIGH <WHAT CAN I DO FOR—>
<YOU.>
<HELLO, NADIA.>
<BEEN AWHILE.>

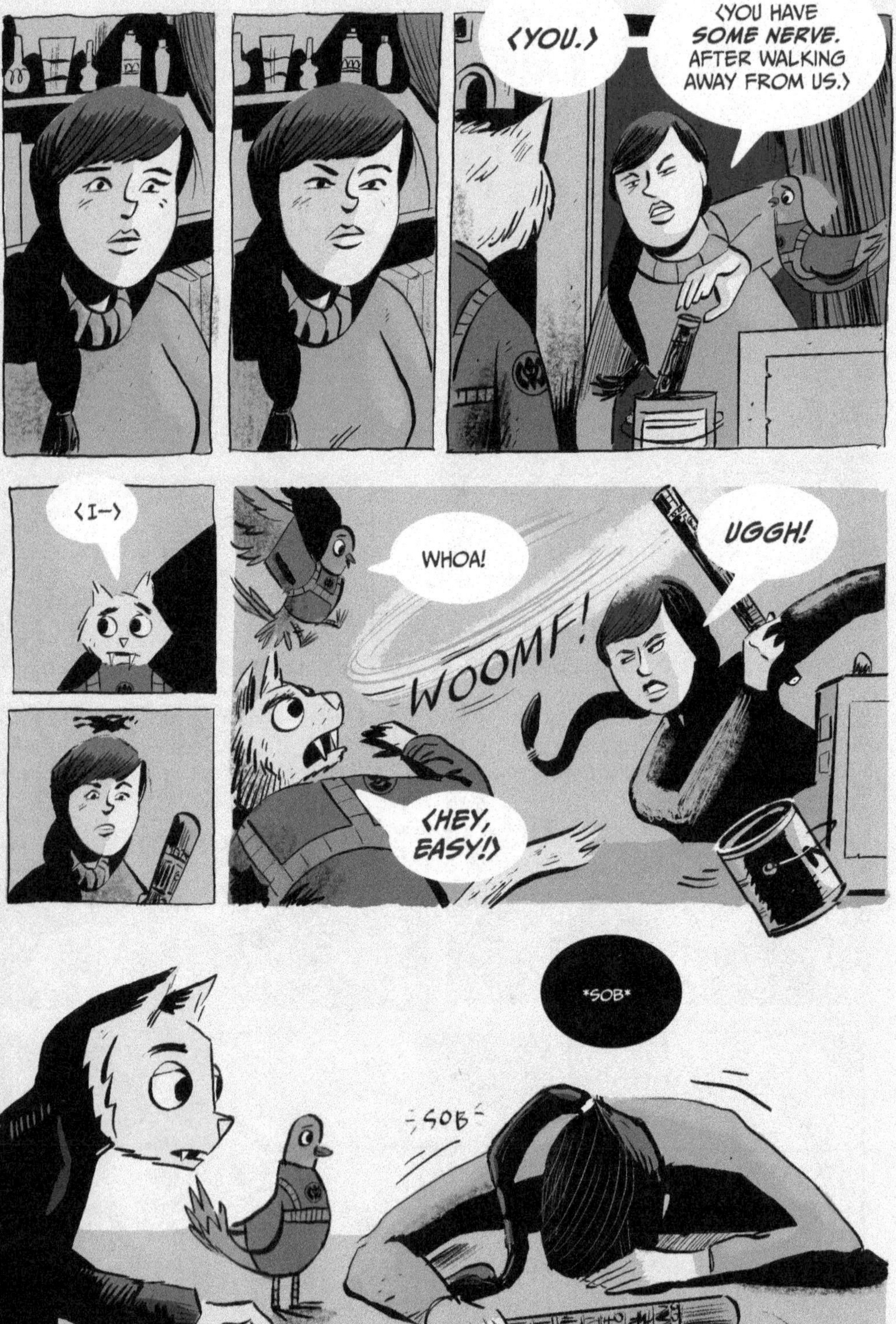
‹YOU.›
‹YOU HAVE SOME NERVE. AFTER WALKING AWAY FROM US.›
‹I—›
WHOA!
UGGH!
WOOMF!
‹HEY, EASY!›
SOB
SOB

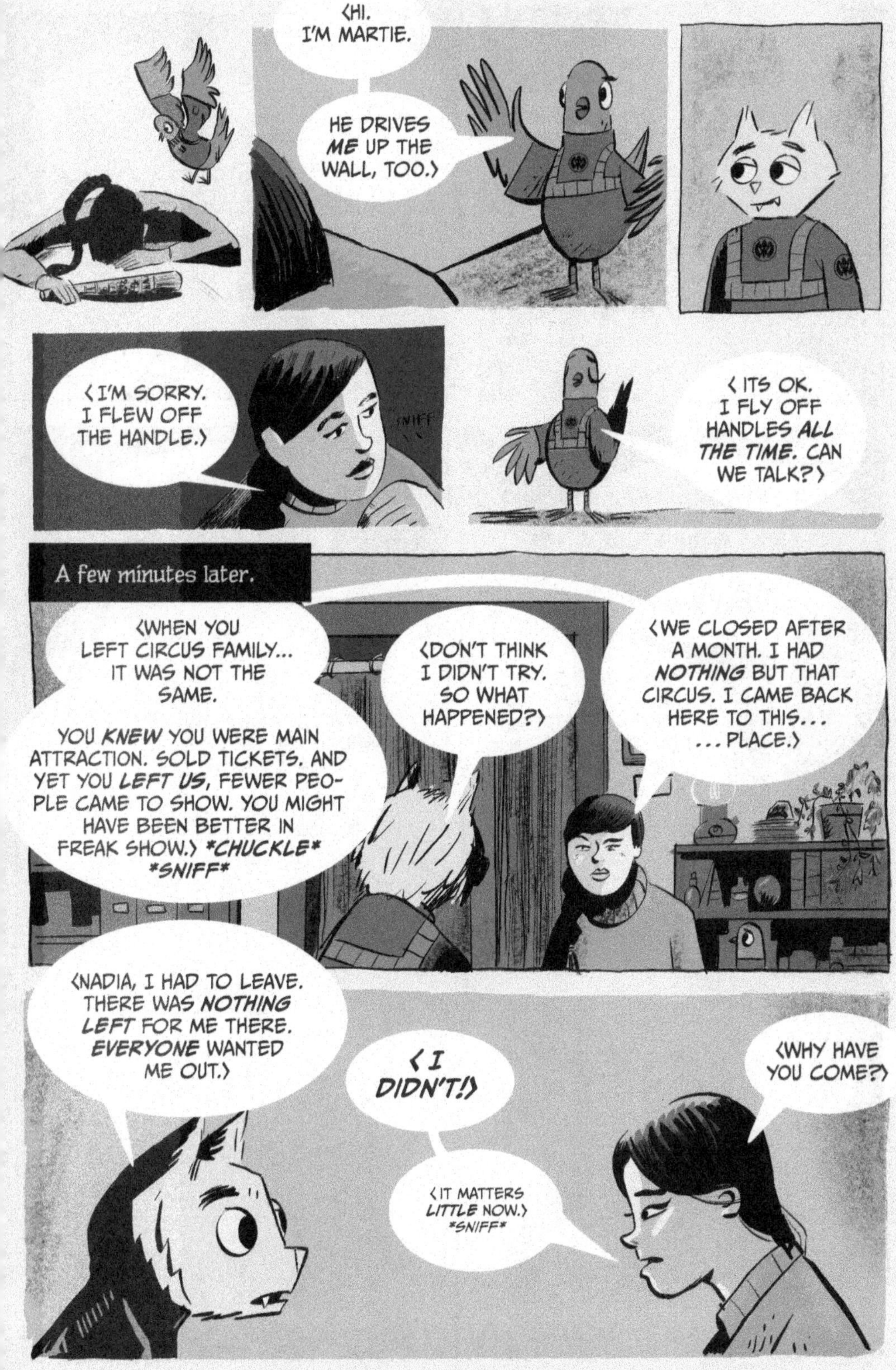

‹HI. I'M MARTIE.
HE DRIVES *ME* UP THE WALL, TOO.›
‹I'M SORRY. I FLEW OFF THE HANDLE.›
SNIFF
‹ITS OK. I FLY OFF HANDLES *ALL THE TIME.* CAN WE TALK?›
A few minutes later.
‹WHEN YOU LEFT CIRCUS FAMILY... IT WAS NOT THE SAME.
YOU *KNEW* YOU WERE MAIN ATTRACTION. SOLD TICKETS. AND YET YOU *LEFT US*, FEWER PEOPLE CAME TO SHOW. YOU MIGHT HAVE BEEN BETTER IN FREAK SHOW.› *CHUCKLE* *SNIFF*
‹DON'T THINK I DIDN'T TRY. SO WHAT HAPPENED?›
‹WE CLOSED AFTER A MONTH. I HAD *NOTHING* BUT THAT CIRCUS. I CAME BACK HERE TO THIS... ...PLACE.›
‹NADIA, I HAD TO LEAVE. THERE WAS *NOTHING LEFT* FOR ME THERE. *EVERYONE* WANTED ME OUT.›
‹I DIDN'T!›
‹WHY HAVE YOU COME?›
‹IT MATTERS *LITTLE* NOW.› *SNIFF*

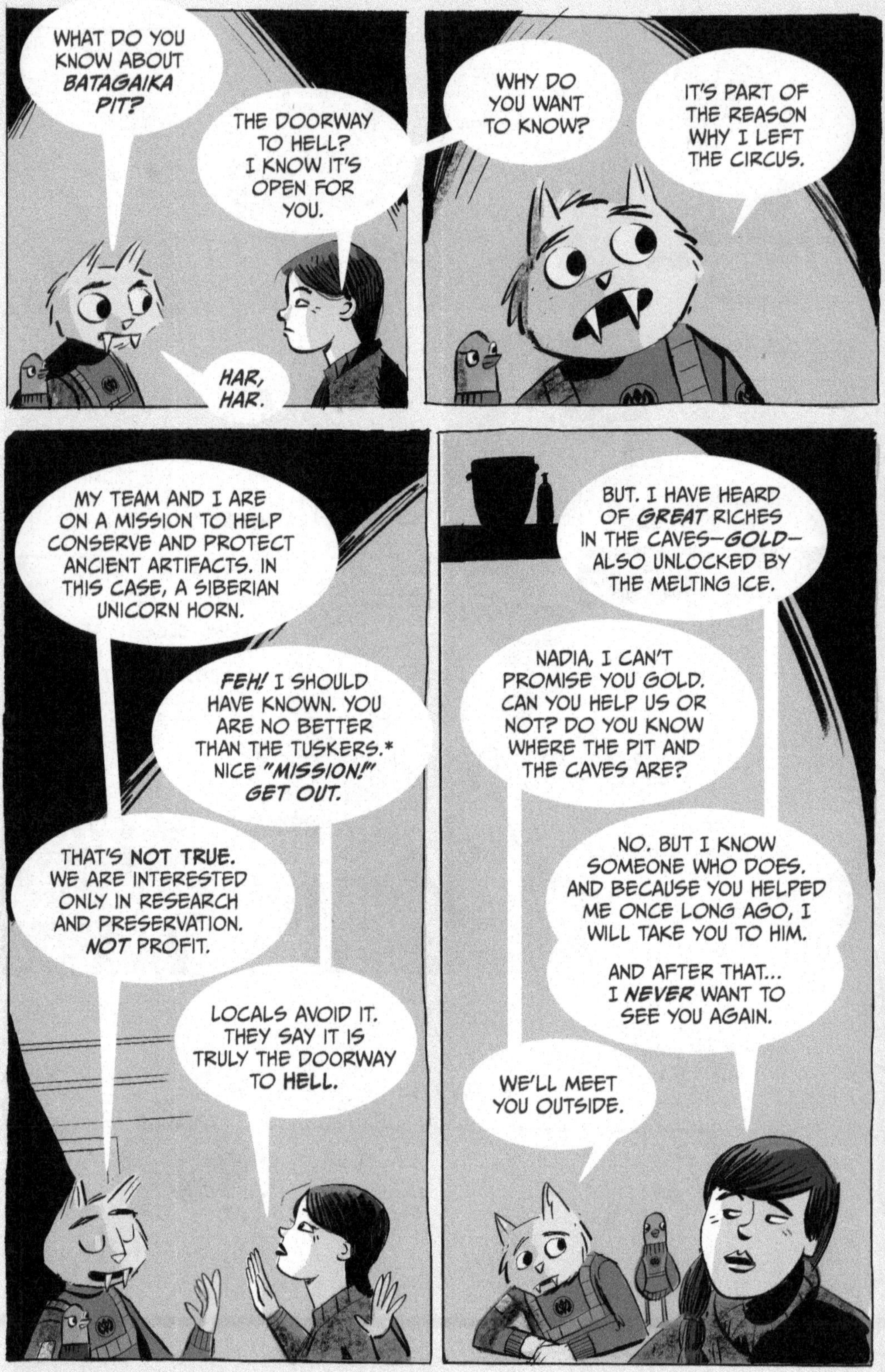
WHAT DO YOU KNOW ABOUT *BATAGAIKA PIT?*
THE DOORWAY TO HELL? I KNOW IT'S OPEN FOR YOU.
HAR, HAR.
WHY DO YOU WANT TO KNOW?
IT'S PART OF THE REASON WHY I LEFT THE CIRCUS.
MY TEAM AND I ARE ON A MISSION TO HELP CONSERVE AND PROTECT ANCIENT ARTIFACTS. IN THIS CASE, A SIBERIAN UNICORN HORN.
FEH! I SHOULD HAVE KNOWN. YOU ARE NO BETTER THAN THE TUSKERS.* NICE *"MISSION!" GET OUT.*
THAT'S **NOT TRUE.** WE ARE INTERESTED ONLY IN RESEARCH AND PRESERVATION. *NOT* PROFIT.
LOCALS AVOID IT. THEY SAY IT IS TRULY THE DOORWAY TO **HELL.**
BUT. I HAVE HEARD OF *GREAT* RICHES IN THE CAVES—*GOLD*—ALSO UNLOCKED BY THE MELTING ICE.
NADIA, I CAN'T PROMISE YOU GOLD. CAN YOU HELP US OR NOT? DO YOU KNOW WHERE THE PIT AND THE CAVES ARE?
NO. BUT I KNOW SOMEONE WHO DOES. AND BECAUSE YOU HELPED ME ONCE LONG AGO, I WILL TAKE YOU TO HIM.
AND AFTER THAT... I *NEVER* WANT TO SEE YOU AGAIN.
WE'LL MEET YOU OUTSIDE.

*Tusk hunters; sell mammoth tusks for profit

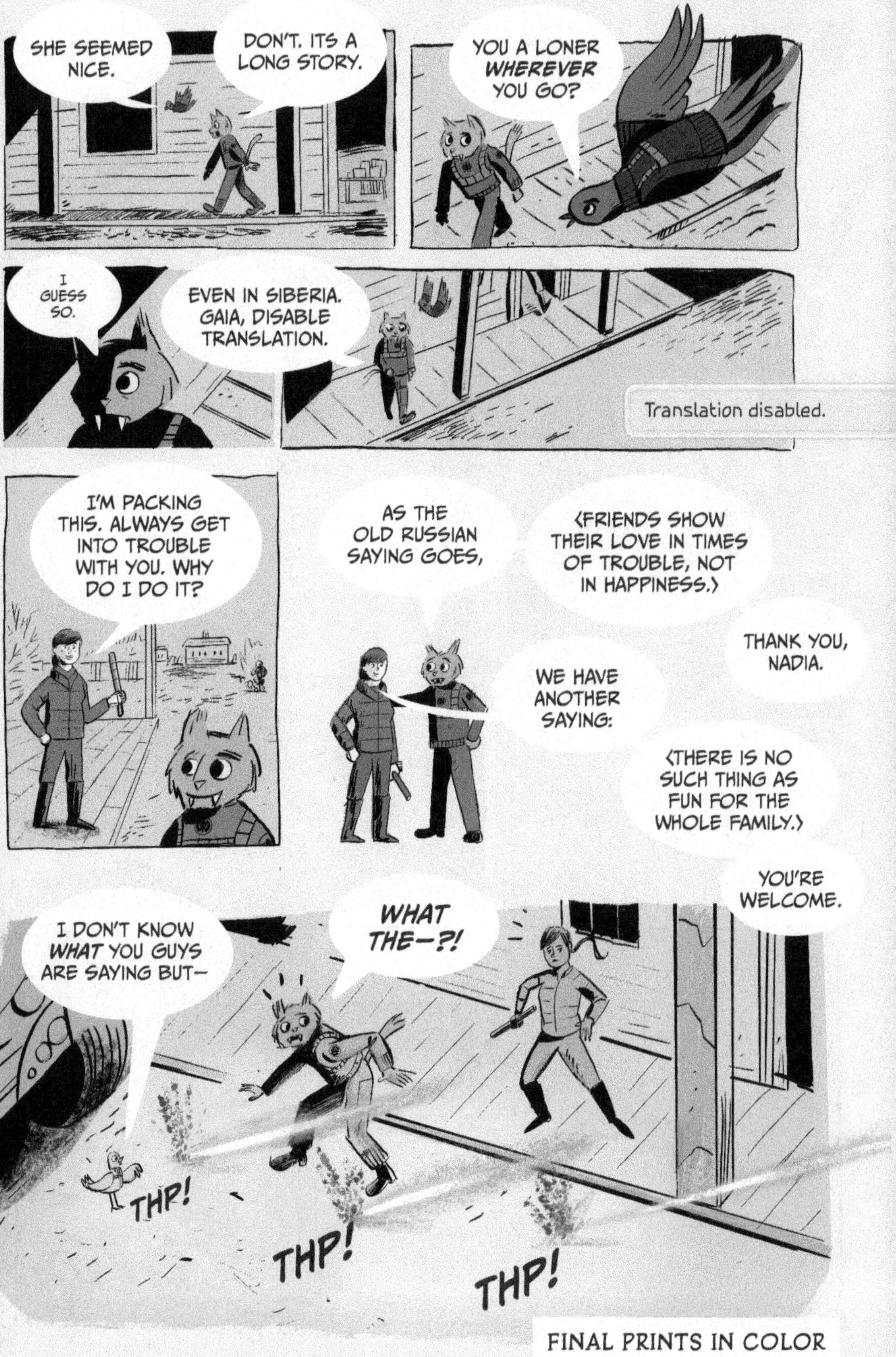
SHE SEEMED NICE.
DON'T. ITS A LONG STORY.
YOU A LONER *WHEREVER* YOU GO?
I GUESS SO.
EVEN IN SIBERIA. GAIA, DISABLE TRANSLATION.
Translation disabled.
I'M PACKING THIS. ALWAYS GET INTO TROUBLE WITH YOU. WHY DO I DO IT?
AS THE OLD RUSSIAN SAYING GOES,
‹FRIENDS SHOW THEIR LOVE IN TIMES OF TROUBLE, NOT IN HAPPINESS.›
THANK YOU, NADIA.
WE HAVE ANOTHER SAYING:
‹THERE IS NO SUCH THING AS FUN FOR THE WHOLE FAMILY.›
YOU'RE WELCOME.
I DON'T KNOW *WHAT* YOU GUYS ARE SAYING BUT—
WHAT THE—?!
THP!
THP!
THP!

FINAL PRINTS IN COLOR

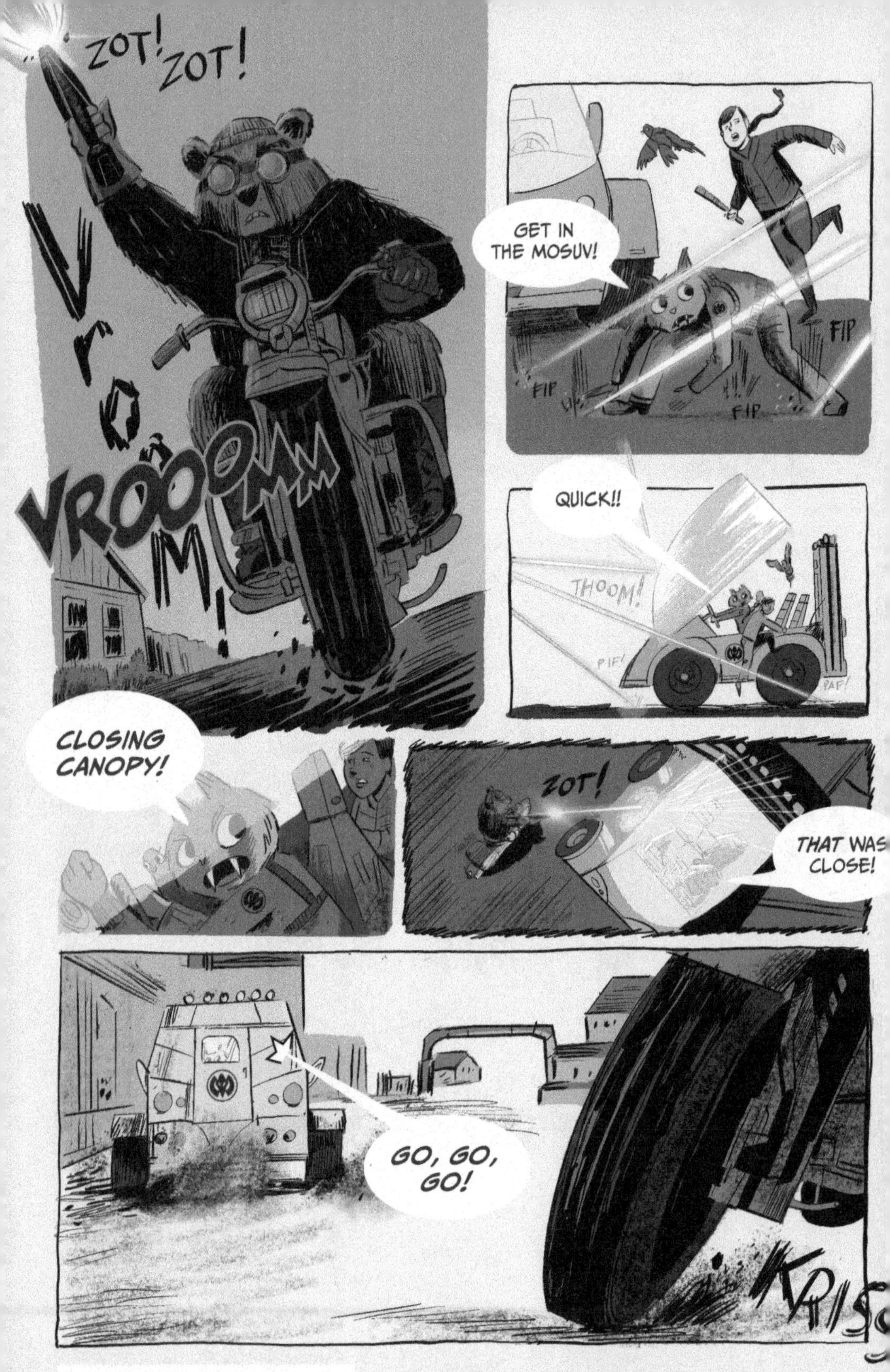
ZOT! ZOT!
VROOM!
VROOOMMM!
GET IN THE MOSUV!
FIP
FIP
FIP
FIP
QUICK!!
THOOM!
PIF!
PAF!
CLOSING CANOPY!
ZOT!
THAT WAS CLOSE!
GO, GO, GO!

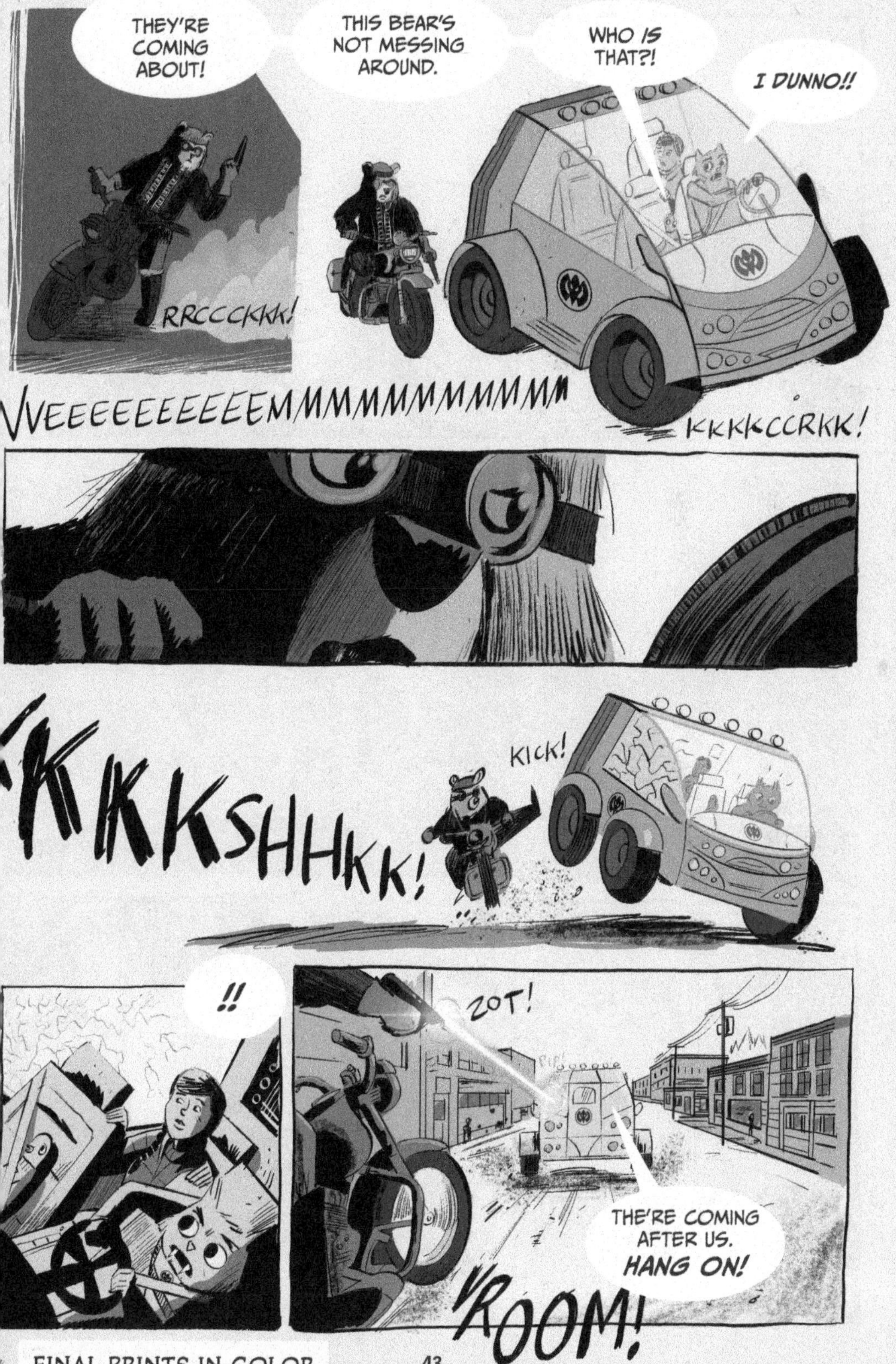
THEY'RE COMING ABOUT!
RRCCCKKK!
THIS BEAR'S NOT MESSING AROUND.
WHO *IS* THAT?!
I DUNNO!!
VVEEEEEEEEEEMMMMMMMMMMM
KKKKCCRKK!
KKKSHHKK!
KICK!
!!
ZOT!
THE'RE COMING AFTER US. **HANG ON!**
VROOM!

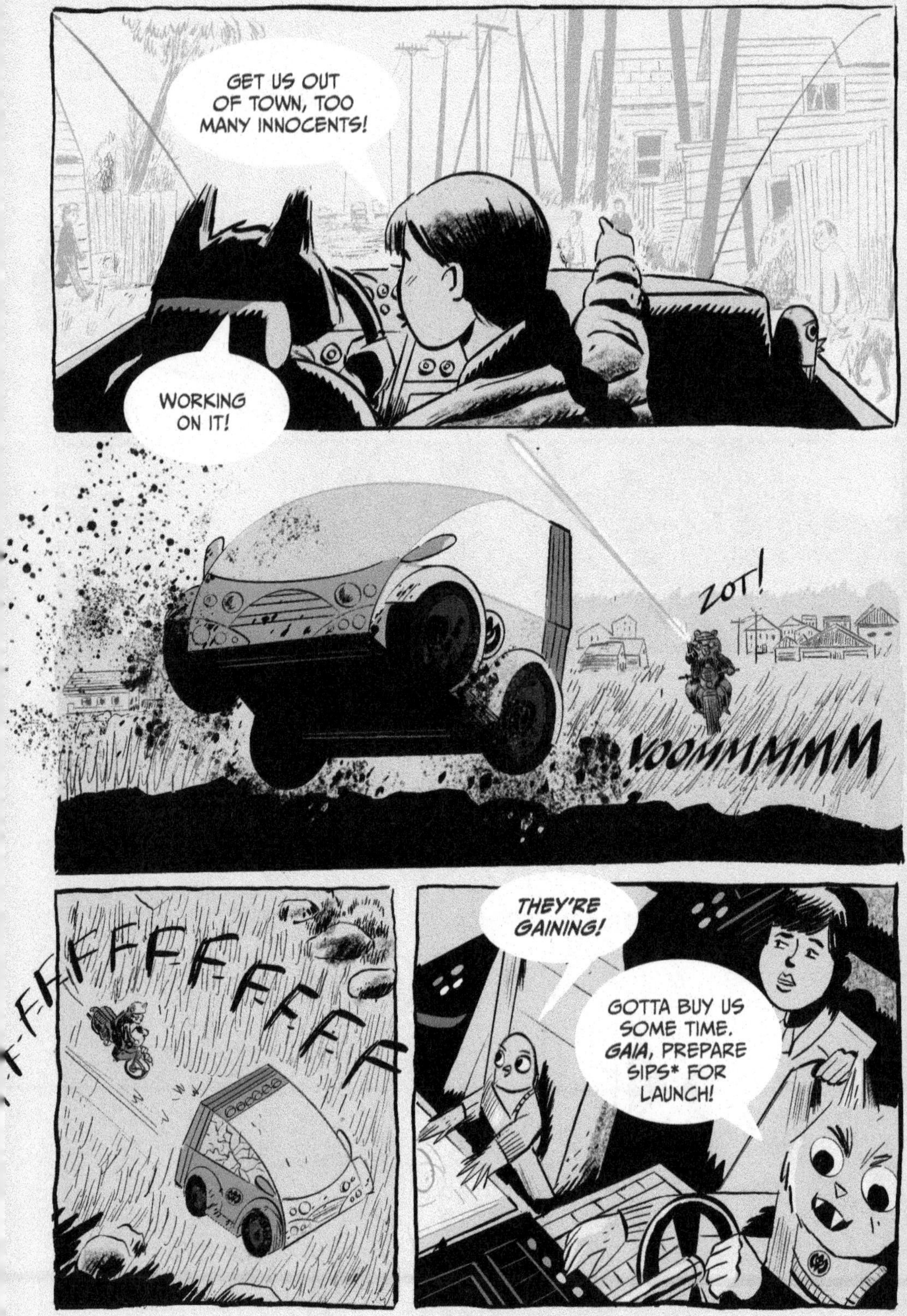
GET US OUT OF TOWN, TOO MANY INNOCENTS!
WORKING ON IT!
ZOT!
VOOMMMMMM
F-F-FFFFFFFFFFF
THEY'RE GAINING!
GOTTA BUY US SOME TIME. GAIA, PREPARE SIPS* FOR LAUNCH!

*SIPs = Squid Ink Pods

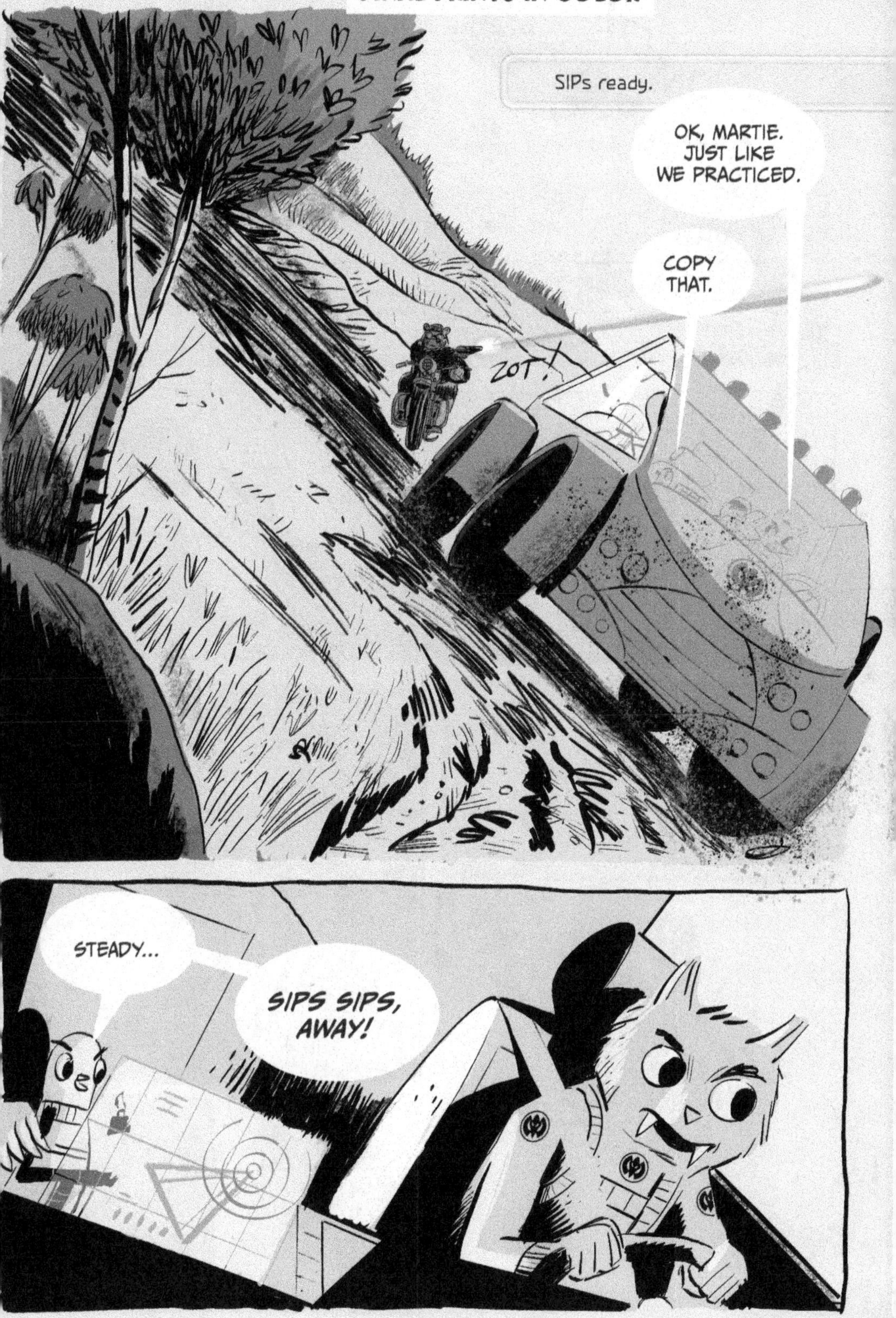
SIPs ready.
OK, MARTIE. JUST LIKE WE PRACTICED.
COPY THAT.
ZOT!
STEADY...
SIPS SIPS, AWAY!

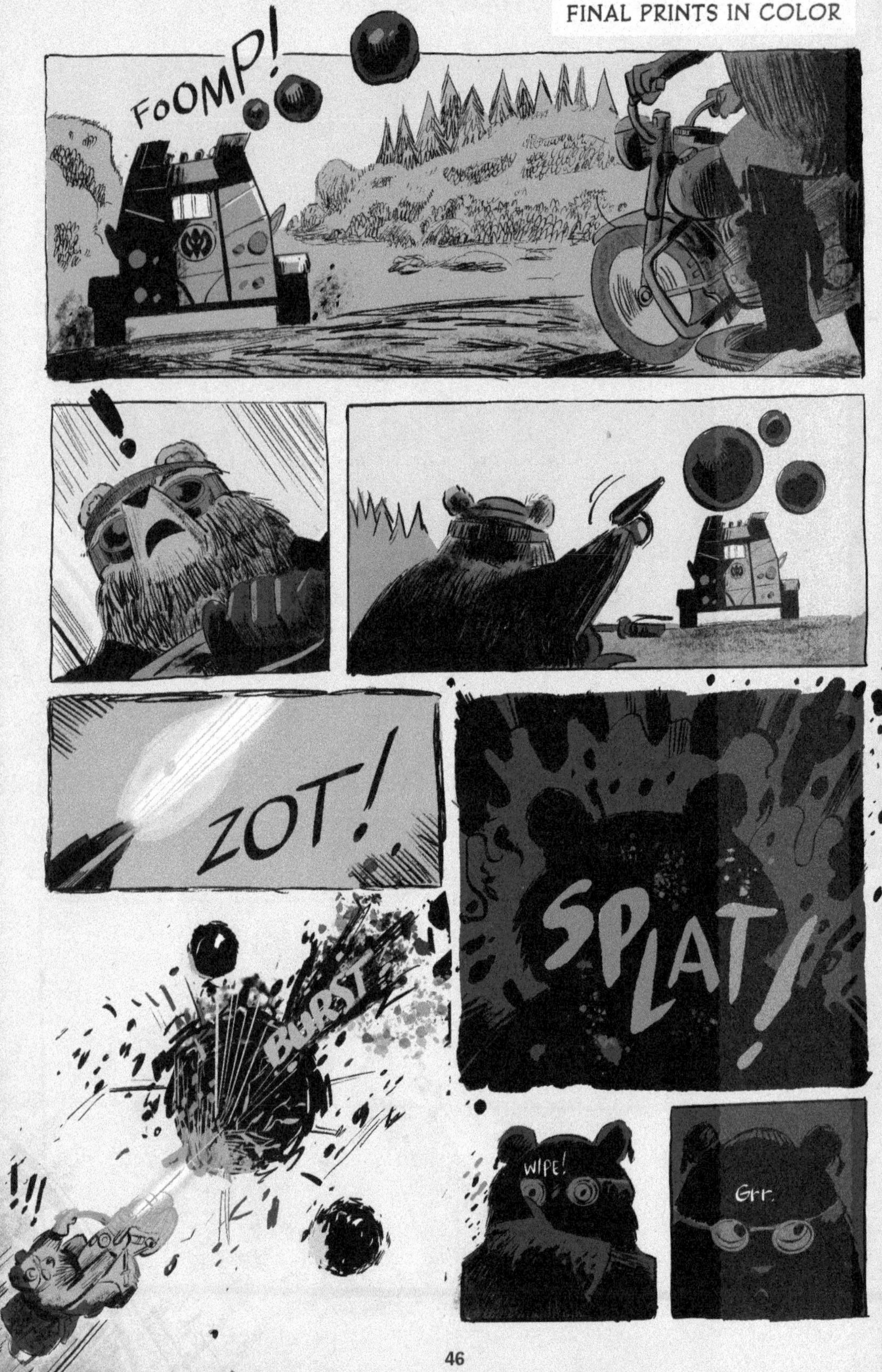
FoOMP!
!
ZOT!
SPLAT!
BURST
!!!
WIPE!
Grr.

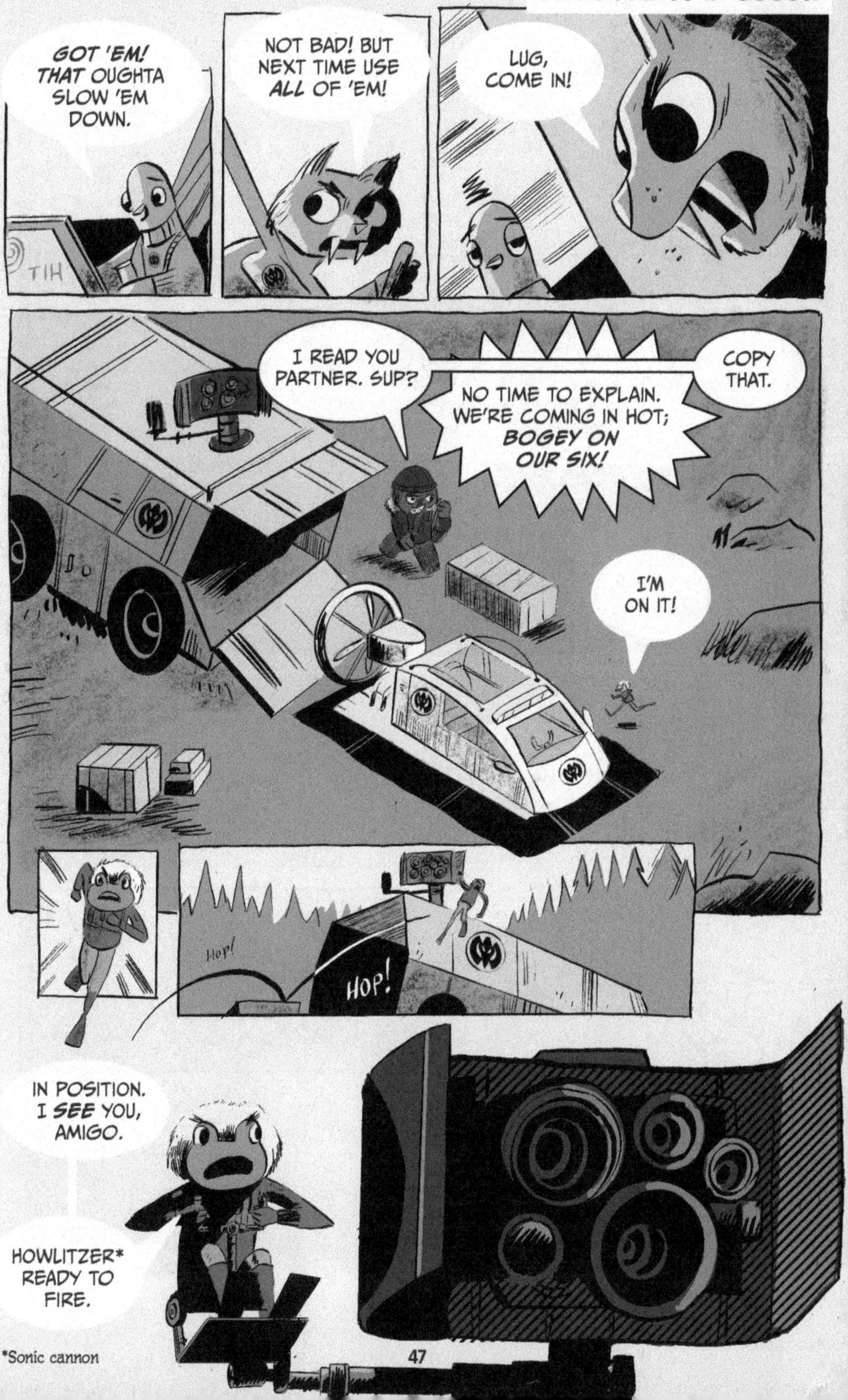
GOT 'EM! THAT OUGHTA SLOW 'EM DOWN.
NOT BAD! BUT NEXT TIME USE ALL OF 'EM!
LUG, COME IN!
I READ YOU PARTNER. SUP?
NO TIME TO EXPLAIN. WE'RE COMING IN HOT; BOGEY ON OUR SIX!
COPY THAT.
I'M ON IT!
Hop!
HOP!
IN POSITION. I SEE YOU, AMIGO.
HOWLITZER* READY TO FIRE.

*Sonic cannon

*Tracking device

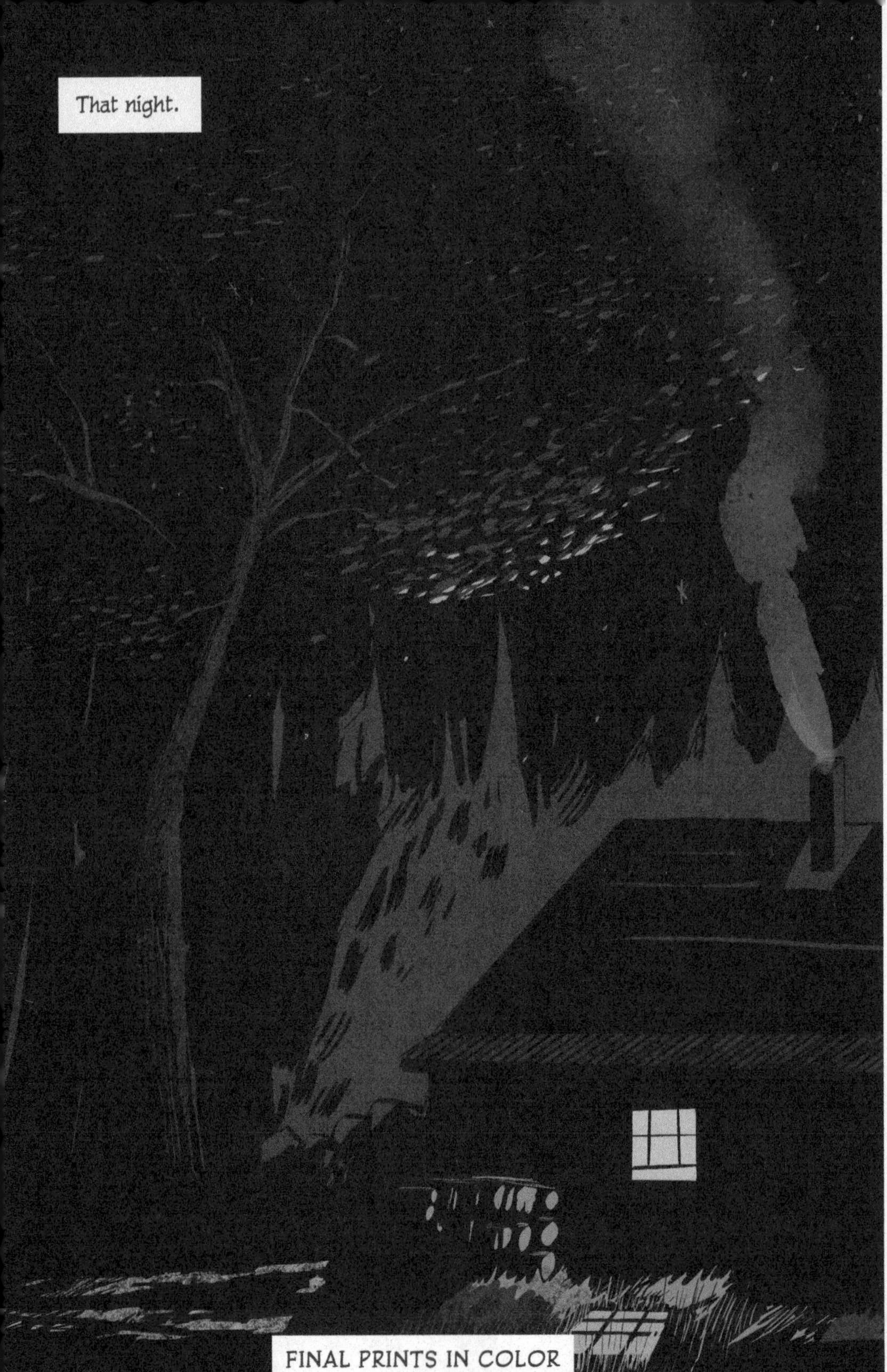
That night.

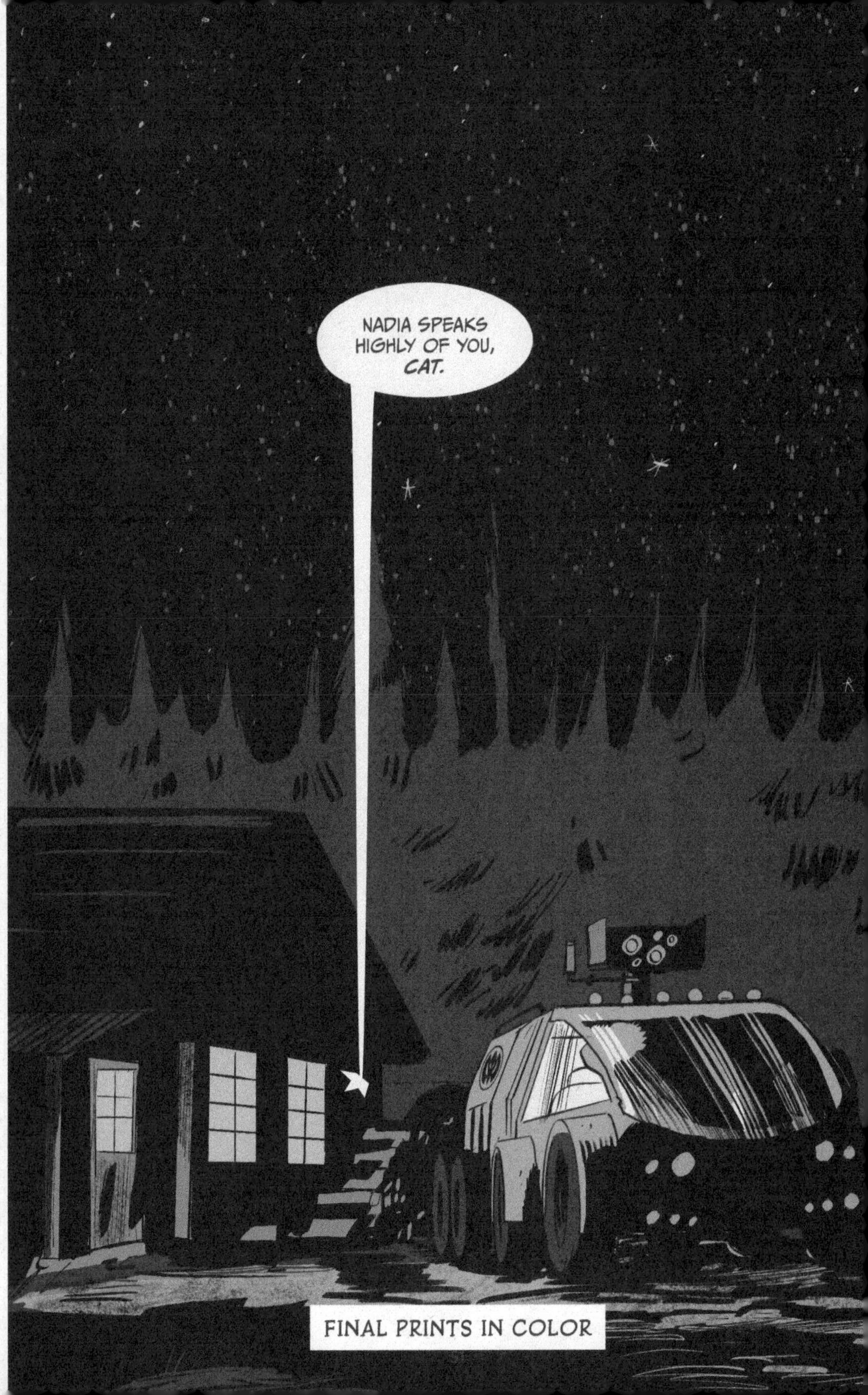

NADIA SPEAKS HIGHLY OF YOU, CAT.
FINAL PRINTS IN COLOR

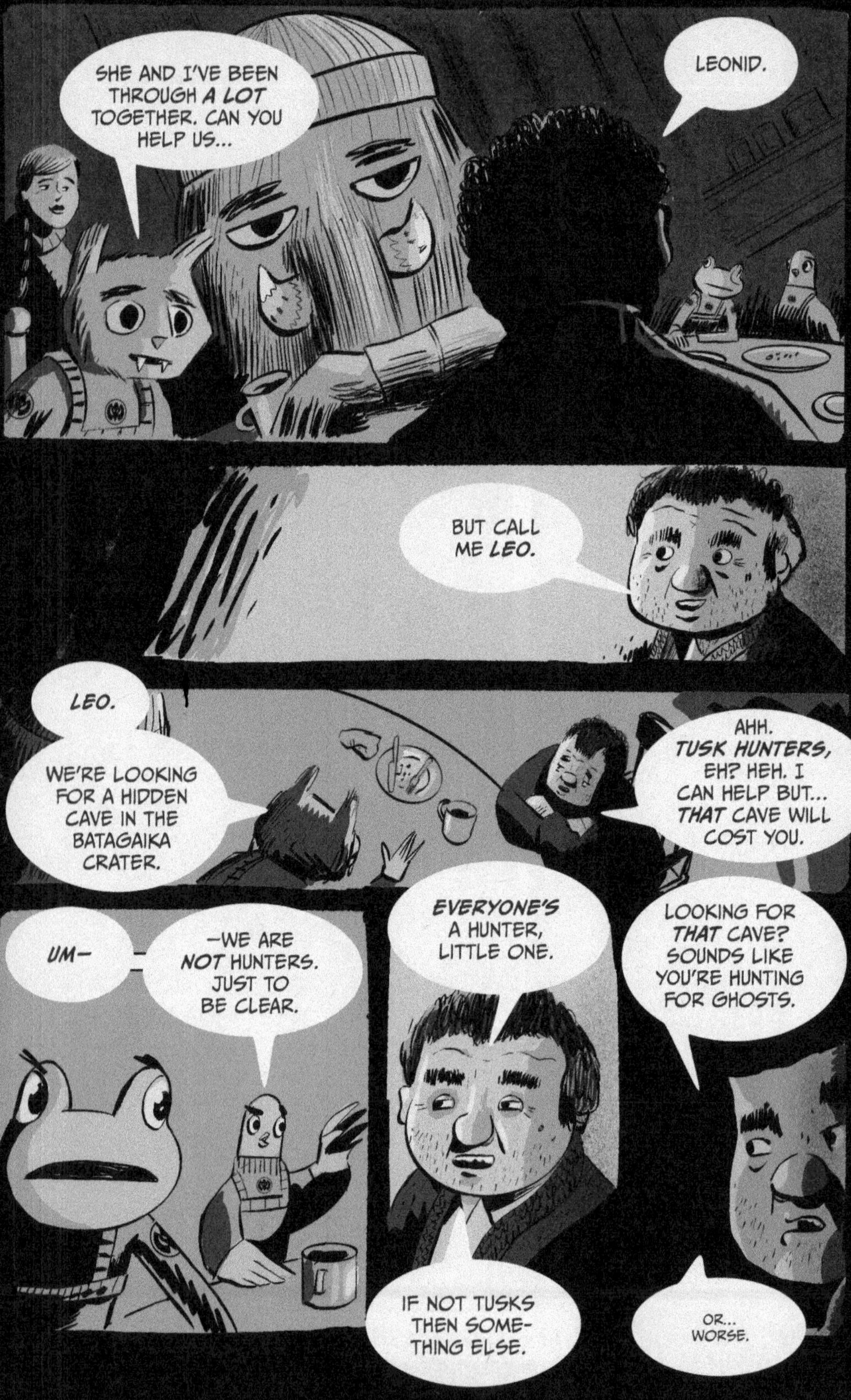
SHE AND I'VE BEEN THROUGH A LOT TOGETHER. CAN YOU HELP US...
LEONID.
BUT CALL ME LEO.
LEO.
WE'RE LOOKING FOR A HIDDEN CAVE IN THE BATAGAIKA CRATER.
AHH. TUSK HUNTERS, EH? HEH. I CAN HELP BUT... THAT CAVE WILL COST YOU.
UM—
—WE ARE NOT HUNTERS. JUST TO BE CLEAR.
EVERYONE'S A HUNTER, LITTLE ONE.
IF NOT TUSKS THEN SOME-THING ELSE.
LOOKING FOR THAT CAVE? SOUNDS LIKE YOU'RE HUNTING FOR GHOSTS.
OR... WORSE.

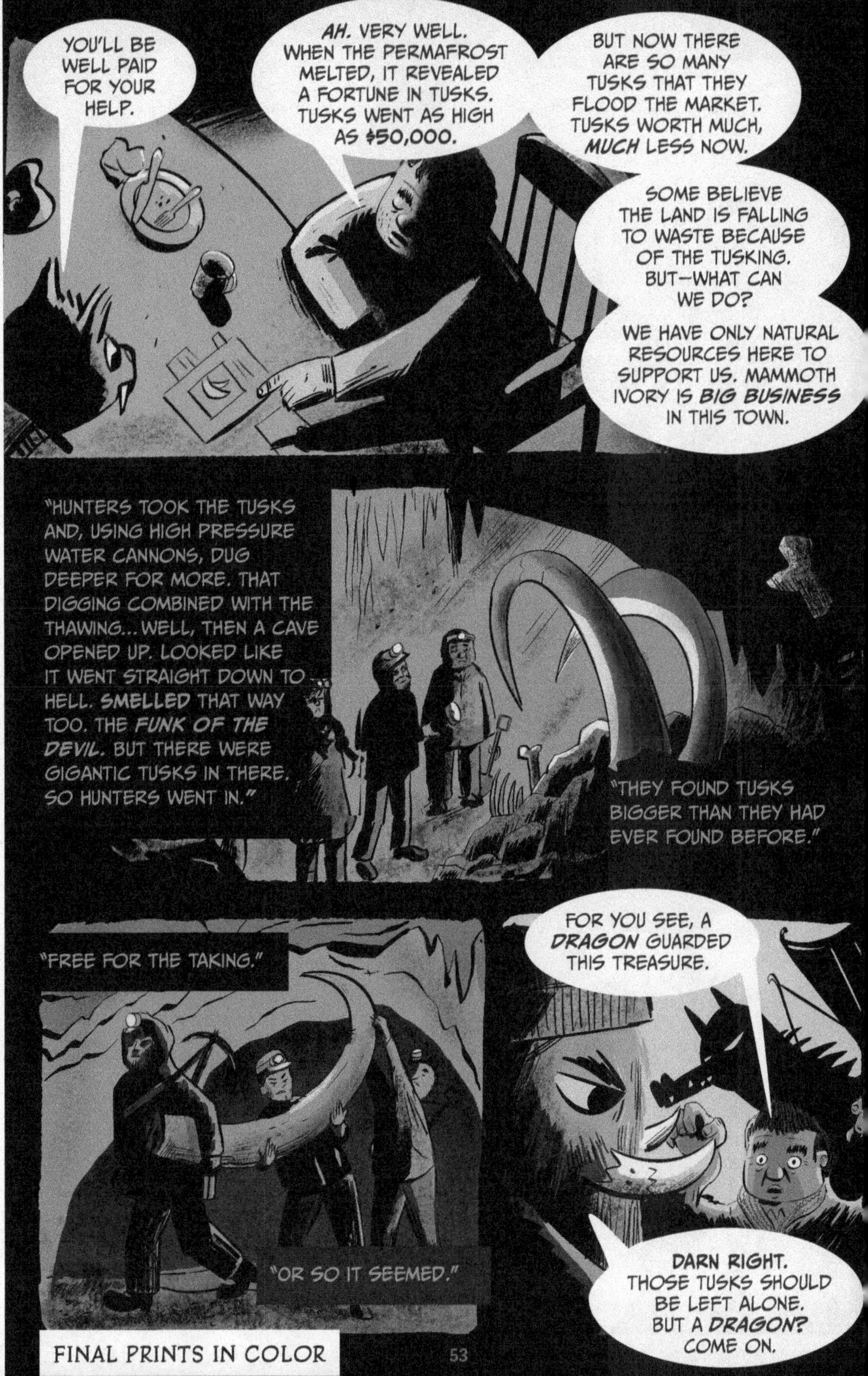
YOU'LL BE WELL PAID FOR YOUR HELP.
AH. VERY WELL. WHEN THE PERMAFROST MELTED, IT REVEALED A FORTUNE IN TUSKS. TUSKS WENT AS HIGH AS $50,000.
BUT NOW THERE ARE SO MANY TUSKS THAT THEY FLOOD THE MARKET. TUSKS WORTH MUCH, MUCH LESS NOW.
SOME BELIEVE THE LAND IS FALLING TO WASTE BECAUSE OF THE TUSKING. BUT—WHAT CAN WE DO?
WE HAVE ONLY NATURAL RESOURCES HERE TO SUPPORT US. MAMMOTH IVORY IS BIG BUSINESS IN THIS TOWN.
"HUNTERS TOOK THE TUSKS AND, USING HIGH PRESSURE WATER CANNONS, DUG DEEPER FOR MORE. THAT DIGGING COMBINED WITH THE THAWING... WELL, THEN A CAVE OPENED UP. LOOKED LIKE IT WENT STRAIGHT DOWN TO HELL. SMELLED THAT WAY TOO. THE FUNK OF THE DEVIL. BUT THERE WERE GIGANTIC TUSKS IN THERE. SO HUNTERS WENT IN."
"THEY FOUND TUSKS BIGGER THAN THEY HAD EVER FOUND BEFORE."
"FREE FOR THE TAKING."
"OR SO IT SEEMED."
FOR YOU SEE, A DRAGON GUARDED THIS TREASURE.
DARN RIGHT. THOSE TUSKS SHOULD BE LEFT ALONE. BUT A DRAGON? COME ON.

FINAL PRINTS IN COLOR

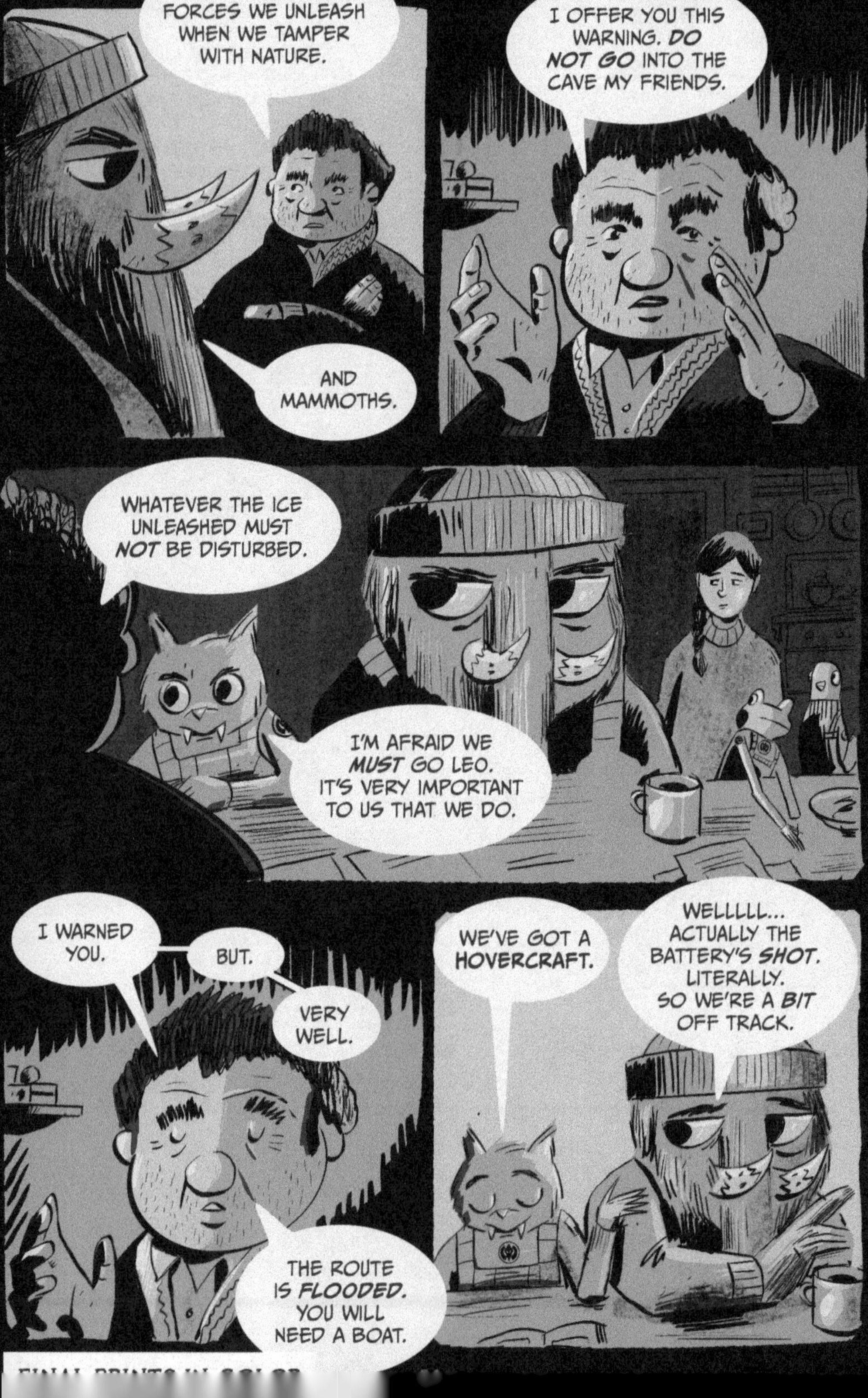
SUCH ARE THE FORCES WE UNLEASH WHEN WE TAMPER WITH NATURE.
AND MAMMOTHS.
I OFFER YOU THIS WARNING. *DO NOT GO* INTO THE CAVE MY FRIENDS.
WHATEVER THE ICE UNLEASHED MUST *NOT* BE DISTURBED.
I'M AFRAID WE *MUST* GO LEO. IT'S VERY IMPORTANT TO US THAT WE DO.
I WARNED YOU.
BUT.
VERY WELL.
THE ROUTE IS *FLOODED.* YOU WILL NEED A BOAT.
WE'VE GOT A **HOVERCRAFT.**
WELLLLL... ACTUALLY THE BATTERY'S *SHOT*. LITERALLY. SO WE'RE A *BIT* OFF TRACK.

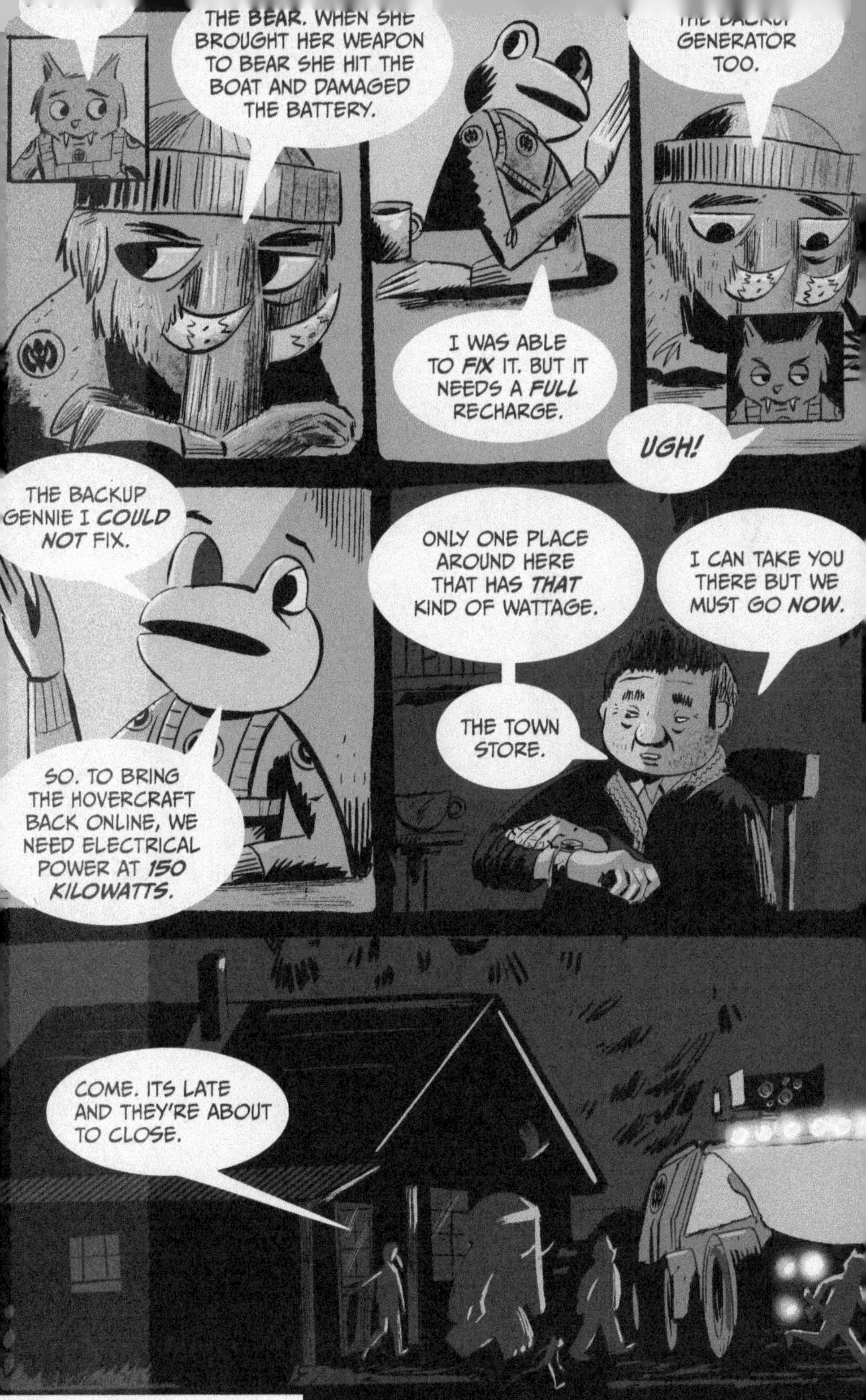
THE BEAR. WHEN SHE BROUGHT HER WEAPON TO BEAR SHE HIT THE BOAT AND DAMAGED THE BATTERY.
I WAS ABLE TO *FIX* IT. BUT IT NEEDS A *FULL* RECHARGE.
GENERATOR TOO.
UGH!
THE BACKUP GENNIE I *COULD NOT* FIX.
SO. TO BRING THE HOVERCRAFT BACK ONLINE, WE NEED ELECTRICAL POWER AT *150 KILOWATTS.*
ONLY ONE PLACE AROUND HERE THAT HAS *THAT* KIND OF WATTAGE.
THE TOWN STORE.
I CAN TAKE YOU THERE BUT WE MUST GO *NOW.*
COME. ITS LATE AND THEY'RE ABOUT TO CLOSE.

WHAT WAS HE TALKING ABOUT BACK THERE? "*EXTINCT FREAKS?*"

WE'RE A RARE BREED, I GUESS? YOU HEARD GAIA SAY IT WAS *BALONEY.*

DUNNO. ITS TOUGH FOR SOME PEOPLE TO DEAL WITH SOMEONE *DIFFERENT.*

Moments later.

SO... WHAT NOW?

STAKEOUT. WE WATCH HIM CLOSE UP SHOP FOR THE NIGHT. THEN...?

THEN WE GET *CREATIVE.*

20 minutes later.

UH, GUYS, I REALLY HAVE TO GO THE BATHROOM. OR THIS STAKEOUT IS GOING TO BE A *STINKOUT.*

THERE'S NO BATHROOM AROUND HERE RIGHT NOW.

I DON'T WANT TO BE THE CANARY IN THE COAL MINE.

PLEASE JUST... GO *OUTSIDE,* LUG.

NO, DON'T GO OUTSIDE, SHOPOWNER WILL *SEE* YOU!

I'VE GOT BAD GAS.

CAN'T YOU JUST HOLD YOUR—

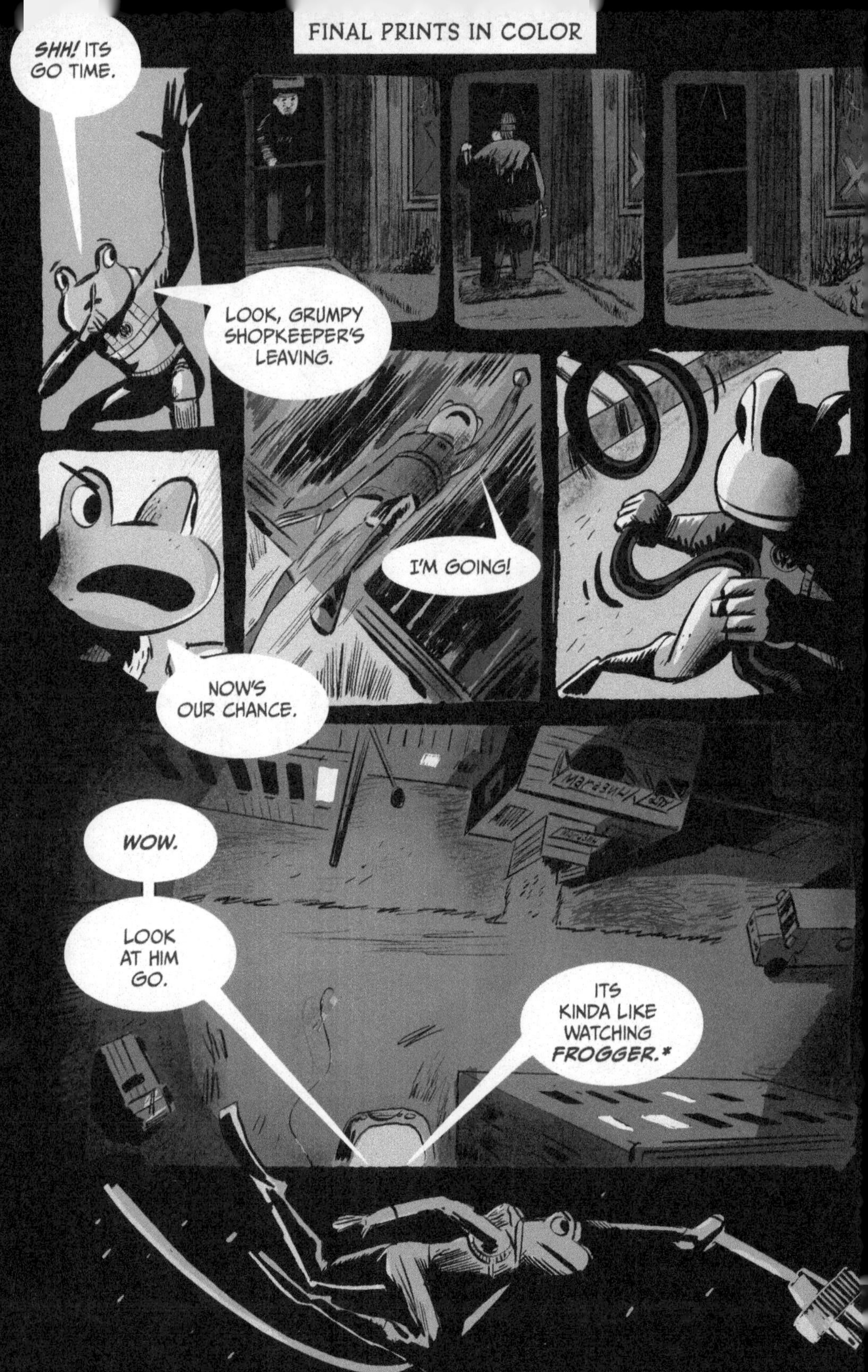
SHH! ITS GO TIME.
LOOK, GRUMPY SHOPKEEPER'S LEAVING.
I'M GOING!
NOW'S OUR CHANCE.
WOW.
LOOK AT HIM GO.
ITS KINDA LIKE WATCHING FROGGER.*

* Just google it.

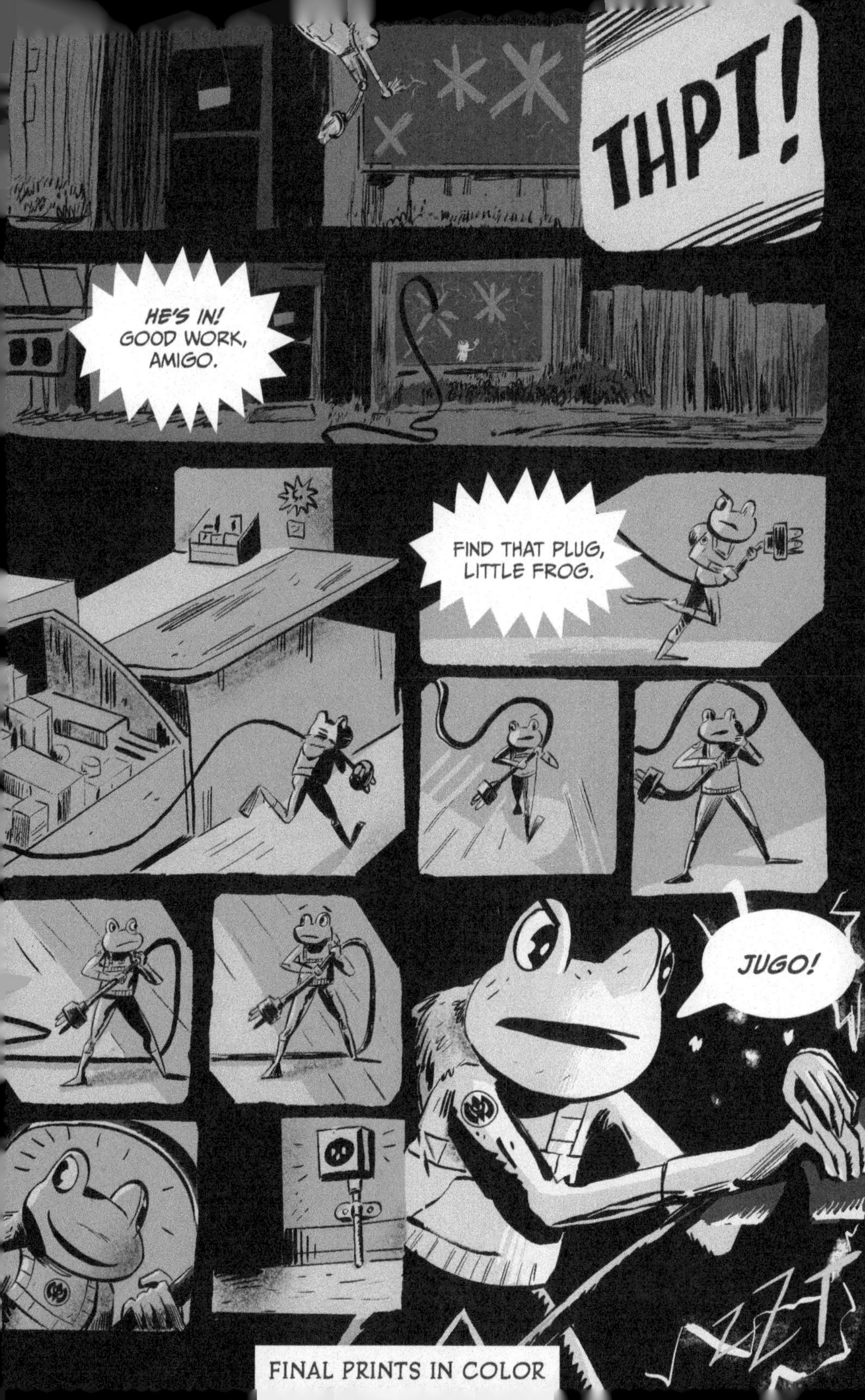
THPT!
HE'S IN! GOOD WORK, AMIGO.
FIND THAT PLUG, LITTLE FROG.
JUGO!

FINAL PRINTS IN COLOR

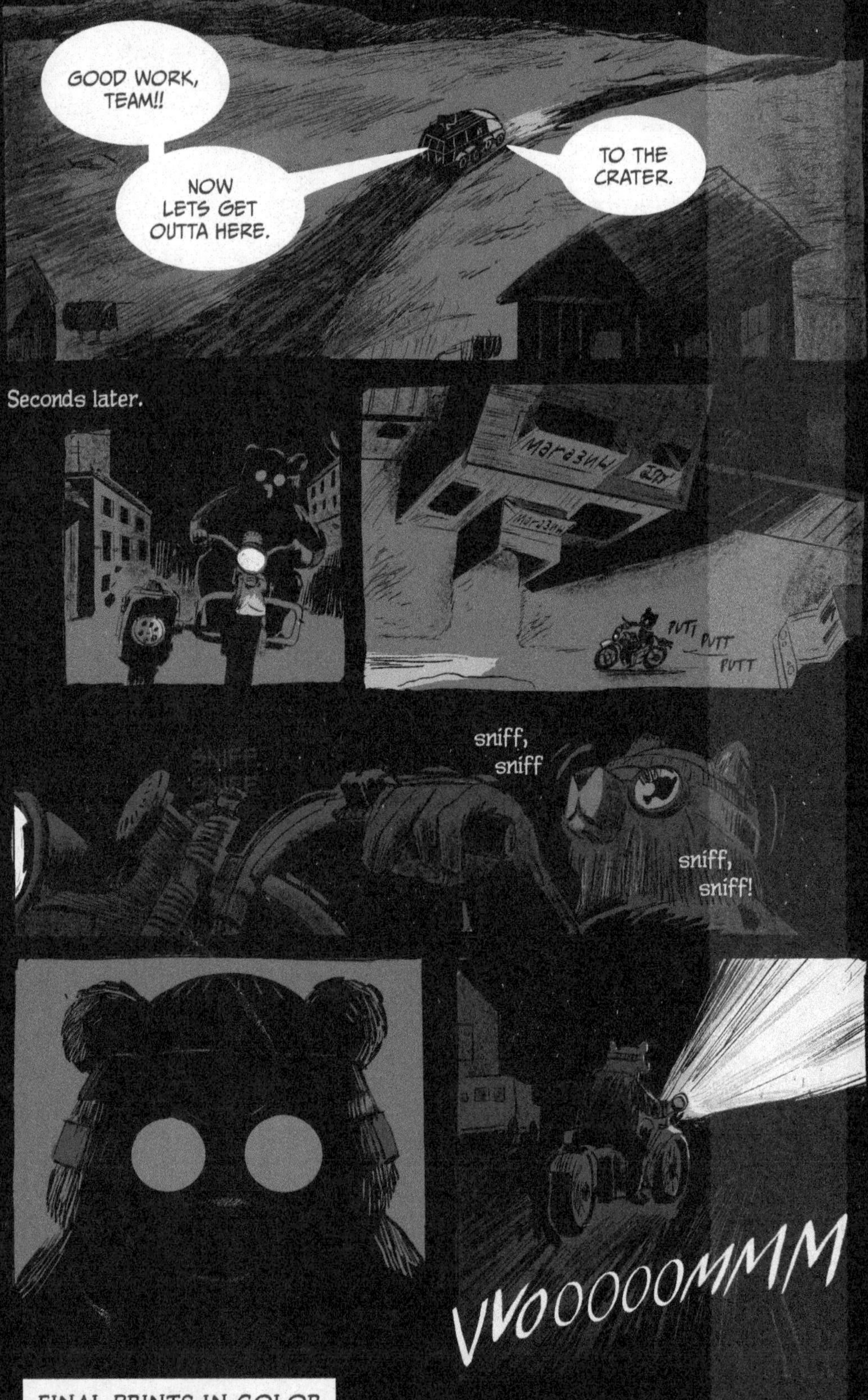
GOOD WORK, TEAM!!
NOW LETS GET OUTTA HERE.
TO THE CRATER.
Seconds later.
PUTT PUTT PUTT
sniff, sniff
sniff, sniff!
VVOOOOOMMM

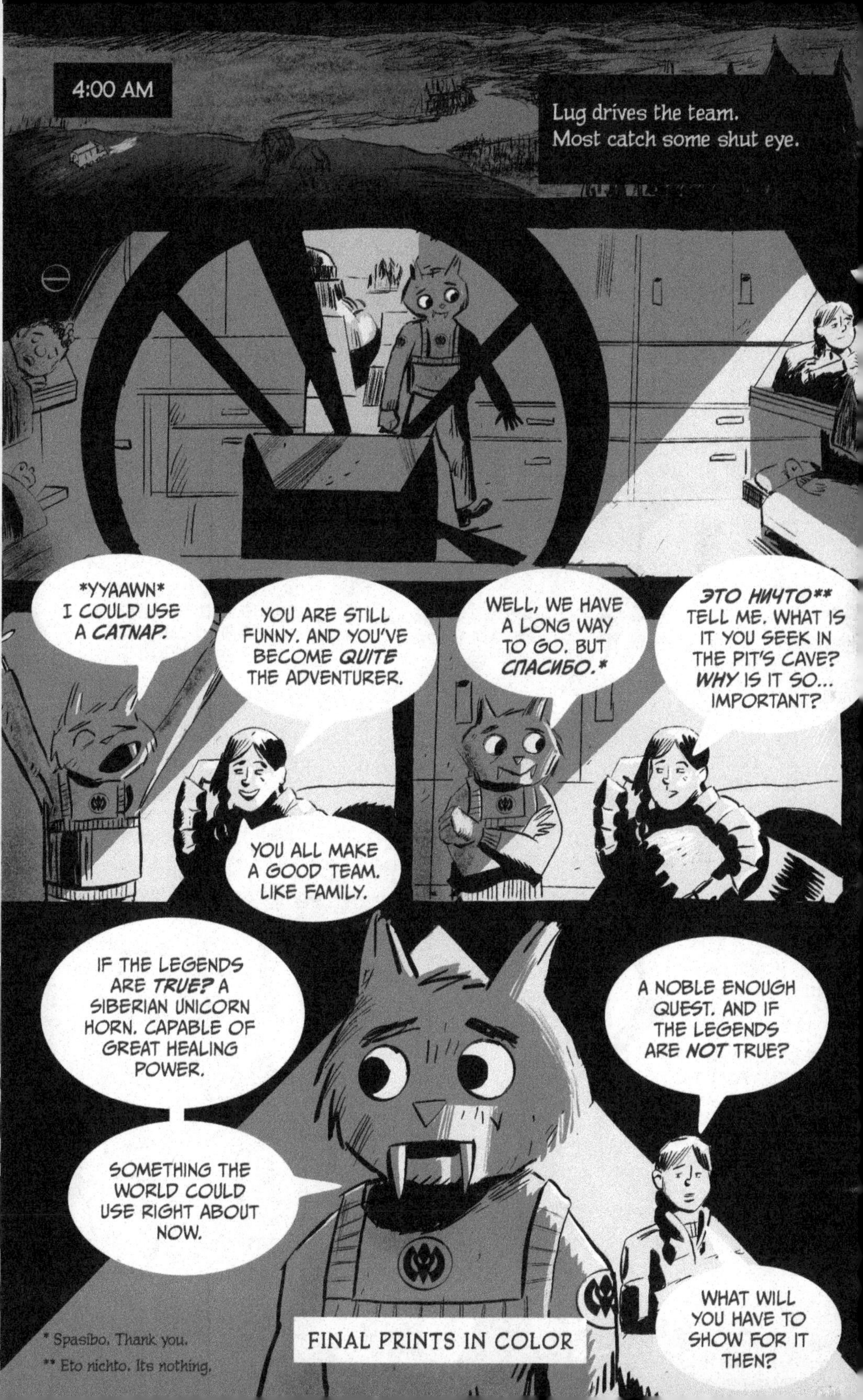
4:00 AM
Lug drives the team. Most catch some shut eye.
YYAAWN I COULD USE A CATNAP.
YOU ARE STILL FUNNY. AND YOU'VE BECOME QUITE THE ADVENTURER.
YOU ALL MAKE A GOOD TEAM. LIKE FAMILY.
WELL, WE HAVE A LONG WAY TO GO. BUT СПАСИБО.*
ЭТО НИЧТО** TELL ME. WHAT IS IT YOU SEEK IN THE PIT'S CAVE? WHY IS IT SO... IMPORTANT?
IF THE LEGENDS ARE TRUE? A SIBERIAN UNICORN HORN. CAPABLE OF GREAT HEALING POWER.
SOMETHING THE WORLD COULD USE RIGHT ABOUT NOW.
A NOBLE ENOUGH QUEST. AND IF THE LEGENDS ARE NOT TRUE?
WHAT WILL YOU HAVE TO SHOW FOR IT THEN?
* Spasibo. Thank you.
** Eto nichto. Its nothing.
FINAL PRINTS IN COLOR

MUDDY BOOTS.

DR. Z BREAKS UP THE TEAM?

I DUNNO.

I...CAN'T THINK THAT WAY.

LOOK, THE WORLD'S FALLING APART. CLIMATE CHANGE. THE SIXTH EXTINCTION.

I GOTTA DO WHAT I CAN TO *HELP* KEEP IT TOGETHER.

WHY DOES IT FALL TO YOU?

NOT JUST *ME*. IT FALLS TO YOU, ME, DR. Z— *EVERYONE*.

BUT—ITS LIKE THAT OLD RUSSIAN SAYING. РАБОТА НЕ ВОЛК— В ЛЕС НЕ УБЕЖИТ.*

I CAN'T WAIT AROUND FOR SOMEONE *ELSE* TO DO IT.

WHO *IS* DR. Z?

SCIENTIST. *GENIUS*. AFTER THEY SOLD DAD, DR. Z TOOK ME FROM THE CIRCUS AND TRAINED ME— HE BECAME LIKE A *FATHER* TO ME.

HE GAVE ME A WHOLE NEW *LIFE*. SOMEONE I *CAN'T* LET DOWN.

IF THIS MISSION SUCCEEDS AND THE HORN CAN HEAL LIKE HE *SAYS* IT CAN?

WE'LL CHANGE THE WORLD FOR THE BETTER. *AND* MAYBE HE'LL KEEP OUR TEAM TOGETHER FOR ANOTHER MISSION.

I SEE. MEANING YOU GET TO KEEP YOUR NEW FAMILY.

MEANING...

I GET TO MAKE A DIFFERENCE.

OK, GANG! COMING UP ON BOAT LAUNCH! LET'S DO THIS.

THAT'S ALL I REALLY WANT.

MAYBE I CAN FINALLY FIND A BATHROOM.

Translation: Work's not a wolf— won't run to the woods.

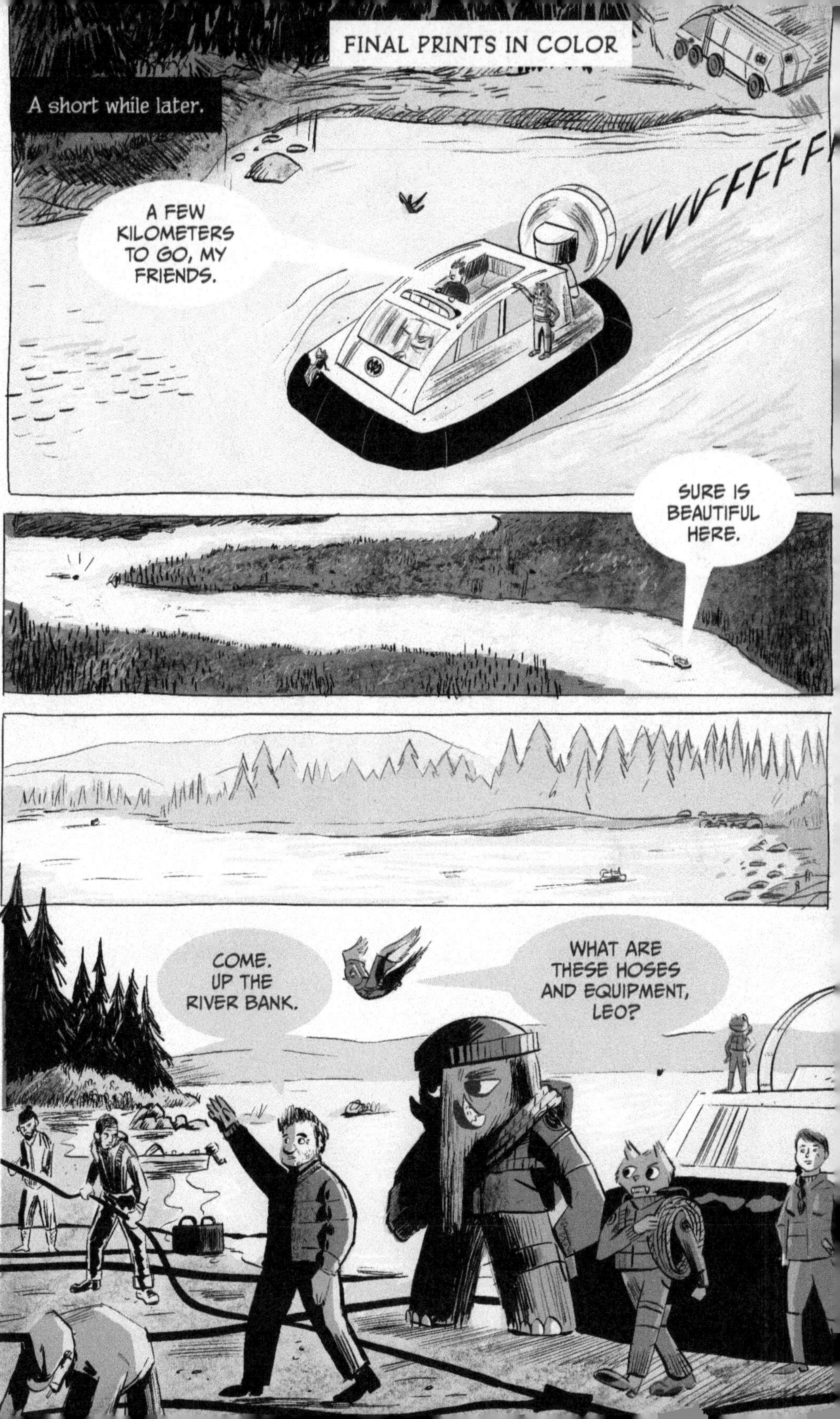
FINAL PRINTS IN COLOR
A short while later.
A FEW KILOMETERS TO GO, MY FRIENDS.
VVVVFFFFF
SURE IS BEAUTIFUL HERE.
COME. UP THE RIVER BANK.
WHAT ARE THESE HOSES AND EQUIPMENT, LEO?

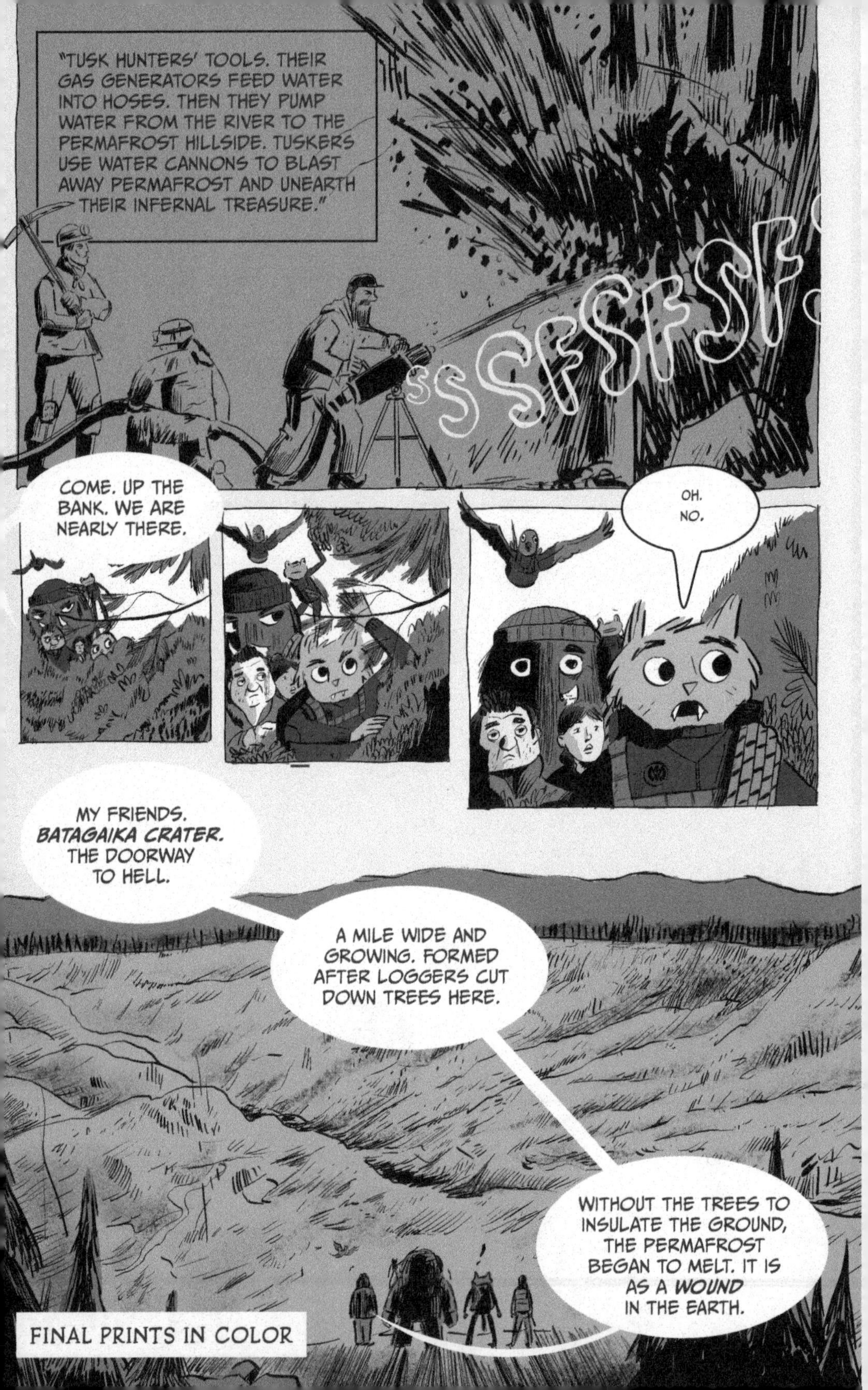
"TUSK HUNTERS' TOOLS. THEIR GAS GENERATORS FEED WATER INTO HOSES. THEN THEY PUMP WATER FROM THE RIVER TO THE PERMAFROST HILLSIDE. TUSKERS USE WATER CANNONS TO BLAST AWAY PERMAFROST AND UNEARTH THEIR INFERNAL TREASURE."
SSSFFSFFSFF
COME. UP THE BANK. WE ARE NEARLY THERE.
OH. NO.
MY FRIENDS. *BATAGAIKA CRATER.* THE DOORWAY TO HELL.
A MILE WIDE AND GROWING. FORMED AFTER LOGGERS CUT DOWN TREES HERE.
WITHOUT THE TREES TO INSULATE THE GROUND, THE PERMAFROST BEGAN TO MELT. IT IS AS A *WOUND* IN THE EARTH.
FINAL PRINTS IN COLOR

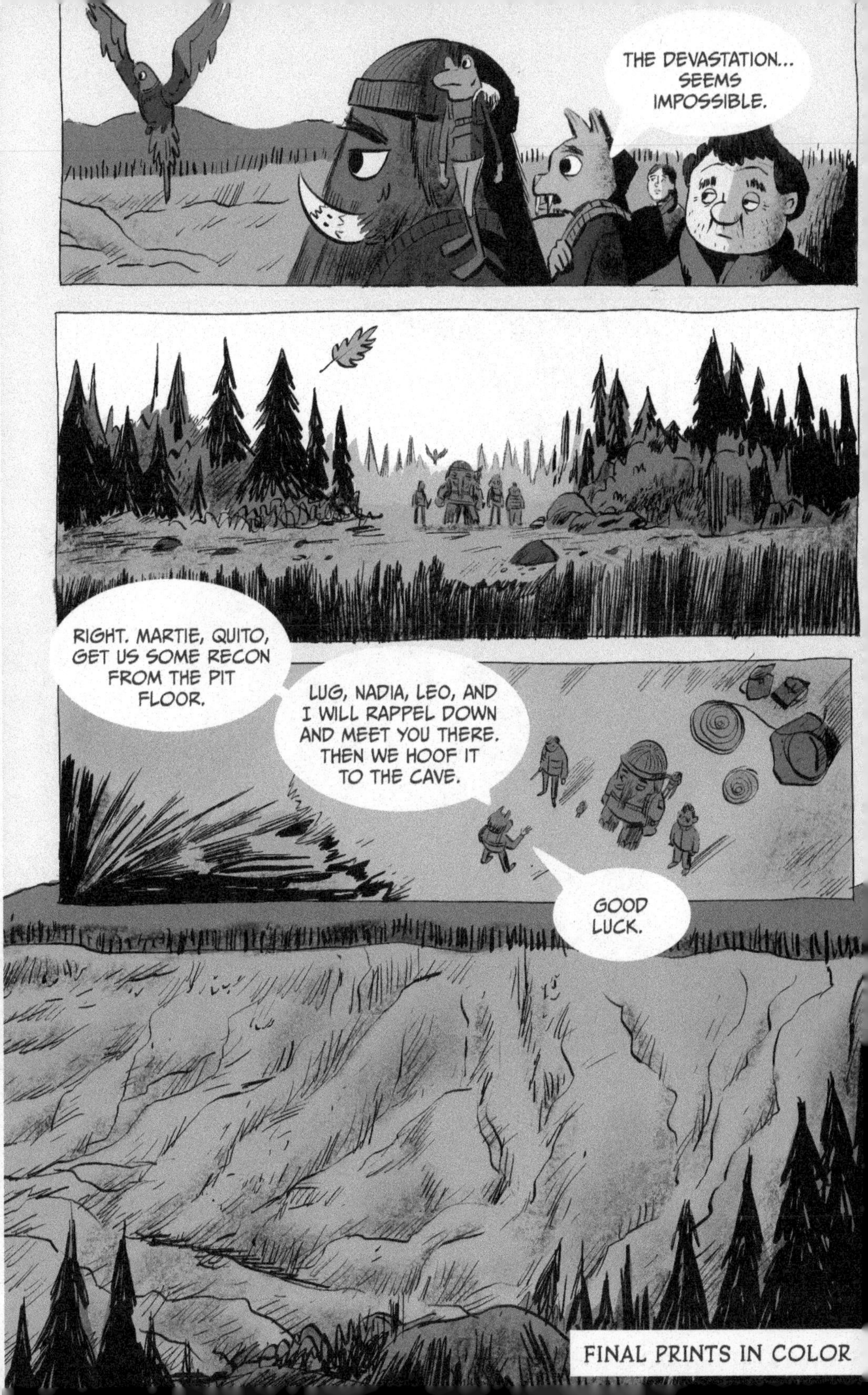
THE DEVASTATION... SEEMS IMPOSSIBLE.
RIGHT. MARTIE, QUITO, GET US SOME RECON FROM THE PIT FLOOR.
LUG, NADIA, LEO, AND I WILL RAPPEL DOWN AND MEET YOU THERE. THEN WE HOOF IT TO THE CAVE.
GOOD LUCK.

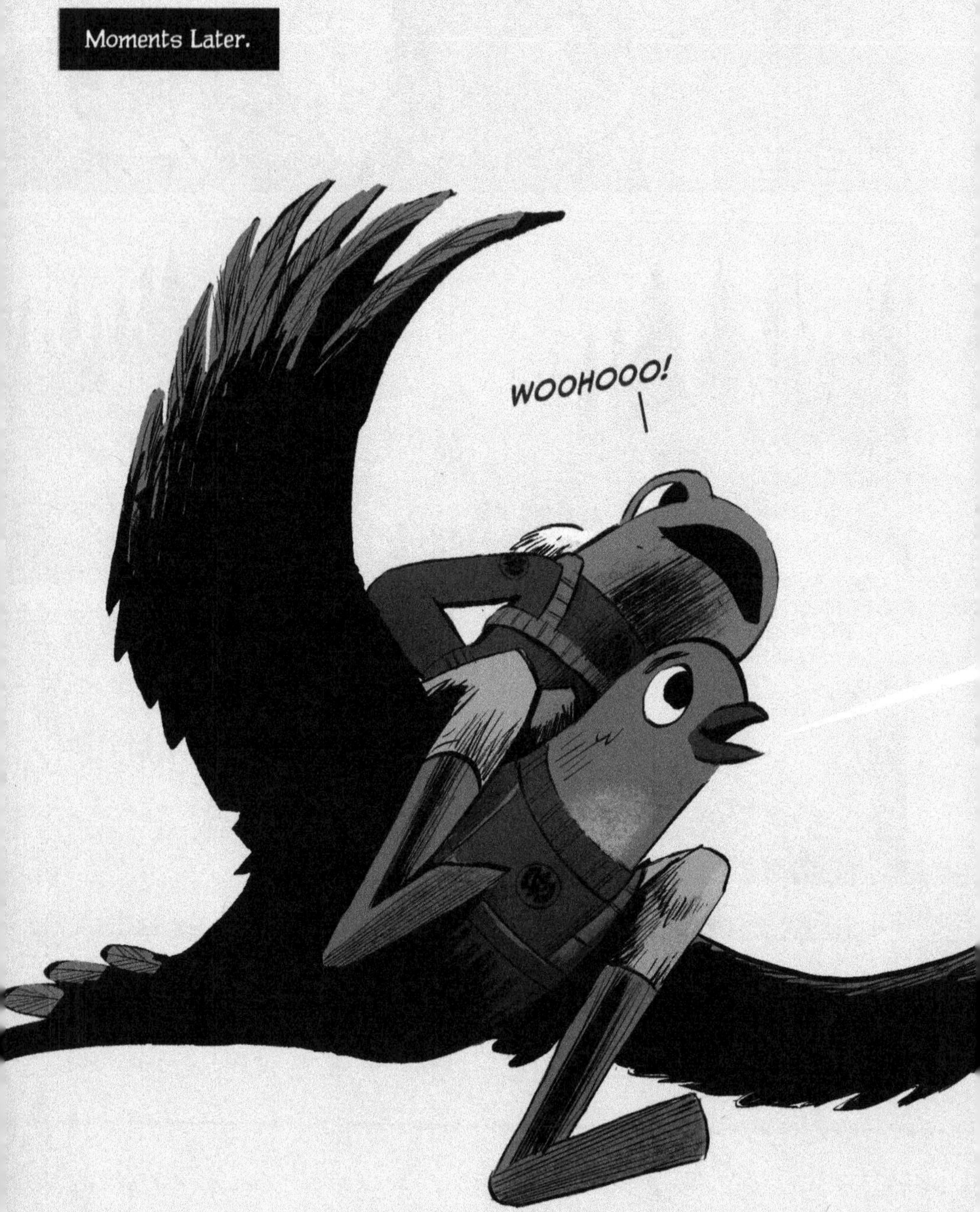
Moments Later.
WOOHOOO!

FINAL PRINTS IN COLOR

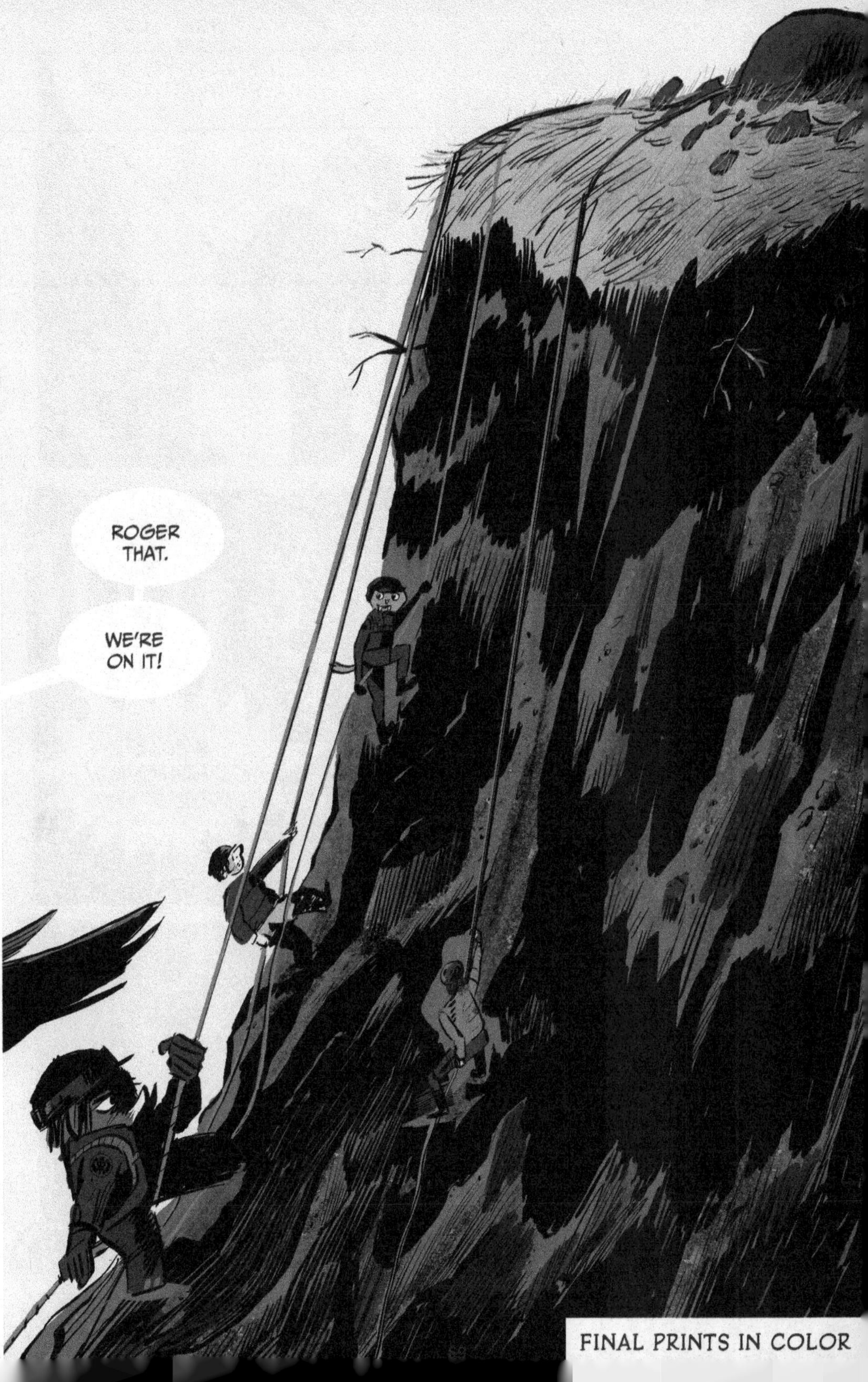
ROGER THAT.
WE'RE ON IT!
FINAL PRINTS IN COLOR

FINAL PRINTS IN COLOR

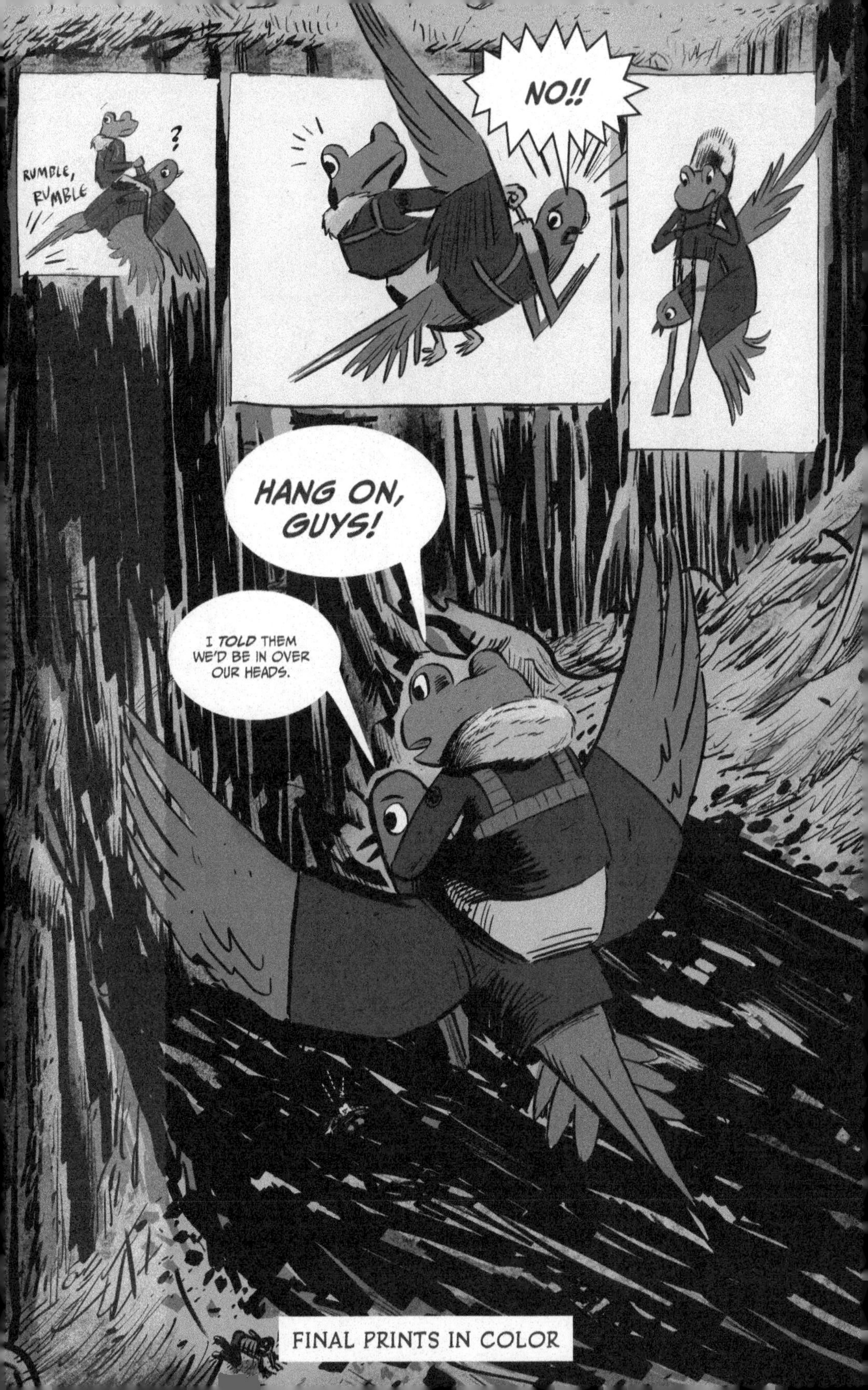

RUMBLE, RUMBLE
?
NO!!
HANG ON, GUYS!
I TOLD THEM WE'D BE IN OVER OUR HEADS.

FINAL PRINTS IN COLOR

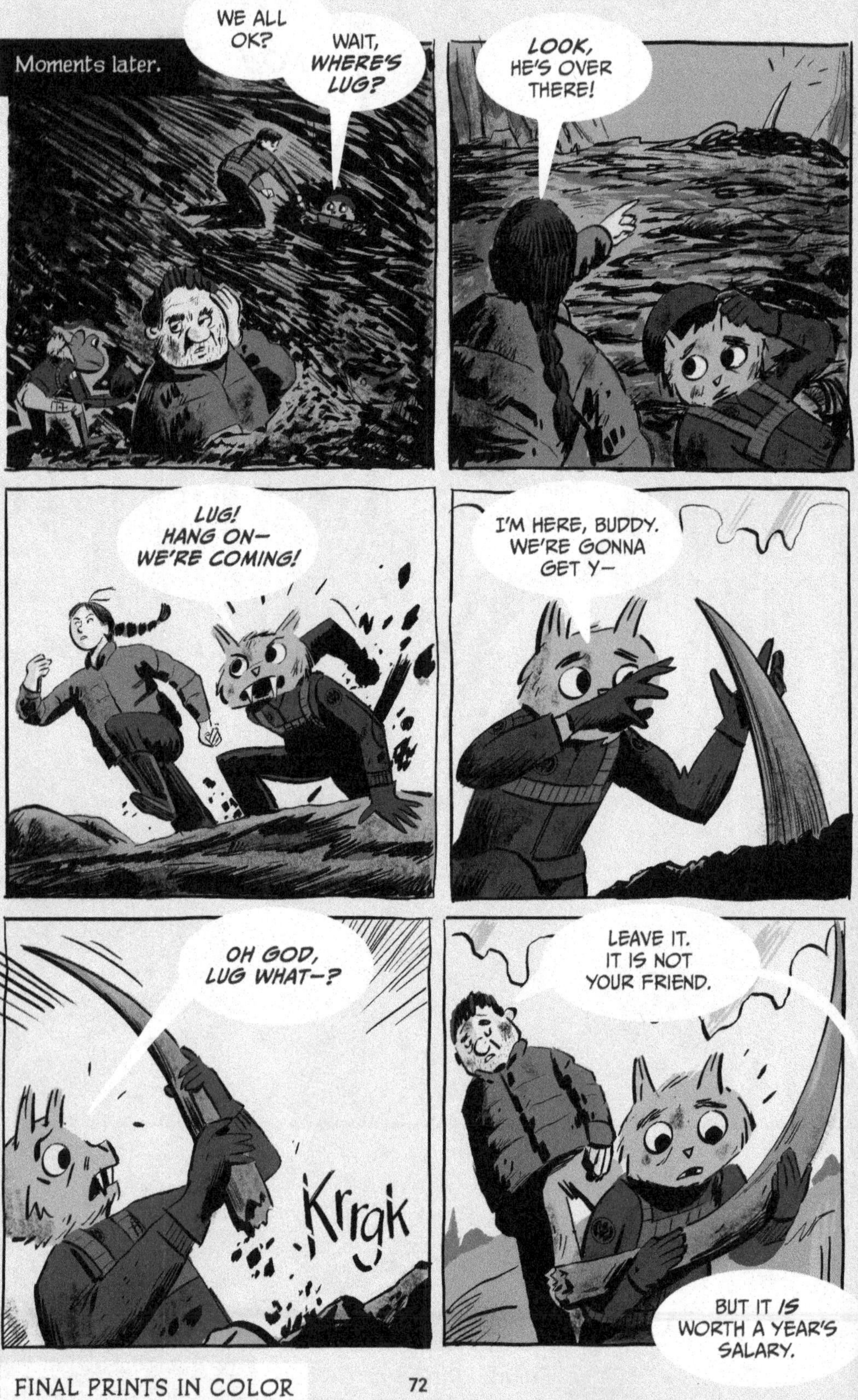
Moments later.
WE ALL OK?
WAIT, WHERE'S LUG?
LOOK, HE'S OVER THERE!
LUG! HANG ON— WE'RE COMING!
I'M HERE, BUDDY. WE'RE GONNA GET Y—
OH GOD, LUG WHAT—?
Krrgk
LEAVE IT. IT IS NOT YOUR FRIEND.
BUT IT IS WORTH A YEAR'S SALARY.

FINAL PRINTS IN COLOR

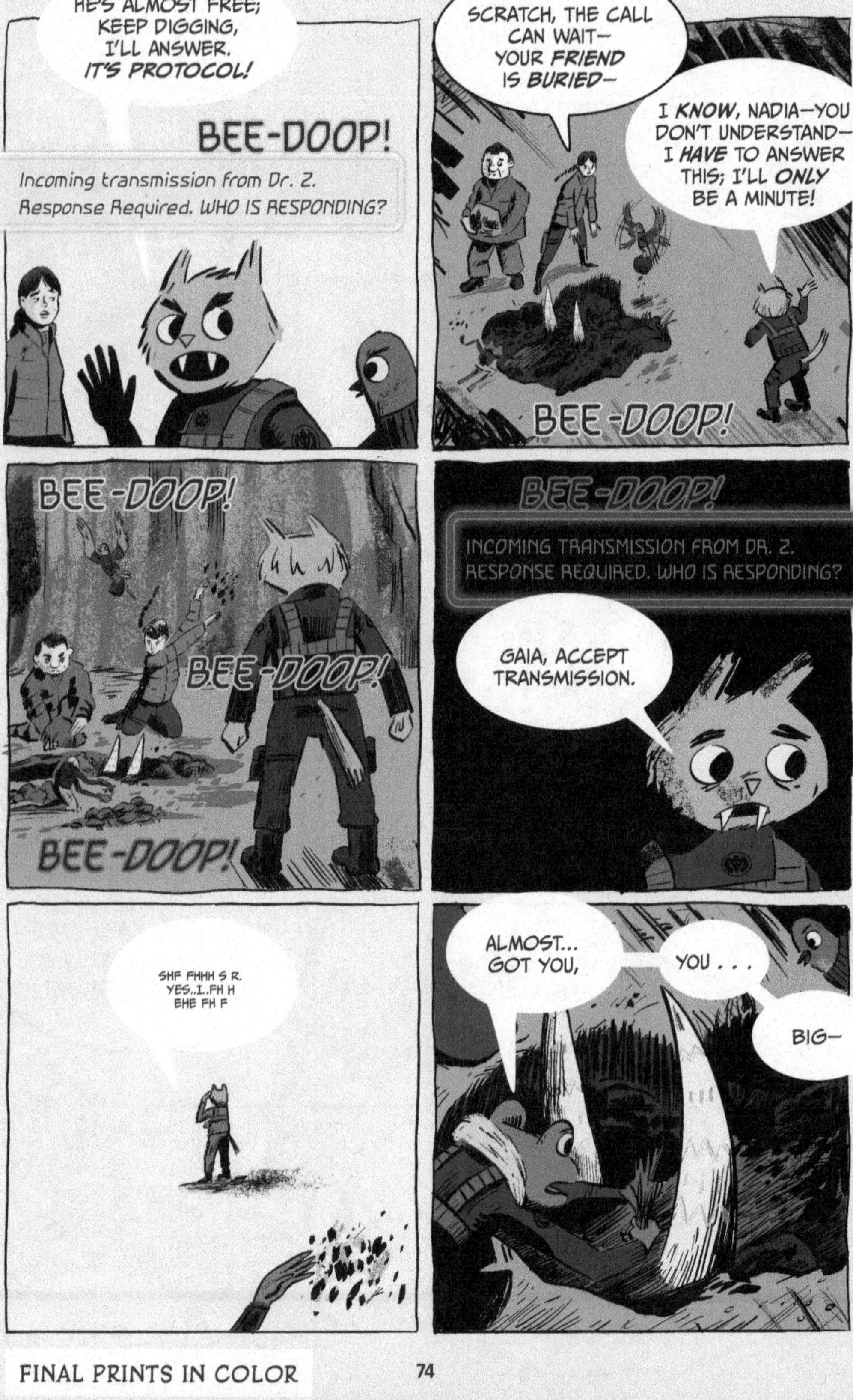
HE'S ALMOST FREE; KEEP DIGGING, I'LL ANSWER. IT'S PROTOCOL!
BEE-DOOP!
Incoming transmission from Dr. Z. Response Required. WHO IS RESPONDING?
SCRATCH, THE CALL CAN WAIT— YOUR FRIEND IS BURIED—
I KNOW, NADIA—YOU DON'T UNDERSTAND— I HAVE TO ANSWER THIS; I'LL ONLY BE A MINUTE!
BEE-DOOP!
BEE-DOOP!
BEE-DOOP!
BEE-DOOP!
BEE-DOOP!
INCOMING TRANSMISSION FROM DR. Z. RESPONSE REQUIRED. WHO IS RESPONDING?
GAIA, ACCEPT TRANSMISSION.
SHF FHHH S R. YES..I..FH H EHE FH F
ALMOST... GOT YOU,
YOU . . .
BIG—

FINAL PRINTS IN COLOR

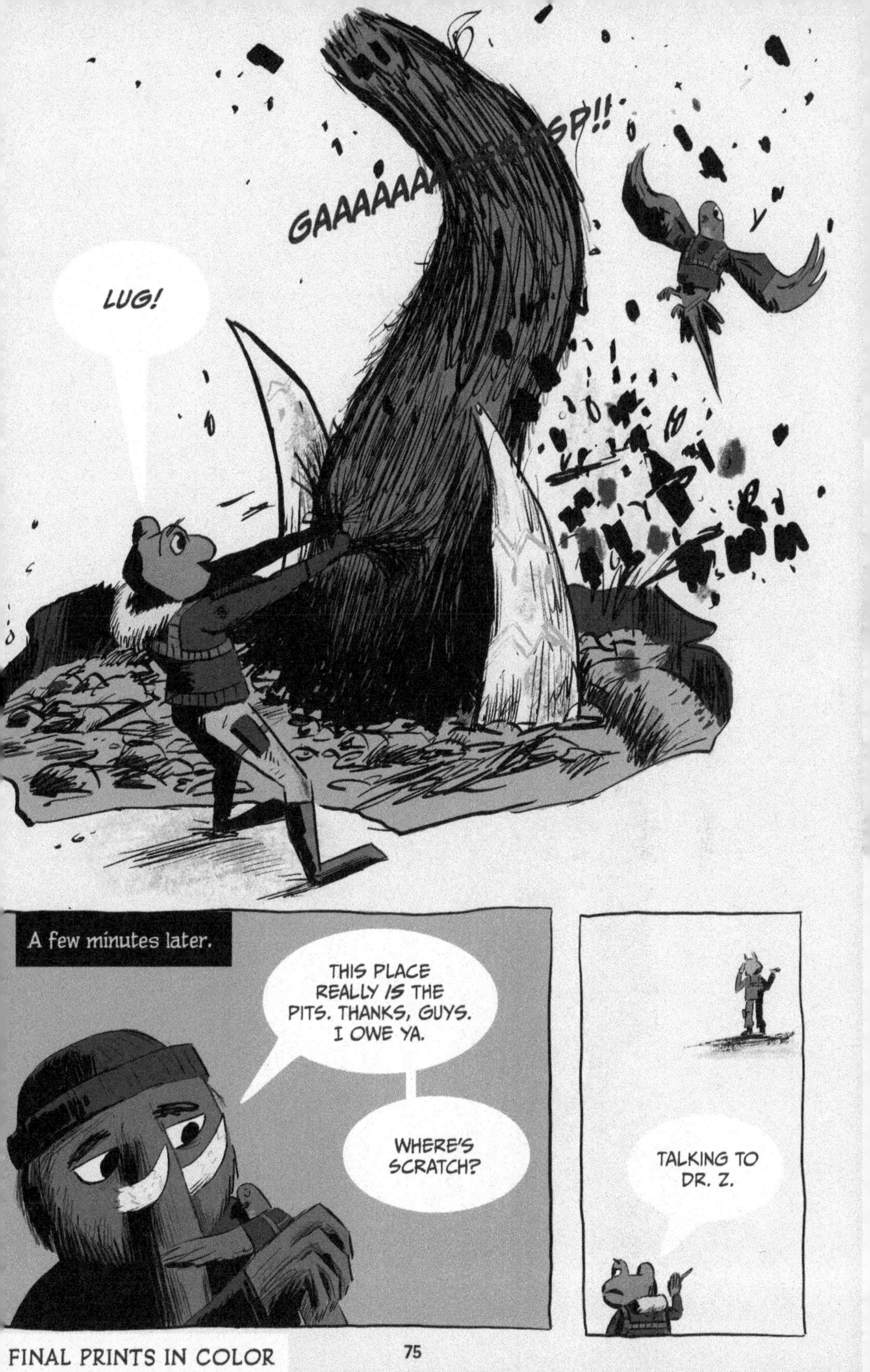
GAAAAAA
LUG!
A few minutes later.
THIS PLACE REALLY IS THE PITS. THANKS, GUYS. I OWE YA.
WHERE'S SCRATCH?
TALKING TO DR. Z.

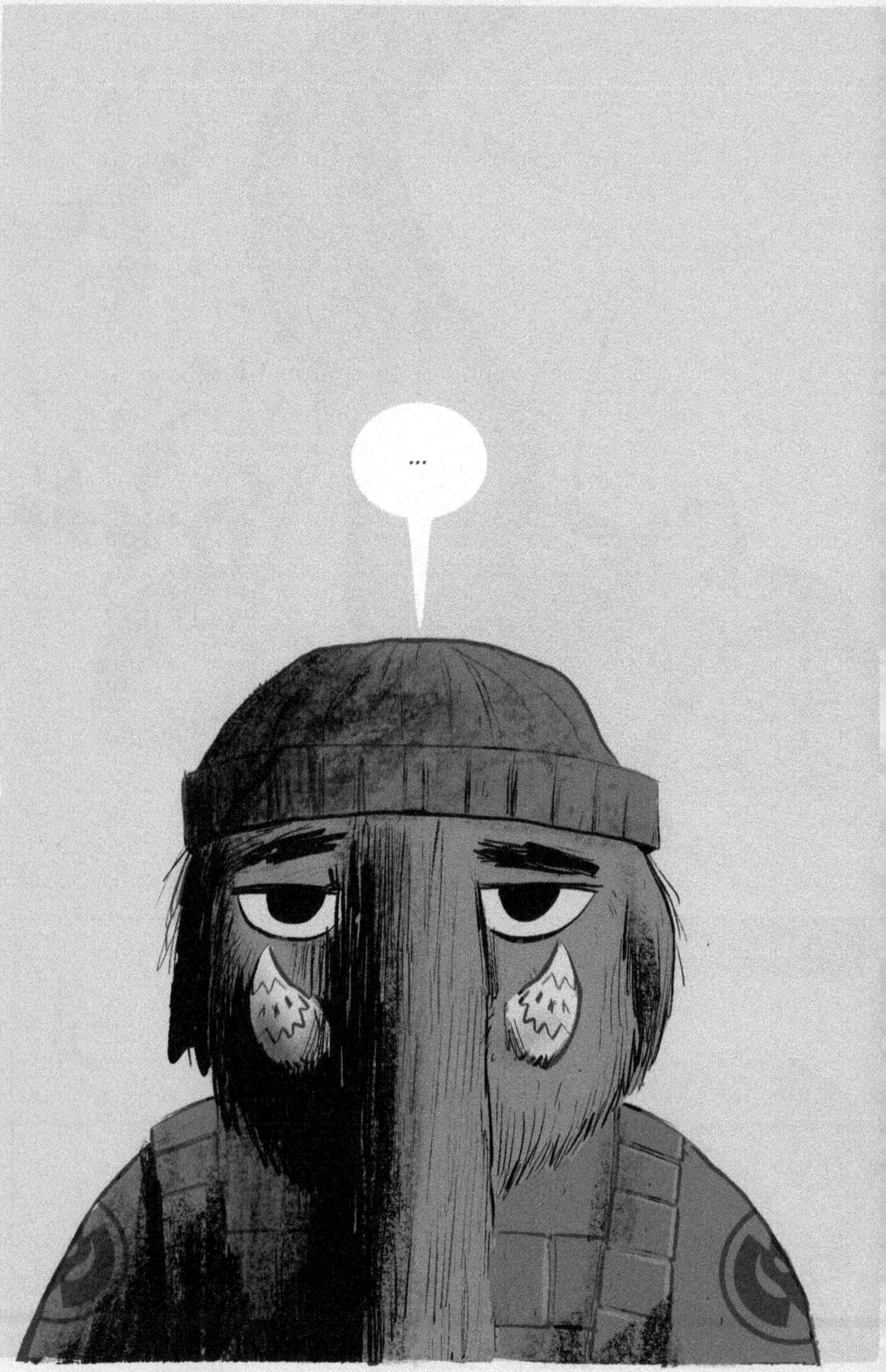
...

77

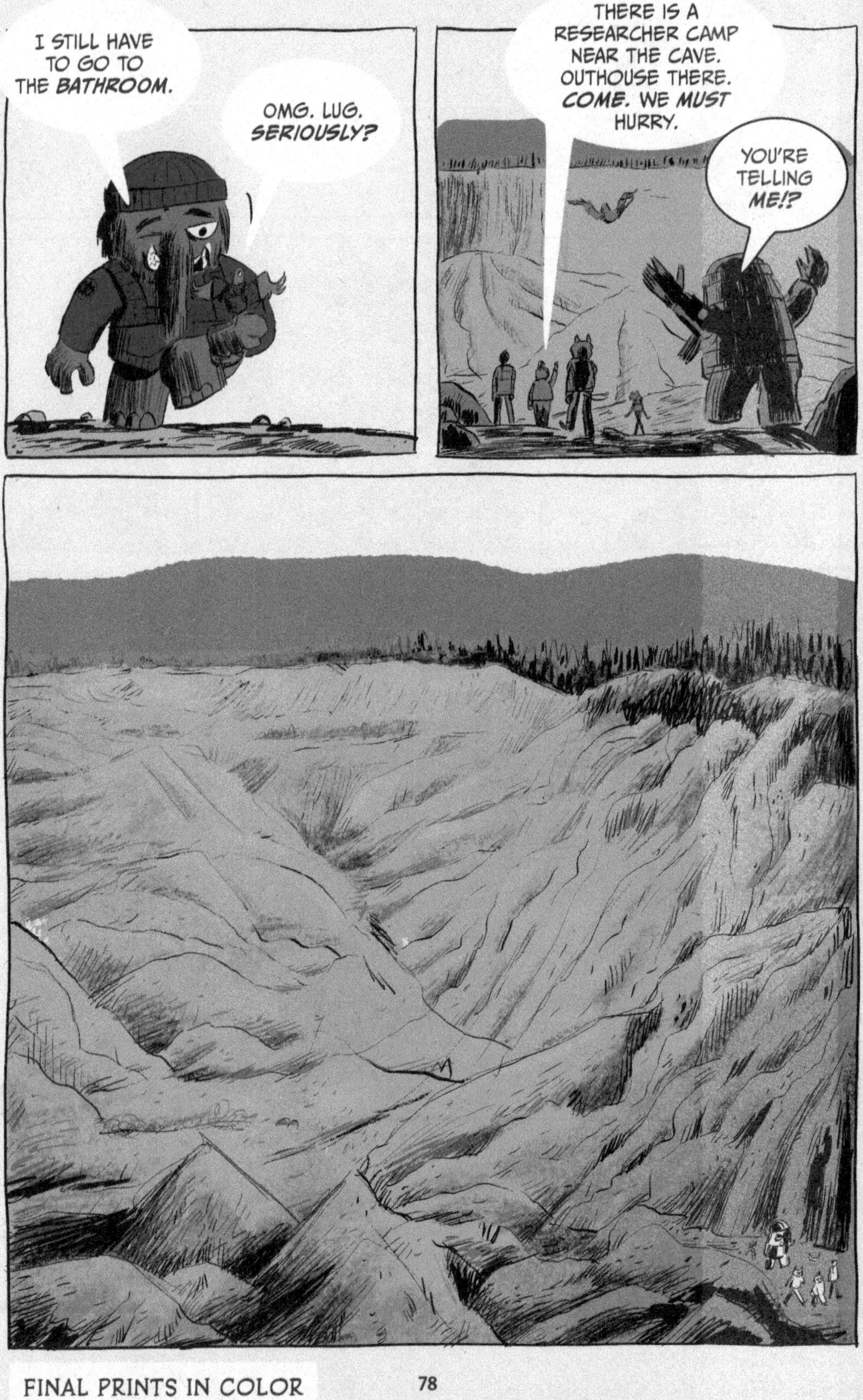
I STILL HAVE TO GO TO THE *BATHROOM*.
OMG. LUG. *SERIOUSLY?*
THERE IS A RESEARCHER CAMP NEAR THE CAVE. OUTHOUSE THERE. ***COME.*** WE ***MUST*** HURRY.
YOU'RE TELLING *ME!?*

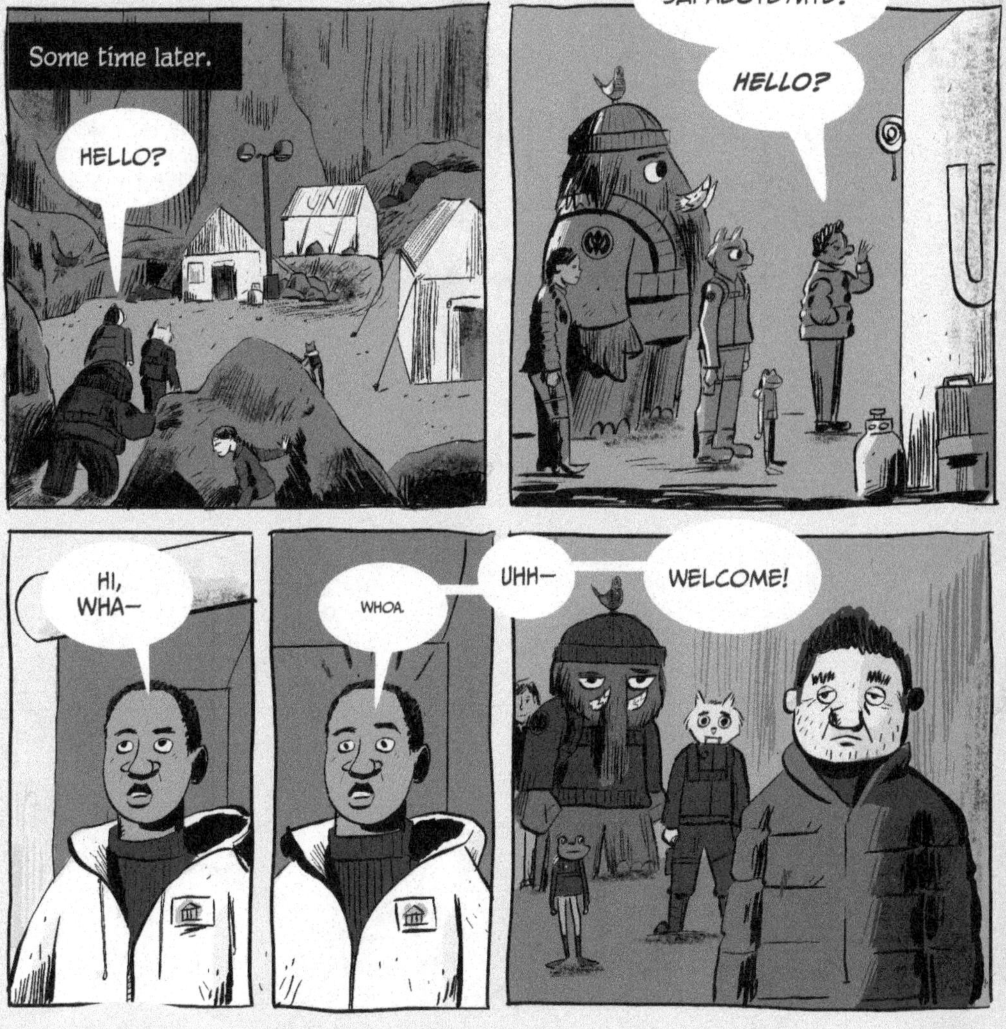
Some time later.
HELLO?
ЗДРАВСТВУЙТЕ?*
HELLO?
HI, WHA—
WHOA.
UHH—
WELCOME!
THANKS. I'M SCRATCH. MY TEAM. WE'RE FROM R.O.A.R.
GOOD TO MEET YOU. DOUG COLEMAN, UNESCO. I'M NOT FAMILIAR WITH R.O.A.R.
D.C.?
THEY ARE FRIENDS OF MINE. THEY ARE GOOD PEOPLE.
ANIMALS.
WHATEVER.

* Zdrastvuyte. "Hello."

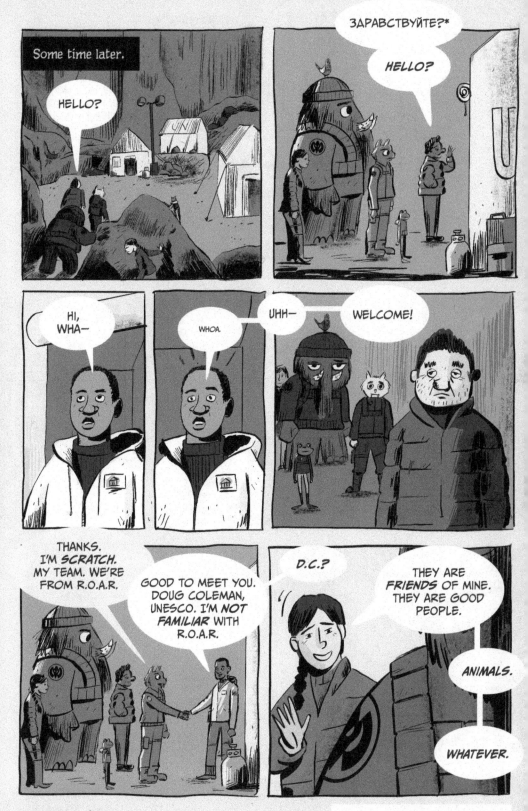

80

FINAL PRINTS IN COLOR

FINAL PRINTS IN COLOR

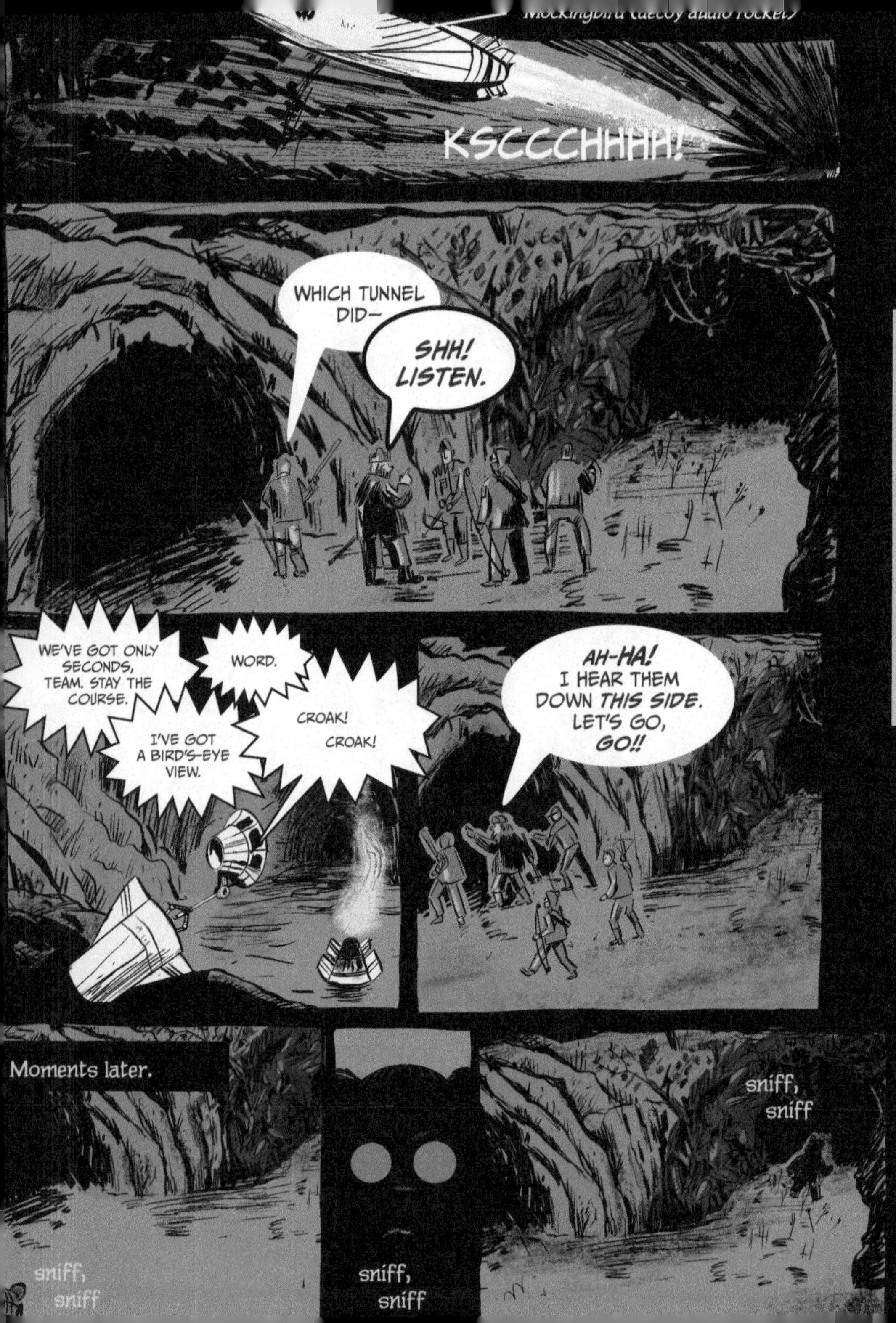

Mockingbird (decoy audio rocket)
KSCCCHHHH!
WHICH TUNNEL DID—
SHH! LISTEN.
WE'VE GOT ONLY SECONDS, TEAM. STAY THE COURSE.
WORD.
I'VE GOT A BIRD'S-EYE VIEW.
CROAK! CROAK!
AH-HA! I HEAR THEM DOWN THIS SIDE. LET'S GO, GO!!
Moments later.
sniff, sniff
sniff, sniff
sniff, sniff

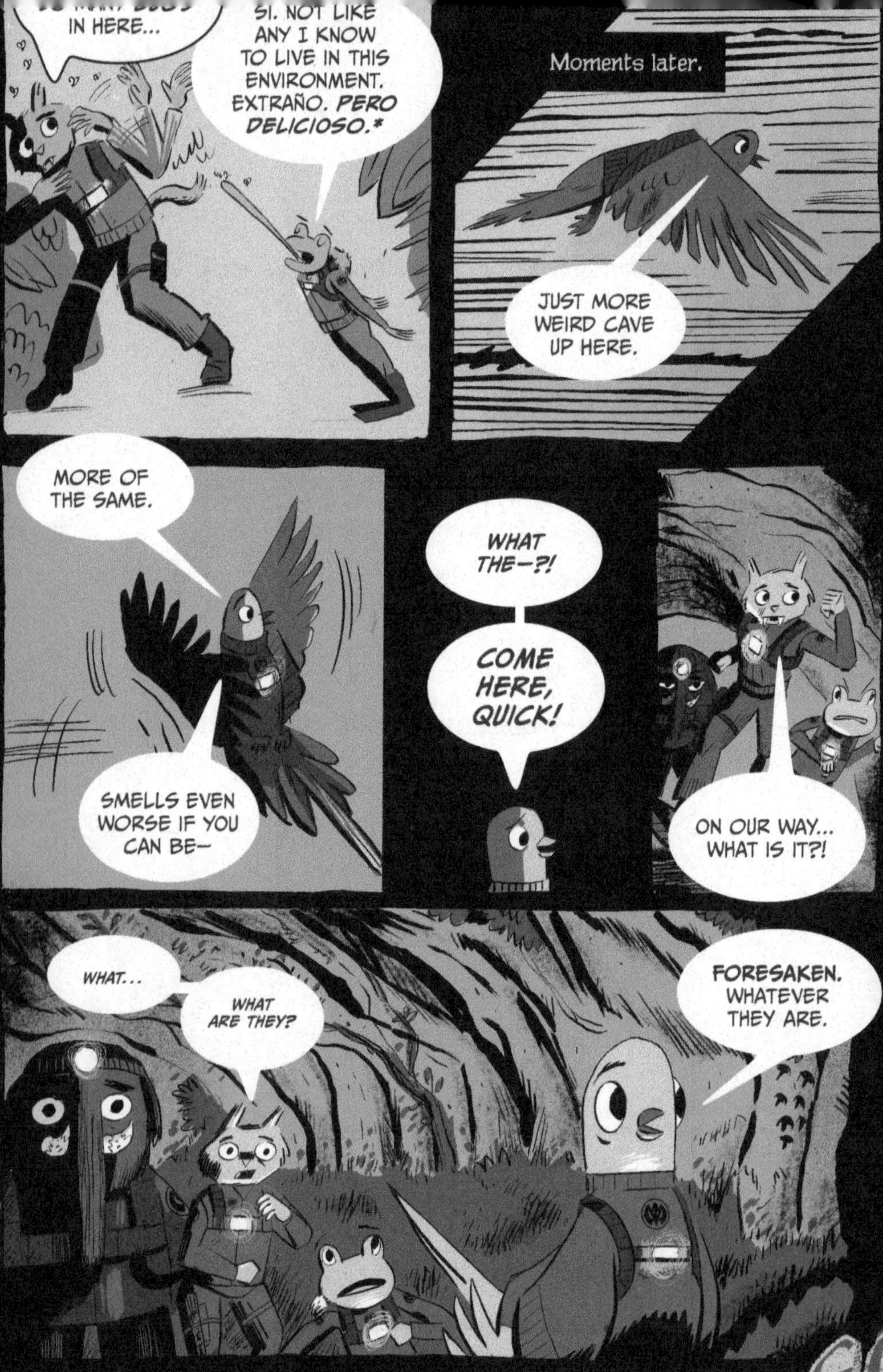

IN HERE...
SI. NOT LIKE ANY I KNOW TO LIVE IN THIS ENVIRONMENT. EXTRAÑO. *PERO DELICIOSO.**
Moments later.
JUST MORE WEIRD CAVE UP HERE.
MORE OF THE SAME.
SMELLS EVEN WORSE IF YOU CAN BE—
WHAT THE—?!
COME HERE, QUICK!
ON OUR WAY... WHAT IS IT?!
WHAT...
WHAT ARE THEY?
FORESAKEN. WHATEVER THEY ARE.

*Strange. But delicious!

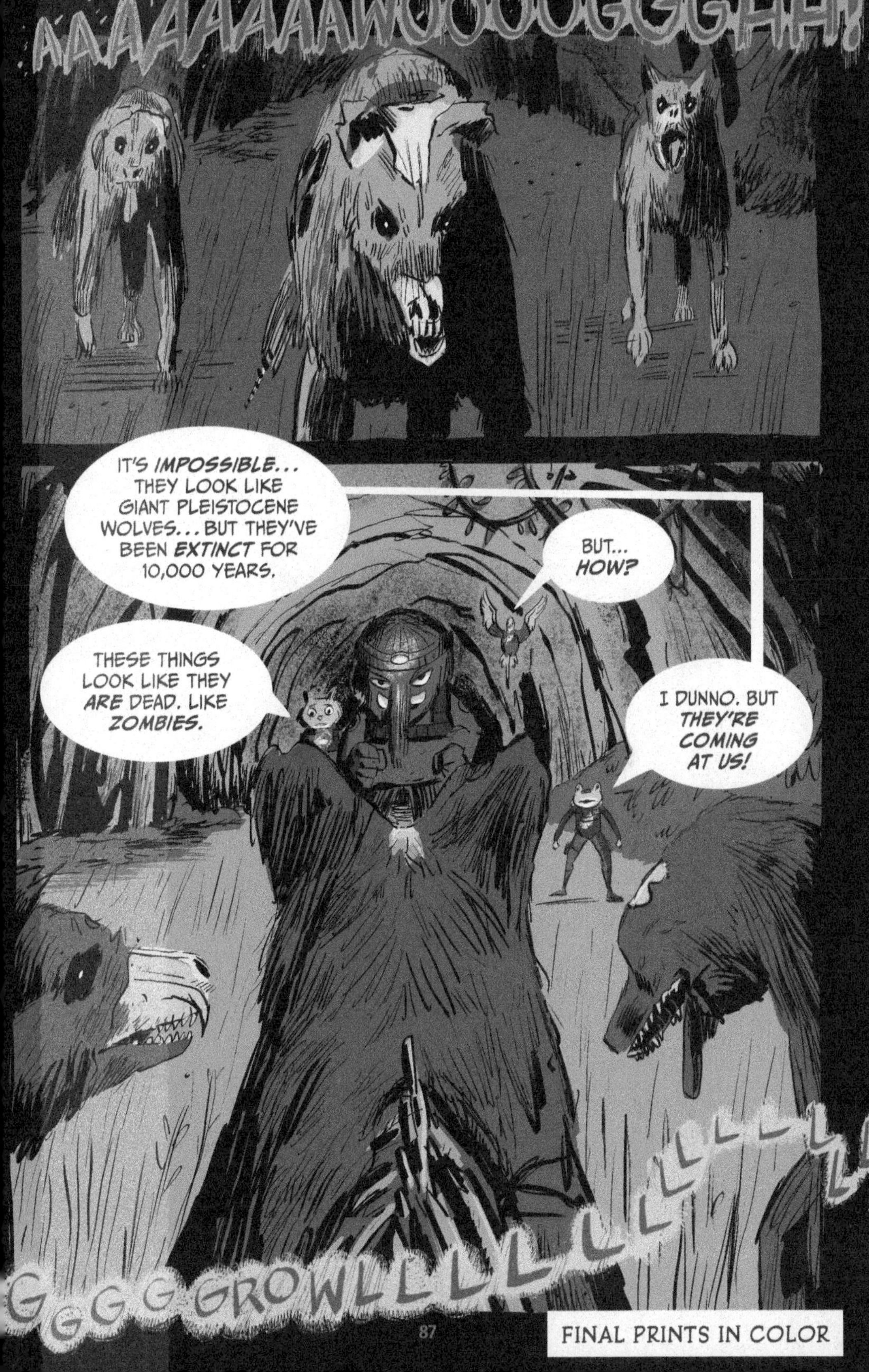
AAAAAAAAWOOOOGGGHH!
IT'S IMPOSSIBLE... THEY LOOK LIKE GIANT PLEISTOCENE WOLVES... BUT THEY'VE BEEN EXTINCT FOR 10,000 YEARS.
BUT... HOW?
THESE THINGS LOOK LIKE THEY ARE DEAD. LIKE ZOMBIES.
I DUNNO. BUT THEY'RE COMING AT US!
GGGGGROWLLLLLLLLLLLL

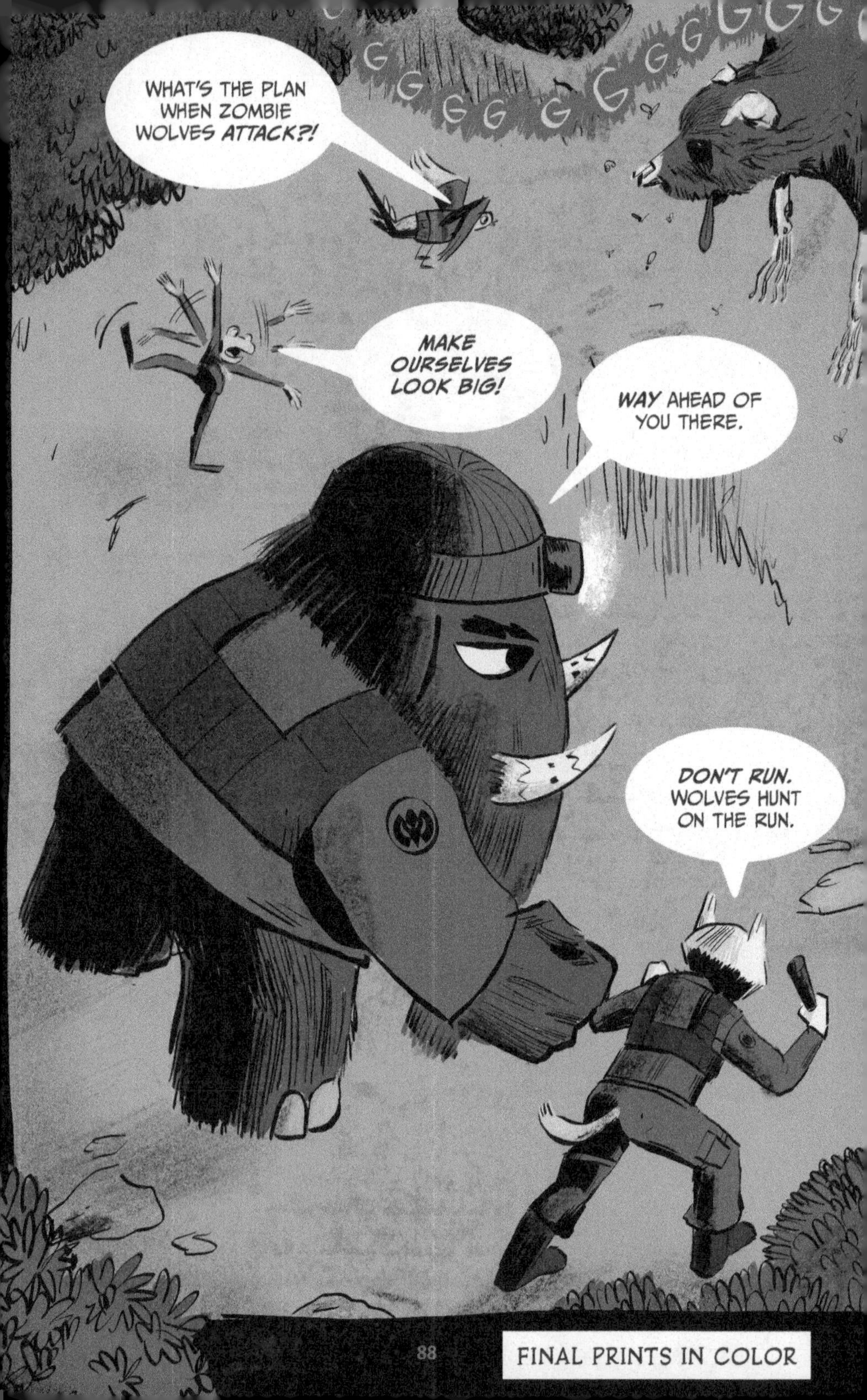
GGGGGGGGGGGGGG
WHAT'S THE PLAN WHEN ZOMBIE WOLVES ATTACK?!
MAKE OURSELVES LOOK BIG!
WAY AHEAD OF YOU THERE.
DON'T RUN. WOLVES HUNT ON THE RUN.

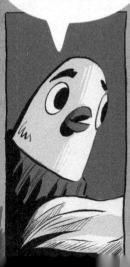

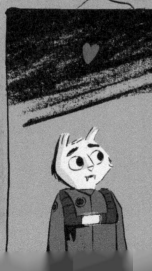

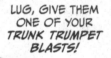

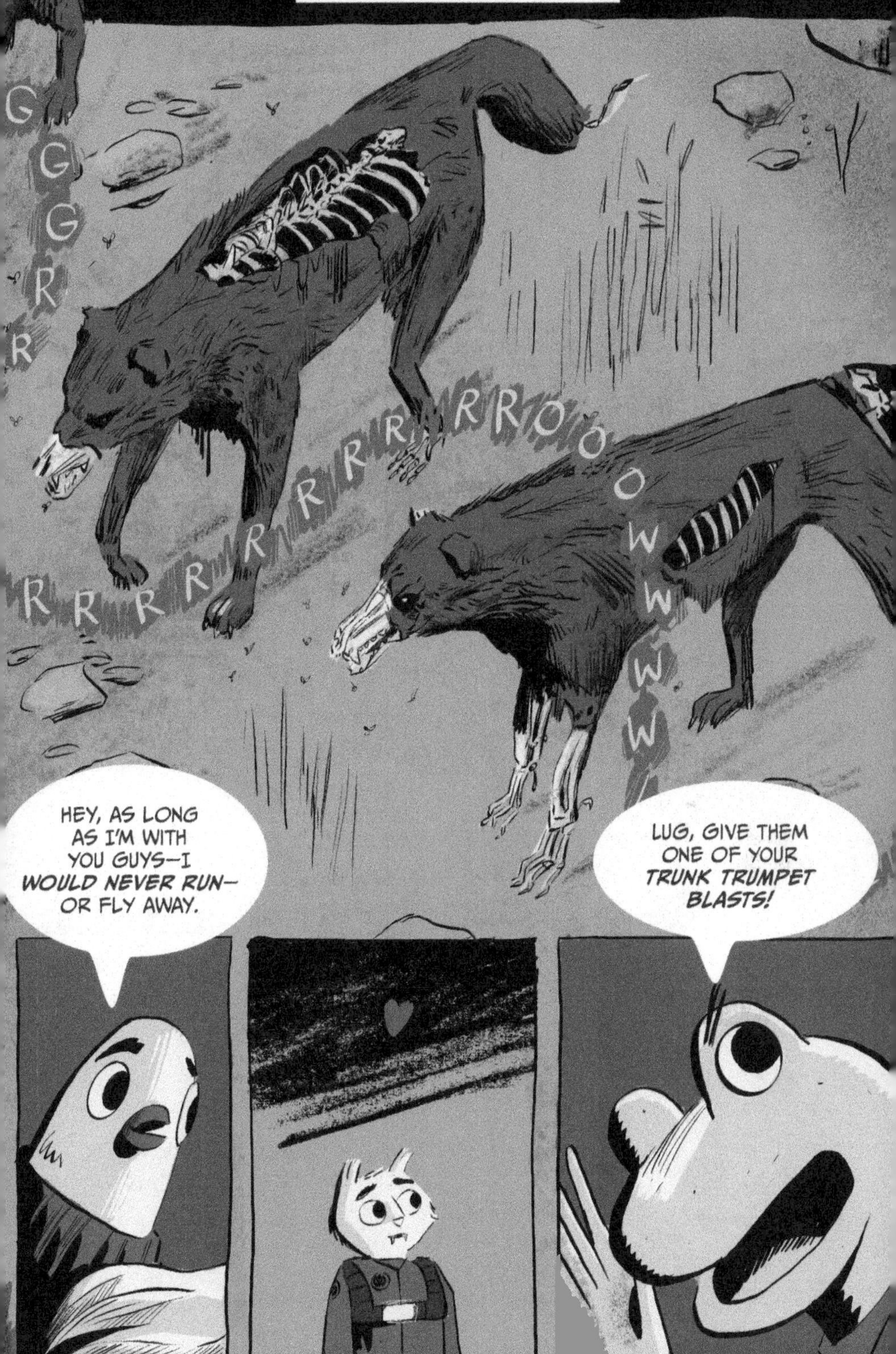
GGGRR
RRRRRRRRRRROOOWWWW
HEY, AS LONG AS I'M WITH YOU GUYS—I WOULD NEVER RUN— OR FLY AWAY.
LUG, GIVE THEM ONE OF YOUR TRUNK TRUMPET BLASTS!

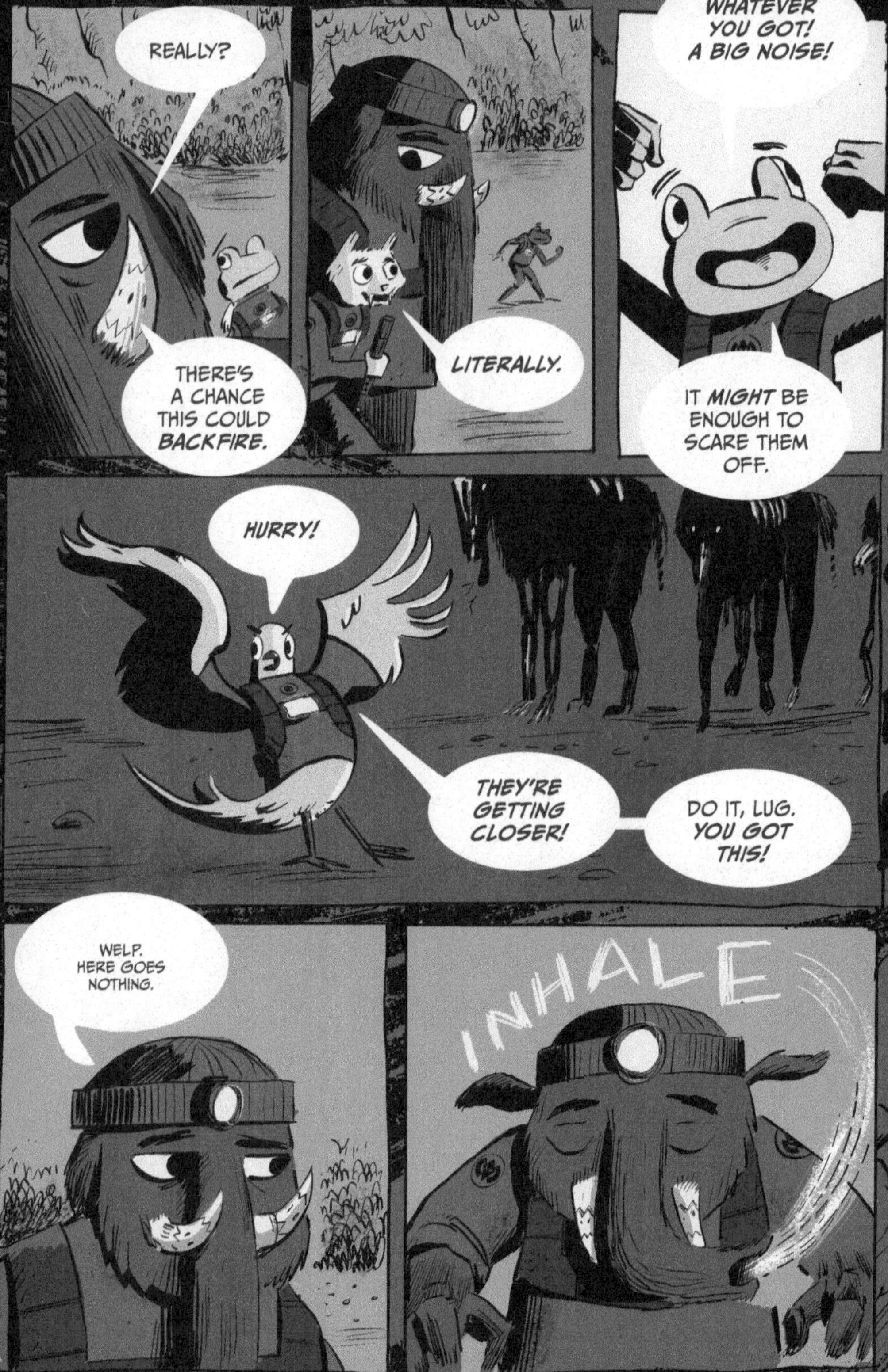

REALLY?
THERE'S A CHANCE THIS COULD BACKFIRE.
LITERALLY.
WHATEVER YOU GOT! A BIG NOISE!
IT MIGHT BE ENOUGH TO SCARE THEM OFF.
HURRY!
THEY'RE GETTING CLOSER!
DO IT, LUG. YOU GOT THIS!
WELP. HERE GOES NOTHING.
INHALE

FINAL PRINTS IN COLOR

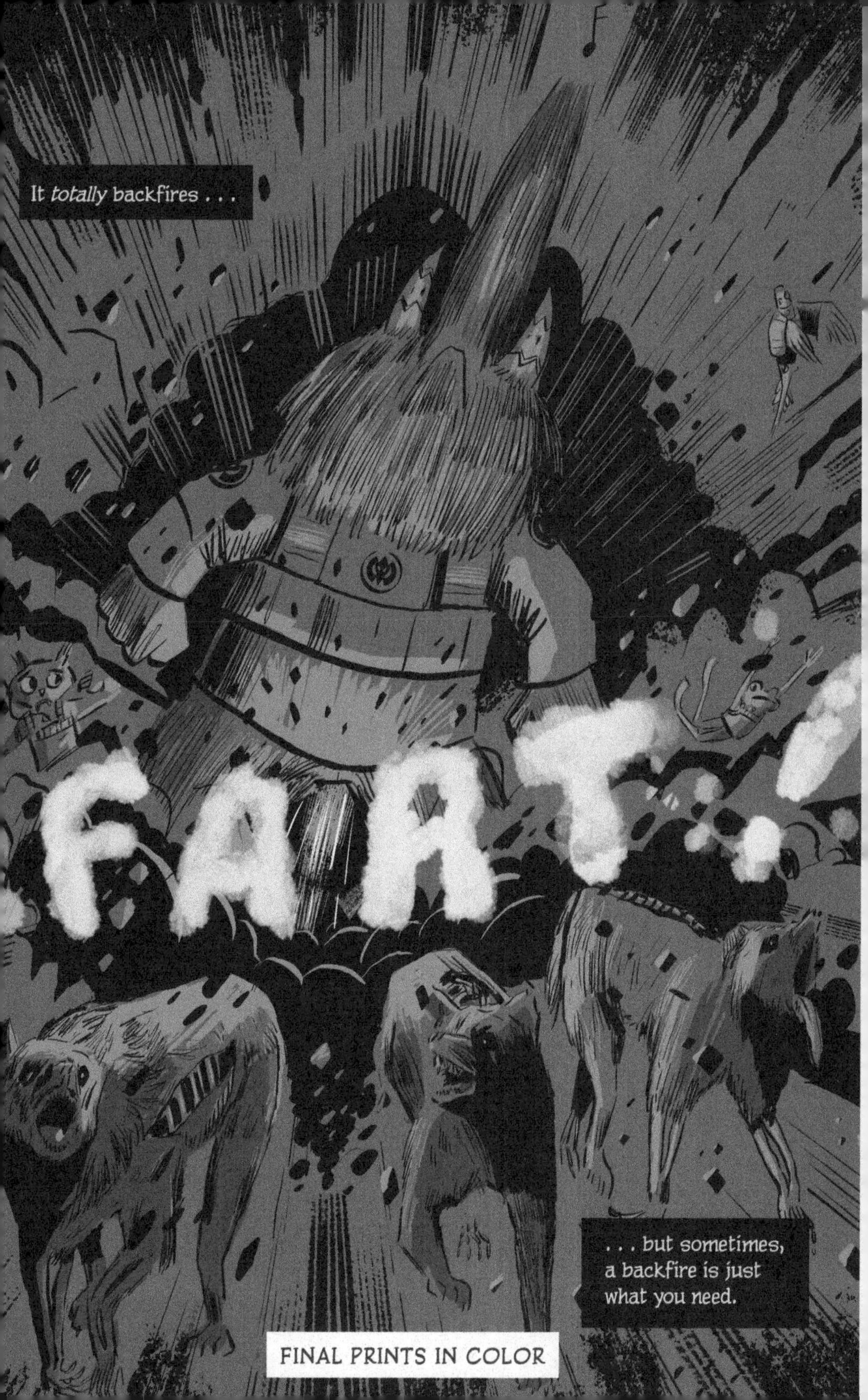

FINAL PRINTS IN COLOR

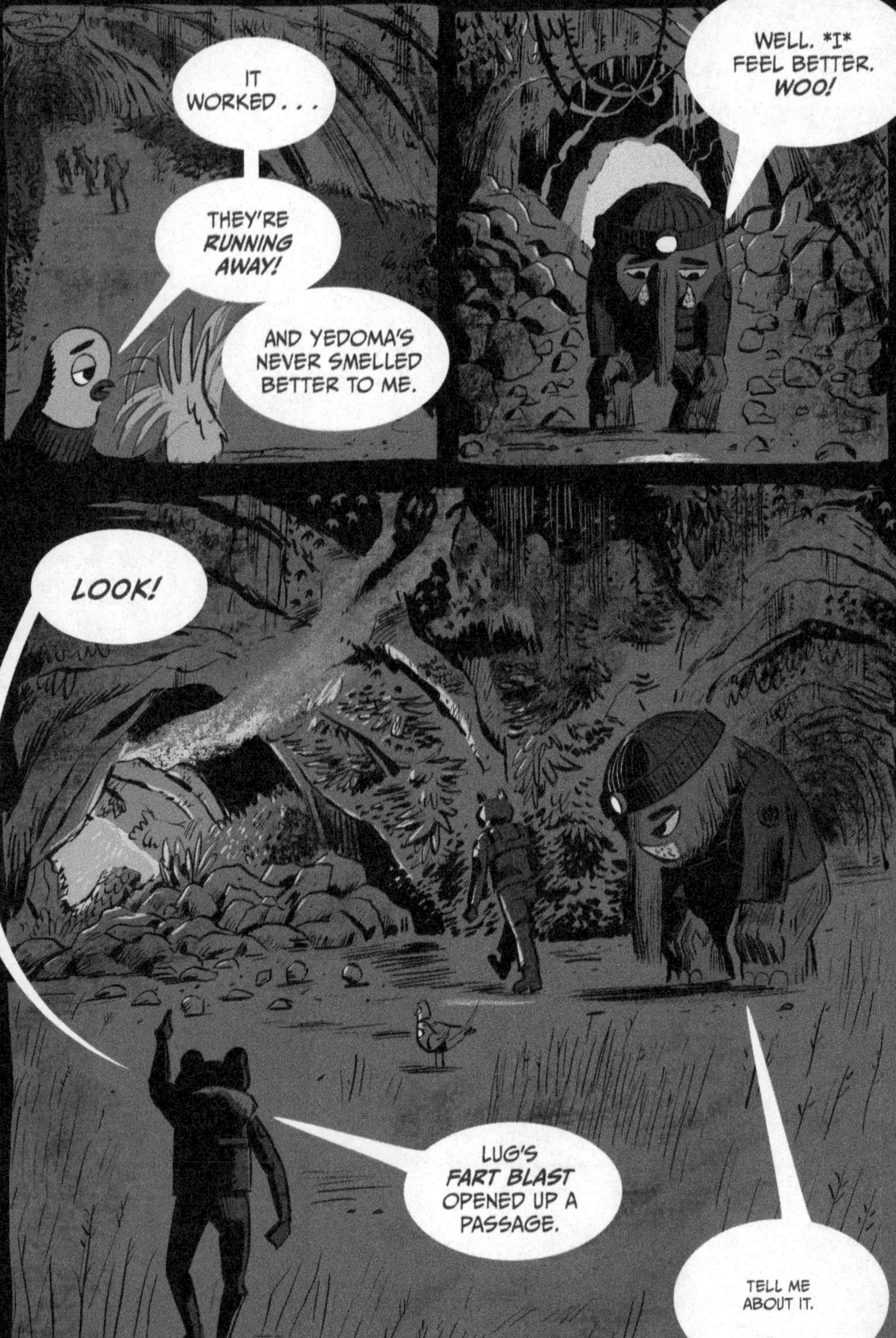
IT WORKED . . .
THEY'RE RUNNING AWAY!
AND YEDOMA'S NEVER SMELLED BETTER TO ME.
WELL. *I* FEEL BETTER. WOO!
LOOK!
LUG'S FART BLAST OPENED UP A PASSAGE.
TELL ME ABOUT IT.

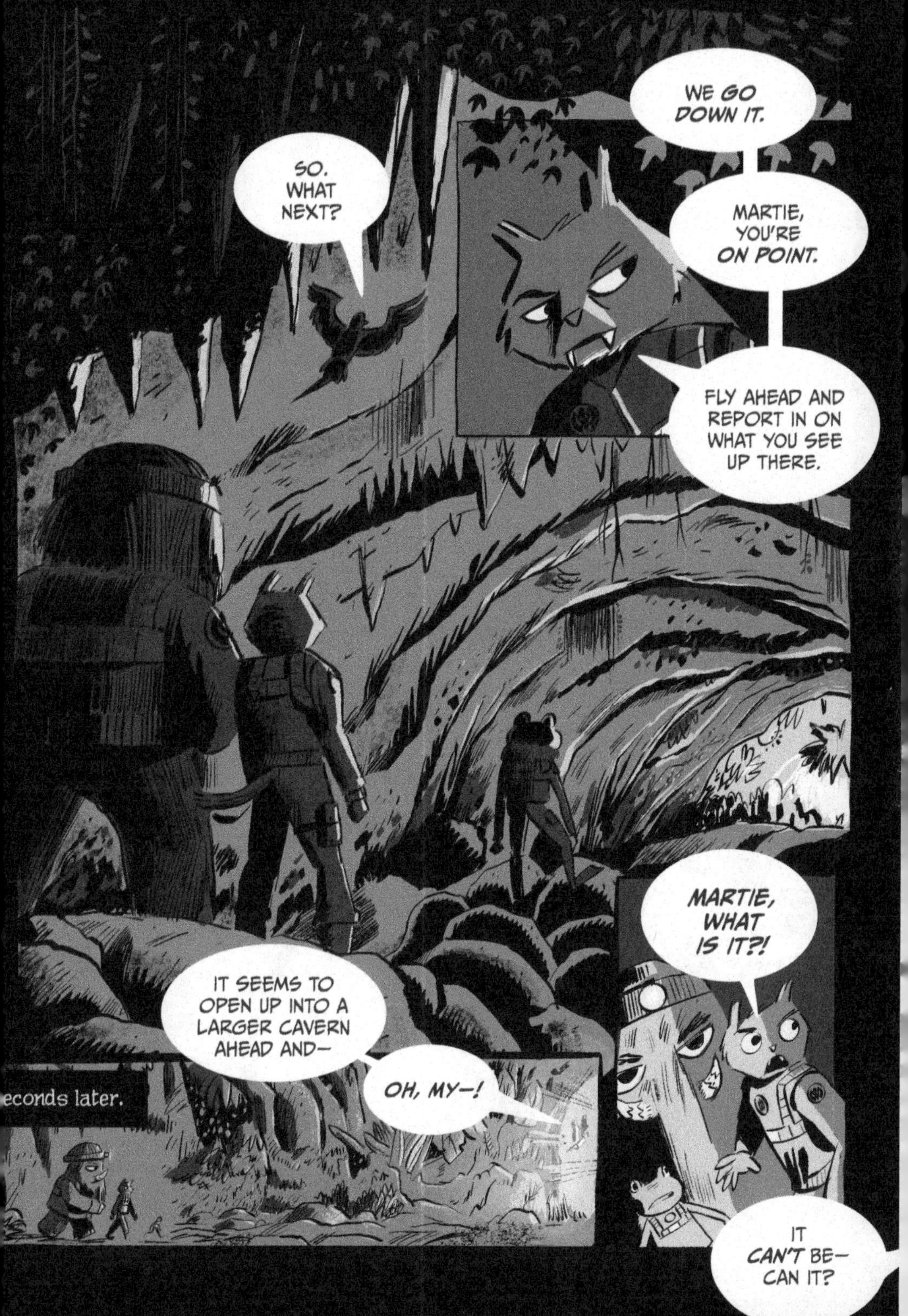
SO. WHAT NEXT?
WE GO DOWN IT.
MARTIE, YOU'RE ON POINT.
FLY AHEAD AND REPORT IN ON WHAT YOU SEE UP THERE.
econds later.
IT SEEMS TO OPEN UP INTO A LARGER CAVERN AHEAD AND—
OH, MY—!
MARTIE, WHAT IS IT?!
IT CAN'T BE— CAN IT?

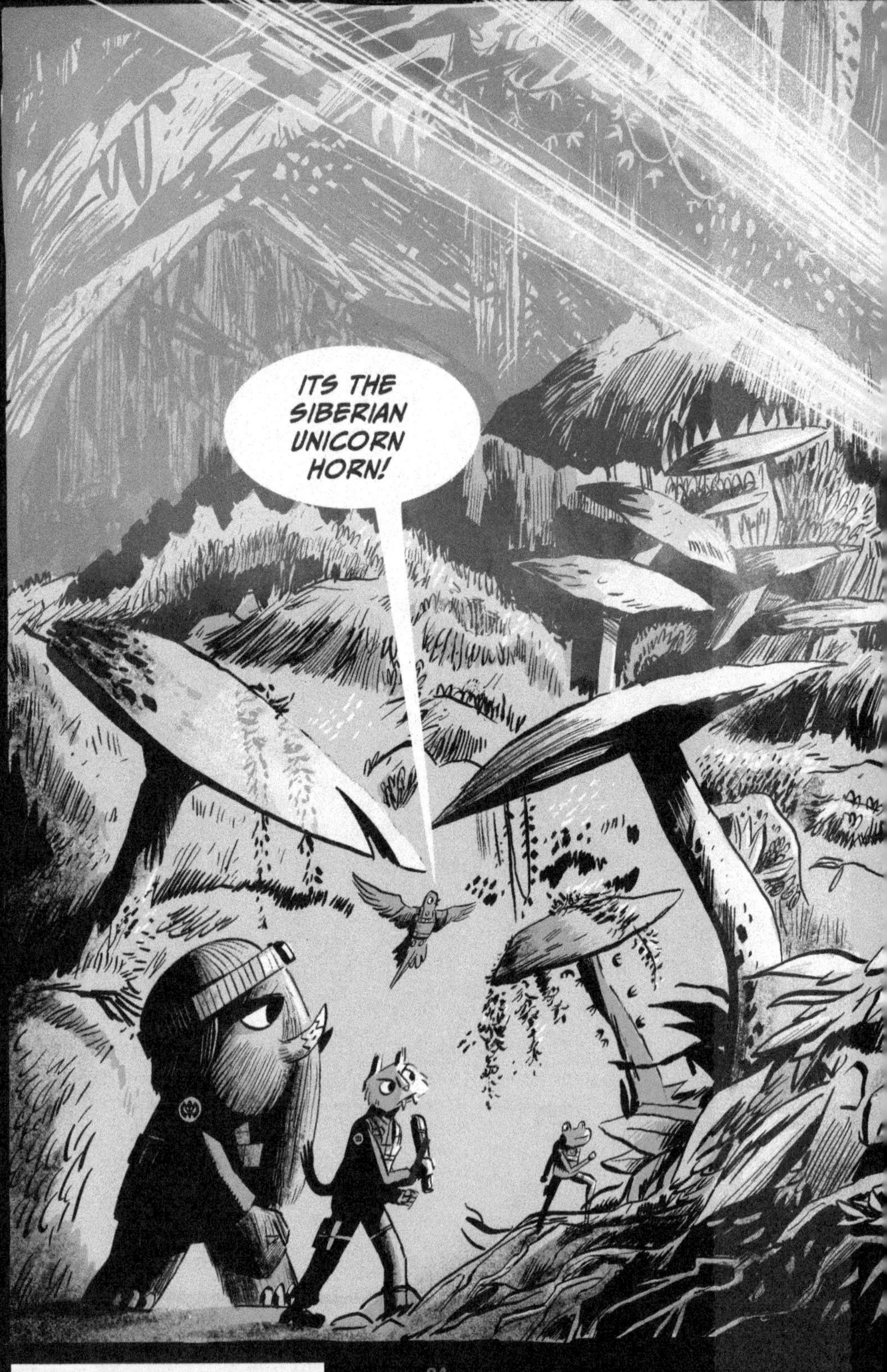
ITS THE SIBERIAN UNICORN HORN!

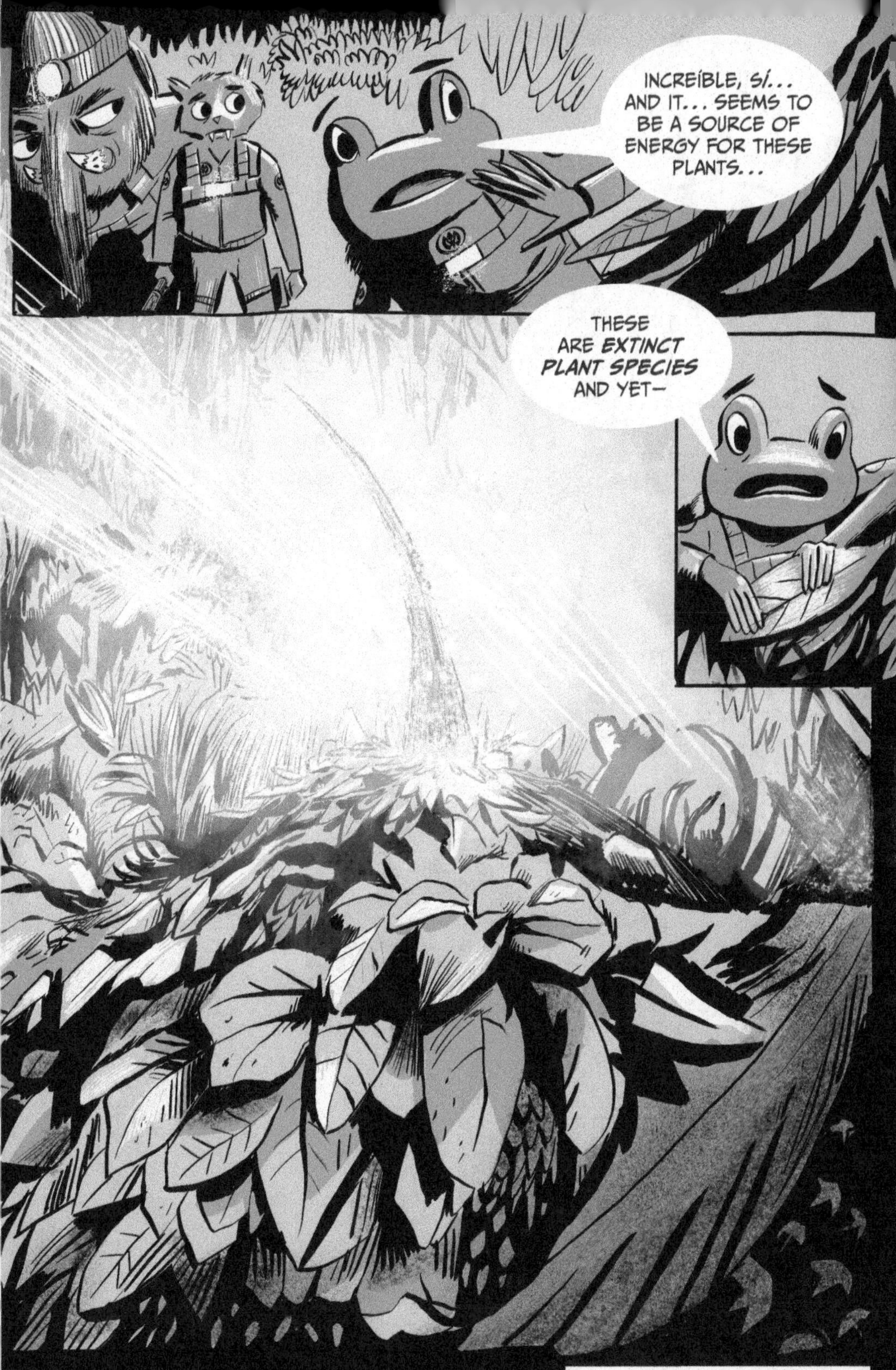
INCREÍBLE, SÍ... AND IT... SEEMS TO BE A SOURCE OF ENERGY FOR THESE PLANTS...
THESE ARE *EXTINCT PLANT SPECIES* AND YET—

FINAL PRINTS IN COLOR

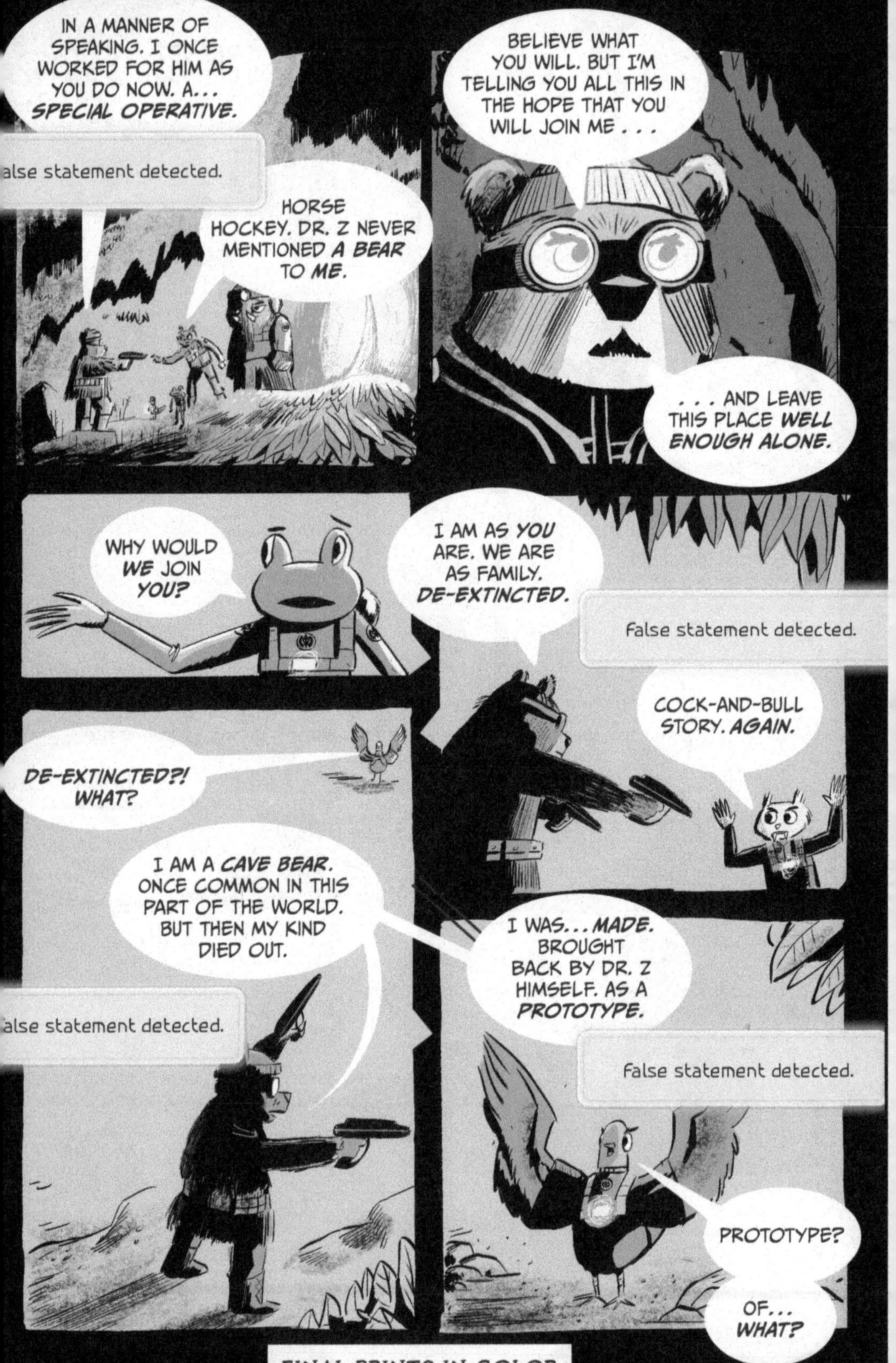
IN A MANNER OF SPEAKING. I ONCE WORKED FOR HIM AS YOU DO NOW. A... SPECIAL OPERATIVE.
alse statement detected.
HORSE HOCKEY. DR. Z NEVER MENTIONED A BEAR TO ME.
BELIEVE WHAT YOU WILL. BUT I'M TELLING YOU ALL THIS IN THE HOPE THAT YOU WILL JOIN ME . . .
. . . AND LEAVE THIS PLACE WELL ENOUGH ALONE.
WHY WOULD WE JOIN YOU?
I AM AS YOU ARE. WE ARE AS FAMILY. DE-EXTINCTED.
False statement detected.
COCK-AND-BULL STORY. AGAIN.
DE-EXTINCTED?! WHAT?
I AM A CAVE BEAR. ONCE COMMON IN THIS PART OF THE WORLD. BUT THEN MY KIND DIED OUT.
alse statement detected.
I WAS... MADE. BROUGHT BACK BY DR. Z HIMSELF. AS A PROTOTYPE.
False statement detected.
PROTOTYPE?
OF... WHAT?

FINAL PRINTS IN COLOR

FINAL PRINTS IN COLOR

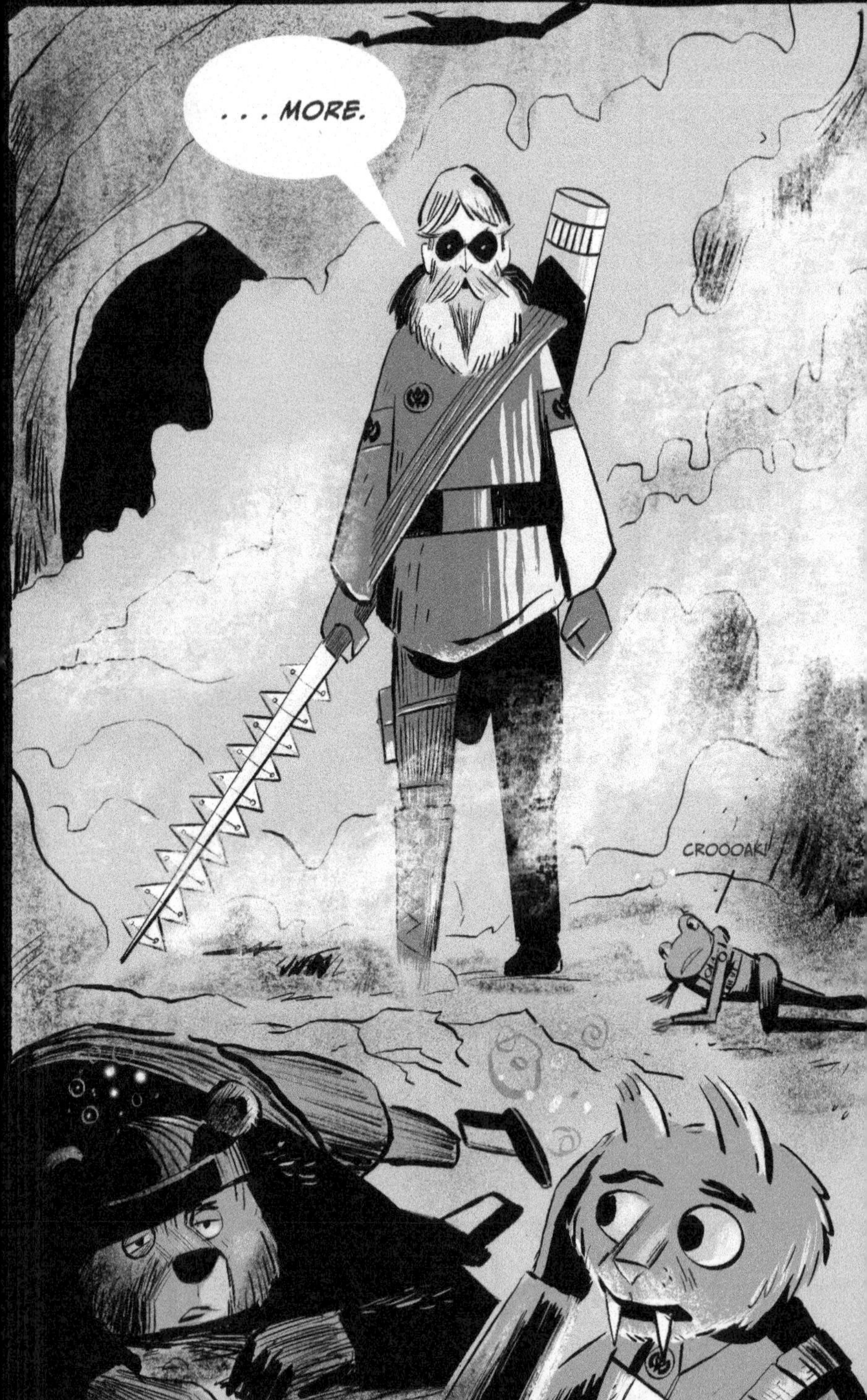
. . . MORE.
CROOOAK!

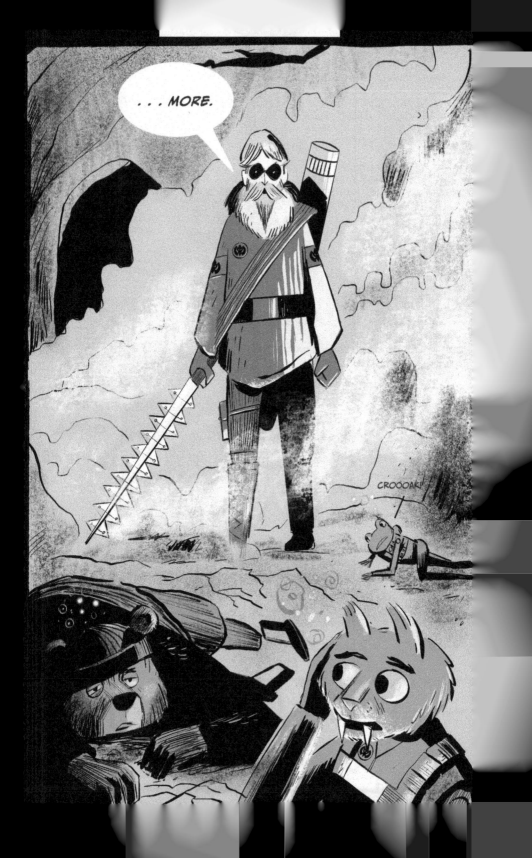

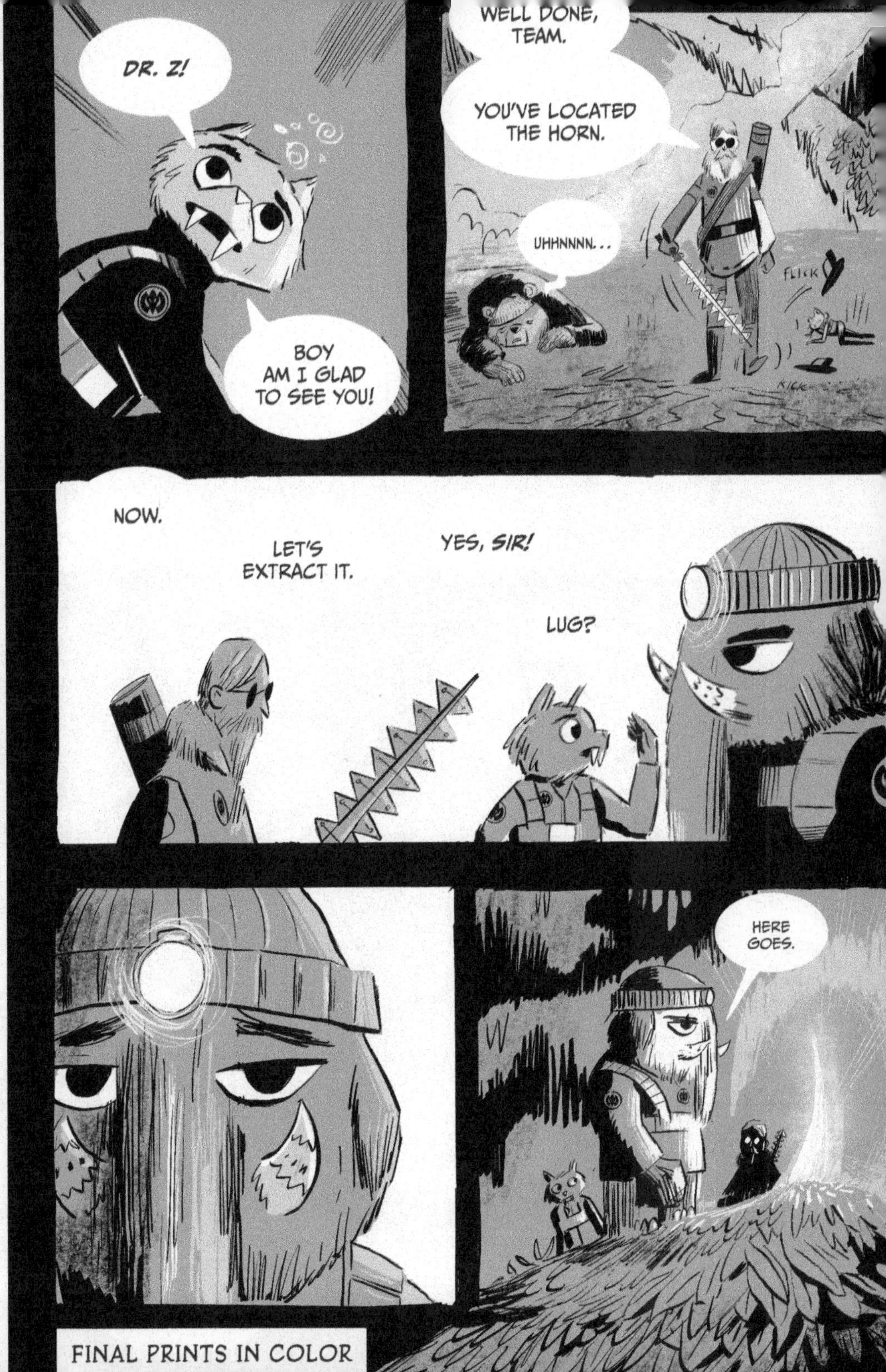
DR. Z!
BOY AM I GLAD TO SEE YOU!
WELL DONE, TEAM.
YOU'VE LOCATED THE HORN.
UHHNNNN...
FLICK
KICK
NOW.
LET'S EXTRACT IT.
YES, SIR!
LUG?
HERE GOES.

FINAL PRINTS IN COLOR

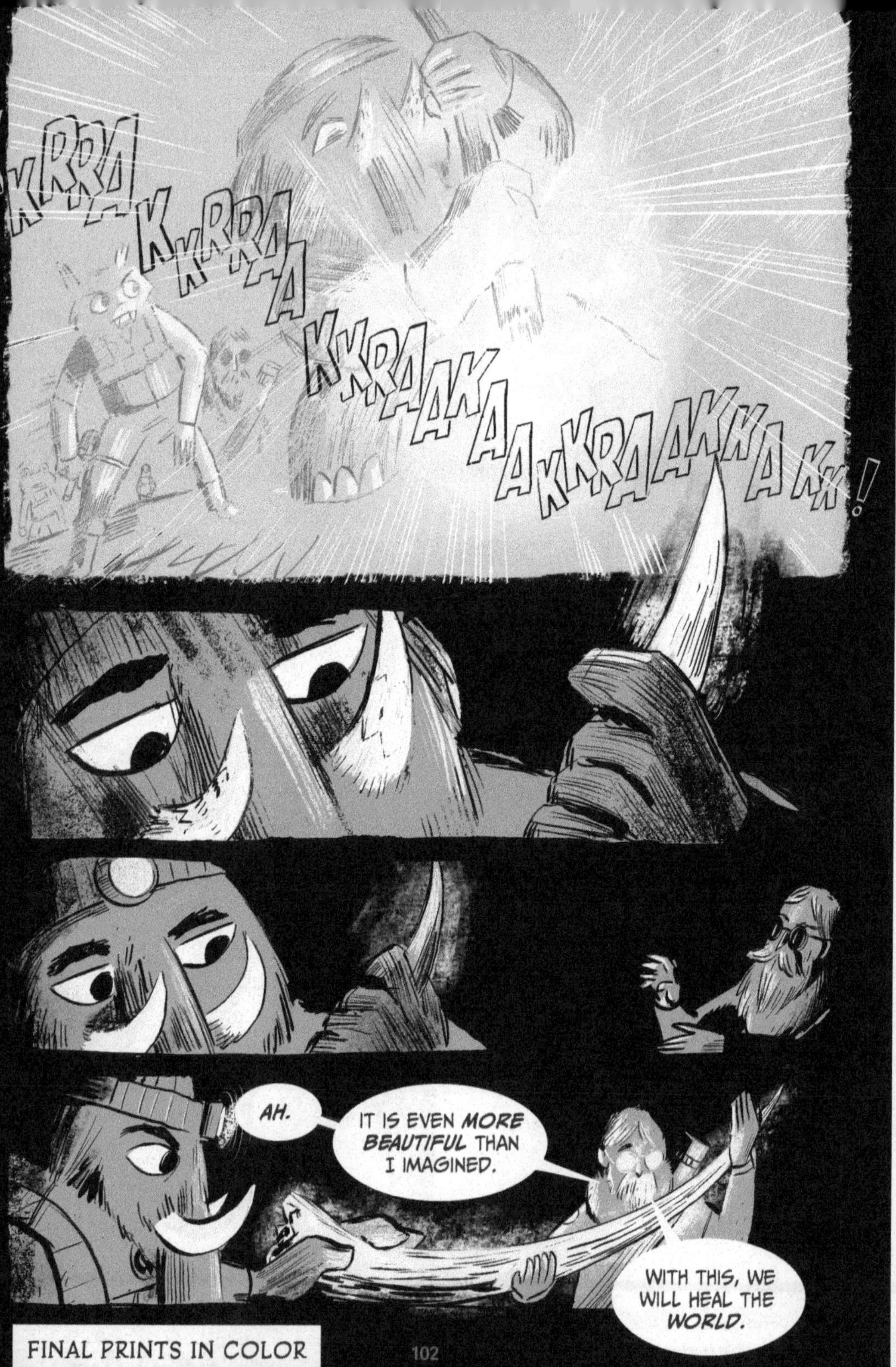
KRRA KRRA KKRAAKA AKKRAAKKAKK!
AH.
IT IS EVEN MORE BEAUTIFUL THAN I IMAGINED.
WITH THIS, WE WILL HEAL THE WORLD.

FINAL PRINTS IN COLOR

FINAL PRINTS IN COLOR

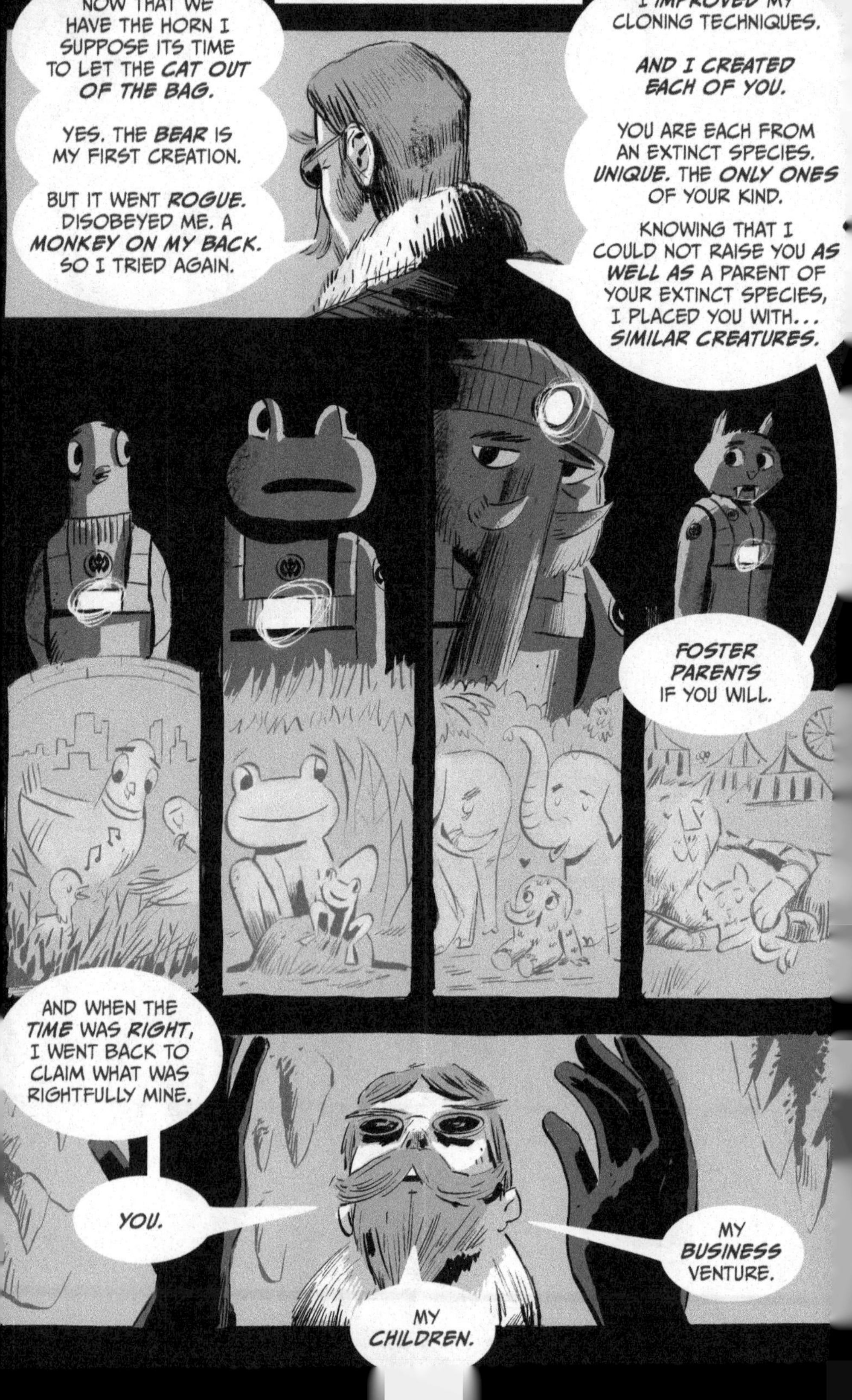
NOW THAT WE HAVE THE HORN I SUPPOSE ITS TIME TO LET THE CAT OUT OF THE BAG.
YES. THE BEAR IS MY FIRST CREATION.
BUT IT WENT ROGUE. DISOBEYED ME. A MONKEY ON MY BACK. SO I TRIED AGAIN.
I IMPROVED MY CLONING TECHNIQUES.
AND I CREATED EACH OF YOU.
YOU ARE EACH FROM AN EXTINCT SPECIES. UNIQUE. THE ONLY ONES OF YOUR KIND.
KNOWING THAT I COULD NOT RAISE YOU AS WELL AS A PARENT OF YOUR EXTINCT SPECIES, I PLACED YOU WITH... SIMILAR CREATURES.
FOSTER PARENTS IF YOU WILL.
AND WHEN THE TIME WAS RIGHT, I WENT BACK TO CLAIM WHAT WAS RIGHTFULLY MINE.
YOU.
MY CHILDREN.
MY BUSINESS VENTURE.

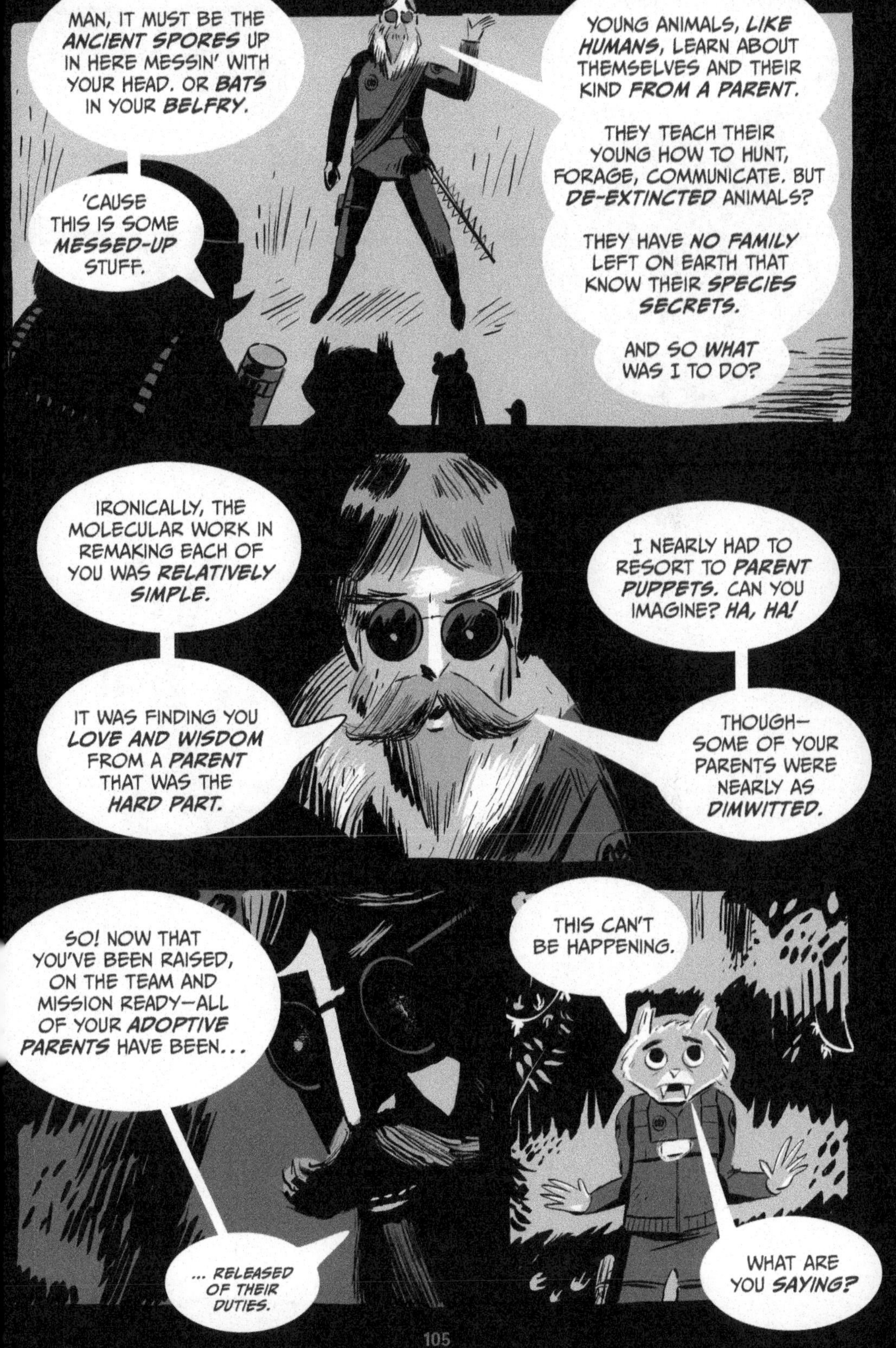
MAN, IT MUST BE THE ANCIENT SPORES UP IN HERE MESSIN' WITH YOUR HEAD. OR BATS IN YOUR BELFRY.
'CAUSE THIS IS SOME MESSED-UP STUFF.
YOUNG ANIMALS, LIKE HUMANS, LEARN ABOUT THEMSELVES AND THEIR KIND FROM A PARENT.
THEY TEACH THEIR YOUNG HOW TO HUNT, FORAGE, COMMUNICATE. BUT DE-EXTINCTED ANIMALS?
THEY HAVE NO FAMILY LEFT ON EARTH THAT KNOW THEIR SPECIES SECRETS.
AND SO WHAT WAS I TO DO?
IRONICALLY, THE MOLECULAR WORK IN REMAKING EACH OF YOU WAS RELATIVELY SIMPLE.
IT WAS FINDING YOU LOVE AND WISDOM FROM A PARENT THAT WAS THE HARD PART.
I NEARLY HAD TO RESORT TO PARENT PUPPETS. CAN YOU IMAGINE? HA, HA!
THOUGH— SOME OF YOUR PARENTS WERE NEARLY AS DIMWITTED.
SO! NOW THAT YOU'VE BEEN RAISED, ON THE TEAM AND MISSION READY—ALL OF YOUR ADOPTIVE PARENTS HAVE BEEN...
... RELEASED OF THEIR DUTIES.
THIS CAN'T BE HAPPENING.
WHAT ARE YOU SAYING?

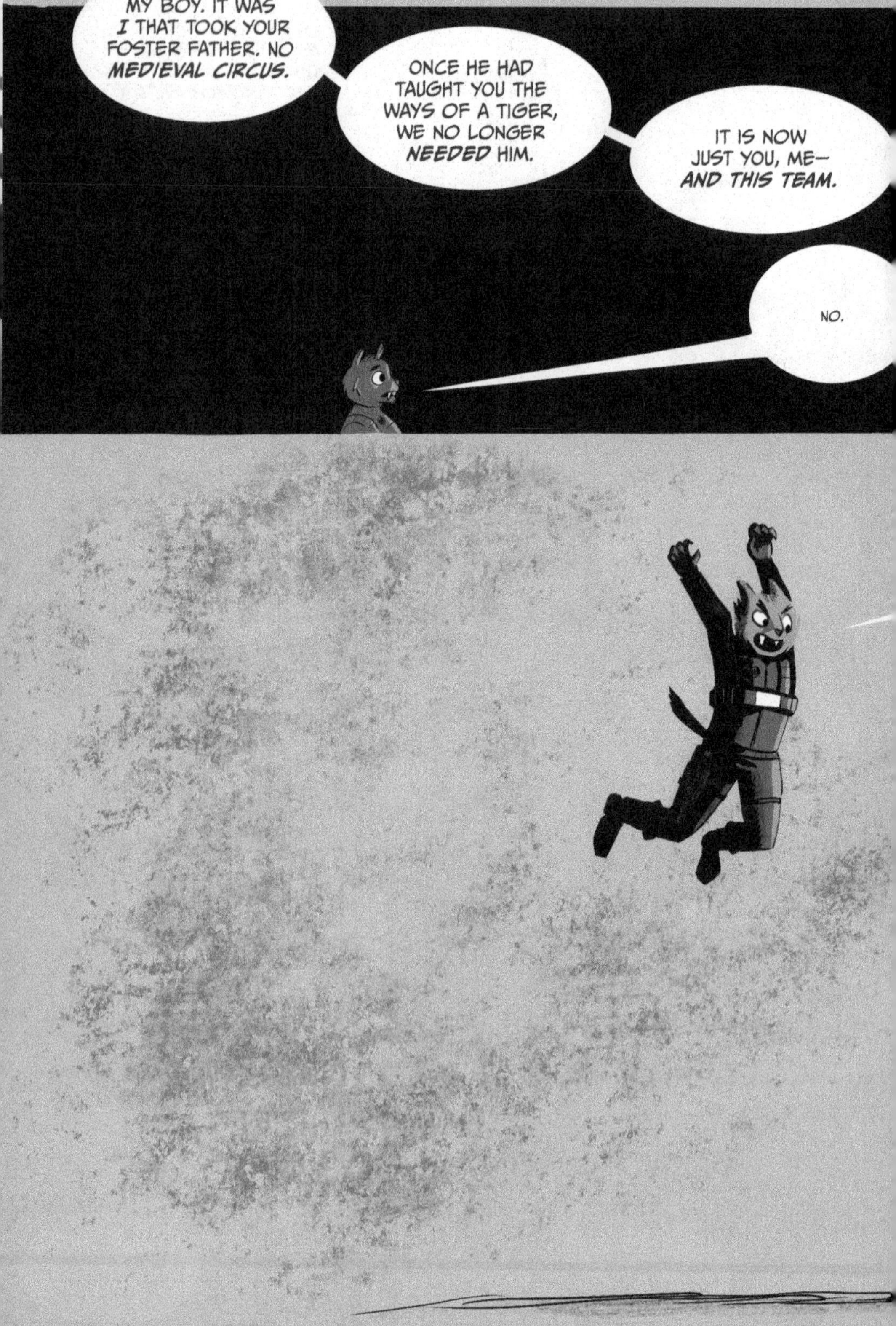
MY BOY. IT WAS *I* THAT TOOK YOUR FOSTER FATHER. NO *MEDIEVAL CIRCUS.*
ONCE HE HAD TAUGHT YOU THE WAYS OF A TIGER, WE NO LONGER *NEEDED* HIM.
IT IS NOW JUST YOU, ME— *AND THIS TEAM.*
NO.

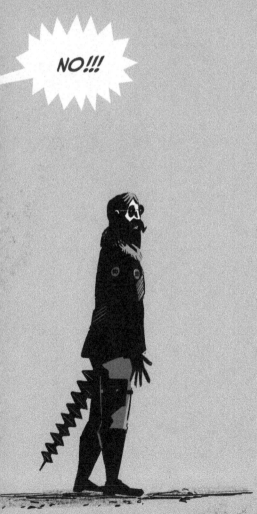

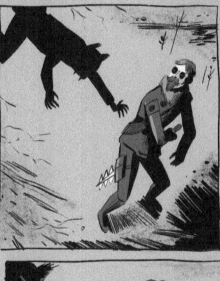

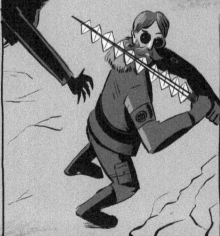

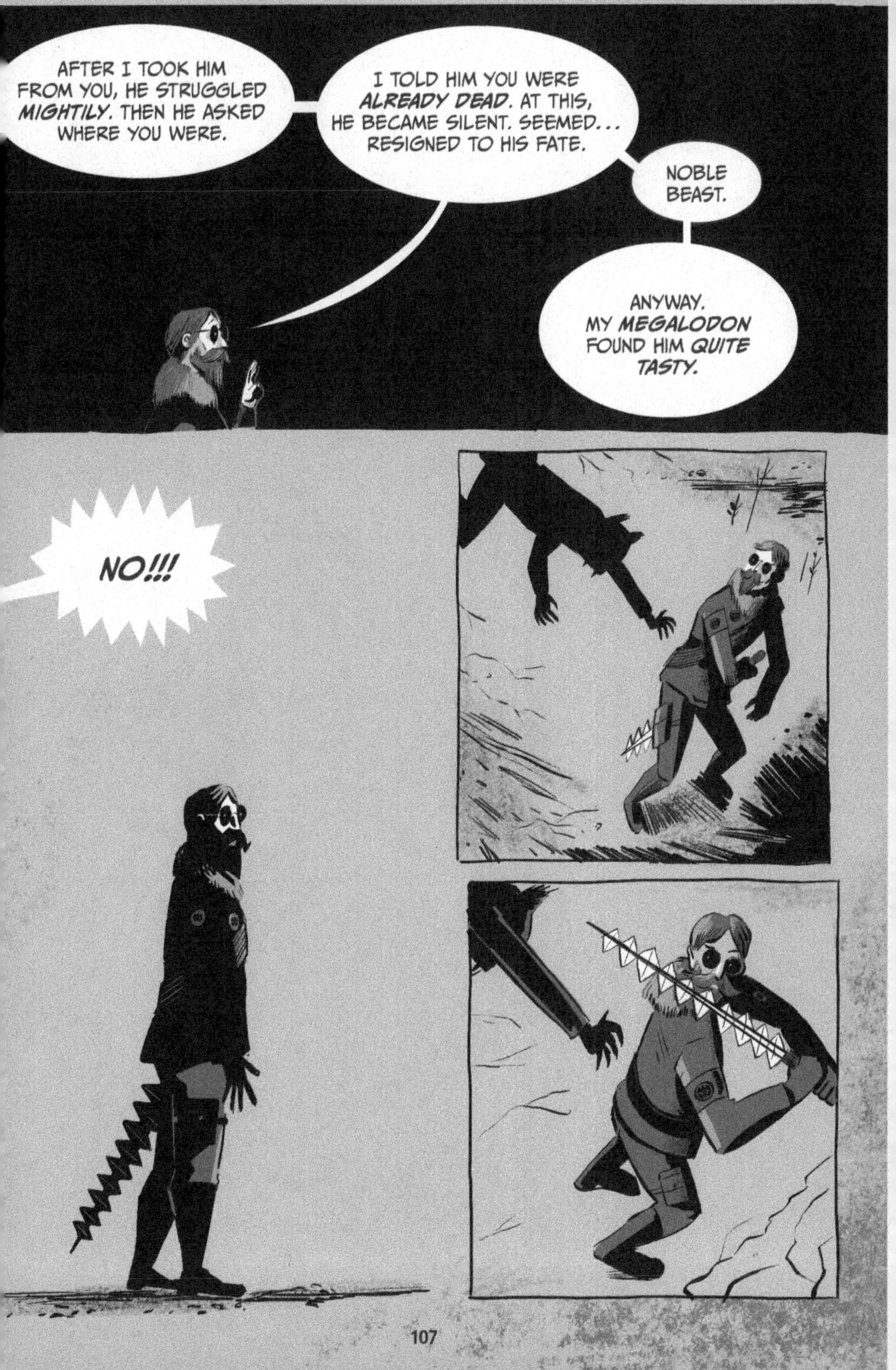
AFTER I TOOK HIM FROM YOU, HE STRUGGLED MIGHTILY. THEN HE ASKED WHERE YOU WERE.
I TOLD HIM YOU WERE ALREADY DEAD. AT THIS, HE BECAME SILENT. SEEMED... RESIGNED TO HIS FATE.
NOBLE BEAST.
ANYWAY. MY MEGALODON FOUND HIM QUITE TASTY.
NO!!!

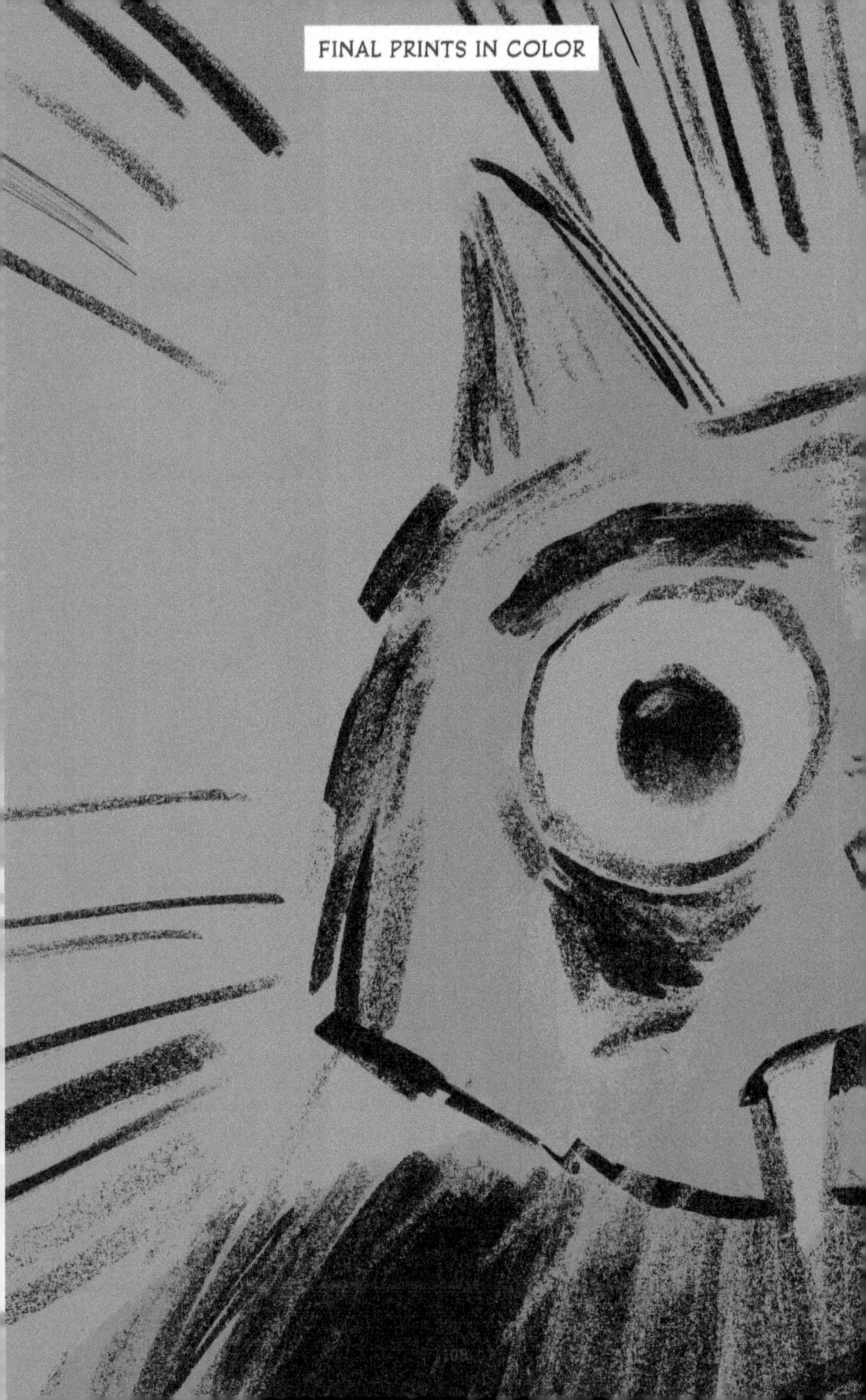

FINAL PRINTS IN COLOR

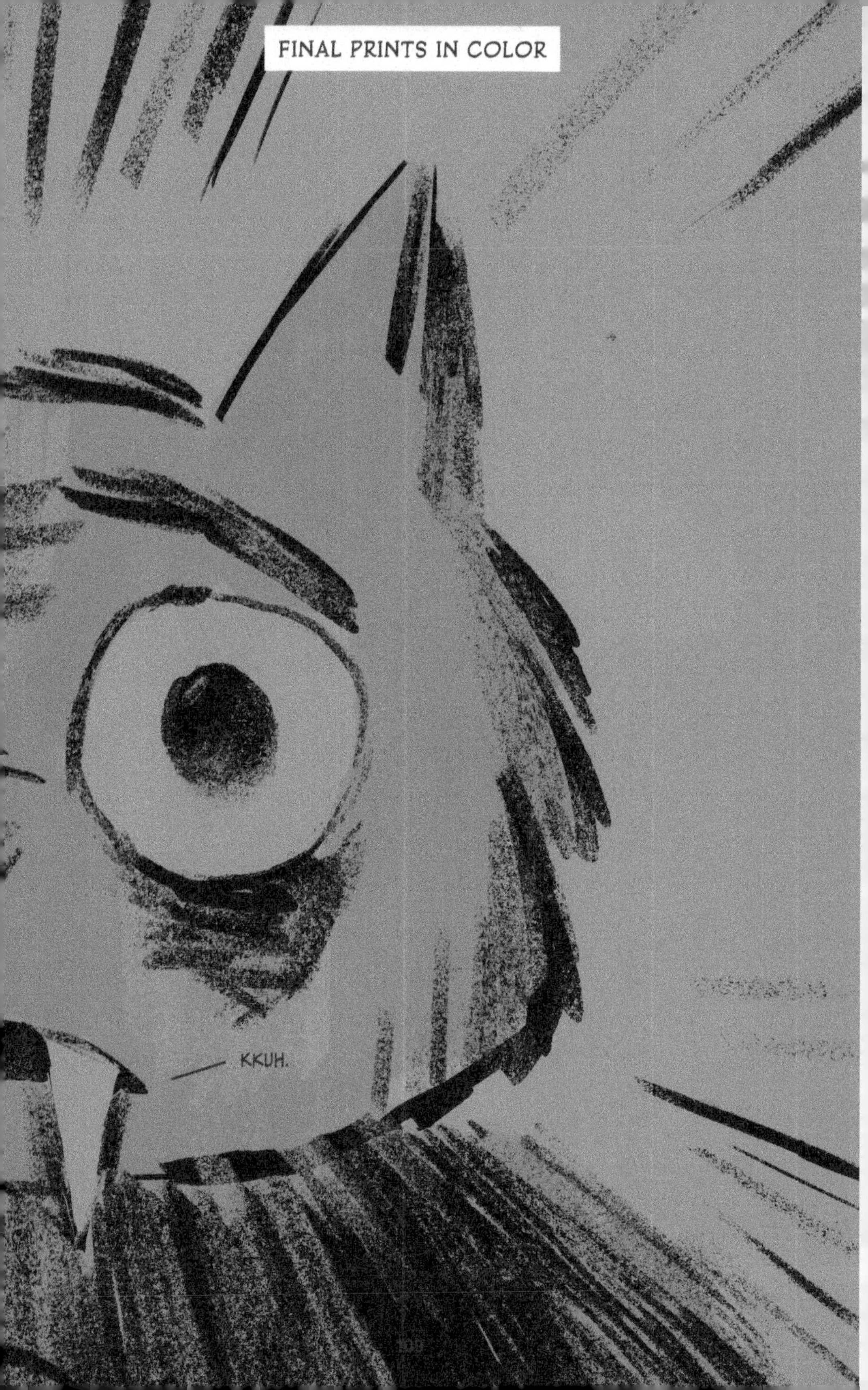
KKUH.

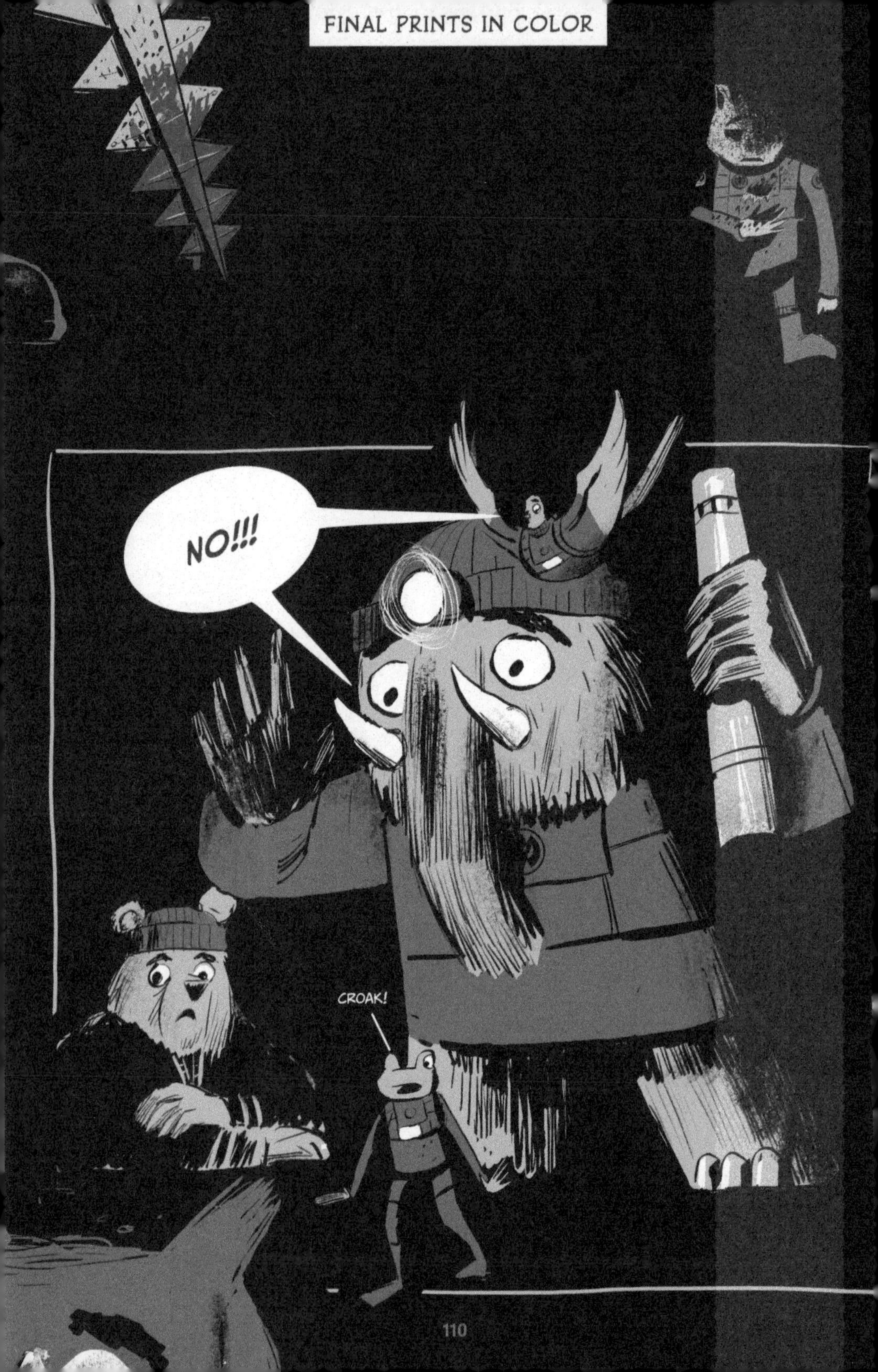
NO!!!
CROAK!

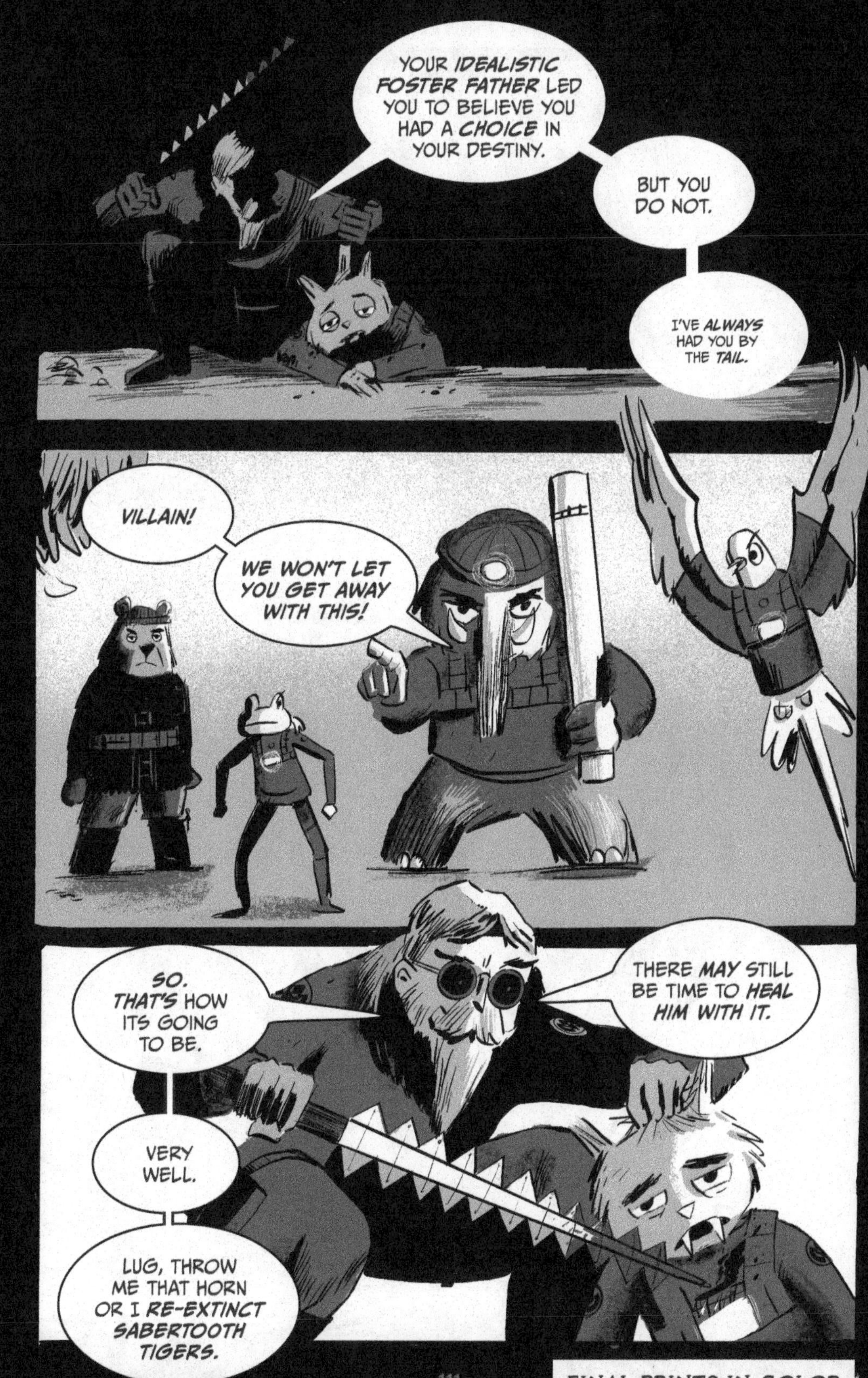

YOUR *IDEALISTIC FOSTER FATHER* LED YOU TO BELIEVE YOU HAD A *CHOICE* IN YOUR DESTINY.
BUT YOU DO NOT.
I'VE *ALWAYS* HAD YOU BY THE *TAIL.*
VILLAIN!
WE WON'T LET YOU GET AWAY WITH THIS!
SO. THAT'S HOW ITS GOING TO BE.
VERY WELL.
LUG, THROW ME THAT HORN OR I *RE-EXTINCT SABERTOOTH TIGERS.*
THERE *MAY* STILL BE TIME TO *HEAL HIM WITH IT.*

FINAL PRINTS IN COLOR

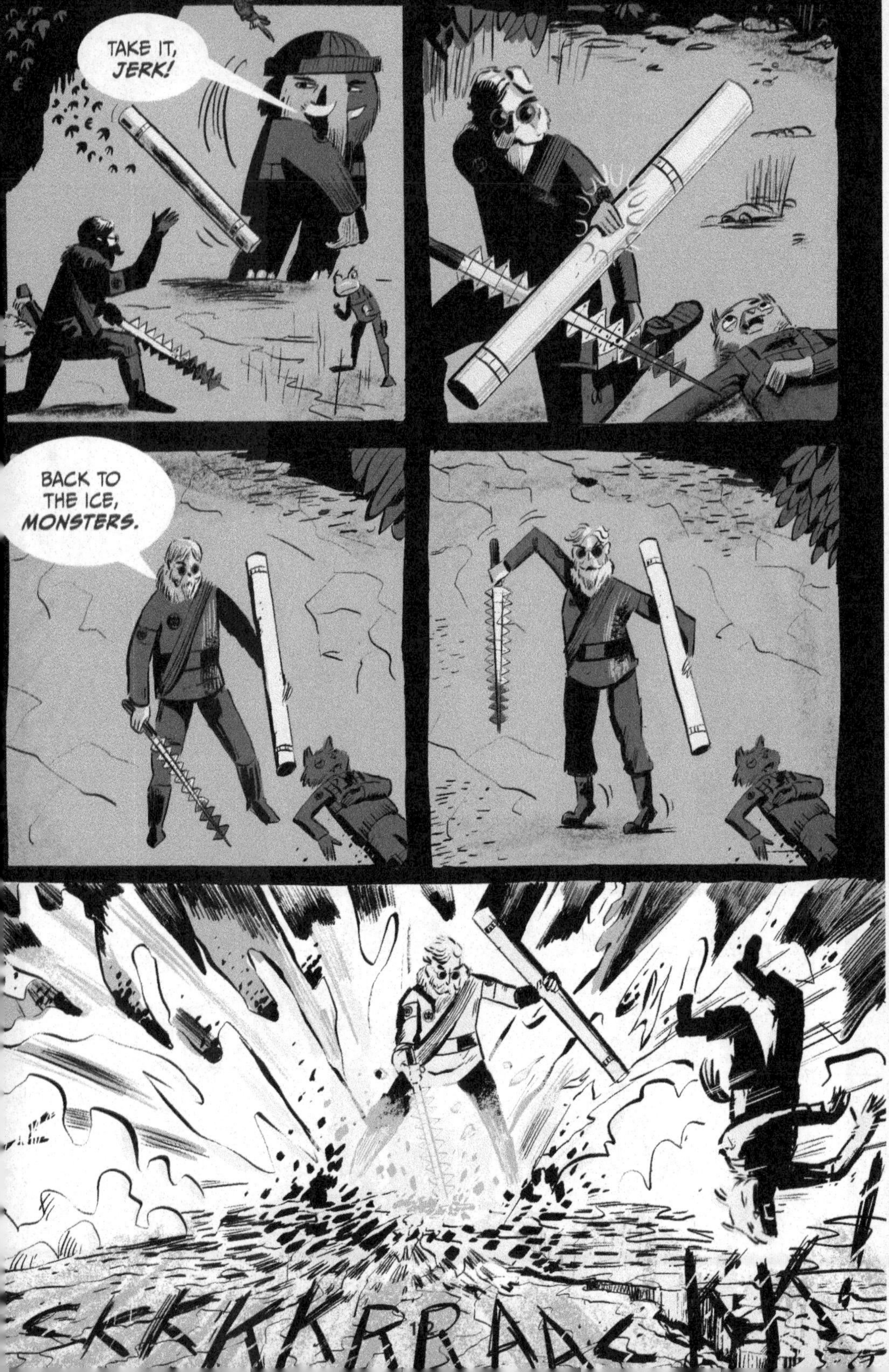
TAKE IT, JERK!
BACK TO THE ICE, MONSTERS.
SKKKRRAACKK!

FINAL PRINTS IN COLOR

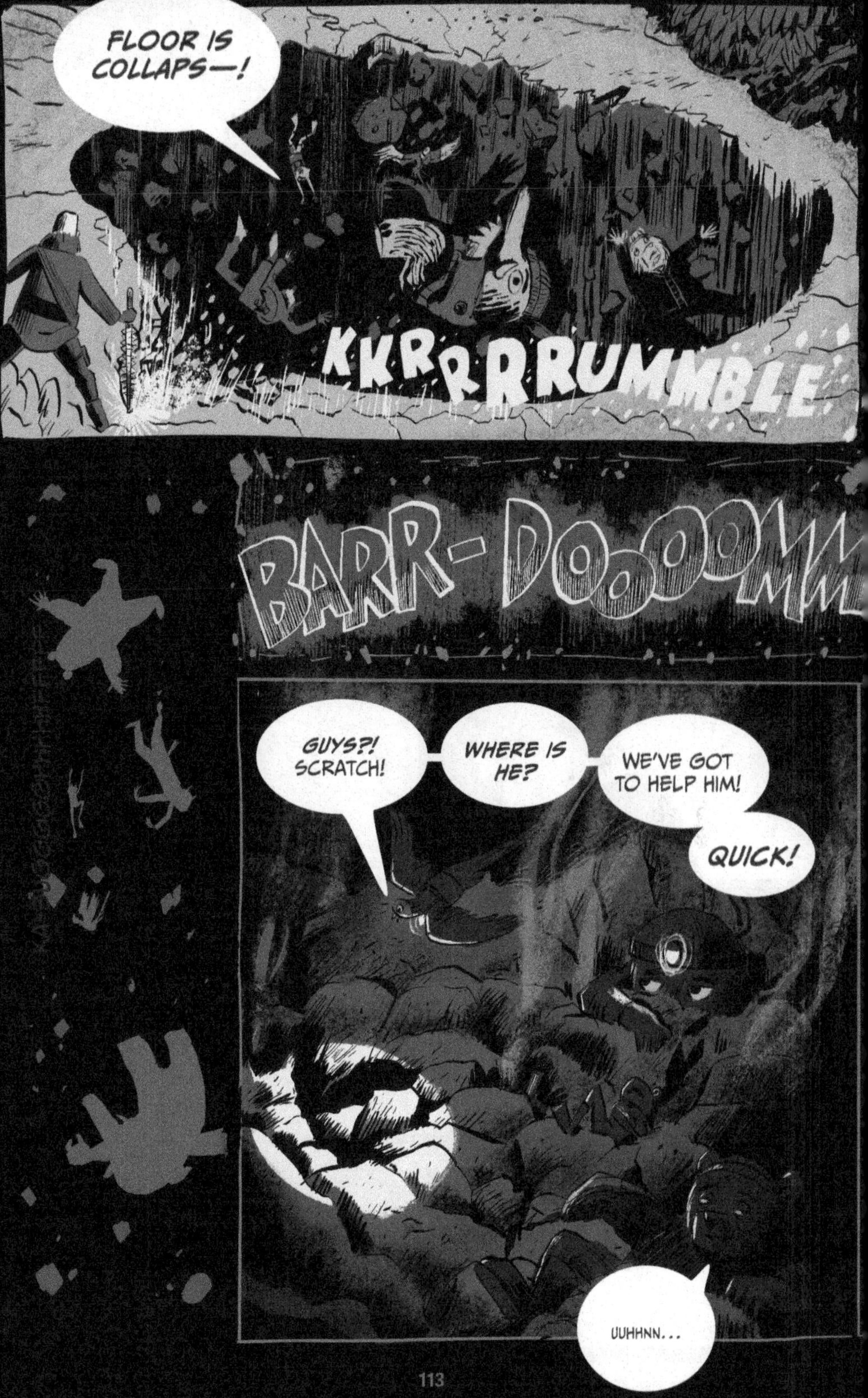
FLOOR IS COLLAPS—!
KKRRRRUMMBLE
BARR-DOOOOMM
GUYS?! SCRATCH!
WHERE IS HE?
WE'VE GOT TO HELP HIM!
QUICK!
UUHHNN...

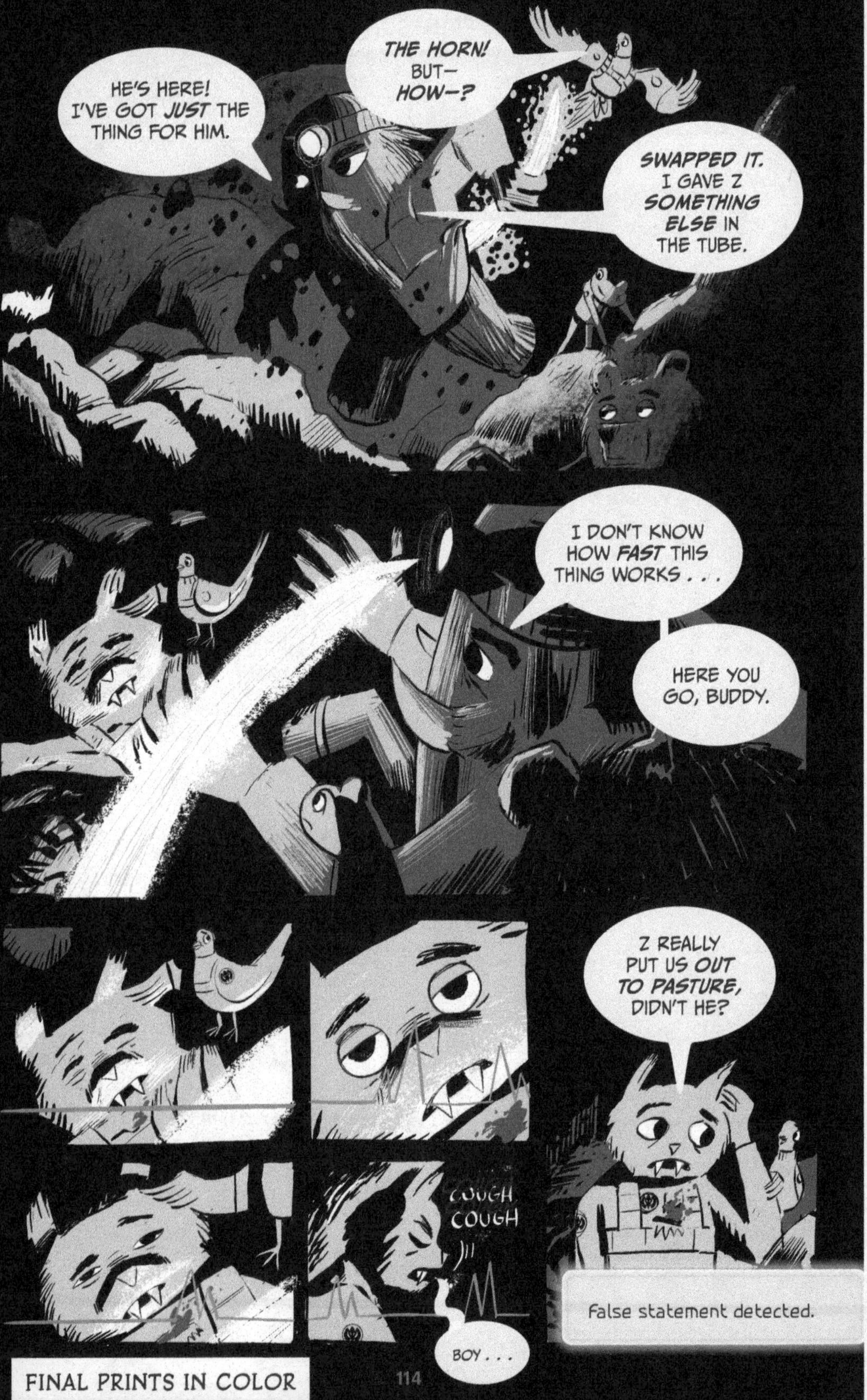

HE'S HERE! I'VE GOT JUST THE THING FOR HIM.
THE HORN! BUT— HOW—?
SWAPPED IT. I GAVE Z SOMETHING ELSE IN THE TUBE.
I DON'T KNOW HOW FAST THIS THING WORKS . . .
HERE YOU GO, BUDDY.
COUGH COUGH
BOY . . .
Z REALLY PUT US OUT TO PASTURE, DIDN'T HE?
False statement detected.
FINAL PRINTS IN COLOR

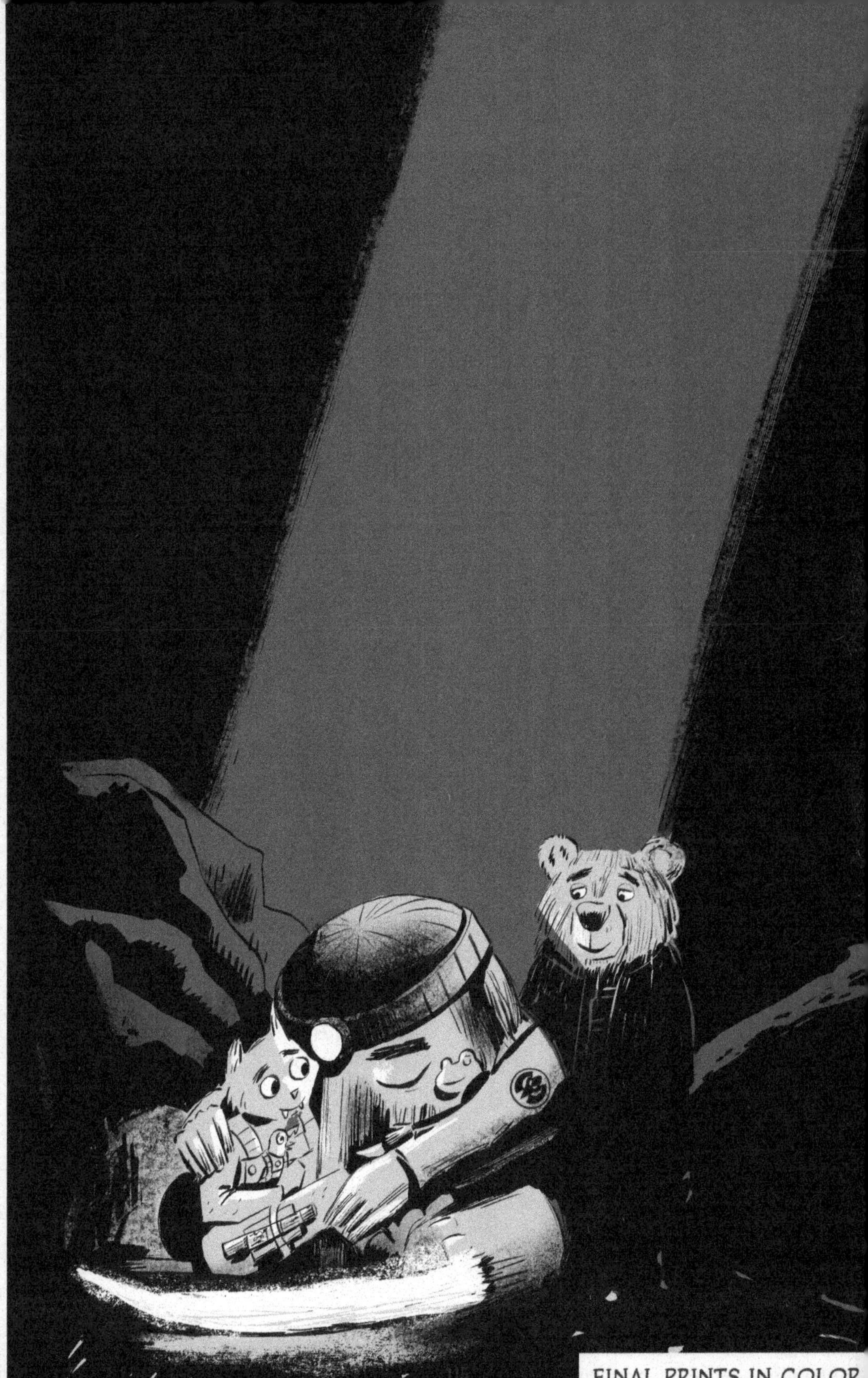

FINAL PRINTS IN COLOR

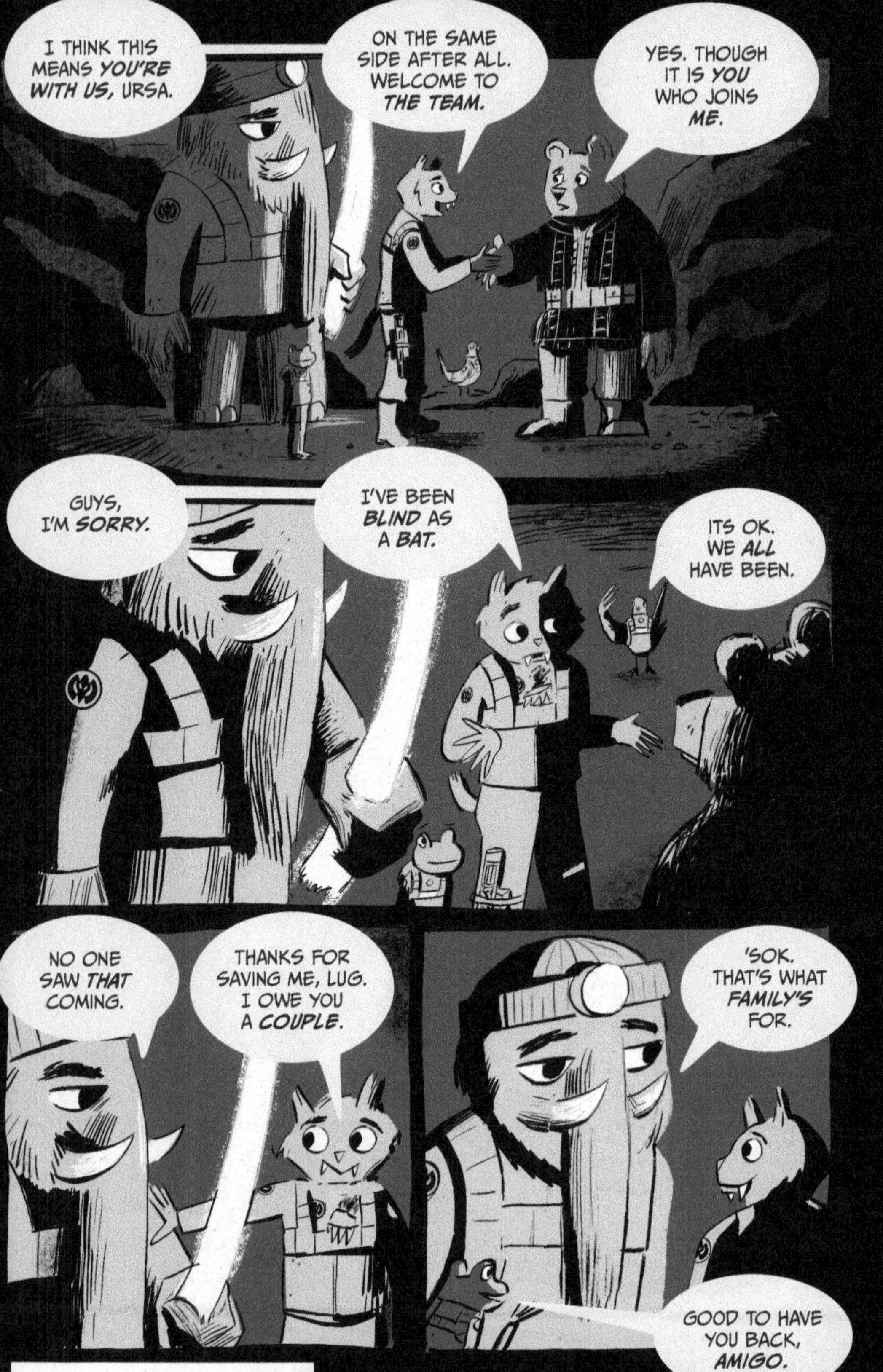

I THINK THIS MEANS *YOU'RE WITH US*, URSA.
ON THE SAME SIDE AFTER ALL. WELCOME TO *THE TEAM.*
YES. THOUGH IT IS *YOU* WHO JOINS *ME.*
GUYS, I'M *SORRY.*
I'VE BEEN *BLIND* AS A *BAT.*
ITS OK. WE *ALL* HAVE BEEN.
NO ONE SAW *THAT* COMING.
THANKS FOR SAVING ME, LUG. I OWE YOU A *COUPLE.*
'SOK. THAT'S WHAT *FAMILY'S* FOR.
GOOD TO HAVE YOU BACK, *AMIGO.*

FINAL PRINTS IN COLOR

FINAL PRINTS IN COLOR

Several minutes later.

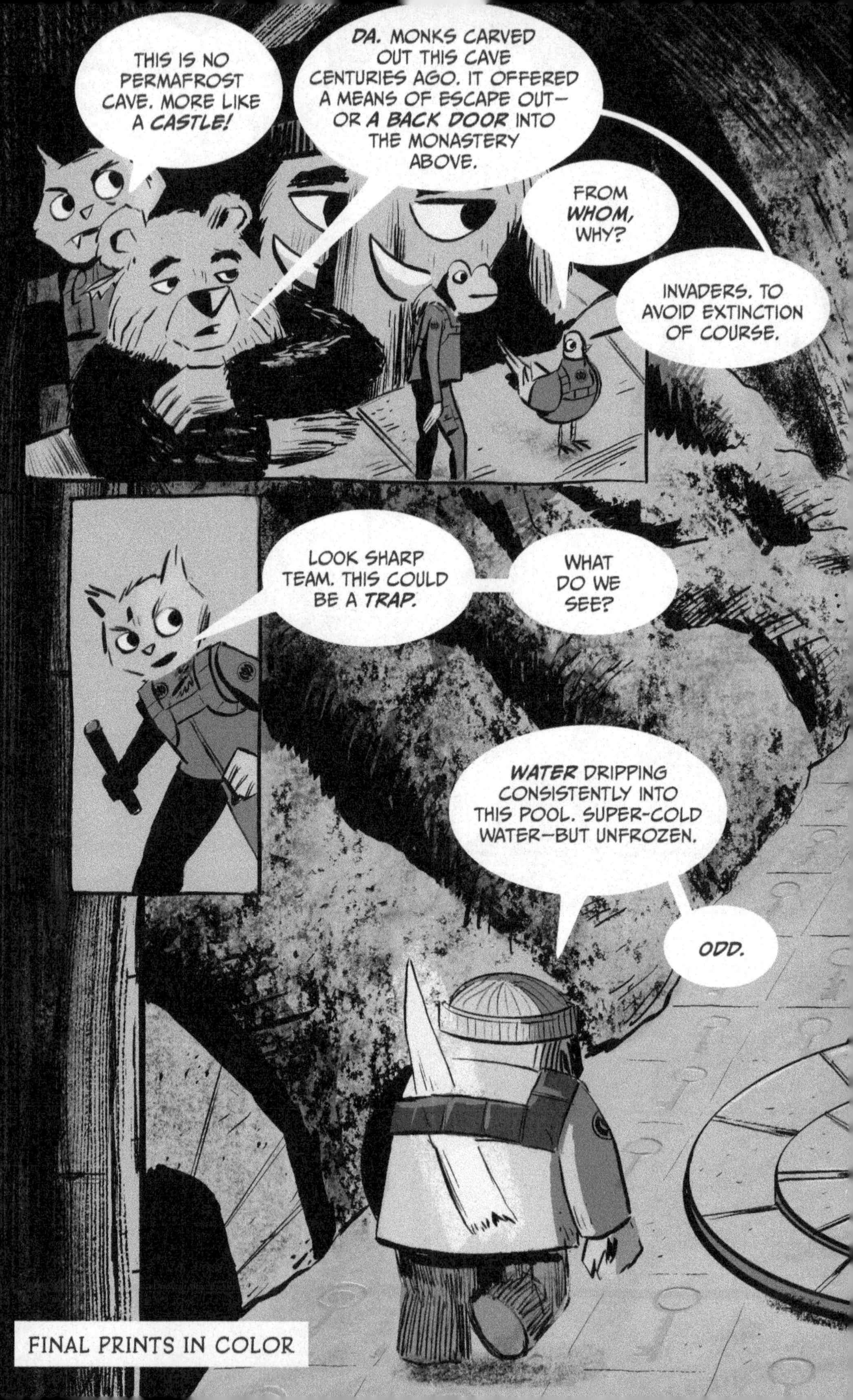
THIS IS NO PERMAFROST CAVE. MORE LIKE A CASTLE!
DA. MONKS CARVED OUT THIS CAVE CENTURIES AGO. IT OFFERED A MEANS OF ESCAPE OUT— OR A BACK DOOR INTO THE MONASTERY ABOVE.
FROM WHOM, WHY?
INVADERS. TO AVOID EXTINCTION OF COURSE.
LOOK SHARP TEAM. THIS COULD BE A TRAP.
WHAT DO WE SEE?
WATER DRIPPING CONSISTENTLY INTO THIS POOL. SUPER-COLD WATER—BUT UNFROZEN.
ODD.
FINAL PRINTS IN COLOR

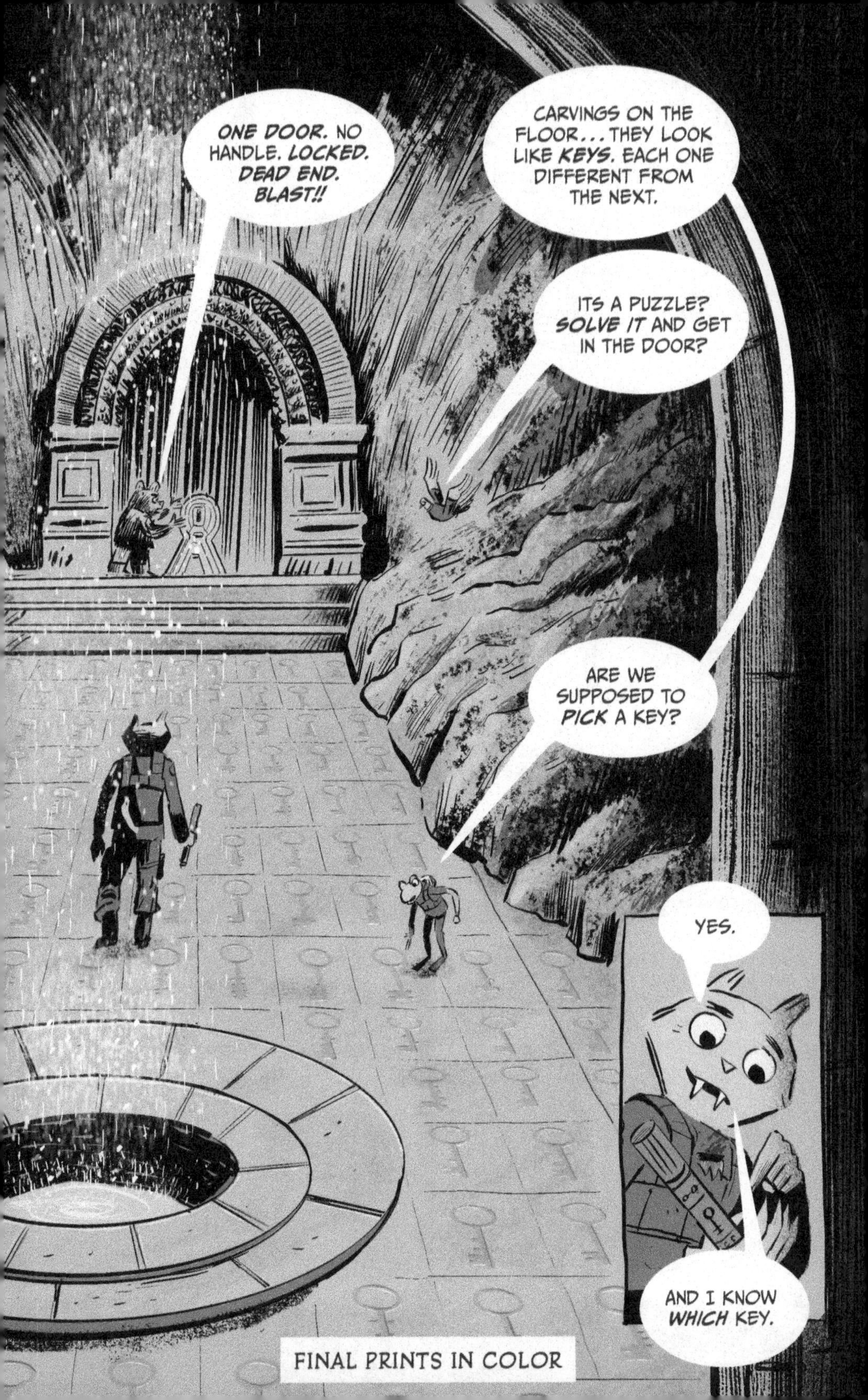
ONE DOOR. NO HANDLE. LOCKED. DEAD END. BLAST!!
CARVINGS ON THE FLOOR... THEY LOOK LIKE KEYS. EACH ONE DIFFERENT FROM THE NEXT.
ITS A PUZZLE? SOLVE IT AND GET IN THE DOOR?
ARE WE SUPPOSED TO PICK A KEY?
YES.
AND I KNOW WHICH KEY.

FINAL PRINTS IN COLOR

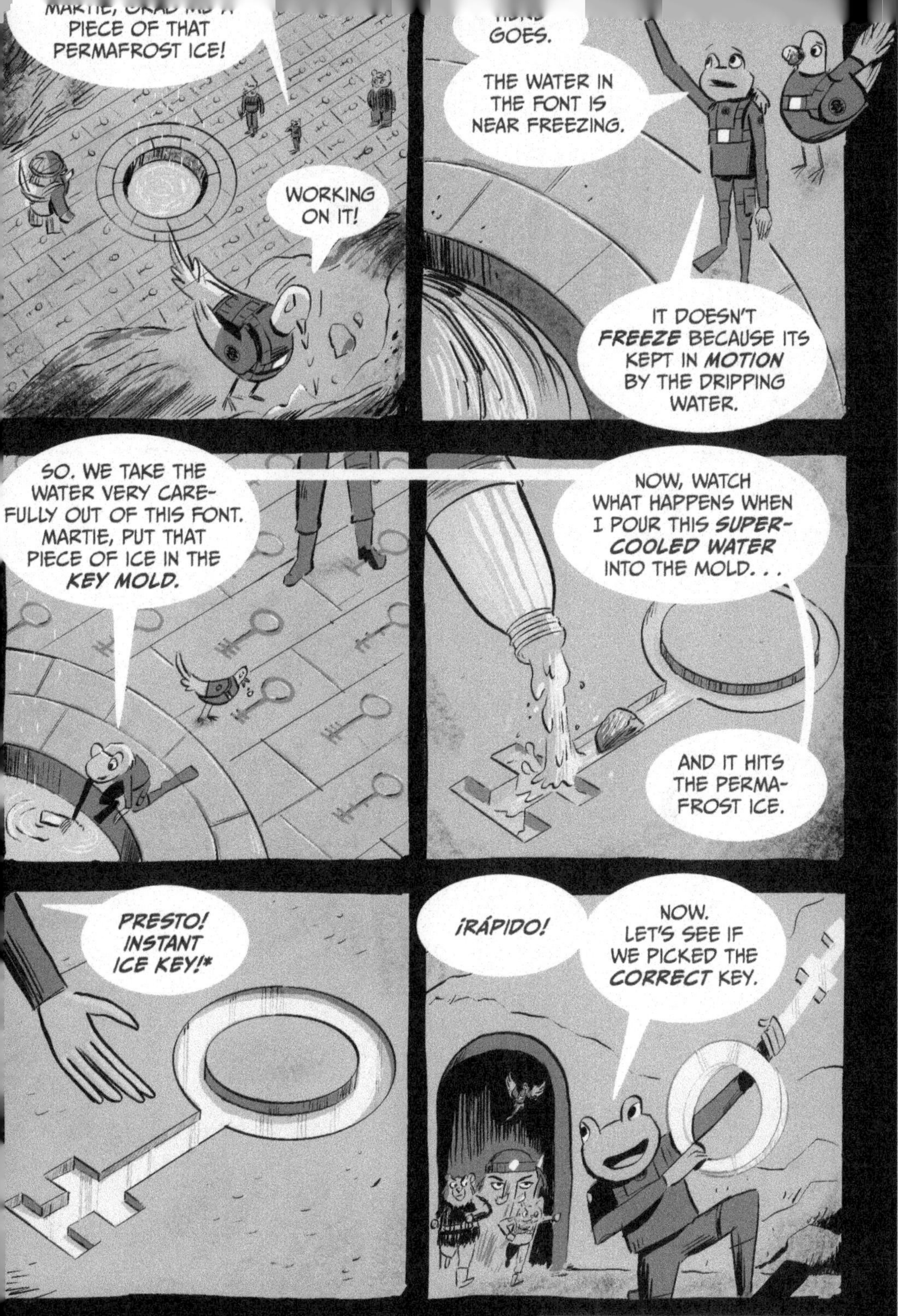
PIECE OF THAT PERMAFROST ICE!
WORKING ON IT!
GOES.
THE WATER IN THE FONT IS NEAR FREEZING.
IT DOESN'T *FREEZE* BECAUSE ITS KEPT IN *MOTION* BY THE DRIPPING WATER.
SO. WE TAKE THE WATER VERY CAREFULLY OUT OF THIS FONT. MARTIE, PUT THAT PIECE OF ICE IN THE *KEY MOLD.*
NOW, WATCH WHAT HAPPENS WHEN I POUR THIS *SUPER-COOLED WATER* INTO THE MOLD. . .
AND IT HITS THE PERMAFROST ICE.
*PRESTO! INSTANT ICE KEY!**
¡RÁPIDO!
NOW. LET'S SEE IF WE PICKED THE *CORRECT* KEY.

*Try this at home! See how at the back of this book.

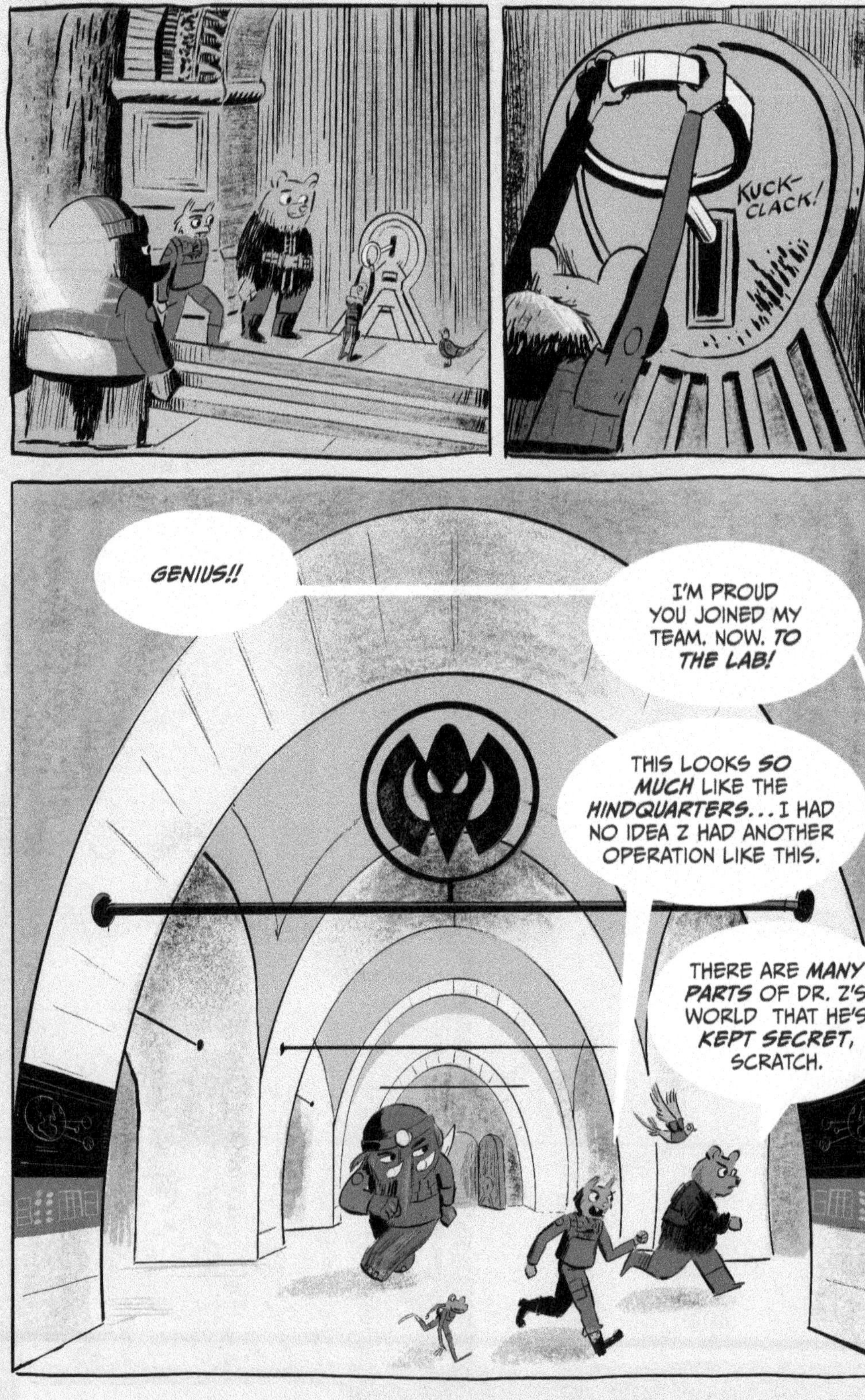
KUCK-CLACK!
GENIUS!!
I'M PROUD YOU JOINED MY TEAM. NOW. TO THE LAB!
THIS LOOKS SO MUCH LIKE THE HINDQUARTERS... I HAD NO IDEA Z HAD ANOTHER OPERATION LIKE THIS.
THERE ARE MANY PARTS OF DR. Z'S WORLD THAT HE'S KEPT SECRET, SCRATCH.

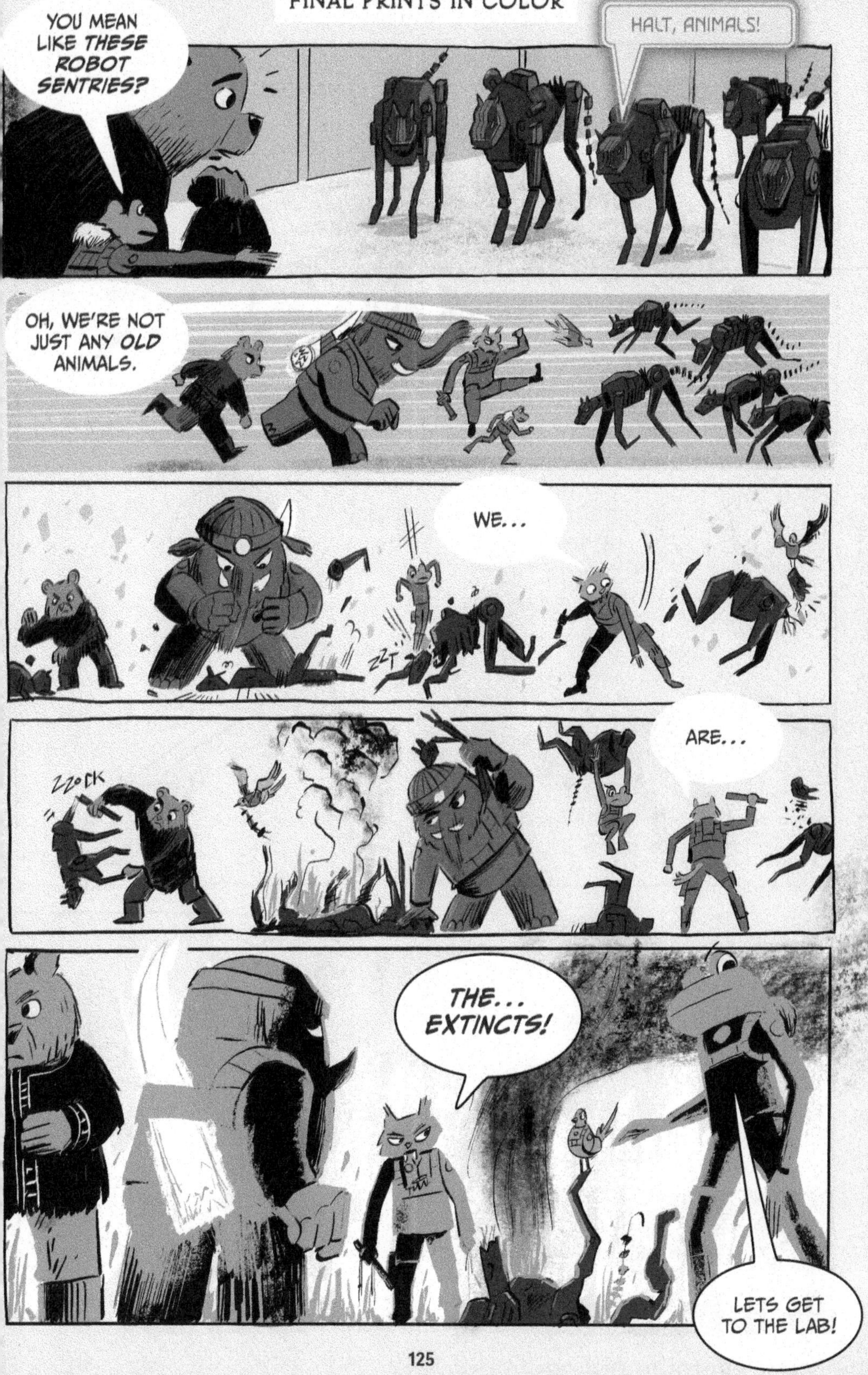
YOU MEAN LIKE THESE ROBOT SENTRIES?
HALT, ANIMALS!
OH, WE'RE NOT JUST ANY OLD ANIMALS.
WE...
ZZT
ARE...
ZZOCK
THE... EXTINCTS!
LETS GET TO THE LAB!

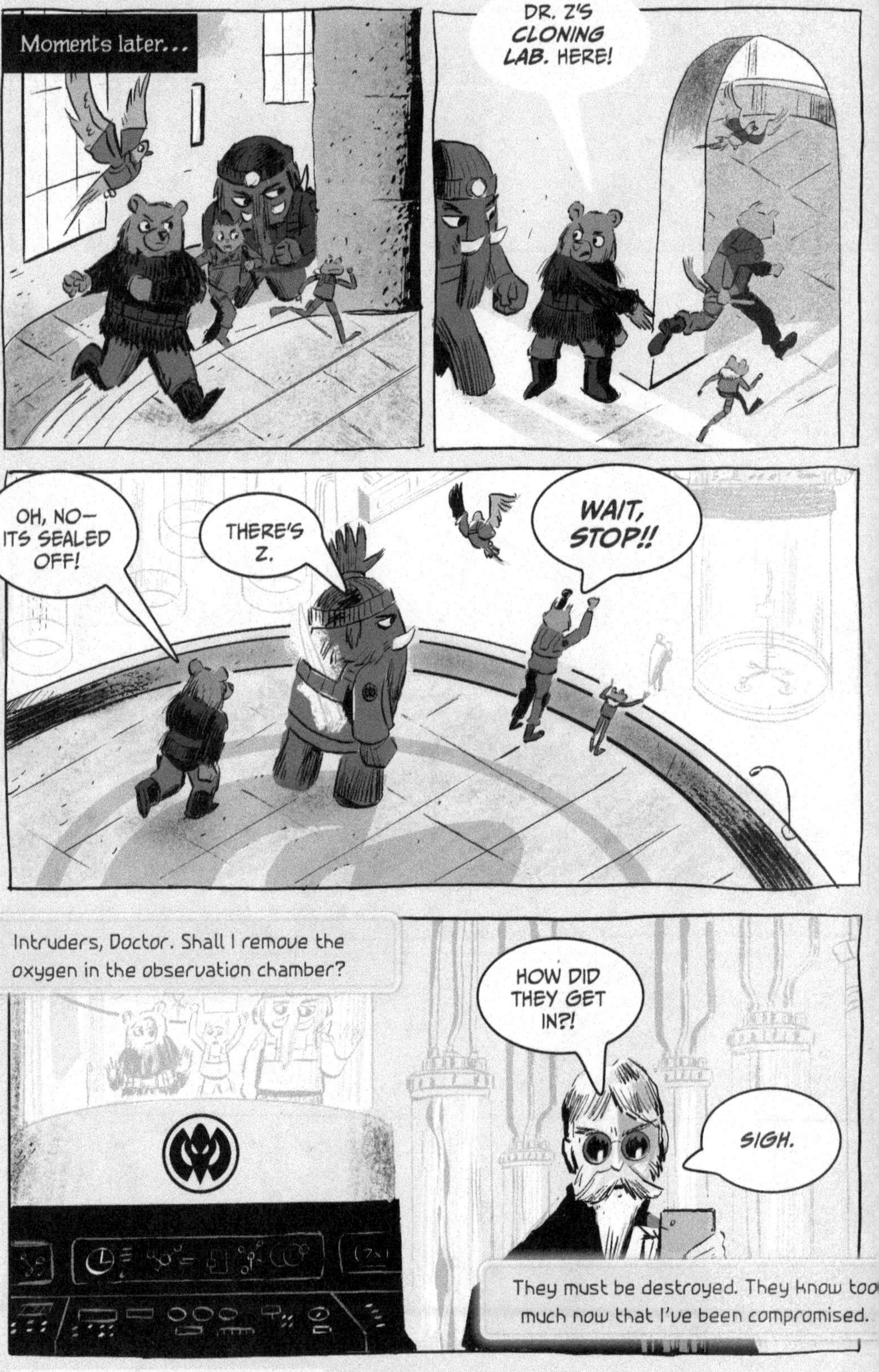

Moments later...
DR. Z'S CLONING LAB. HERE!
OH, NO— ITS SEALED OFF!
THERE'S Z.
WAIT, STOP!!
Intruders, Doctor. Shall I remove the oxygen in the observation chamber?
HOW DID THEY GET IN?!
SIGH.
They must be destroyed. They know too much now that I've been compromised.

FINAL PRINTS IN COLOR

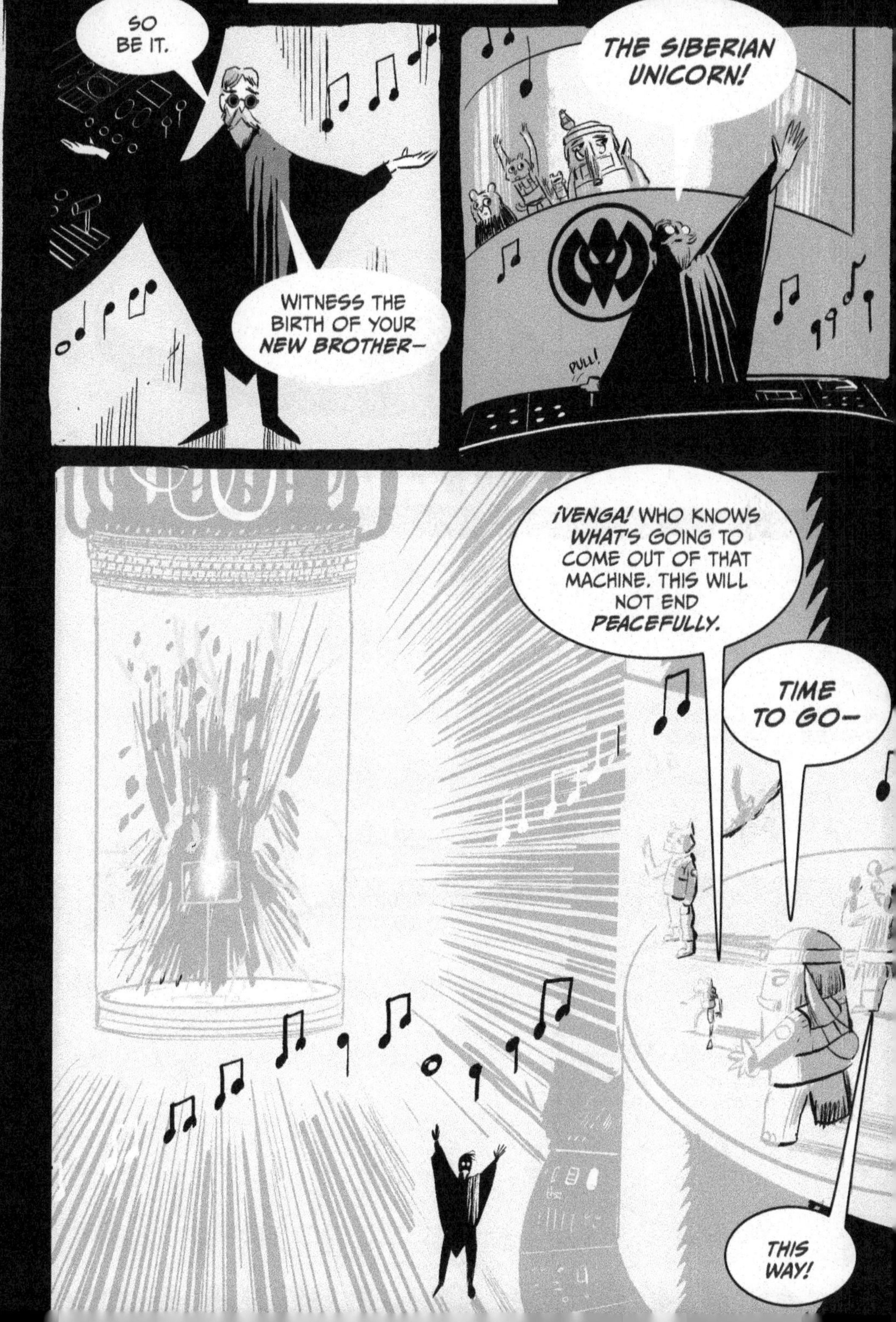
SO BE IT.
WITNESS THE BIRTH OF YOUR NEW BROTHER—
THE SIBERIAN UNICORN!
PULL!
¡VENGA! WHO KNOWS WHAT'S GOING TO COME OUT OF THAT MACHINE. THIS WILL NOT END PEACEFULLY.
TIME TO GO—
THIS WAY!

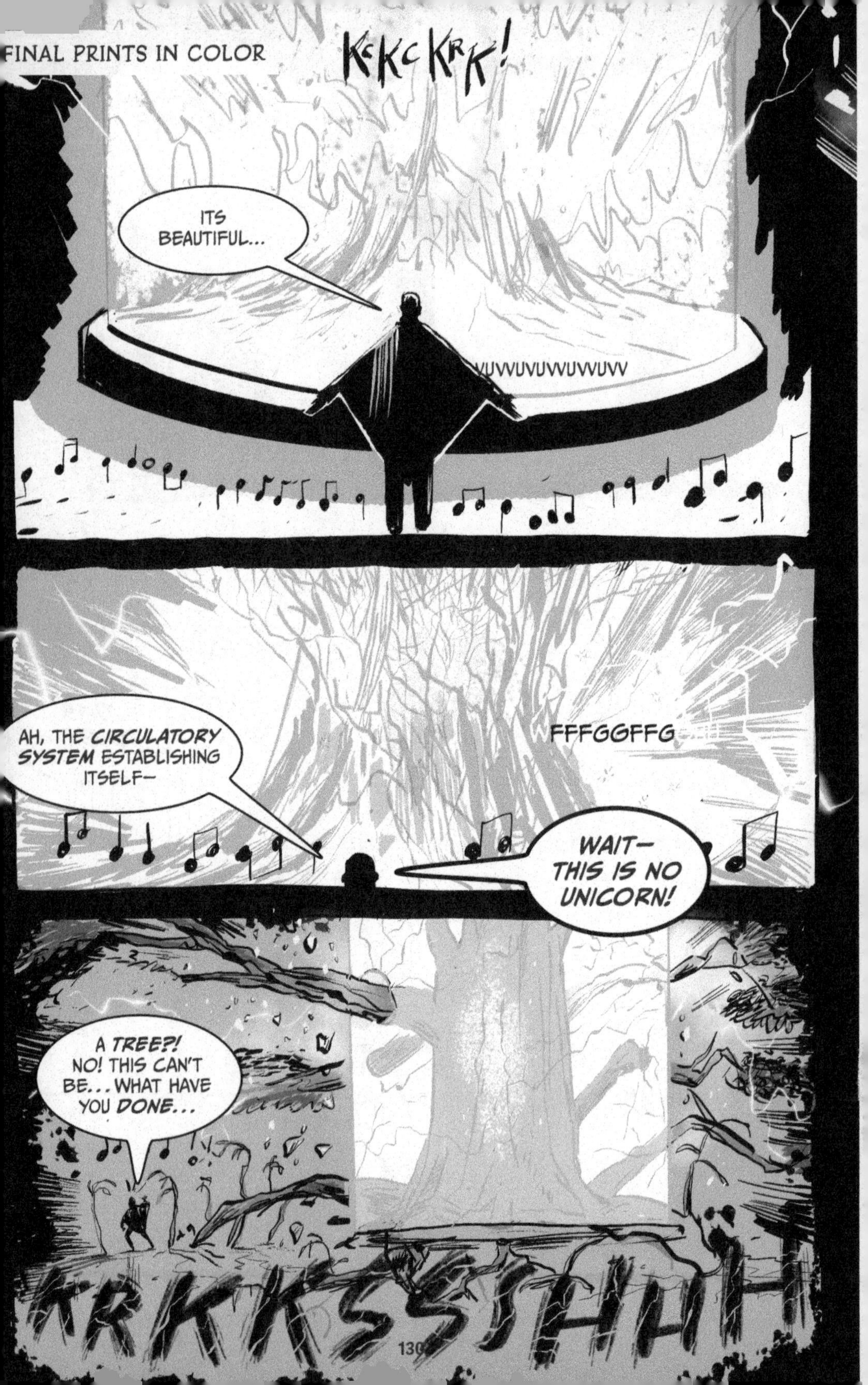
KcKcKrK!
ITS BEAUTIFUL...
VUVVUVUVVUVVUVV
AH, THE *CIRCULATORY SYSTEM* ESTABLISHING ITSELF–
WFFFGGFFG
WAIT– THIS IS NO UNICORN!
A *TREE?!* NO! THIS CAN'T BE... WHAT HAVE YOU *DONE...*
KRKKSSSHHH

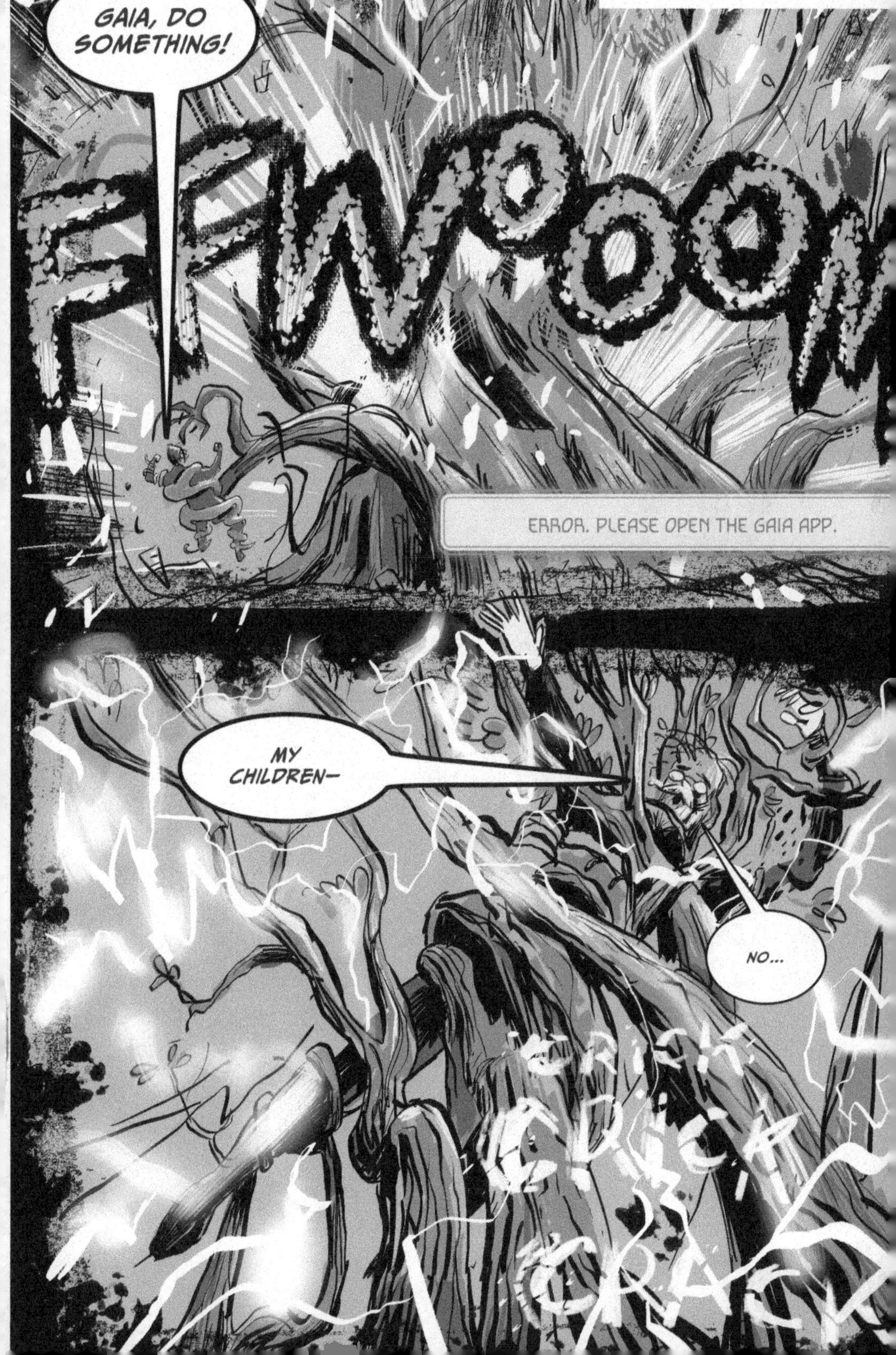
GAIA, DO SOMETHING!
ERROR. PLEASE OPEN THE GAIA APP.
MY CHILDREN—
NO...

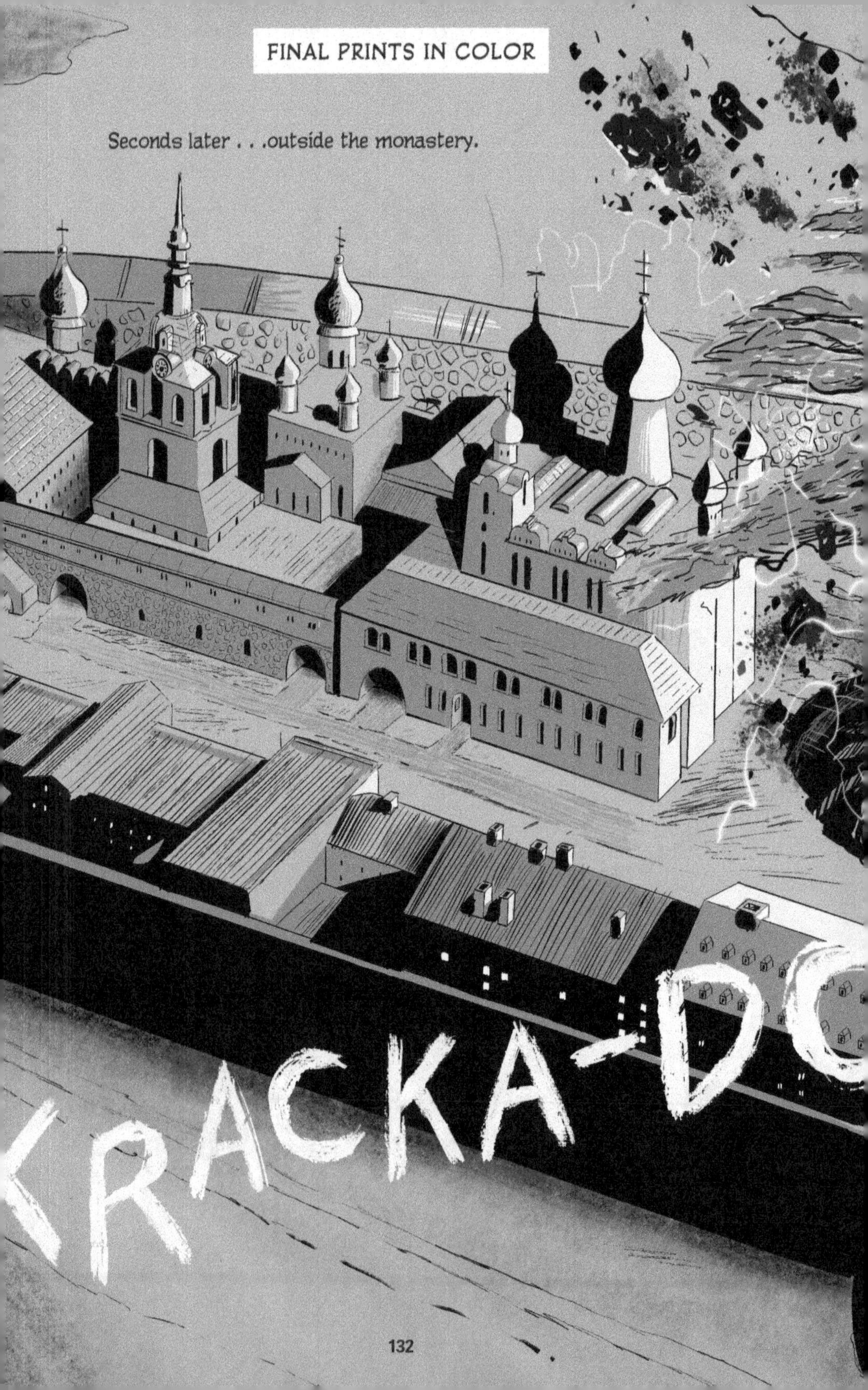
Seconds later . . .outside the monastery.
KRACKA-DO

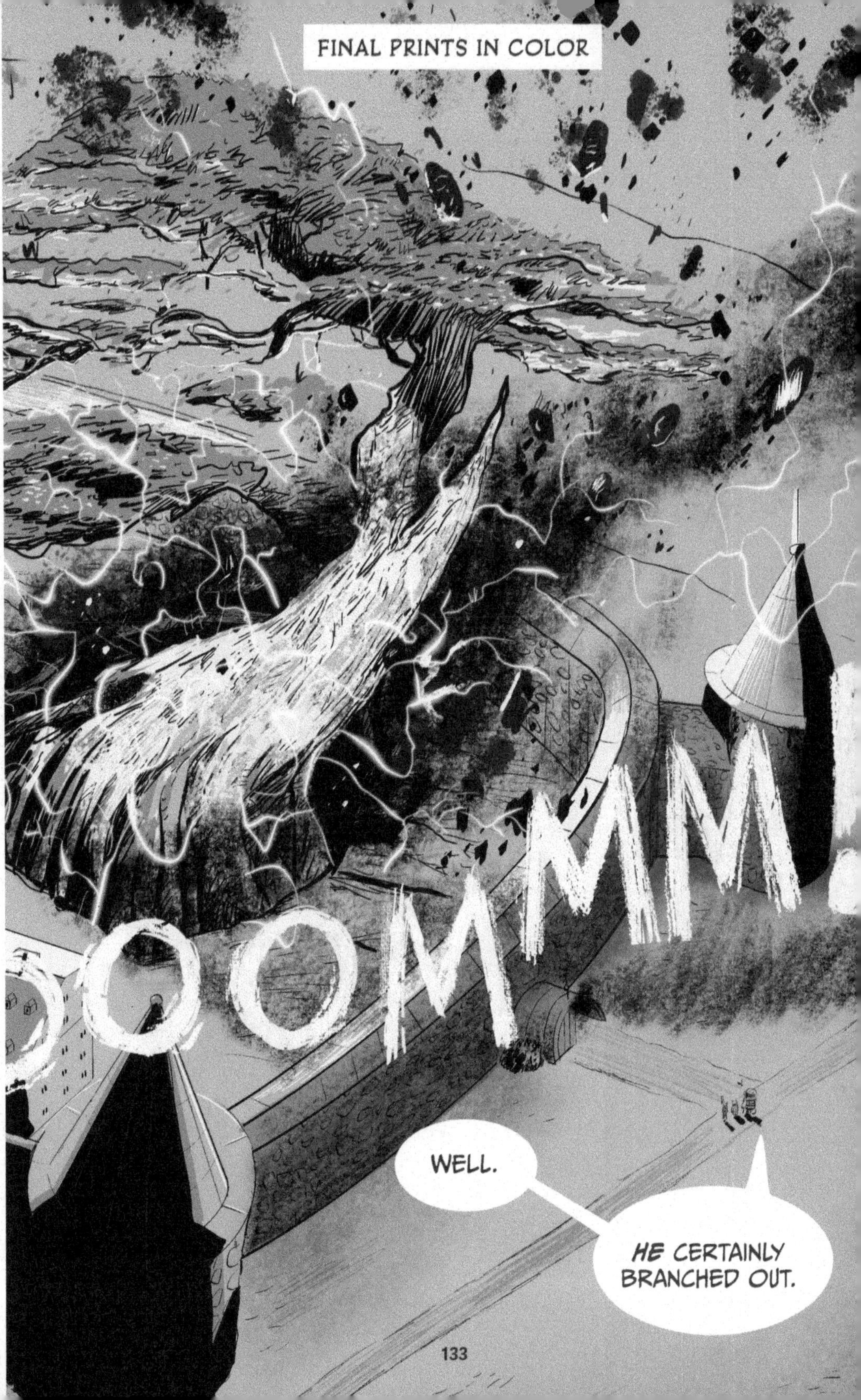
OOOMMM!
WELL.
HE CERTAINLY BRANCHED OUT.

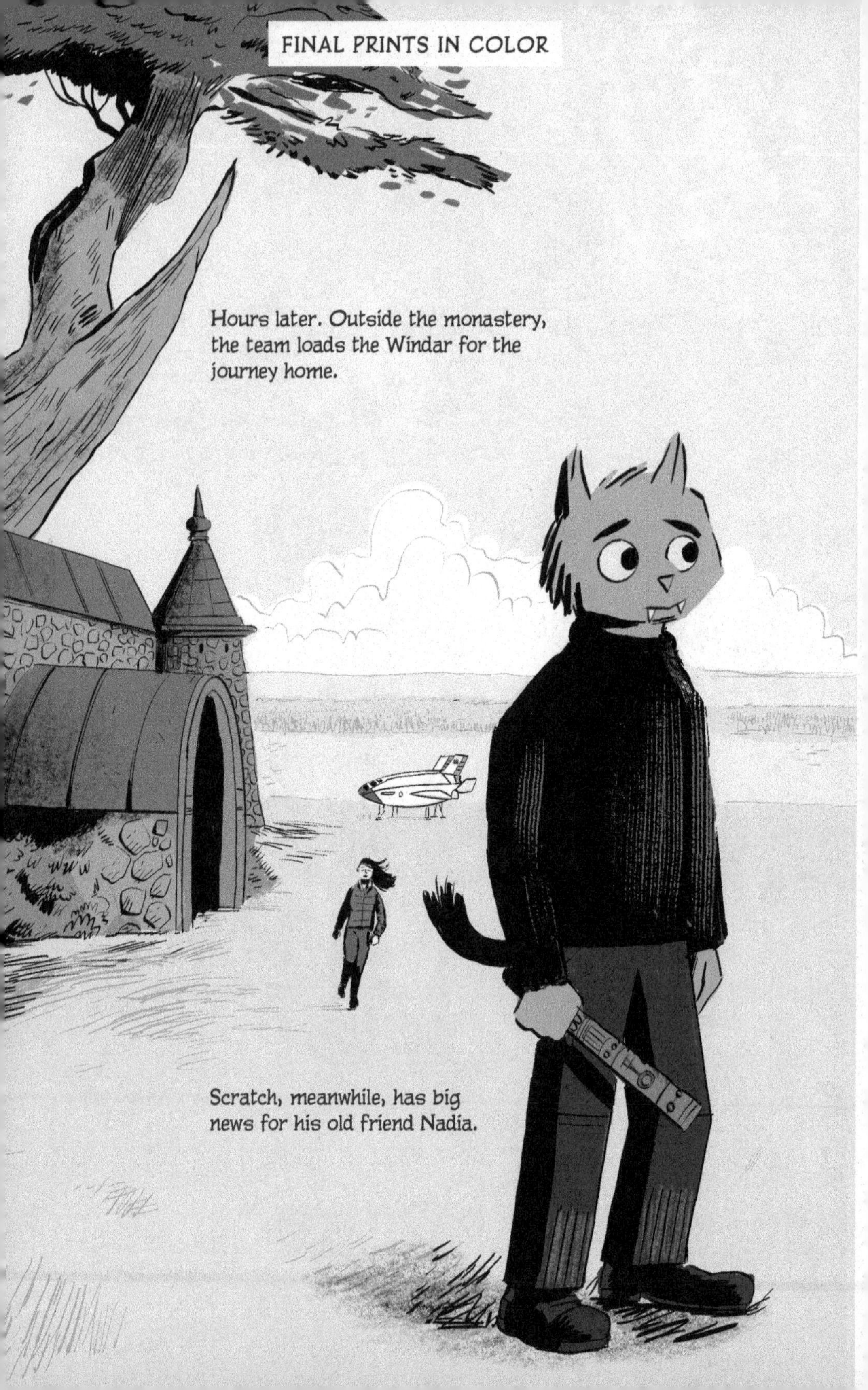
Hours later. Outside the monastery, the team loads the Windar for the journey home.
Scratch, meanwhile, has big news for his old friend Nadia.

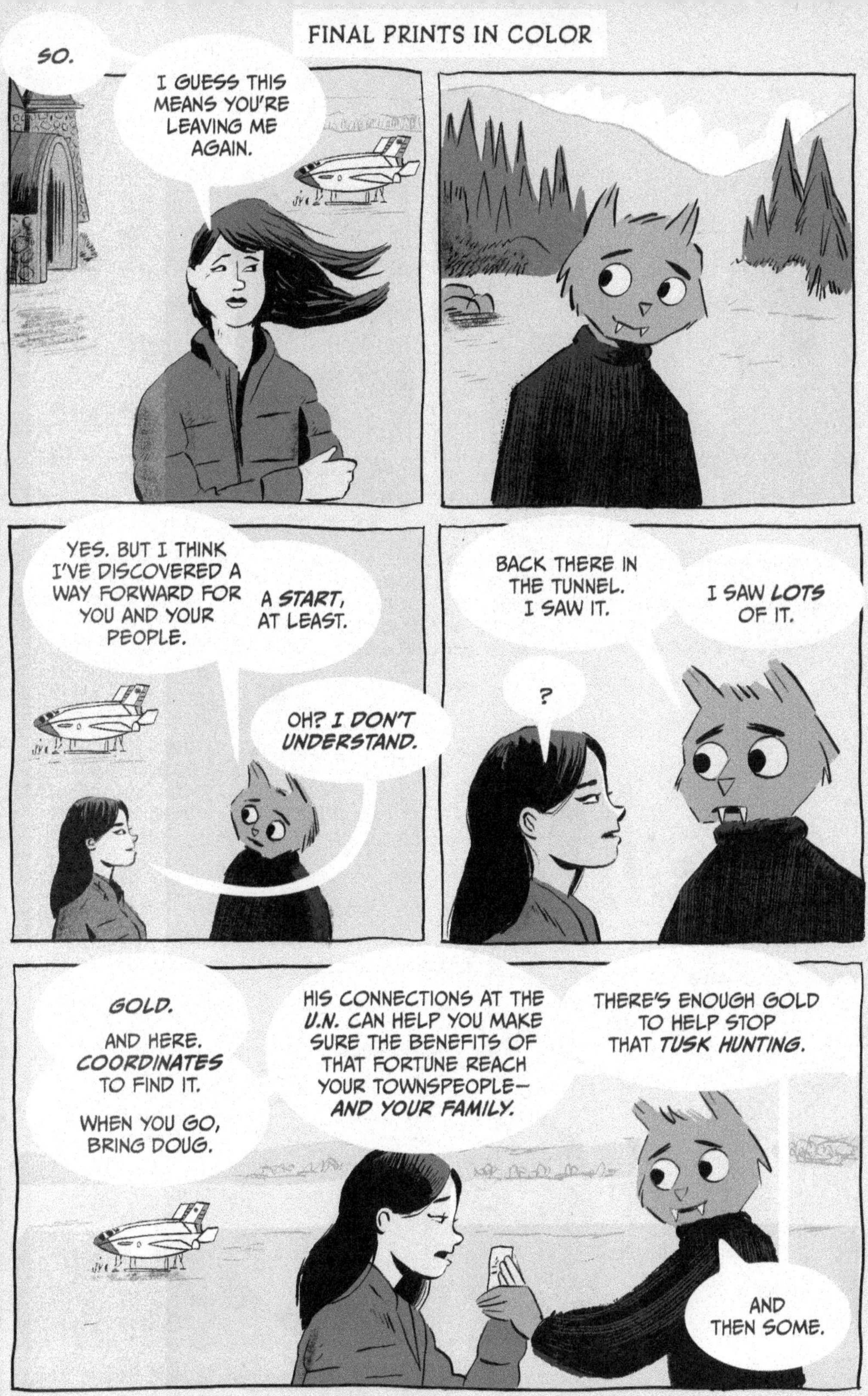
SO.
I GUESS THIS MEANS YOU'RE LEAVING ME AGAIN.
YES. BUT I THINK I'VE DISCOVERED A WAY FORWARD FOR YOU AND YOUR PEOPLE.
A *START*, AT LEAST.
OH? *I DON'T UNDERSTAND.*
BACK THERE IN THE TUNNEL. I SAW IT.
I SAW *LOTS* OF IT.
?
GOLD.
AND HERE. *COORDINATES* TO FIND IT.
WHEN YOU GO, BRING DOUG.
HIS CONNECTIONS AT THE *U.N.* CAN HELP YOU MAKE SURE THE BENEFITS OF THAT FORTUNE REACH YOUR TOWNSPEOPLE— *AND YOUR FAMILY.*
THERE'S ENOUGH GOLD TO HELP STOP THAT *TUSK HUNTING.*
AND THEN SOME.

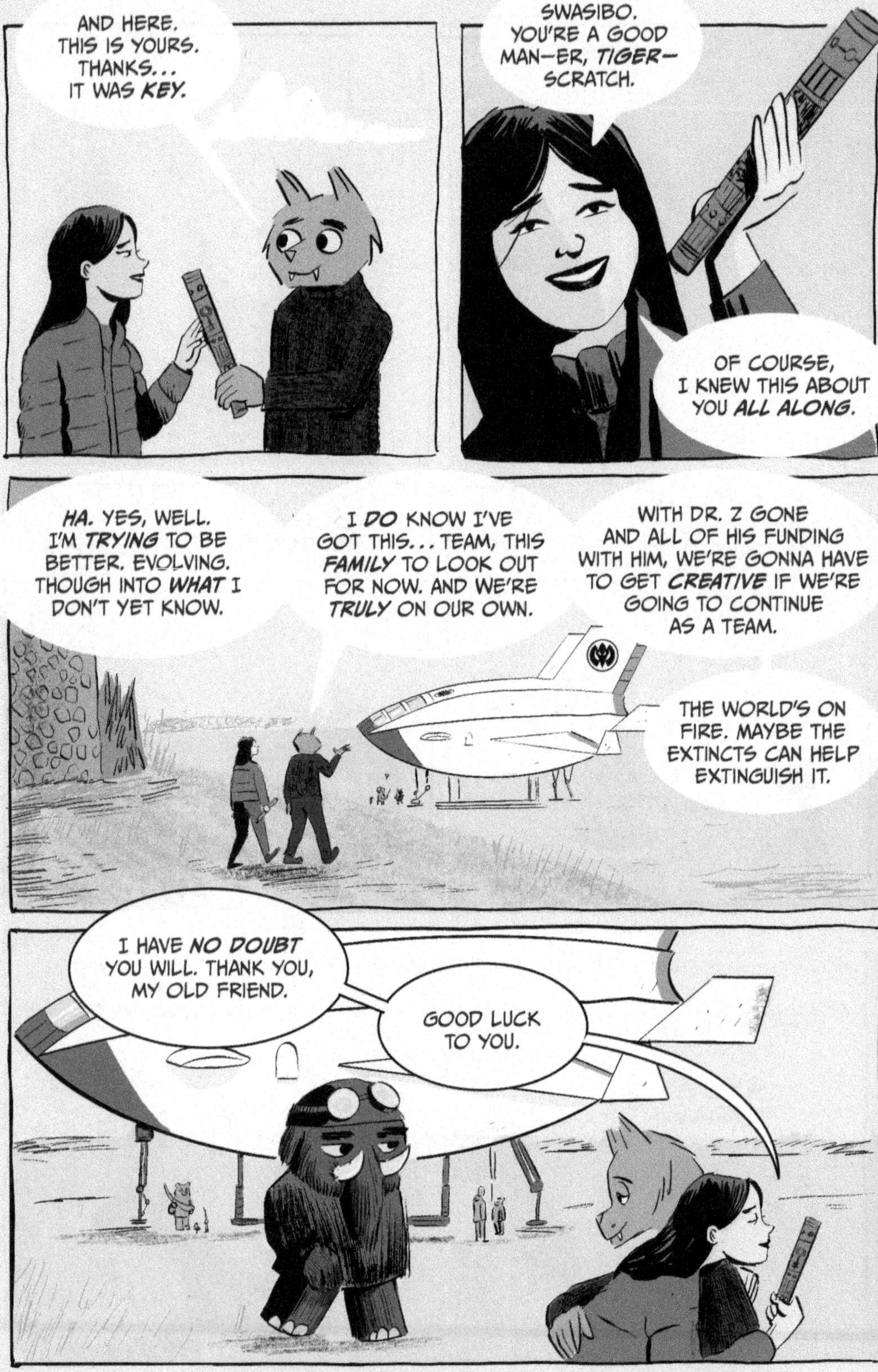
AND HERE. THIS IS YOURS. THANKS... IT WAS KEY.
SWASIBO. YOU'RE A GOOD MAN—ER, TIGER-SCRATCH.
OF COURSE, I KNEW THIS ABOUT YOU ALL ALONG.
HA. YES, WELL. I'M TRYING TO BE BETTER. EVOLVING. THOUGH INTO WHAT I DON'T YET KNOW.
I DO KNOW I'VE GOT THIS... TEAM, THIS FAMILY TO LOOK OUT FOR NOW. AND WE'RE TRULY ON OUR OWN.
WITH DR. Z GONE AND ALL OF HIS FUNDING WITH HIM, WE'RE GONNA HAVE TO GET CREATIVE IF WE'RE GOING TO CONTINUE AS A TEAM.
THE WORLD'S ON FIRE. MAYBE THE EXTINCTS CAN HELP EXTINGUISH IT.
I HAVE NO DOUBT YOU WILL. THANK YOU, MY OLD FRIEND.
GOOD LUCK TO YOU.

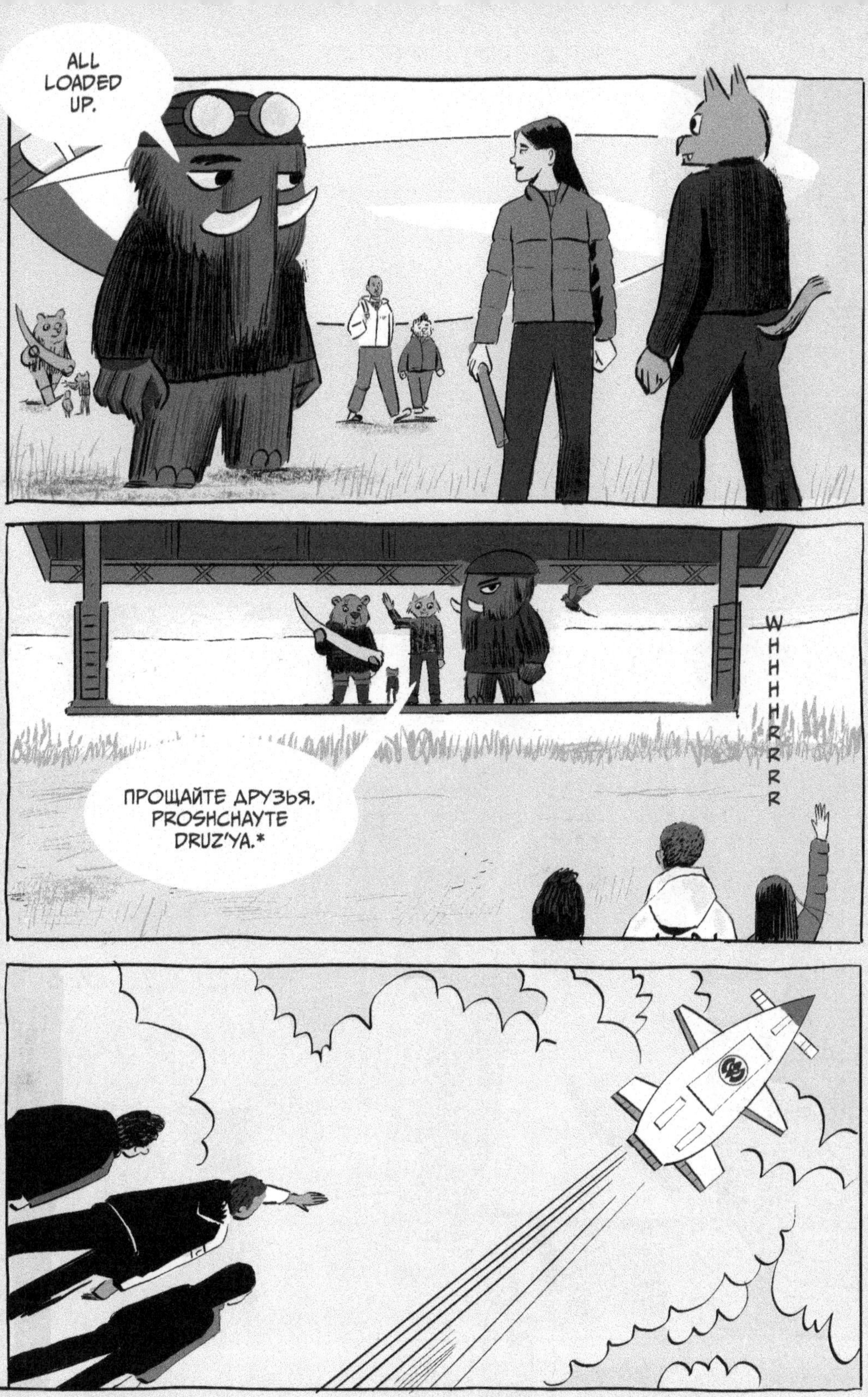
ALL LOADED UP.
WHHHRRRR
ПРОЩАЙТЕ ДРУЗЬЯ. PROSHCHAYTE DRUZ'YA.*

*Farewell, friends.

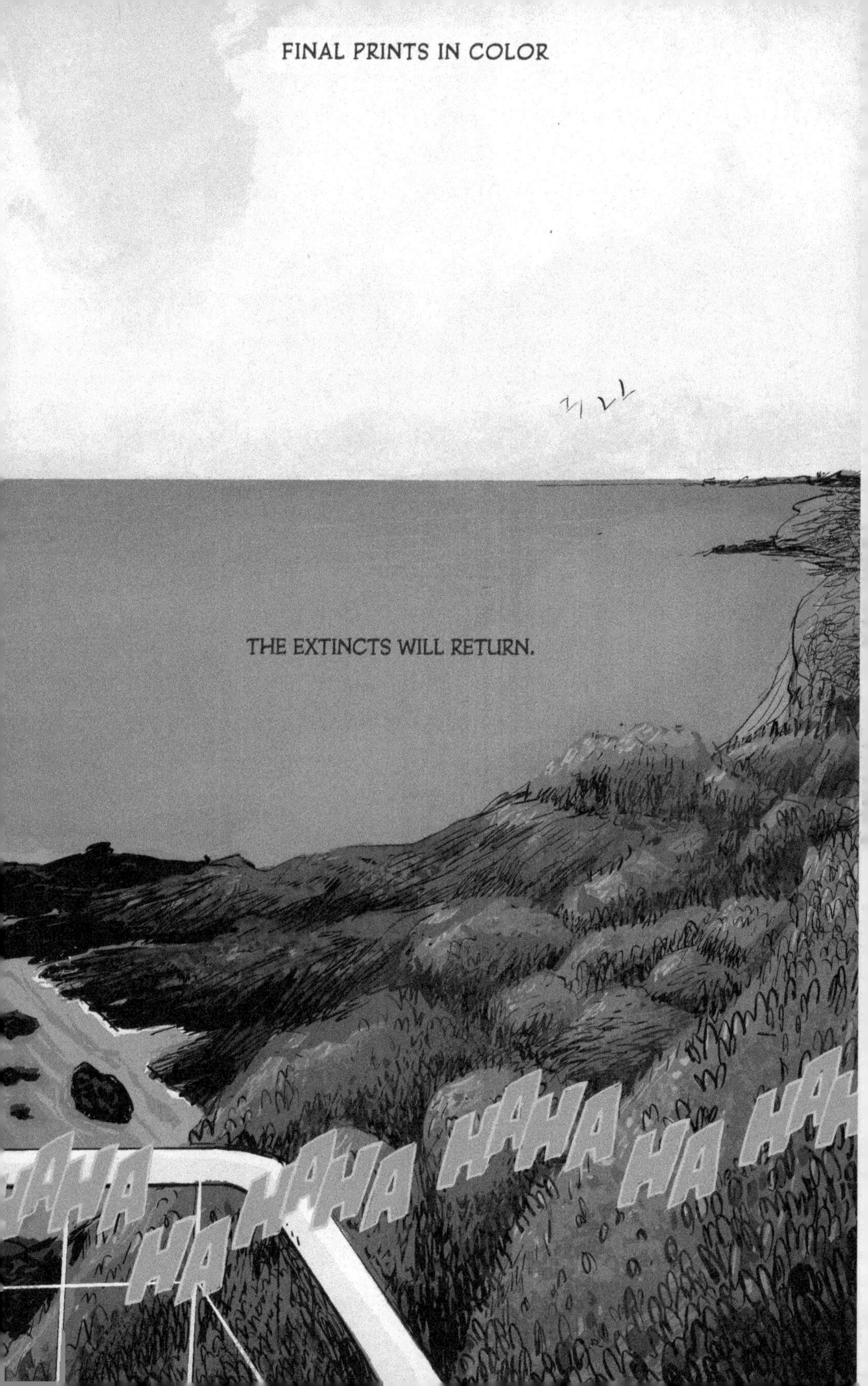
FINAL PRINTS IN COLOR
THE EXTINCTS WILL RETURN.
HAHA
HA
HAHA
HAHA
HA

THE EXTINCTIARY

Your field guide to the extinct creatures & concepts featured in this book*

* *Don't worry, GAIA didn't write it.*

CAVE BEAR *U. spelaeus*

HABITAT: FORESTED LOW MOUNTAINOUS AREAS
TEMPORAL RANGE: Chibanian to Upper
Pleistocene (129,000-11,000 years ago)
DISTRIBUTION: Europe and parts of Eurasia
SIZE: 11.5' standing on hind legs, 5.5' at
shoulder on all fours, up to 1500 lbs
LIFESPAN: Probably fewer than 20 years
WHY EXTINCT: Food loss due to climate
change/competition with humans for caves in
which to hibernate
FUN FACT: A 1917-1923 excavacation of the
Drachenloch cave in Switzerland uncovered more
than 30,000 cave bear skeletons.

NONE SHALL BEAR WITNESS

Thousands of winters ago, as Cave Bears hibernated in their cave homes, Cave Lions snuck in to hunt them. A great idea—until the bears awoke to fight off the cats, their only predator. Explorers discovered the cats' bones in caves years later, and the creatures became known, ironically perhaps, as Cave Lions.

Still, dying during hibernation was common for the Cave Bear. If it was sick, old or did not feast to prepare for the cold winters then it wouldn't awaken in Spring.

Like its modern Eurasian brown bear cousin, the Cave Bear was an omnivore but loved eating plants. Unfortunately, the ice age shortened or eliminated plant-growing seasons, likely starving the bears.

Cave Bears were among the first megafauna to go extinct in the late Pleistocene era, around 27,000 years ago. Most other megafauna survived the ice age and died out 10-15,000 years ago.

For ages, people assumed the remains of Cave Bears were those of apes, large dogs, cats—even dragons. But by the end of the 19th century scientists identified the cave bear as a member of the ursine—or bear—family.

Today, scientists collect frozen and well-preserved Cave Bear DNA. In late 2020 Siberian reindeer herders unearthed a well-preserved frozen cave bear carcass. They turned it over to a local university that specializes in studying ancient megafauna. For the first time ever, scientists are able to study the bear's soft tissues, inner organs—and even its nose.

SEE A SKELETON
American Museum of Natural History New York, NY
Field Museum, Chicago, Illinois

FURTHER READING
Hehner, Barbara. *Ice Age Cave Bear. The Giant Beast That Terrified Ancient Humans*. New York, NY: Random House Publishers, 2002.
Kurtén, Björn. *The Cave Bear Story: Life and Death of a Vanished Animal*. New York, NY: Columbia University Press, 1995.

COLLINS' POISON FROG *Andinobates Abditus*

HABITAT: Dense humid forest
TEMPORAL RANGE: Cretaceous? to Holocene
(100 million years — modern era)
DISTRIBUTION: Ecuador, in the eastern base of
the Reventador stratovolcano, in Napo Province
SIZE: Approx. 0.4 to approx. 1.5" long, .2 -.14 oz
LIFESPAN: 4-6 years
WHY EXTINCT: Habitat loss, possible fungal infection
FUN FACT: Its poison comes from diet of poison insects

HOPPED OUT

Andinobates Abditus is a species of poison dart frog currently listed as extinct in its only known home. It may survive elsewhere in areas not surveyed.

Poison dart frogs are among the most toxic creatures on earth. We've come to know these creatures as "poison dart" frogs because native peoples reportedly rub the frogs and hunting darts together to infuse the darts with poison. However, scientists identified only a few of the nearly 200 species are actually used for this purpose, including the golden poison frog. That specie is the most toxic of all poison dart frogs, secreting enough poison to kill several humans! Some poison frogs secrete the alkaloid toxin batrachotoxin that medical researchers (very carefully) use in promising research of muscle relaxants, heart stimulants and anesthetics.

These frogs do not create their own poison. Instead, like us, they are what they eat. Using sticky, retractable tongues, the frogs catch and eat specific poisonous insects that ate poisonous plants. The frogs digest the insects—but keep their poison in their skin and use it to protect themselves from predators. By contrast, poison frogs in captivity on a diet of crickets and other non-poisonous insects are not poisonous themselves.

Poison frogs' beautiful skin colorings are a visual warning to would-be predators. "Don't eat me!" the colors seem to shout. Indeed, if a predator tries to eat a colorful frog and it finds it unappetizing, it will then it recognize that creature and not attack it in the future.

Scientists can identify species of poison frogs by their calls. Frogs use these calls to attract mates, mark their territories or express distress.

SEE A POISON FROG
Smithsonian National Zoo, Washington, DC (green-and-black, tri-colored and blue poison frogs)
Detroit Zoo, Detroit MI (Golfodulcean, green-and-black, dyeing, mimic and yellow-headed poison frogs)
San Diego Zoo, San Diego, CA (green and black poison, dyeing, splash back, and black-legged frogs)

FURTHER READING
Bredeson, Carmen. *Poison Dart Frogs up Close.* Berkeley Heights, NJ: Enslow Elementary, 2012.
Carney, Elizabeth. *Frogs!* Washington, D.C.: National Geographic, 2009.
Davey, Owen. *Fanatical about Frogs.* London, UK: Flying Eye Books, 2019.
Owings, Lisa. *Poison Dart Frogs.* New York, NY Scholastic/Children's Press, 2012.

MEGAFAUNAL WOLF *Canis Cf. lupus (where cf. in Latin means uncertain)*

HABITAT: Multiple, across the Holarctic
TEMPORAL RANGE: Upper Pleistocene to Holocene
(About 45,000-7,500 years ago)
DISTRIBUTION: Northern continents of the world
SIZE: About 3.5'–5.3' in length and about 2.75' at
shoulder. Weighed up to 180 lbs.
LIFESPAN: 6-8 years
WHY EXTINCT: Loss of food
FUN FACT: Today's wolves are not descendants
of these prehistoric ones, which must
have died out completely

ONE BIG BAD WOLF

The megafaunal wolf was similar to the gray wolf we know today but there are subtle
differences. The megafaunal wolf had a shorter and wider mouth with larger rear teeth in
relation to the size of its skull. This adaptation allowed it to prey and scavenge on Pleistocene megafauna. Analysis of the isotopes in these wolves' bones reveal that their diet
included bison, horse, muskox and scavenged woolly mammoths.

Compared to gray wolves, megafaunal wolf samples show moderately-to-heavily worn
teeth, as well as frequent broken teeth. The place where the teeth broke is also different.
Megafaunal wolves had more fractures of incisors, cheek teeth, and molars than gray
wolves. Scientists observed a similar pattern in hyenas' teeth, suggesting that increased
fang and side teeth breaks meant these megafaunal wolves, like hyenas, often ate bone,
because wolves gnaw bones with fangs and then crack them with their cheek teeth.

Scientists examined specimens of all of the carnivore species from the La Brea tarpits in
California, including remains of dire wolves which was also a megafaunal hypercarnivore.
That evidence suggests that these carnivores were well-fed just before they went extinct,
and that scavenging was less common than among large carnivores today. Tooth breaking
was probably from the catching and eating of larger prey and not from scavenging.

In 2019, a head of the world's first adult Pleistocene-era wolf was unearthed in Siberia.
The wolf had thick mammoth-like fur, intact fangs and two to four years old when it died.
It was the first found with soft tissue preserved. Russian scientists will compare it to
modern-day wolves to better understand its evolution and to reconstruct its appearance.

SEE A GRAY WOLF
Detroit Zoo, Detroit, MI
San Diego Zoo, San Diego, CA
Stone Zoo, Stoneham, MA

FURTHER READING
Dutcher, Jim, and Jamie Dutcher. *Living with Wolves!: True Stories of Adventures with Animals.*
Washington, D.C.: National Geographic, 2016.
Marsh, Laura F. *Wolves.* Washington, D.C.: National Geographic, 2012.

MEGALODON *Carcharocles megalodon*

HABITAT: Warm coastal waters
TEMPORAL RANGE: Burdigalian to Zanclean
(About 20-3.6 million years ago)
DISTRIBUTION: Nearly worldwide.
Fossils found globally except Antarctica
SIZE: Average estimates 33' long, possibly larger.
Weighed up to 65 tons
LIFESPAN: Up to 25 years
WHY WENT EXTINCT: Climate change,
competition from Great White Shark
FUN FACT: Its name in Latin means "big tooth"

JAWESOME

Thought by paleontologists to be one of the largest and most powerful predators ever. Its bony jawbone and teeth preserved in the fossil record give scientists scant clues as to what Megalodon looked like—and just how big it grew. There are theories that it resembled a massive great white shark, a large sand tiger shark or even a basking shark. Scientists estimate the Megalodon's size based on the size of its teeth and jaw. Maximum length estimates puts the leviathan at 59 feet—longer than a tractor trailer!

Given their enormous size, the shark most likely preyed on large animals like whales, seals, sea turtles—and maybe, given its 6-foot-wide jaws, some of them in a single bite.

The long-standing uncertainty about sharks led humans throughout history to make wild assumptions about it. People used shark teeth as jewelry and as medicine. In the Middle Ages, Europeans even thought shark teeth to be petrified tongues of dragons and snakes.

Today, there are a number of theories about how the Megalodon died out. A warmer water fish, Megalodon might've met its match in the cooling of oceans at the dawn of the ice age. With so much water frozen as ice, sea levels worldwide lowered—and the resulting loss of acceptable areas to raise young could have contributed to Megalodon's extinction.

Their prey also began to disperse into cooler waters. Baleen whales moved into polar seas and reduced the Megalodon's main food source. Then there was the competition—the Great White shark, smaller and more nimble might have literally eaten the Meg's lunch.

SEE A SPECIMEN
Jaws at the American Museum of Natural History New York, NY
Life-size model in the Smithsonian Museum of Natural History Washington, DC
Reconstructed skeleton at Calvert Marine Museum in Solomons, MD

FURTHER READING
Skerry, Brian, Elizabeth Carney, and Sarah Wassner. Flynn. *The Ultimate Book of Sharks: Your Guide to These Fierce and Fantastic Fish*. Washington, D.C.: National Geographic, 2018.
Harvey, Derek. *Super Shark Encyclopedia: and Other Creatures of the Deep*. New York, NY: DK Publishing, 2015.

PASSENGER PIGEON *Ectopistes Migratorious*

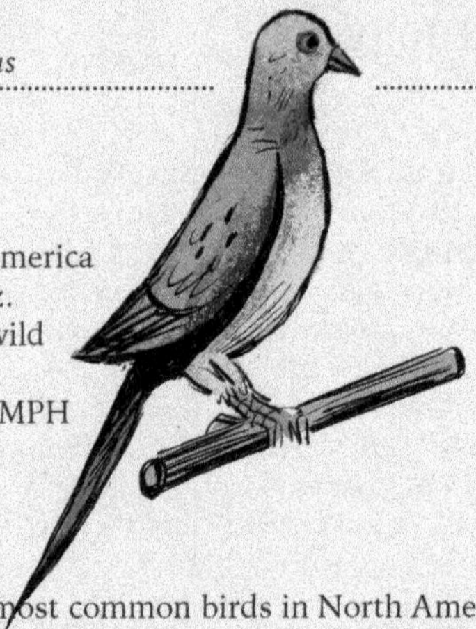

HABITAT: Deciduous forests
TEMPORAL RANGE: Zanclean to Holocene (3.6 million years ago-1914)
DISTRIBUTION: Midwest & Eastern North America
SIZE: 15-16" length, 7-8.5" Wingspan, 9-12 oz.
LIFESPAN: 15 years in captivity, unknown in wild
WHY EXTINCT: Hunting, loss of habitat
FUN FACT: Fast! Could fly at speeds up to 62 MPH

NO MORE PASSENGERS

Long ago, the Passenger Pigeon was one of the most common birds in North America. At 3-5 billion birds, their population was so large that gigantic flocks of them darkened the sky, sometimes taking days to pass by overhead. It must've seemed unbelievable at the time that humans could wipe out billions of birds. But we did—in less than a century.

Pigeon meat was tasty and purveyors sold it as a cheap and plentiful food. Humans hunted the birds on a massive scale for many decades, enabled by new and emerging technology. The telegraph spread word about pigeon nestings to hunters who would flock to the flocks. Trains carried tons of ice-packed barrels of dead birds to distant diners. Sportsmen shot at live pigeons in shooting competitions. There's at least one instance of them used as cannon fodder. Hunters chopped down trees full of nesting birds to net them before they could escape. Widespread deforestation also destroyed the pigeons' habitat. All of this reduced the large breeding population necessary for its species survival.

The decimation of the Passenger Pigeon and other species led to some of the nation's first natural conservation laws. But it was too little, too late. A hunter shot the last confirmed wild bird in 1901. The last Passenger Pigeon, Martha (for whom Martie in this book is named) died in captivity the Cincinnati Zoo on September 1, 1914. It was the first time we witnessed the extinction of a species by our own hand. You can see the specimen made from Martha's remains at the Smithsonian in Washington D.C.

There are efforts underway to 'de-extinct" a passenger pigeon—but some people believe resources would be better spent conserving existing endangered creatures. Indeed, today many of our extant birds are at risk. North America lost nearly 3 billion birds of hundreds of species over the past fifty years. Its an enormous loss revealing an "overlooked biodiversity crisis," according to a study by scientists and government agencies.

SEE A SPECIMEN

Cleveland Museum of Natural History, Cleveland, OH
Harvard Natural History Museum, Cambridge MA
Smithsonian Museum of Natural History, Washington D.C.

FURTHER READING

Avery, Mark. *A Message from Martha: the Extinction of the Passenger Pigeon and Its Relevance Today.* London, UK: Bloomsbury, 2014.
Benchwick, Greg. *Martha: the Last Passenger Pigeon.* Castroville, TX: Black Rose Writing, 2019.
Greenberg, Joel. *A Feathered River Across the Sky: The Passenger Pigeon's Flight to Extinction.* New York, NY: Bloomsbury USA. 2014
Timberlake, Amy, and David Homer. *One Came Home.* New York, NY: Scholastic, 2014.

SABERTOOTH TIGER *Smilodon*

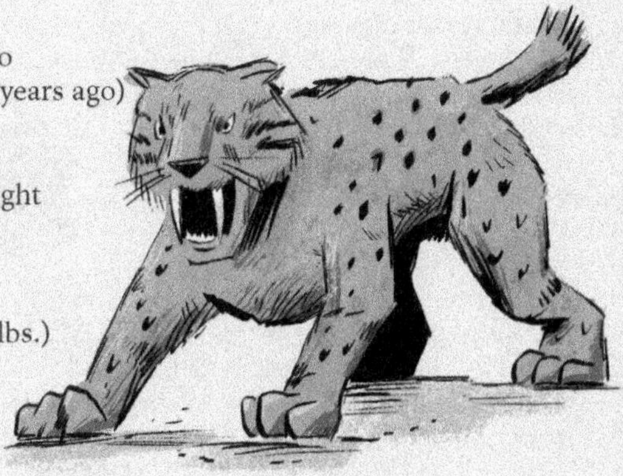

HABITAT: Forests, bush
TEMPORAL RANGE: Early Pleistocene to Early Holocene (About 2.5 million-10,000 years ago)
DISTRIBUTION: The Americas
SIZE: Varied, depended on species:

- *S. gracilis* 120 to 220 lbs.; unknown height & weight, Jaguar-sized.
- *S. Fatalis,* 350-620 lbs., 3.25' tall, about 5.8' length. Modern lion-sized
- *S. populator* 220 to 400 kg (490 to 880 lbs.) 4' shoulder height; unknown length Footprint larger than of Bengal Tigers'

LIFESPAN: 20-40 years
WHY EXTINCT: Loss of food
FUN FACT: Smilodon's name comes from the Greek word for "knife" and "tooth"

A REAL BIG MOUTH, LONG IN THE TOOTH

Its huge mouth made Smilodon the legendary apex predator of its age. It featured a special jaw that could open very wide, unleashing its 7-inch long serrated fangs. The cat sank those dagger-like fangs into prey's neck or belly to cause it to bleed to death. Prey included bison, horses, giant sloths, American camels and mammoths.

Smilodon was probably not as fast as modern cats because it had somewhat bear-like legs—strong and heavy. It also had a very short tail, only 14 inches or so. Like modern cats though, it had retractable claws to help it hold down large prey.Even though we think of the fierce Sabertooth as a tiger, it was not closely related to tigers or even lions. Instead, most species descended from the jaguar-like Megantereon.

Smilodon's exact appearance and behavior remain something of a mystery. For instance, we're not sure what the Smilodon's coat looked like. Nor is it known for certain whether Smilodon lived a solitary life or was a more social creature. Shedding some light on that question are Smilodon fossils that show healed wounds. Wounds that, before they healed, would have crippled the cat and kept it from hunting. Yet, somehow the creature continued to eat while it recuperated. This could mean that other Smilodons provided food for injured or old members of their pack. It could also mean that Smilodons raised their young in packs and were more social than solitary.

SEE A SKELETON

Harvard Natural History Museum, Cambridge MA
La Brea Tar Pits Museum, Los Angeles, California

FURTHER READING

Antón, Mauricio. *Sabertooth*. Bloomington, IN: Indiana University Press , 2013.
Bailey, Gerry, and Trevor Reaveley. *Sabre-Tooth Tiger.* St. Catharines, Ont.: Crabtree Pub., 2011.
MacPhee, R. D. E., and Peter Schouten. *End of the Megafauna: the Fate of the World's Hugest, Fiercest, and Strangest Animals.* New York, NY: W.W. Norton & Company, 2019.
Zoehfeld, Kathleen Weidner., and Franco Tempesta. *Prehistoric Mammals.* Washington, D.C.: National Geographic Kids, 2015.

SIBERIAN UNICORN *Elasmotherium Sibiricum*

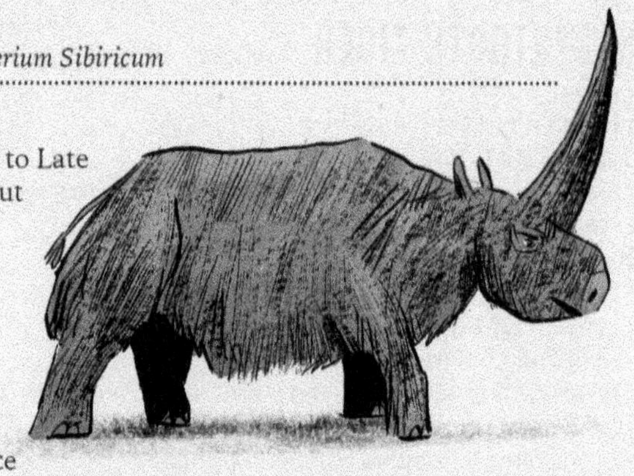

Habitat: Tundra
Temporal Range: Late Pliocene to Late Pleistocene (About 2.5 million to about 10,000 years ago)
Distribution: Siberia, Russian Federation
Size: 15' length, 6-7' at shoulder, 3.8 tons (7,716 lbs)
Lifespan: Unknown
Why went extinct: Climate change: fall in temps killed food source
Fun Fact: Also known as the giant rhinoceros, the steppe rhinoceros, and the giant Siberian rhinoceros

YOU'RE NEVER GOING TO SEE NO UNICORN

Interestingly, of the Siberian Unicorn skeletons unearthed so far none of them include a preserved horn. Why? Part of the reason may be because the horn was probably keratinous—the same softer material of which hair, nails, claws, hooves are made—and likely to decay over thousands of years. Under the right conditions though, paleontologist found hair, horns and claws of other ancient creatures. As more permafrost melts reveals more megafaunal remains it may just be a matter of time before a horn is discovered.

How do we know the unicorn even had a horn? By studying its skeleton. Paleozoologists look to a significant cranial vertebrae, hunched back, a furrowed and domed skull. From this they theorize that each of these features would have allowed for the creature to support a massive horn—estimated to be about three feet in diameter and 3-6 feet long.

The bones give us other clues. A genetic analysis of 23 unicorn bone specimens' DNA revealed that the Siberian Unicorn was the last surviving member of a unique subset of rhinos. The bones also showed that the species survived much later than previously thought: 39,000 years ago—which means they co-existed with modern humans and Neanderthals.

The Siberian unicorn fell on hard times by the start of the ice age in Eurasia when a dramatic fall in temperature led to frozen ground, reducing the grasses it fed on and impacting herds of the creatures over an entire region.

Some theorize that modern man's collective unicorn myth-making might've stemmed from this creature but the unicorn myth originated in India, far from the Siberian Unicorn's nature known habitat or range. Its possible that the discovery of a narwhal's horn was the start of the unicorn myth.

See A Skeleton

Azov Museum in Azov, Russia

Further Reading

Prothero, Donald R., and Mary Persis. Williams. *The Princeton Field Guide to Prehistoric Mammals.* Princeton, NJ: Princeton University Press, 2017.
Zoehfeld, Kathleen Weidner., and Franco Tempesta. *Prehistoric Mammals.* Washington, D.C.: National Geographic Kids, 2015.

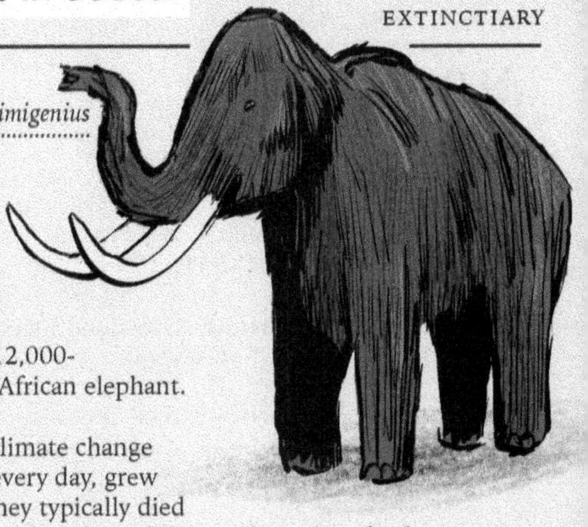

WOOLLY MAMMOTH *Mammuthus primigenius*

HABITAT: Tundra
TEMPORAL RANGE: Middle Pleistocene—Early Holocene (About 400,000-4,000 years ago)
DISTRIBUTION: Northern Asia, parts of Europe, northern North America
SIZE: 11.5"high at shoulder, 6-8 tons (12,000-16,000 lbs). About the size of a modern African elephant.
LIFESPAN: 60-80 years
WHY EXTINCT: Hunted by humans, climate change
FUN FACT: Ate about 500 lbs of food every day, grew six sets of teeth during their life span. They typically died after they lost their last set of teeth and with it their ability to chew their food

A TRUNCATED HISTORY

For eons, the Woolly Mammoth ruled the frozen tundra. A two-layer shaggy coat of hair kept them warm while their 6-foot-long trunk and two massive 10-foot long curved tusks foraged for grasses under winter snow and ice. If food became scarce, they used large humps of fat stored on their back as—quite literally—a back-up source for energy. They traveled in herds of matriarchal family units, caring for their young, sick and old. Mammoths were mammoth (some over 12 feet tall!) and, owing to this great size, had no predator for thousands of years.

But then humans invented the spear. Emboldened by the weapon, hunters began to prey upon the mammoth for meat and other resources. Traces of mammoths are found in prehistoric art, tools, dwellings and in ancient ceremonial burials.

The last known population of mammoths died out around just 4,000 years ago, probably hunted to extinction by humans. The woolly mammoth was the last of its kind of mammoth. Its closest living relative is the Asian elephant.

Today, human's exploitation of the woolly mammoth continues with efforts to clone the creature, effectively bringing it back to life. The scientists intent on this face serious obstacles however. A mammoth cannot be exactly re-created from DNA. Instead, scientists work to create a mammoth-elephant hybrid using frozen mammoth DNA and an Asian Elephant mother. The eventual possibility of this has profound ethical, environmental and scientific implications. In addition, people question the need to de-extinct a species when so many living species are currently threatened.

SEE A SKELETON
American Museum of Natural History New York, NY
Field Museum, Chicago, Il
La Brea Tarpits & Museum Los Angeles, CA

FURTHER READING
Lister, Adrian, Paul G. Bahn, and Jean M. Auel. *Mammoths: Giants of the Ice Age*. New York, NY: Chartwell Books, an imprint of Book Sales, 2015.
Shapiro, Beth. *How to Clone a Mammoth: the Science of De-Extinction*. Princeton, NJ: Princeton University Press, 2016.

GLOSSARY

CARBON DIOXIDE An invisible, odorless gas produced by organic compounds, burning carbon and by breathing. It is about 0.03% naturally present in air. Plants absorb it in photosynthesis. See also *Greenhouse gases, photosynthetic*

CASCADE EFFECT An unavoidable and sometimes unexpected sequence of events caused by one act that affects an entire system.

CLIMATE The combined or regular weather conditions of a region. To determine climate, Scientists measure air pressure, winds, temperature, precipitation, humidity, sunshine, cloudiness for a year. Then that data is averaged over a series of years.

CLIMATE CHANGE A long-term change in the average weather patterns of Earth's established local, regional and global climates.

DE-EXTINCTION The process of creating an organism of an extinct species or one that looks like an extinct species. Also known as species revivalism or resurrection biology.

ECOSYSTEM A community of living organisms interacting with the nonliving components of their environment. These living and and nonliving components are connected by nutrient cycles and energy flows.

EXTINCTION The end of a member of a species or a group of species. Scientists consider the moment of extinction to be the death of the last individual of the species. However, the species may have lost the ability to reproduce and rebuild the species before that point.

GLOBAL WARMING The ongoing rise of the average temperature of Earth's climate. It is a part and a major aspect of climate change. In addition to rising global surface and atmosphere temperatures, global warming also includes its effects, like precipitation changes. See also *Climate Change*.

GREENHOUSE EFFECT The process by which radiation from the sun is absorbed and re-radiated by greenhouse gases. While some energy radiates back into space, some is sent towards the surface. This warms the planet's atmosphere and surface to a temperature higher that what it would be without this effect.

GREENHOUSE GASES Like glass on a greenhouse, a greenhouse gas absorbs and then radiates energy within the thermal infrared range. Greenhouse gases cause the greenhouse effect on planets. The main greenhouse gases in Earth's atmosphere include water vapor, carbon dioxide, methane, nitrous oxide, and ozone.

MEGAFAUNA The large mammals of a certain region, habitat, or geological era.

METHANE An odorless, invisible, flammable gas, a principal component of marsh gas and the dangerous firedamp of coal mines. It is obtained commercially from natural gas. See also *Greenhouse gases*

PALEOGENETICS The examination of the past by studying of preserved genetic material from the remains of ancient organisms.

PERMAFROST A thick layer of subsurface soil that remains frozen throughout the year for at least two consecutive years, occurring primarily in polar regions.

PHOTOSYNTHETIC The process by which green plants, algae and certain bacteria convert carbon dioxide, water, and salts into carbohydrates using chlorophyll and energy from the sun.

RESURRECTION ECOLOGY An evolutionary biology technique whereby researchers hatch old dormant eggs from lake sediments to study animals as they existed in the past. Others have used this technique to explore the evolutionary effects of a lake's excessive nutrients due to runoff from the land, predation, and contaminants.

SIXTH EXTINCTION, THE An ongoing extinction event of species during our present day Holocene epoch as a result of human activity. Also known as the Holocene extinction, or Anthropocene extinction. See also *Extinction*.

THERMOKAST terrain formed by the melting of the permafrost sublayer. The melting ice leaves small pits, marshes, valleys, hummocks and uneven ground.

TUNDRA A flat or gently rolling treeless plain typical of arctic and subarctic regions. Soil is black and mucky with a permanently frozen subsoil called permafrost, and supports a dominant vegetation of herbs, mosses, lichens, and dwarf shrubs. See also *Permafrost*.

WEATHER A short-term (as in minutes, hours or days) atmospheric change in conditions that occur in a local area. Examples include rain, snow, clouds, winds, floods or thunderstorms. See also *Climate Change* and *Global Warming*.

YEDOMA An organic-rich Pleistocene-age permafrost with of 50–90% ice content by volume. Yedoma are abundant in the regions of eastern Siberia, such as northern Yakutia of the Russian Fedaration, as well as in Alaska in the U.S. and Canada's Yukon province.

MORE ABOUT THE BATAGAIKA PIT

We can learn a great deal from the Batagaika pit. Certainly, this "megaslump" and others like it reveal well-preserved remains of ancient creatures for scientists to study. But more importantly—given climate change's urgency—they also study the pits for the impacts of our warming world.

The pit is both a result of a warming climate *and a cause* of more warming temperatures to come. Geologists estimate that up to 50 percent of the earth's methane gas may be locked up in Arctic permafrost. As it thaws, permafrost releases the greenhouse gas methane—and then microbes consume the dirt's unfrozen organic matter. After they eat, the microbes release methane and carbon dioxide as waste into the atmosphere, speeding up warming even more. In short, the megaslumps are huge greenhouse gas emitters.

Thanks in part to their Arctic research, scientists have a better idea of the ways permafrost changes can contribute to greenhouse gas emissions—and how large that contribution is. That work helps us to know what we're up against in our changing climate.

The Arctic may fortell global environmental changes to come. But it does so while we still have time to apply what we learn at Batagaika and places like it. The question is, then, will we take action in time? That's up to you and me.

HELP THE EXTINCTS SAVE THE WORLD

HERE ARE SOME WAYS YOU CAN GET INVOLVED TO HELP PROTECT THE ENVIRONMENT

ON YOUR OWN

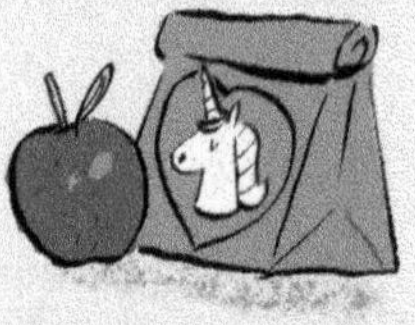

- Reduce trash. Take your lunch to school in a reusable container. Avoid using throw-away containers.
- Conserve water. Turn off the faucet whenever you're not using the water—when you're brushing your teeth for instance. Avoid long showers.
- Keep reusable resources out of the trash. Glass, aluminum and plastics can be used again—recycle them.

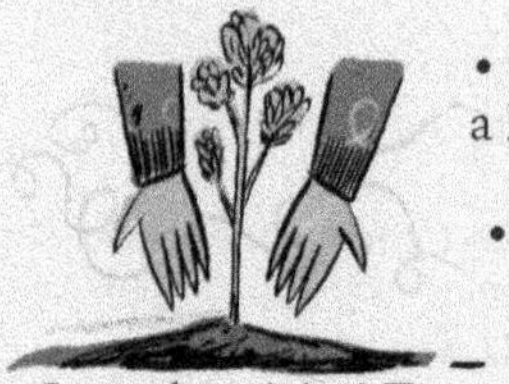

- Plant a tree to put more oxygen in the air and birds a home.
- Use reusable drink containers instead of disposable ones.
- Save electricity! Turn off the lights and TV when you leave the room. Unplug chargers you're not using.

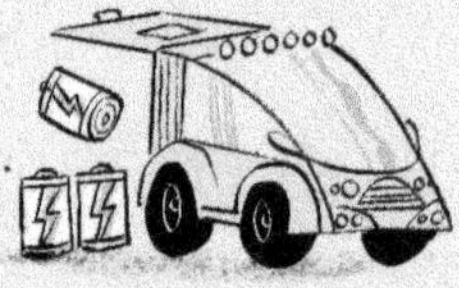

- Collect your baby books for a book drive.
- Use rechargeable batteries in your devices, toys and games.
- Use paper straws instead of plastic ones.
- Use both sides of your paper or old newspapers and magazines for art projects.

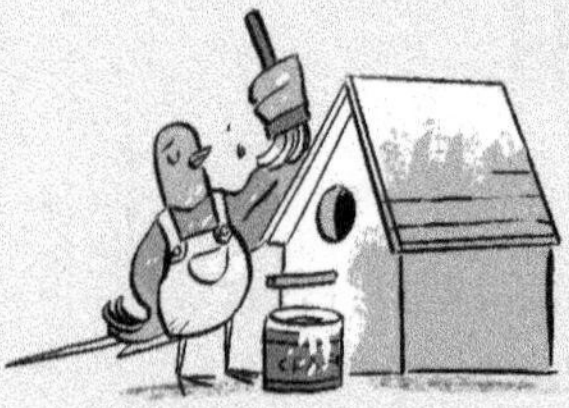

- Check out and read library books about the environment.
- Ask your teachers about starting a bottle recycling program at your school.
- Make gifts for others instead of buying them.
- Don't waste food—or anything for that matter. Make maximum use of stuff.

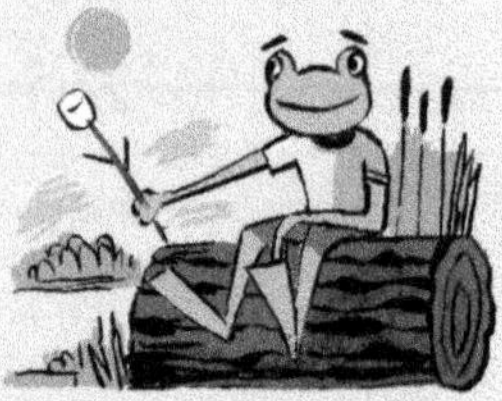

- Ask your teachers about your school 'adopting' an endangered animal. They can contact your local zoo or or visit the World Wildlife Fund's website for more info on this.
- Ask your school about hosting a "solar cookout." Cook s'mores with the sun with solar ovens you make.
- Ask your school about taking an environmental-related field trip.
- Share these lists with your friends and family. They may have even more ideas!

WITH YOUR PARENTS

- Grow a vegetable garden. Or plant pollinator-friendly plants to help struggling butterflies and bees.

- Create a compost pile from table scraps and yard clippings. It'll make great fertilizer for that garden you just made!

- Write a letter together for your member of Congress about environmental issues.

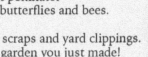

- Donate your old clothes so that they will be worn by someone else.

- Volunteer or organize community cleanup or recycling drive.

- Carpool. Create a rideshare with friends and family.

- Spend time in nature. Try birdwatching or geocaching!

- Go electric! Ask your parents about solar panels for your home or an electric car to reduce greenhouse gas emissions.

- Replace incandescent lightbulbs with more energy efficient LED ones.

- Walk or ride a bike whenever possible instead of driving.

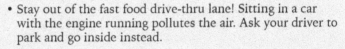

- Stay out of the fast food drive-thru lane! Sitting in a car with the engine running pollutes the air. Ask your driver to park and go inside instead.

- Hang a bird feeder or birdbath in your backyard to help local bird species.

- Ask your parents to help you research your local endangered creatures—and what you can do to help conserve them. Many states have endangered species watch-lists. Learn more at goextincts.com.

FURTHER READING:
French, Jess. *What a Waste: Trash, Recycling, and Protecting Our Planet.* New York, NY: DK Publishing, 2019.
Montez, Michele, and Lorraine Bodger. *The New 50 Simple Things Kids Can Do to Save the Earth.* Kansas City, MO: Andrews McMeel Pub., 2009.
Siber, Kate, and Chris Turnham. *National Parks of the U.S.A.* Minneapolis, MN: Wide Eyed Editions, an imprint of The Quarto Group, 2018.

TRY THE QUICK-FREEZE TRICK

WHAT YOU'LL NEED:

- 3-4 17 oz. unopened spring water bottles
- 1 ice cube, chipped
- A clear plastic cup
- A freezer

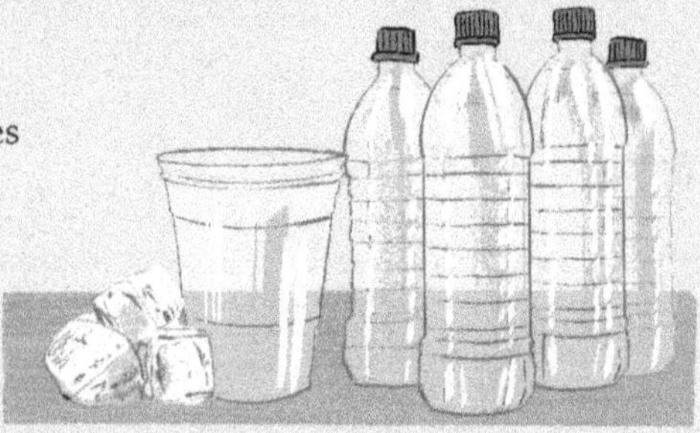

HOW TO MAKE INSTANT ICE

1. Leave the unopened water bottles at room temperature for about 4 hours. Then put them in the freezer for about 2.5-2.45 hours. (You might have to experiment with the amount of time. This is not an exact science!)

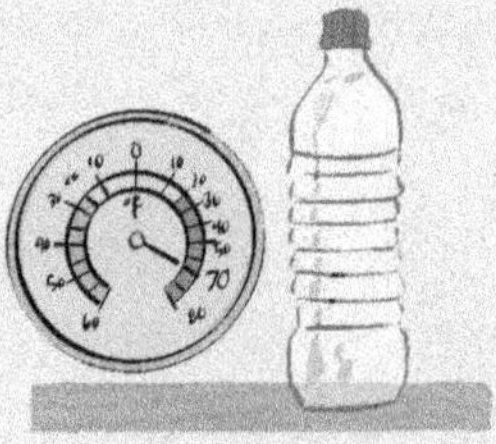

2. After taking the bottle from the freezer, test it to make sure its cold enough. Hit the super-chilled water bottle onto a hard surface. If your water is super cooled, ice crystals inside the bottle will form and the water inside should turn opaque white as it flash freezes. Proceed to step three. If not, put your bottle back in the freezer for another 10-15 minutes.

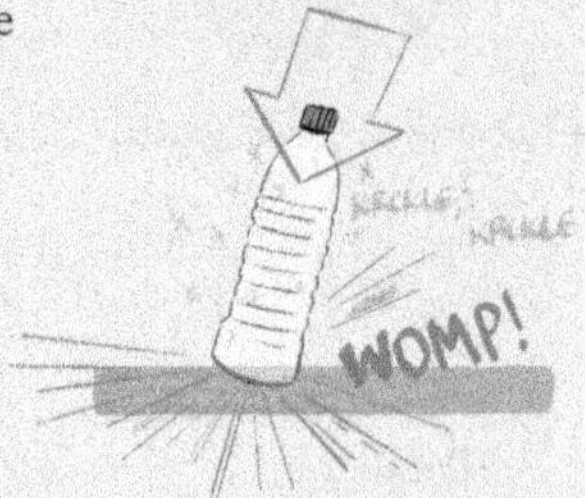
WOMP!

The next 2 steps should happen in quick succession:

3. Take a supercooled bottle from the freezer and open slowly, —be careful not to jostle it!

4. Next, put the ice chip into the plastic cup. That ice chip is going to be your nucleation point, the point at which the liquid water starts to form crystals—and become ice.

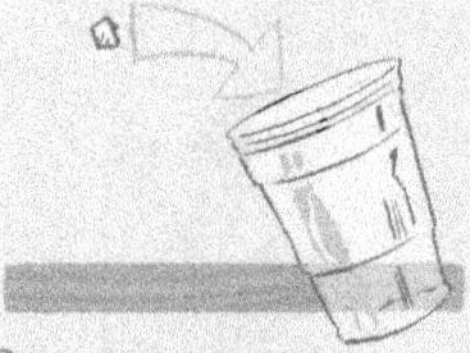

5. Gently open the bottle water pour the water very slowly. Ice should begin to form around the ice chip. Cool! Instant ice!

6. Recycle or re-use those plastic bottles and cups.

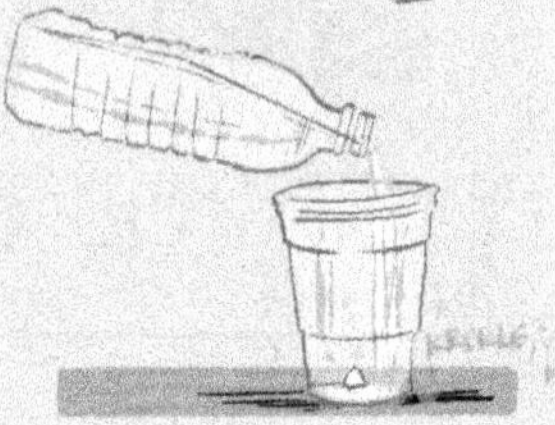

HEY, QUITO, WHY DOES IT DO THIS?

WHEN WATER FREEZES, INTERCONNECTED CRYSTALS FORM LIKE SNOWFLAKES ON TINY LITTLE IMPURITIES IN THE WATER. SINCE YOU'VE USED FAIRLY PURE SPRING WATER AND SLOWLY SUPERCOOLED IT INTO A METASTABLE STATE, ITS HARDER FOR ICE CRYSTALS TO FORM. WHEN YOU INTRODUCED THE ICE CHIP YOU DESTABILIZED THE WATER AND TRIGGERED THE FORMATION OF THE CRYSTALS. ICE CRYSTALS THEN BUILD ON THEMSELVES UNTIL YOU SEE THE MINI ICE AGE IN YOUR CUP.

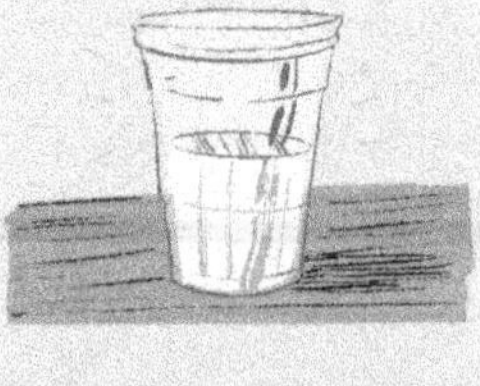

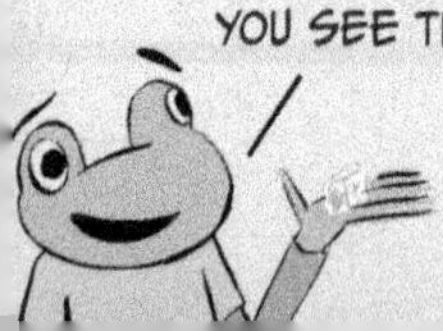

FURTHER READING

BOOKS FOR YOUNG READERS:

Herman, Gail, John Hinderliter, and Kevin McVeigh. *What Is Climate Change?* New York, NY: Penguin Workshop, an imprint of Penguin Random House, 2018.
Hoare, Ben, and Tom Jackson. *Endangered Animals.* New York, NY: DK Publishing, 2010.
Sabuda, Robert, and Matthew Reinhart. *Enclycopedia Prehistorica: Mega-Beasts.* Somerville, MA, MA: Candlewick Press, 2007.
Sewell, Matt. *Forgotten Beasts: Amazing Creatures That Once Roamed the Earth.* London, UK: Pavilion, 2019.
Torday, Piers. *The Last Wild.* New York, NY: Puffin Books, 2015.
Zoehfeld, Kathleen Weidner., and Franco Tempesta. *Prehistoric Mammals.* Washington, D.C.: National Geographic Kids, 2015.

BOOKS FOR OLDER READERS:

Carson, Rachel, Linda J. Lear, and Edward O. Wilson. *Silent Spring.* Boston, MA: Mariner Books/Houghton Mifflin, 2012.
Greenberg, Joel *A Feathered River Across the Sky: The Passenger Pigeon's Flight to Extinction.* New York, NY: Bloomsbury USA. 2014
Kalmus, Peter. *Being the Change: Live Well and Spark a Climate Revolution.* Gabriola Island, BC: New Society Publishers, 2017.
Kolbert, Elizabeth. *Sixth Extinction: an Unnatural History.* New York, NY: Picador Usa, 2015.
O'Connor, M. R. *Resurrection Science Conservation, De-Extinction and the Precarious Future of Wild Things.* New York, NY: St. Martin's Press, 2015.

WEBSITES

https://kids.nationalgeographic.com
http://www.passengerpigeon.org
https://reviverestore.org
https://www.worldwildlife.org

BIBLIOGRAPHY

Wray, Britt, and George M. Church. *Rise of the Necrofauna: the Science, Ethics, and Risks of De-Extinction.* Vancouver, BC: Greystone Books, 2019. Macfarquhar, Neil, and Emile Ducke.
"Russian Land of Permafrost and Mammoths Is Thawing," August 4, 2019. https://www.nytimes.com/2019/08/04/world/europe/russia-siberia-yakutia-permafrost-global-warming.html.
Expedition Unknown, Season 4 Episode 5, "Cloning the Woolly Mammoth." Written by Thomas Quinn. Aired on December 28, 2016 on Travel Channel.
Expedition Unknown, Season 4 Episode 6, "Journey to The Ice Age." Written by Thomas Quinn. Aired on January 4, 2017 on Travel Channel.

ACKNOWLEDGMENTS

The book you hold in your hands is my attempt to raise awareness of climate change and species extinction. Mercifully, I had a team as great as the Extincts to help me with it.

This book would not exist without my brilliant & beautiful wife Christy and my brave boys Owen and Daniel. In addition to their endless patience with me, they read early drafts and shared their thoughts. I hope this book is worthy of all that time we were apart. My parents for instilling in me a deep appreciation for nature and for their support as I worked on this book. Thank you, I love all of you.

My agent Paul Rodeen—your early and ongoing enthusiasm for this project was a key part of its genesis. To my editor Russ Busse who gave me wide-open creative fields in which to roam, mammoth-like, I am grateful. Andrew Smith for remembering me, the old days in Cambridge and giving me this opportunity. The whole team at Abrams Books for Young Readers for bringing the Extincts to life. Heartiest thanks to all of you.

My brother Zach, my friends Jon D., Sean T., Dave L., Geoff L., and Chris S. for sitting through countless descriptions of what this book was going to be. Just think, we can do it again with book 2.

Matt Tavares for his *Hoops* graphic novel camaraderie "And Ryan Higgins also, I guess." You guys are the best.

For Patrick McGee for giving my comic strip *Duct Tape Man* a chance all those years ago at the Northeastern News. One thing lead to another and here we are.

Jerry Jamowski for not taking it from anyone. WFUZ's music kept me drawing late into Thursday nights. Thanks, man!

The teams at my local public library and town forest. Liz Whitelam and her team at Whitelam Books—and indie booksellers everywhere.

George Lucas, Larry Hama for the inspiring imaginary adventures and Josh Gates for the real ones. Isabella Stewart Gardner for getting me out the door. Or maybe it was in the door.

And a special thank YOU for reading my words and looking at my pictures. I hope you'll be back for Extincts book two.

AUTHOR/ILLUSTRATOR *Scott Magoon*

HABITAT: New England
TEMPORAL RANGE: Late Holocene
DISTRIBUTION: Worldwide
SIZE: 6'1", approx. 190 lbs.
AGE: Late 40s
FUN FACT: Collects vintage Star Wars and GI Joe action figures and vehicles.

WRITING AND DRAWING FOR AGES

Scott was born back in the 1900's. He earned a B.A. in English Literature from North-eastern University sometime before the dawn of the 21st century. More recently, he was a children's book art director at major American publishers. Now he writes and illustrates books full time. He's a lefty and, like his ancestors, enjoys running long distances, good food and good music. He and his nomadic family travel to new places together from their Boston-area home.

He's illustrated 30 picture books and written five. This is his first graphic novel.

Visit scottmagoon.com to learn more about him, his books and get in touch. Sign up for his newsletter *The Magoon Tribune* while you're there for quarterly updates on all the latest and greatest.

You can also visit goextincts.com to find out more about extinct and endangered creatures, teacher's guide, behind-the-scenes stuff from the Extincts, free downloads and special Extincts merchandise—the profits of which benefit environmental causes.

It is not the strongest
of the species that survives,
nor the most intelligent
that survives.

It is the one that is most
adaptable to change.

–Charles Darwin

For the Earth and her endangered species
–S.M.

Library of Congress Control Number: 2021932219

Hardcover ISBN 978-1-4197-5251-3
Paperback ISBN 978-1-4197-5250-6

Text and illustrations copyright © 2022 Scott Magoon
Book design by Heather Kelly

Printed and bound in China
10 9 8 7 6 5 4 3 2 1

ABRAMS The Art of Books
195 Broadway, New York, NY 10007
abramsbooks.com